Assimilation

James Stryker

First published by Momentum in 2016
This edition published in 2016 by Momentum
Pan Macmillan Australia Pty Ltd
1 Market Street, Sydney 2000

A CIP record for this book is available at the National Library of Australia

Assimilation

EPUB format: 9781760302481
Mobi format: 9781760302498
Print on Demand format: 9781760302504

Cover design by Pat Naoum
Edited by Tara Goedjen
Proofread by Lauren Choplin

Macmillan Digital Australia: www.macmillandigital.com.au

To report a typographical error, please visit momentumbooks.com.au/contact/

Visit www.momentumbooks.com.au to read more about all our books and to buy books online. You will also find features, author interviews and news of any author events.

For Jayme, her favorite since she's my favorite.

Chapter 1

His consciousness was reborn in a sea of fog. He wouldn't have described it as black or dark. With no sense of light, there was only emptiness as he crossed from "unbeing" to "being." He vaguely remembered having a body, but now nothing extended beyond his thoughts. Without sensory input, he felt like a brain in a jar, which, of course, he had been for the past sixteen months.

Where am I? What am I? What's the last thing I remember?

Talking to the first responder crouched by a car.

"Where's my baby? I can't hear him crying."

"We got him out." The man had smiled, but his eyes betrayed him.

He remembered the agony this lie had caused. In his mind he'd seen the image of a George Minne sculpture. The woman's arms cradled the body of her child, its head lolled forward with the chin to her hand. Her own head tilted to the sky, her neck elongated and mouth parted to release her anguish.

Mother grieving over her Dead Child. And it's no longer a plaster statue in a Belgium museum. It's me.

With this thought, the pain overcame everything else. The anxiety for the other boy, the physical suffering, the terror that he was going to die. His child was dead.

If the EMT had been more convincing, would he have had the strength to go on? As the building ache boiled from his stomach, it went too fast. He couldn't scream. He couldn't speak. He opened his mouth like the grief-stricken sculpture to release the pain. But instead the pressure foamed into his head.

A weight cut through as if he'd collapsed into himself, and he struggled with it at first. He knew that he should want to live, that he was expected to. No one wanted to die when they were young and healthy. Not when they had so much to live for. But his resolve slipped as the heaviness drained him of everything. So at last he allowed the weight to crush him.

This had been death. And whether from the severe injuries, or loss of the child, he knew he'd died, passing from one plane of existence to another. Wherever this place was.

So there's no great light. There are no angels or paradise. Death is just being recreated into a new life.

And whatever he was now, he knew he wasn't the same.

She was far away, this woman he'd been. Distant enough that in combination with the clearing haze, he couldn't recall her name or what she'd looked like. He knew her children's and husband's names. He could see their faces. But she was a ghost. So impersonal that he was unable to fully connect with her feelings. Even the suffering from realizing the baby was dead. He felt sad about it in general. But Michael might've been a dead pigeon in the gutter, and the statue was just a piece of art once more.

These people are shadows to me. They might've mattered to her, but she's over. I imagine, as I can't remember any life before her, I'll forget about being her altogether. I'm new.

2

A sense unlike anything he'd experienced before as the woman rippled outward from the concept of "new." At death, the paintbrush had been lifted and a linen canvas was switched for a panel of masonite. The tip of the brush touched the fresh material and the texture was unyielding. Smooth without the acrylic seeping into the weave, the density gave the paint a different control. Him. This life would be created as a *him*.

And he had a name. Heard somewhere in the old life, or in a prior existence. His thoughts paddled in a tranquil circle and it surfaced:

Andrew.

He relaxed as the last wisps of creeping mist evaporated. And because it was difficult to be detached, his mind wandered to a place. He envisioned a bench before a large black painting and thought of being immersed in the swirling brush strokes. He wasn't sure how much time would pass before he'd be reborn, but he was content to wait.

He didn't have long.

A faraway voice was calling a name.

You'll have to come to me, Voice. Wherever I am.

The voice spoke again. It sounded closer this time, which was exciting. That something could be approaching him meant he held a position in the universe.

"Natalie Keller. Natalie, can you hear me?"

The name was strange but familiar, like putting on an old shoe that hasn't been worn in a while. He felt no ownership, but he tossed it around.

That could've been your name. Is Natalie still here?

"She hears us!" Another, higher voice.

"Thank God. With that chunk of crystallization in the frontal lobe, I thought she might be veg."

Andrew wanted to pull away, but there was no physical body to move, let alone a sense of where it might be possible to escape to. Something gnawed at him, and the comforting grasp he had on the painting in his mind faded.

"Natalie Keller." The first voice was stern and close. "This is Dr. Mitchell Brigman speaking. You're located at the Cryobiotic Treatment Center in Savannah, Georgia."

Anxiety struck through him. A machine beeped.

Let me be a speck of dust on a wall. A molecule in a window shade. A self-aware atom on the floor!

"Mrs. Keller, I need you to calm down."

Though the fog was gone, his thoughts thrashed in the sea – chopping the water in desperate, volatile struggles to stay above the crest. The woman had never had an anxiety attack. She'd gracefully bent under pressure, but Andrew's panic was a fire striker hitting over and over.

He remembered:

The Cryobiotic Treatment Center.

CryoLife.

The rider on the joint life insurance policy – taking advantage of medical technology's latest and crowning achievement.

"Sedate her! She's going to stroke!"

It'd seemed like a good idea. The amazing CryoLife scientists and doctors had extinguished the failing systems of the past and brought society into the future. Peace of mind by preventing death from wedging apart a family.

The woman had selected the option for her children. Andrew remembered her thinking of them as she signed the legal document, and her relief that Michael and Simon would never be without their mother.

But she'd also opted in for Robert. The smiling family on the brochure that'd last forever would be them.

"*I'd want you back, Rob.*"

"*I'd want you back too.*" Robert had curled a piece of long blond hair around his fingertips. "*You're my everything.*"

And Andrew was gone.

*

When he crawled back into awareness, it wasn't how previously waking had been. This time he'd been washed ashore. His fingers dug into a sandy beach as he dragged himself from the waves. He felt hazy, but bruised. And he heard the voice immediately.

"Showtime."

He raised his face from the grainy rocks.

"Natalie Keller. This is Dr. Mitchell Brigman speaking. You're currently located at the Cryobiotic Treatment Center in Savannah, Georgia."

As Andrew remembered where he was, the anxiety built. Beeping. Beeping as his thoughts flew.

No, this feels wrong. Wrong. I'm not her. I'm me!

"Mrs. Keller. I don't want to sedate you again. I need to read you this statement before we proceed. You'll feel better once your eyes are open."

Think of anything. Paintings. Think of the fourteen black canvases. Of being inches from them. Absorbed in them. Part of them.

And the beeping slowed.

"Thank you." A piece of paper crinkled, and the words rolled from Dr. Brigman's mouth. "Mrs. Keller, you were involved in a vehicular collision and declared imminently dead approximately sixteen months ago. Thanks to the research and development at the Cryobiotic Treatment Center and your enrollment in the CryoLife program, you've been successfully reanimated.

"Per the terms of the legally binding agreement you entered with CryoLife, and in accordance with United States law, a conservatorship has been established wherein your conservator may grant you the full benefits and entitlements of your previous identity after a period of six months.

"You'll remain at the Cryobiotic Treatment Center for rehabilitation until you're released to your conservator, Robert Keller. Further instructions will be provided when necessary, and you'll be given the opportunity to ask questions once you regain the ability to speak."

There was a pause, as if the doctor anticipated a response. And where the pliable Natalie would've waited for the next move, the flint and high carbon steel of Andrew lit a spark on the tinder.

Obviously I can't say anything! You said it yourself, fucking moron!

"Bring in the husband."

His outrage iced over as the cage he found himself in expanded to admit another prisoner.

He heard a door opening. A motor murmured, and his mind tipped with vertigo as the beeping machines changed position. Fast breathing filled the room.

"For now, Mrs. Keller, welcome back."

Andrew met the light. The room was dim, but while his eyes strained to adjust he could only look straight ahead, as if his nerves and muscles were frozen.

It seemed like any normal hospital room. He sensed the machines to his right and the doctor standing next to an IV on the left. Flowers and brightly colored balloons crowded the windowsill and table across the room. But much to his upset, his vision centered on the man sitting on his bed.

It was the Robert he'd seen in the emptiness, though thinner and more care worn. Tears ran down his gaunt face, for all that his eyes glowed. And while this was the man the woman had loved enough to dedicate her life to him, when Andrew looked at Robert, he felt nothing. Except perhaps pity.

I'm sorry. I don't know what happened, Robert, but you're not looking at your wife. I don't feel like Natalie, I don't think I'm her anymore. I'm not even a woman.

Robert didn't divert his gaze, but he took a hand that'd been lying on the bed.

"She can't feel you yet, Mr. Keller."

Andrew was grateful that he could only watch Robert smooth his short fingers over the hand's knuckles. If he'd been able to feel the touch, he would've vomited. Or maybe stroked. And he'd rather have that. Wasn't nausea in the brain? It didn't have much to do with the stomach. Which would explain why, though Andrew felt no physical part of the body, there was a churning sickness at the idea of Natalie's husband holding his hand.

"That's okay." Robert's voice crackled. "Thank God you're back. I missed you so much, Nat."

The panic ratcheted higher when Robert brought the hand to his face.

Stop touching me.

Andrew knew the hand was his. Robert pressed it to his cheek and closed his eyes.

Stop touching me, Robert.

He imagined the sticky, freshly shaven texture of the man's skin.

Stop fucking touching me! Get—

A tremor passed through Robert's body and hulking sobs poured from him. The last sixteen months of pain had been bottled, and it looked like his insides were being torn from his mouth in thick, raw strips.

The omnipotent machines sounded their urgent, furious code.

"Mr. Keller." The doctor touched Robert's shoulder, and Andrew recognized the voice he'd heard in the thick mist as belonging to Dr. Brigman. "She's temperamental. If she gets too anxious, she could stroke."

Robert bolted up and, in gulping too much air, launched into a coughing fit. He accepted a cup of water and sputtered until he could speak.

"I'm sorry." He stared at Andrew, and his aching flooded the room with steam. "It's been so hard. But that's over. You're alive."

No, Robert. She's dead. I'm not Natalie.

"When can she come home? When can I bring Simon to see her?"

Simon. Andrew thought of the boy with Robert's dark hair. Simon running, Simon laughing, Simon playing. Sitting between them to watch television. Crawling into his parents' bed in the middle of the night. The knees of his pants caked in mud from unearthing bugs in the yard. And Simon as a baby. The way his skin smelled of powder and freshness. How it'd been to hold him, feed him, hear him gurgle, and feel they were the only people in the world.

He remembered these things, but with detachment. Simon wasn't his. He was a random child on the playground.

But better a child than a dead pigeon.

"She needs to stay for observation and physical therapy before we can release her. The process usually doesn't take long."

Robert brought the hand to his lips and talked around it. "She'll want to be home with us as soon as possible."

The machines restarted their beeping as Andrew thought about going with Robert. Unsettling snippets of filling Natalie's role spun in his mind. Feeling Robert's touch and being expected to return it – not with neutrality, but with love.

"It goes faster than you'd think. Just coaxing the nerves and neural pathways to reactivate. It's easier than with your original body." Brigman laughed. "Shattered my knee two years ago; took me months to run. Give her a few days and she'll be talking. Then we can discuss what comes next. I wouldn't recommend bringing your son until she has full upper body control."

"But I'll be here every day." Robert bit his lower lip. "I can't stop looking at you. I can't believe you're alive."

Dr. Brigman glanced at the flashing monitor lights.

"We need to let her rest, Mr. Keller. It's been a lot for today."

From the corner of his eye, Andrew watched the doctor fill a syringe. Robert's grip tightened on the hand.

"She's afraid of shots. Don't you have a smaller one?"

Andrew remembered the woman's phobia, but a hypodermic needle seemed pathetic. A brief stick was only that. What awaited him beyond the reactivation of neural pathways was unthinkable.

Put me out. Please put me out. I can't deal with this. I want to go back. I want to go back!

"She can't feel anything, remember? She can't feel she has arms, let alone a syringe going into one." Brigman shifted his focus to Andrew. "You do have arms, Mrs. Keller. You're absolutely, completely perfect."

You don't understand. There's something wrong, there's—

"It's true. You look just like yourself."

9

The doctor still held the filled needle, but the hospital room blurred. Though Andrew couldn't close his eyes, he concentrated on the outlines of his vision as he thought about Natalie. Unlike before, her image came clearly to him as if she'd strode into the room and sat beside Robert on the hospital bed.

The imaginary Natalie ran her manicured hand through her golden hair and looked at Andrew. She crossed one knee over the other in an elegant motion and leaned toward him, the clingy fabric of a low-necked blouse hugging her curves. When she smiled, a nauseating sweetness lit her delicate features.

Whatever I am, whoever I am. This is not me.

"I'll be here when you wake up, Natalie. I love you."

Robert's voice grew muddled and the room fell dark.

Chapter 2

Robert came every day, as he said he would. And if he wasn't there when Andrew woke, the first thing Andrew saw was Robert's face in a framed portrait on the side table. His hand clasped Simon's shoulder, and the woman was in it too.

I'm in it. I'm the woman. I'm she. I remember when that photo was taken. I remember being Natalie. But I don't feel like her.

The will to regain the ability to move his head and eyes came from the desire to turn away from that picture. Upon feeling himself coming back, he'd keep his eyes closed and feel for which cheek was on his pillow. If it was the right, he'd turn his head and open his eyes to the wall.

The reprieve was never long.

"Good morning, Nat! How are you? Dr. Brigman says you're ahead of where most people are. Always the overachiever." Robert sat by the bedside.

Only days later Andrew could feel when Robert kissed his forehead or caressed his cheek, and each touch was accompanied by a rock in his stomach. He was still unsure what to do – what he'd say, when he could say anything.

The eventual revelation occupied his thoughts when he was awake and Robert wasn't there to touch him, talk to him, and generally unnerve him.

I know how crazy this sounds. The woman in that picture, Natalie, died. I can't be your wife.

He'd stop rehearsing the confession. In real, un-cryogenically reanimated life, a person could wake one morning and decide not to be with their partner. But what clouded Andrew with uncertainty was the reason he didn't feel he could be Robert's wife.

I feel like a man. Please believe me – No, no. He would shake his head. *You don't have to beg. You didn't do anything wrong. It feels wrong, but it's not your fault.*

But did he comprehend the situation enough himself to be able to explain? Did he *believe* it enough?

It has to be possible. Something changed. Something more than a name.

Being called Natalie was horrible. And other feminine names he could be called induced a similar wriggling, slimy feel. He felt there was a different substance at his core. An alternative lens interpreted the world and a new material was being built upon.

Maybe that's how it'll make sense to him. Like a building moved to another foundation. Doesn't the base make all the difference in the world? On this new ground I can't be your wife, Robert. The place I am feels like Andrew.

He couldn't imagine hiding his aversion to the name, to pronouns, or Robert's affection. In his current frozen state, whenever his hand was petted or his hair caressed Andrew would wind tighter and tighter. A similar scenario would then play out as the machines revealed what he couldn't by their frantic beeping.

"Nat, are you okay?" Robert would squirm. "You can't tell me. Oh, God. Oh, God."

Robert's panicking actually played a role in releasing the agitation to calm Andrew's mind.

If you genuinely love me, there's a good chance you'll understand, right? That you'll try to help me figure out this mess.

Robert's anxiety was also better proof of his care than physical gestures or constant verbal adoration. It made Andrew feel more powerful. If he had control over nothing else, he could influence Robert, because he was so invested.

The noise of the machines usually waned by the time Brigman arrived.

"What's wrong?" He'd bluster in.

"Nothing, now. I was holding her hand, and they started going off. Does everything look okay?"

The doctor turned to the screens behind Andrew's bed, giving them an unnecessary level of scrutiny.

"Everything's fine."

I feel like I'm a paralyzed man trapped in a woman's body. What part of this is fine?

Brigman would look from Robert to Andrew. The doctor's eyelids came closer together as he scanned Andrew's face, and he gave a broad, though thin-lipped smile, causing lines to pile in the corners of his mouth.

"You're all right, Mrs. Keller, aren't you?" Knowing one wouldn't come, he'd still wait for a reply. When he turned to Robert, the smile relaxed, releasing a crinkle or two. "See, perfect. Like always."

And not realizing more lurked beneath the surface, Robert would agree.

*

Andrew knew that Robert hoped their one-sided conversations would end soon. And sometimes the feeling was mutual.

To reveal anything frequently felt like it would be better than nothing. The simple request to stop calling him Natalie would be a relief, even if a response to the inevitable "why" was still muddled and confusing.

You'll help me work it out. You'll tell me what happened to me, and then maybe it will all make sense.

Why had he died as one person – Natalie – but been reanimated as another – Andrew? Maybe the answer had been in the smiling family pamphlet or buried in the legal document. Like a list of side effects on a medicine bottle.

But who reads that shit? And it's not as easy as the doctors having switched my brain with another since I remember being Natalie. I don't remember this feeling of Andrew.

The possibility that he may be unable to shake the masculine feeling was terrifying with its consequences, and the limited options for resolution had been trudging through his head one afternoon during visiting hours.

"Nat, are you okay?" Robert had lowered the magazine he'd been browsing. "You looked sad. Were you thinking of something sad?" There was no response, but he paused like Brigman and everyone else. Despite trying to ignore it, being treated and talked to like a toddler caused that internal sparkwheel to strike the ignition button.

I may be mute for now, but I'm not an idiot.

"I know what will cheer you up!"

Andrew watched Robert's shoulders move as he rummaged through a bag at his feet. He remembered how Natalie had liked the way they moved – muscles working under the overly starched cotton shirts he wore. Robert's powerful shoulders made her feel safe and protected. They made Andrew want to upchuck the sludge he'd involuntarily ingested.

"I can't believe I forgot. Simon asked if you liked it this morning, and I had to say you did. But you will, so it wasn't much of a lie."

Robert shuffled his chair closer and held a large, folded piece of construction paper in front of Andrew's face. A sloppily written "To: Mom" was etched on its cover and scrawls of flowers decorated the bottom. A lot of care had gone into a particularly intricate flower, which resembled a cat that'd swallowed a beehive.

Andrew nodded for Robert to open the card. When he saw the contents, everything changed.

A house was drawn on the right half. Smoke curled from the chimney in the shape of a heart, and the door's window looked like a deflated hexagon.

A peach colored creature hovered to the house's left, and it took Andrew a minute to identify the airborne thing as an angel. When this occurred to him, he recognized the blue smudge on the blob's face was a pacifier.

Michael.

His gaze moved from the sad depiction to three figures standing under a sun as big as the house.

Simon had recreated a family portrait Andrew couldn't look away from. Robert held hands with a small boy wearing glasses, who was holding hands with the figure of a woman. Of any drawing on the page, the most attention had been paid to her. He'd drawn the laces on her shoes, the rings on her fingers, the lashes on her eyes. While Robert was missing an ear.

Above the family, the words in purple crayon: "Come home soon." And like an afterthought, squeezed at the bottom in cramped writing: "Please."

Despite the whirl of emotions – the waves of anger and anxiety where he felt split in half, Andrew hadn't cried. He wasn't sure if he hadn't been physically able to, or if Simon's card was his breaking point.

While technically he'd survived death, he'd been spat out as a fraction of the whole person he'd been before. Hardly anything of Natalie felt okay, let alone those feminine traits completely lost. But as angry as he became when he was called Natalie, or when Robert touched him, he couldn't deny that those things were familiar. The state of Natalie wasn't home, but it was a place he'd been before. A sofa with plastic on the cushions. Uncomfortable, but still a place to sit.

And there was Robert. How was he going to feel when he knew that something was wrong, and not "perfect like always"?

Andrew would try to console himself, cringing as Robert smothered him with worshipful stares. *Look how much he loves her. He could find someone else who won't die and come back feeling like a man.*

But this fine rationale couldn't fit for Simon. Sure, the boy could have a stepmother, grandmother or any number of maternal figures, but it'd never be the same. He was only eight years old, and for a child too old to forget but too young to move on, no one could take Natalie's place. It was an idea Andrew hadn't considered until reading the simple plea on the card. How would he tell Simon?

I look like your mom, but I'm not her. I may not know completely who I am yet, or what kind of future I'll have, but I don't want a family with you or your dad. I'm sorry, and this sucks for you—

"Come home soon. Please."

A boy's innocent appeal for nothing more than his mother to return. Natalie could be horribly deformed. She may never talk or walk. She might not remember who he was. But Simon didn't care. He only wanted her back.

Andrew's eyes ached. Michael was the dead pigeon, and Simon could be any child in a playground. There may not be attachment, but Andrew wasn't a selfish monster. Was he?

Ugly, gasping sounds came from his mouth, but he couldn't stop them.

"It's okay, Nat." Robert sat on the bed, and Andrew felt himself rocked. "You'll be home soon. Don't cry. It's okay."

*

So above everything, you're a monster. How does that feel?

The evening after receiving Simon's card, Andrew woke in the middle of the night.

You're a regular 22nd century fucking Frankenstein.

He visualized how the scenario had played out. Dramatically pulled from the wreckage, Natalie had died, and Dr. Brigman wheeled her lifeless body into a dark tower. Green and blue Tesla coils spiraled to an open ceiling, and Brigman snapped a pair of jumper cables onto the exposed bolts from her neck. He pulled the switch, and fifteen million volts coursed through the body, jump-starting the heart. Brigman raised his hands to the sky, cackling that his creation lived.

At two in the morning, it could've been real.

They electrocuted her brain and zapped the part that made Natalie, Natalie. I'm what's left over. He tipped his head, but couldn't feel any bolts. Not that they couldn't have removed them afterward.

Stop being stupid. You may not know exactly what happened, but this isn't a horror movie. It's a legitimate medical procedure that has saved countless lives. Maybe a surgeon just dropped his watch in me.

But whether due to electric shock, freezer burn, or masculinity-inducing metal poisoning, the result remained the same.

Robert had left Simon's card on the side table, and it called to him. It reached out with illusory arms, brushing his face and coaxing him to remember who'd made it, and what revealing another identity would do to the child.

Andrew closed his eyes, and there she was – Natalie. The specter. Worse than imagining her sitting on the hospital bed, or seeing her smiling face in the portrait. She was in the purple dress with the meticulously drawn shoelaces. And he saw Simon at the kitchen table with his crayons. The tip of his tongue out between his lips, and his brow furrowed in concentration. With a combination of urgency and precision, he'd make the card *perfect* so his mother would come home.

If I could walk out now, they'd never find me. I'd disappear. God, give me the strength to get out of this bed. Prove you don't want that boy to suffer.

But the Almighty was as unresponsive as usual. There was nothing Andrew could do to help his own situation, let alone Simon's. He had to lie there and rot. And worry.

Where would you go? You're so brave in the daylight. Creating passionate speeches to deliver to Robert and Brigman, then storming out. But where would you actually go?

It was a sobering reality that besides Robert and Simon, he had nobody. Natalie had been an only child and her parents were dead. But even if they'd been alive, they weren't *his*.

Andrew had no family. He had no friends. They all belonged to the real Natalie, not the person imprisoned in her skin.

Not much else was in his favor either. Nowhere and nothing. There was knowledge, though. For some reason, while many of her other qualities were empty chalk outlines, Natalie's comprehension of art had remained with Andrew. But what good did that do? Parents wouldn't be okay with a freak teaching their brats, so he'd have no way to support himself.

Yes, it'd be honesty. He'd be true to the world and who he felt he was. What people on the outside expected of a hero. But how courageous was it to be alone? To be on the streets? To destroy the lives of those around him. And for what?

You think Robert would help and understand. But the person he loves isn't you. What you are, is the thing that's replaced his Natalie. Not only will you hate yourself because of what you'll do to them, but they will hate you.

Andrew couldn't remember a time when Robert had been angry with Natalie. He was a man who managed his life from sets of blueprints – straight lines and exact ninety degree angles. And Natalie had always allowed him to take the lead, preferring to operate placidly within his instructions. The infrequent deviations from Robert's plans were only met with frustration, and then quickly resolved. But a hole being burned into one's favorite slacks with an iron paled in comparison to one's wife being substituted with a man.

He'll hate me. And I do care about being hated. Isn't that a type of love?

Though even if he had the support of anyone, or somewhere to go:

The existence I have is unnatural. I'll always be mismatched. Who'd want anything to do with me?

His only hope seemed to hinge on CryoLife recognizing a mistake had been made and correcting it by removing his brain and putting it in a different body. For the thousandth time, why hadn't Natalie invested in understanding the legal document? Or read the pamphlet. Past the bullets highlighting CryoLife benefits.

If you'd pinched off your ovaries for ten goddamn minutes to look at the facts and not focus on your children's prematurely weeping faces.

But he was sure CryoLife must've inserted a clause limiting their liability. It would've been foolish not to. Admitting their error and fixing it was a slim possibility at best. And this took him back to where he'd started.

Does this thing you are merit any value? Is Andrew worth it?

Robert's lovesick mauling annoyed him, but the actions came from a genuine place. Andrew would forfeit the safety and security Robert could represent if he admitted his feelings. He had a ready-made family if he wanted. It might not feel like his, but nothing except his conscience stopped him from taking it.

Natalie was happy. I was happy as her. Maybe I could be again. How do I know I'm not crazy? I feel different, but feeling isn't the same as being. How is it possible to wake up a different person, with the memories of someone else?

The medication.

It hit him. That IV bag had been hanging on the drip pole since he'd opened his eyes. He had no idea what they'd been dosing him with. Who's to say that disassociation with Natalie's identity, masculine feelings, and unstable emotions weren't side effects of the drugs? What if he revealed his confusion to Robert, crushing him and the boy, and then became normal after he got off the medication?

The more he considered the idea, the more sense the answer made. "Andrew" was a medically induced identity disorder. These delusions would clear when CryoLife left him alone, and the gulf separating her would disappear. He couldn't throw away the life and relationships he'd built as Natalie due to being drugged out of his fucking mind.

I want to be at peace, to be happy, and to be loved. All these things are her. He closed his eyes. *I've been giving into hallucinations, that's what this has been – an imaginary struggle and a waste of time.*

He had to resist the perverted thoughts. Perhaps like regaining mobility, he'd have to relearn being Natalie. She was another neural pathway that needed to be reactivated by continuous movement.

I can learn to love you, Robert. She – no I, must be in here.

He was eventually able to drift back to sleep with his mind set to the task of forgetting he ever woke feeling like a man named Andrew.

Chapter 3

Like most CryoLife staff and visitors, Robert entered the Cryobiotic Treatment Center by way of the indoor entrance. These secure double doors separated the Center from the east wing of Savannah General Hospital. The main doors were manned by two armed guards, but they were also stage to constant and occasionally belligerent demonstrations.

Activists fanned cardboard signs with biblical verses through the air, churning the sticky Georgia humidity with the scent of black markers. Fortunately, they were prevented from assembling inside the private property of the hospital, but their roaring proclamations from God could sometimes be heard within the building as they shouted down a naïve deliveryman. Robert chose not to think much about them.

They have no idea what they're talking about. Here's what God wants: families that aren't broken by accidents or disease. He'd swipe his visitor's pass through the eastside card reader and the steel doors would slide aside. *They're hypocrites anyway. Where were the protesters when CryoLife solved the organ donation crisis? This is the same. Giving life and hope. These are wonderful people. They gave me back my Natalie.*

Even if he still worried about her.

Before going in to see his wife, he always stopped by the nurse's station. Those women had their fingers on the pulse of everything.

"How has she been today?"

"Oh, fine, Mr. Keller. Doing very well." A nurse would close her laptop and immediately come around the counter to speak with him. The service and attention of every CryoLife staff member had been unparalleled.

I wish I could find subcontractors this sharp.

"Any anxiety attacks?"

"No, just quiet, like an angel. But, honey, she has a lot she wants to say and can't. What would upset her about not being able to talk to me? She doesn't know me from Adam."

It was as if the nurses read his mind. He wasn't stupid; he saw the patterns.

Every time I touch her, those machines erupt.

"Did she look unhappy?" he'd ask.

"She looked tired, but pay no mind to it, Mr. Keller. If you were stuck in a bed, unable to move so much as your finger, wouldn't you look angry too?"

"Yes, I suppose."

Robert would feel better for a while. He'd decide to wait and see. And trust that CryoLife was right, and his gut feeling was wrong.

But after Natalie's breakdown from Simon's card, his worry reached an intensity that drove him directly to Dr. Brigman. The rapid improvements she'd been making had stopped and she no longer seemed present in her body. When he dropped a glass in the room and she didn't turn her head to the noise, his patience crumbled. He had to talk to Brigman. Privately. In his office.

"I don't think she's sleeping. Did you change her medication?"

"We stopped the sedation. She needs to acclimate to normal sleep, as we discussed."

"Maybe it's too soon. She's lethargic. She looks like she's dying."

"Mr. Keller, it's extremely difficult to re-develop a healthy sleep cycle after being on sleep aids. Give it time."

"Can't you test something, scan something?" Robert asked.

"I assure you, her care is our highest priority. If anything in the slightest was wrong, alarms all throughout this wing of the building would go off." The doctor tipped his head slightly, his mouth curved in a gentle smile. "Your wife is attached to more machines than a space shuttle."

Robert felt his left eyelid twitch, but he kept his voice level. "Do you think this is funny? I'm telling you, something—"

"Certainly not." Brigman pushed back his leather chair and stepped in front of the desk. "Your concerns are important to us, and I appreciate you telling me how you feel."

"This isn't about how I feel. It's not about me. It's—"

"I know, I know." The soothing, easy tone in the man's voice made the interruption less irritating. "It's about your wife. I didn't mean anything else, or to have upset you."

"I'm fine. I just don't want my wife to suffer unnecessarily. She's been through enough, and we're only talking about sleep. If she needs help sleeping in order to continue making progress, maybe you should consider tapering off the medication instead of cutting it all at once."

Robert shuffled his feet, somewhat regretting the boldness. However, the question of which medical school Robert had graduated from remained unasked. Brigman's cold frown reverted to the warm, grandfatherly smile.

"We don't want her to suffer either, Mr. Keller, but you have to trust we're going about her rehabilitation in the right way. Believe me, I understand where you're coming from, and what you're thinking." He put a hand on Robert's arm. "Here I am, fancy degrees but a perfect stranger to you and Mrs. Keller. You're more in tune with her than any expert, aren't you?"

Robert allowed himself to be nudged toward the door. "I married her when she was only eighteen and haven't spent a single day apart from her in almost ten years. Until, of course, the accident." He cleared his throat. "No one knows her like I do."

"Absolutely. So let's do this – you allow us two more days. If she isn't on schedule by then, we'll reintroduce the sleeping aids, as you requested." The man turned the handle and held the door. "Surely you'll give forty years of medical experience forty-eight hours of leeway."

Maybe I'm being irrational. He's right, Natalie's not dying. But I can't shake the feeling that there's something—

Robert's eyes had been wandering the office. Certificates hung in gilded glory on the far wall, but the rest were lined by bookshelves, their tiers stocked with thick tomes and various plastic brain models. His thoughts broke off as the doctor removed the room's only photograph from a shelf.

"Here's especially why you can trust me, Mr. Keller."

Brigman held out the small framed picture of a boy with light brown hair and a wide smile. He wore an oversized doctor's coat, complete with stethoscope, and his arms were in the air as if about to hug the photographer.

Robert returned the boy's captured smile. "Your grandson? He looks about the same age as our Simon."

"No, he's my son." Dr. Brigman chuckled. "It's a common misconception. I only like to think of him as a little boy." He sighed and replaced the picture on its shelf. "You've spent ten years loving your wife. I've spent over thirty loving that boy. And he was a patient here."

"Was he?"

"Yes. So I know what you're going through. It's awful to see a loved one suffering. And it's not easy to have some old expert ask you to bear with us. But I promise you, every patient who comes through CryoLife's doors is family to me. And I'll continue to give Mrs. Keller the same care I gave to my son."

As with the friendly nurses, Brigman had said exactly what Robert needed to hear. He thought of the idiot demonstrators parading outside on the sidewalk.

See, what this man has done is a gift direct from God. These people understand values and ethics. And priorities. Family above everything else.

"Thank you." Robert extended his hand, and the doctor gave it three jovial pumps. "And I hope nothing I've said will be taken out of context. I just want to ensure my wife is taken care of and no mistakes are—"

Brigman dropped Robert's hand as if the magnetic poles of their palms had reversed. The frosty expression of his face resembled his earlier reaction to Robert's questioning. "CryoLife doesn't make mistakes."

The lingering intensity of the doctor's eyes made Robert step back, crossing the threshold into the hallway. But his motion served to break Brigman's gaze, and instantly the empathetic exterior returned.

"Two days, Mr. Keller." He gave his relaxed smile, the satin swagger of his voice erasing the minor slipup. "Your worries are admirable, but unnecessary. You can trust me. Everything will be better than all right. It'll be perfect. I'd give you nothing less. Like family, remember?"

Robert nodded.

"And please, don't hesitate to stop by again if there's anything I can assist you with. The pleasure is entirely mine."

Before he could answer with another head gesture, Brigman gently shut his office door and the deadbolt slammed into place.

The doctor's parting behavior caused Robert to have a restless night – he spent that evening tossing and turning. He closed his eyes, and there was Natalie: trapped in the hospital room, wasting away. Dying. Brigman stood at her IV, his hands folded at the small of his back.

"Aren't you going to do anything?" Robert shouted in his dream. "She's dying! Do something!"

But the doctor remained motionless with the plastic smile on his face. "There's nothing to do. Everything's perfect. Perfect."

The color drained from Natalie's face, her eyes drifting closed. Robert wanted to reach out to Brigman – grab him by his collar and push him forward, force him to save her. But he felt fixed to the spot.

And then into the dream ran the boy with light brown hair, the ends of the large white coat trailing the vinyl tiles. He was some combination of the doctor's son and Simon, as he climbed into the bed with Natalie and began shaking her.

"Mom, wake up. Wake up, Mom." The Simon-hybrid turned to Robert, his face red with crying. "She's cold, Dad. She won't wake up, and she's cold."

Robert continued to be a helpless spectator. He couldn't make Brigman act. He couldn't comfort the boy. He couldn't move to save Natalie himself. And she grew cold. Again. Lifeless. Again. And there could be no bringing her back.

The nightmare was so real he launched halfway out of bed, sweat running down his face.

"Dad, are you okay? What's wrong?"

Simon, prone to night terrors since the car accident, had taken to sleeping in bed with his father. The boy hadn't only been in the vehicle and walked away unharmed, but he'd also witnessed the beginning of the preservation procedure. Simon had described how the doctor had sunk the scalpel into his mother's throat. Her blood had gushed over the doctor's hands, spurting onto his surgical mask. He'd only been six years old.

"Yes, it's okay." Robert tried to calm his breaths as he lay down to stare into the darkness. "Go to sleep."

A thin arm curled around his chest.

"I have them too. I know what it's like."

Despite the unfortunate reality of that statement, Robert felt more peaceful after it was said aloud that he wasn't alone. He pulled Simon close and spent the night lying awake, petting his son's hair.

Upon arriving at the Cryobiotic Treatment Center the next day, his disheveled appearance prompted the nurses to question him instead.

"Mr. Keller, are you okay? Can we get you anything?"

"I didn't sleep well."

"You poor man. Let me straighten your tie. You can't let her see you like that."

Robert allowed the knot at his neck to be straightened and pieces of hair to be patted into place. Natalie didn't care how he looked, but it was nice they thought she did. She'd be upset no matter how straight his tie was.

"The dear was awake most of the night. She's sleeping now."

"That's okay."

In a way he preferred to be at her bedside when she slept. He didn't feel the hostility or panic from her, and he could pretend that everything was normal. Her languidness had him missing even the negative interaction though.

I'd rather you be angry or anxious or whatever you are than be dead. Please don't be dead.

But he didn't think he could take another day of her lying defeated and nearing the edge of death. Thank God she was asleep. It'd help her feel better.

I can't give him two days. He watched Natalie's sleeping face and thought of the dream. *If there's no improvement today, she needs the sleeping aids. I won't take no for an answer.*

Robert sank into the chair by her bed with a sigh. He pulled a magazine from his bag, opened the cover, and promptly fell asleep.

*

He woke when he felt eyes on him.

"I'm sorry, Nat. I didn't sleep well." Robert sat up from where he'd slouched in the chair. "How are you feeling? I'm glad you got some rest."

Her lips were closed, and she just stared at him.

God, I can't do this. I can't.

But then her head rose and, lowering her chin, Natalie moved her eyes toward him.

"Me?"

The corners of her mouth curled into a frown. But as she nodded there was something about the way her eyes looked at him – the skin around them not tight in displeasure.

"You're worried about me?"

Another nod. His chest thumped.

"You don't need to worry about me."

Natalie shook her head.

Robert wasn't sure what to do. She'd never tried to communicate concern toward him. Now there was kindness in her eyes. There was the first real sign that his Natalie was in there.

He raised a hand to her cheek, ready for her to pull away and the machines to howl. Her jaw tightened, but she leaned into his hand. He forgot the tenseness and melted.

*

For the rest of the visit the machines had remained quiet. Robert hadn't been given annoyed looks, and Natalie was engaged in everything he had to say. There were times when he caught a twist of her lips, or the rigidity of her cheek, but he chose not to think about these things.

So in returning the next day, Robert was intent on keeping positive to continue the promising direction things were headed. He opened the door to her room feeling upbeat.

"Good morning, Robert," Natalie said.

It was clichéd, but after the accident he'd saved her phone messages. He'd kept their voicemail the same and grouped every video of her, including those where she was filming. He would listen to his wife's light, silvery voice. Despite the reassurance by CryoLife that they'd be reunited he knew there was a chance he'd never hear her again.

He'd been told that her original body had been so mangled he couldn't be allowed to view it. So there'd been no goodbye to that either. It'd been a shock to see the new body – his flawless Natalie, even if it was a shell. But then her eyes had opened and he'd watched her progress. If the accident had happened two decades earlier, she'd have been moldering in a grave. But now she was sitting up. And she was talking to him.

"Good morning, Nat." He blinked away the tears.

"Come. In." She spoke in two separate sentences. "And. Close. The door."

He rushed in. He'd light himself on fire if she asked.

"I'm not. Stupid. I have to concentrate. To get. The words out. I'm not thinking slowly."

"I wouldn't care if you were. You're alive." Robert took her hands in his. "You must have so much to say. Talk to me. Tell me how you are, and if there's anything I can do for you."

She hesitated and glanced toward Simon's card on the side table. It made him smile. This was Natalie. Her first thoughts were for her children.

"I have things to ask," she said and he could tell that she was doing her best to speak evenly.

"Ask anything of me."

Natalie stared at the thin blanket covering her lower body. When she looked back at him, the words came in rapid succession.

"Robert, tell me what happened to me."

The accident was a topic he avoided, so he hadn't mentioned it since she'd woken. Dr. Brigman had read the statement before they opened her eyes, but that was it. There'd been no telling how much she knew. Perhaps she'd been knocked unconscious and knew nothing.

To wake completely paralyzed, and not know what happened. No wonder you've been so upset. I'm so sorry, Nat. I should've told you.

"You were in a car accident. A car crossed the—" Robert stopped as she shook her head.

"Tell me what they did to me."

"You were dead, and they brought you back."

"How'd they do it?"

"They removed your brain and kept it preserved until they rebuilt your body."

"But how exactly did they do it?"

For Natalie this was an odd question. She'd always been queasy about medical things. Besides the needles, she fell apart at the sight of blood.

On the other hand, Robert had no such hang-ups, and he'd been curious about the procedure. He hadn't found much on the exact methods and tools CryoLife used, but an image search yielded plenty of gory photographs taken from smart phones. Simon wasn't exaggerating when he described what he'd witnessed as the doctor cut off his mother's head.

Robert had also seen the storage facility once the extraction procedure was over. Row after row of metal canisters, their exteriors frosted and individual temperature gauges reading exactly -162 degrees fahrenheit. Each container bore a silver plate engraved with a number. He'd been told Natalie was CRYO-03877.

This is you, Robert had thought. Not your skin, your smile, your beautiful hair … you're really just a brain. Everyone is.

The CryoLife staff had assured him this was true, even though he struggled to believe it while walking through the storage facility that day. The essence of Natalie was a 3-pound organ, indistinguishable from the others save for the number they'd assigned her. And she'd wait with these other brains until Robert could afford to free her. For up to five long years

CryoLife would hold them in this limbo. If he was unable to finance the reanimation by then ...

He'd imagined a cryonicist popping the top of canister CRYO-03877 and dumping its contents into a furnace as if it were a piece of trash. Whether his wife was more than just the brain or not, everything would then be over.

Don't worry. I'll bring you back. I promise, Natalie.

And he had. He'd triumphed as usual, since here she was – not a brain in a metal container. His Natalie was alive—

"Robert." Natalie's voice brought him back to her hospital room, and he realized he'd forgotten what she'd even asked him. "Tell me how they brought me back."

"Nat, I'm not a doctor. I'm not sure."

"Do you have the pamphlet? And the document I signed? Can you get them for me?"

"I've read them, hon. Don't worry about it," Robert said.

"Do you know what medication they're giving me?"

"No, why would I?"

"Can you find out what it does, and what the side effects are?"

"Are you not feeling well? Is there a problem?"

I knew it. I knew there was something wrong that—

"I want to know what they're giving me. I have the right to know."

As with what he knew of the CryoLife procedure and preservation, Natalie didn't need her mind cluttered with irrelevant information.

"I'm sure we'll discuss everything with Dr. Brigman. Remember he said we'd talk when you could be part of the conversation?"

She agreed with a small nod.

"I'll take care of everything, Nat. You have more important things to concentrate on. Like getting better."

After a delay, she nodded again, devoid of emotion. Her resignation to end the topic relieved him, and his heart lit once more.

"What else do you want to know? Ask me what I can answer."

He waited for Natalie to ask about Simon or Michael. Or him. What about their friends, his family, or their jobs? To ask what changes had taken place in the world. But she relaxed into her pillows.

"There's nothing else." They studied each other before she continued. "What magazine did you bring?"

Robert's smile faded. She'd been gone for more than a year and had been conscious, yet mute, for days. Now that she was finally speaking, he'd hoped to get more out of her.

"If you'll hold it, let me read to you. If you can stand to hear it slowly," Natalie said.

She knew. Through the joy of hearing her voice he was likely to lose the meaning of her actual words.

"If I can stand it? There's nothing I'd rather hear than your voice."

Robert nudged the side table and lowered the rail to her bed. He sat halfway on it, and bent the magazine's spine to hold in front of her. He could smell her hair and feel the warmth from her skin. Both were worth the mildly uncomfortable position.

Chapter 4

The promised discussion took place in Dr. Brigman's office the next day, and it was the first time Andrew had been allowed to leave the hospital room. After staring at the same four walls for weeks, the excitement of a new place temporarily mashed down the weight of his internal conflict.

Robert pushed his wheelchair out into the hall. And what a hall! Had there ever been such a hall? Unlike his bleached room, the walls were sectioned in a cream colored molding. The tile was different too. White but patterned with streaks of black, splotches of yellow, daubs of—

"Nat, what are you doing? You're going to tip the chair over." Robert paused.

Thank God. Twisting from side to side as he tried to study the floor was making him dizzy.

"Look." Andrew pointed to a square.

"It's tile."

"Doesn't it remind you of anything?"

"Tile."

"Jackson Pollock. The colors and the marbling. It reminds me of *White Light*. Don't you think?"

The look on Robert's face revealed his thoughts before he spoke. "I think it reminds me of vinyl tile. Stop squirming, hon."

No matter. Andrew took a breath and swallowed. Natalie hadn't needed Robert to be interested in art for them to get along. It hadn't mattered before, so it shouldn't matter now. As the wheelchair moved forward he locked an image of the abstract tile in his mind for solitary consideration later. *There are other things to enjoy. Such as:*

"After the meeting, why don't we go outside? The nurse opened the blinds this morning and it's so bright—"

"No."

Andrew turned his head. "Why not?"

"Nat, you remember how there's that sect that doesn't understand anything about CryoLife?" Robert stopped again outside a door. A gold plaque in the middle proclaimed it to be the office of Dr. Brigman. "They have a troop outside to heckle people to cause trouble."

"Why? I mean, on what basis do they oppose CryoLife?"

"It doesn't matter what basis."

"Sure it does. What—"

"They're uneducated religious fanatics with nothing better to do than clog sidewalks."

Robert's eyebrows were pulled together and his tone had a clipped feel. Natalie had been inquisitive about the world, but her questions never went three deep. Her husband gave an answer and things moved on. But despite Robert's frustration, Andrew couldn't curb his curiosity. People opposing CryoLife? Why? And what did they know?

"They must feel passionately about—"

"Much good it does them." Robert smiled and appeared to push aside his annoyance. When he ran a hand through Andrew's hair, Andrew tried not to lean away. "They're waiting for us, Nat."

Before he could say anything further, Robert pushed open the door and wheeled him into the office.

Andrew watched as Robert shook hands with the two men and one woman in the room. Dr. Brigman introduced his colleagues as Mr. Tweed, legal representation of the Cryobiotic Treatment Center, and Dr. Zuniga, head of the CryoLife psychiatric board. Once they'd all taken their seats, Brigman spread his hands apart like a benevolent God, and the meeting began.

"I speak on behalf of CryoLife when I say this is why we do what we do. Reuniting beautiful families that would've been otherwise torn apart by tragedy." The way the doctor looked between the two of them gave Andrew an unsettling feeling.

"We're so pleased to be part of your recovery journey." Dr. Zuniga smiled at Andrew. He didn't return it. There was something exaggerated about her expression. Like she'd read somewhere that the wider the smile, the higher and rounder the eyebrows, the more trustworthy a person appeared. The result resembled an overinflated balloon.

And who can trust a balloon? An honest person doesn't need to try so hard to look honest.

"We appreciate everything your staff has done." Robert placed his hand on Andrew's arm.

In his head, Andrew began to count.

1 Mississippi. 2 Mississippi. 3 Mississippi.

Robert's touch still felt awful, but the only way he'd relearn to like it was by endurance. Yesterday, he'd let it go for ten seconds. Today, he was trying to hold out for fifteen.

"There are some things we need to outline as part of the six-month recovery plan—"

Andrew cleared his throat and pulled away from Robert at only seven seconds. He couldn't concentrate on training when he was on the brink of having answers. The three professionals focused on him as he spoke. "I have questions first."

"By all means, Mrs. Keller." Brigman drew his fingertips together in an upside down "V". "Ask us anything."

"I'd like to know what happened to me."

"You were in a car accident and declared imminently dead. We were able to preserve your brain and reanimate you."

"I want to know *how* it happened."

"Our organization doesn't review or file police reports, ma'am." While Mr. Tweed's face remained neutral, the lack of an overcompensating smile like Zuniga's or Brigman's thin-lipped grin didn't make Andrew feel differently about him. Something about these CryoLife people – they couldn't be trusted. "I'd recommend contacting the Savannah Police Department for that information."

"I don't mean what happened in the accident."

Andrew felt his shoulders stiffen and in his peripheral vision, the psychiatrist's balloon appearance shrunk slightly as she made a note in the portfolio on her lap.

Always scrutinized. Always being watched. But I wouldn't get so fucking pissed off if you'd stop dicking me around and just answer—

Robert touched his shoulder. "Nat, you don't want the technical details."

1 Mississippi. 2—

"Yes, I do." Andrew shrugged him off. "I wouldn't ask otherwise."

"It's too graphic for you." Robert nodded and touched him again. "Way too—"

"How would you know? You're not a doctor, remember? You weren't sure when I asked you before."

This time, Robert's hand withdrew of its own accord and he broke Andrew's eye contact, turning his head away.

You lied to me. Even if it was because the old Natalie wouldn't have wanted to know, I did. I still do. And you deliberately withheld information from me, you son-of-a-bitch.

"Mrs. Keller," Tweed interrupted the angry silence. "Our processes are also patented and classified."

Andrew looked from Robert to the attorney. "I need to know what happened to me."

Dr. Zuniga clicked the top of her pen and set her folder of notes on the corner of Brigman's desk. "I think a general outline could be given if it'd help with the trauma. Not full disclosure, but understanding more can be an effective coping tool." She sucked in a breath to re-inflate her face and smiled at Robert. "Assuming that's okay with you, Mr. Keller, of course."

Andrew shot a glare to Robert, but before he could speak, Robert answered. "Okay. But please keep it general. That type of thing makes her uncomfortable."

"I'm fine." Andrew crossed his arms tightly and looked across the desk as Dr. Brigman began.

"You're aware of the CryoLife guidelines and candidacy in time of need?"

Tweed broke in, reciting from memory: "As referenced in article 1–5: 'For redemption of benefits, CryoLife participants must be between the ages of 18 and 35 at time of crisis. As determined by a licensed CryoLife technician, participants must have minimal to no existent brain injury associated with crisis. Participants must be declared imminently dead by a licensed CryoLife technician, or pronounced dead no more than two full minutes before extraction proceedings begin. Participants—"

"What does that mean, 'declared imminently dead'?" Andrew asked. "You said I was declared imminently dead."

"You were still alive, but anticipated to die," Brigman said.

Isn't that the general human condition? "Aren't you alive but anticipated to die? Can I extract your brain?"

Zuniga pushed a pair of eyeglasses farther up the bridge of her nose, took her portfolio, and jotted something else.

That's right, bitch. Note it all up. Everything was so frustrating. Andrew knew he was already failing. Old Natalie had been demure and accommodating. But he couldn't help that he wasn't easily dominated or reserved. The words rolled out before he could stop them.

Brigman seemed to take the venomous comment in stride. "Tweed?"

"As deemed by a licensed CryoLife technician, 'imminently dead' is defined by the anticipated death of an individual within five minutes or less due to trauma."

"One can never be absolutely positive, but I'm relatively certain I don't fit that criteria." Brigman smiled.

"Well, as you said – 'one can never be *absolutely positive.*'"

"Natalie, enough." Robert took his hand. "I apologize, she's not usually like this."

"Don't apologize for me, I—" Andrew stopped as Robert curled his fingers sharp into his palm.

"No, no, don't you worry about it, Mr. Keller. She's right – one can never be absolutely positive." Brigman leaned forward with a smile before continuing. "But I certainly hope I make it to lunchtime. It's pizza Thursday in the hospital cafeteria."

Pizza? Are you serious?

Amid the polite chuckles all around, Andrew managed to pull his hand from Robert. He folded his arms again and gave Brigman a concentrated stare.

"Anyway, once a participant is determined to be qualified, our technician jumps into action. We provisionally connect the body with a machine to continue circulation and oxygen while the blood is replaced with a stabilizer reducing freezing damage. We then extract the brain. It's kept in storage and cooled by liquid nitrogen for up to five years, or until the beneficiary waives benefits, or provides the deductible to begin reanimation."

"You said 'reducing freezing damage.' The freezing causes damage?"

"The brain is delicate, Mrs. Keller, damage could result from many things. This goes back to the cryonic concept that surfaced two hundred years ago – preserving the body at low temperatures with the ultimate goal of revival in a more medically advanced future. And that future is now."

"But that wasn't—"

"My team is comprised of the best cryonicists in the world, the *best*," Brigman interrupted. "And we've conquered every physical and neurological challenge in the field. First for simple organ recreation, which eliminated the need for organ donation, ending an epidemic that plagued mankind for—"

"You're not answering—"

"We're at a completely different level than the primitive techniques where they'd basically hang a body in an icy sleeping bag. Reminds me of ..."

Andrew felt himself shaking, and his cheeks burned. This was his medical care. HIS. He had a right to know what had happened to him. He should not have to—

"Dr. Brigman, I think my wife is trying to ask you something."

He glanced over at Robert, who offered an almost imperceptible smile.

For what? Lying to me? Pinching my hand? Getting this douche bag to shut up does not make—

"I apologize, Mrs. Keller." The head doctor pulled his lips into his professional smirk and looked at Natalie. "I'm just very proud of the work we do here. Please, go ahead with your question."

"I want to know if the freezing causes damage. Does your procedure cause brain damage?"

Tweed coughed. "Per section 14–8, 'Participant and beneficiaries agree the CryoLife corporation and associated staff are not liable for perceived or actual damage. Participant and beneficiaries waive rights to all litigation."

Dr. Brigman laced his fingers and rested his hands on his stomach, rocking in his chair. "We've implemented many new methods to reduce the impact of the temporary loss of circulation and oxygen, the stabilizer, and cooling process. Nonetheless, it's inherent that minor brain tissue damage occasionally occurs due to crystallization, lack of oxygen, et cetera." He lifted a hand and gave a lilting gesture. "And we can't forget that this procedure isn't being performed with a healthy person. There may be undetected impairment resulting from the crisis."

To his surprise, when Andrew looked to Robert, one of his eyebrows was lifted. *You did know something, but not that much. Maybe that's why you held back from me.*

And he felt a little better about Natalie's husband, which was a relief in many ways. Abhorring his touch was one thing, but if Andrew couldn't trust Robert, then who did he really have? He turned to the doctors and attorney.

Certainly not these so called "care providers."

"Brain damage?" Andrew snapped. "You cause people brain—"

"If you're considering the daily function of an individual, Mrs. Keller, 'damage' is probably an overstatement," Brigman replied. "Yes, there's tissue alteration, but we're talking about minor changes."

"Changes?"

"If I may?" Dr. Zuniga rose and took a plastic brain model from a shelf beside Brigman's desk. Andrew saw that it was sectioned into hundreds of colorful places like a mosaic, or a stained glass window. Larger pieces were labeled with abbreviations, but there were other portions smaller than a pinhead.

Pointillism, kind of. A Seurat brain.

Dr. Zuniga crouched to be at his eye level and drew a line with her fingertip around a section the size of a golf ball.

"We've isolated crystallization here, so anything affected won't be debilitating to the individual," she said. "You see, Natalie, most people think the brain is infinitely complex, but it comes down to groups of cells. There's an exact pattern of cells responsible for everything you like and dislike. Your greatest joys and deepest sorrows are a bit of brain matter. Tissue damage to this area only impacts things like that."

I hate being spoken to like I'm in preschool. Where's that group of cells? I'm not going to shove your pen up my fucking nose, so stop treating me like a five-year-old.

"I had a patient years ago." Dr. Brigman nodded. "Loved Chinese food. When we reanimated him, he couldn't stand the stuff. Another woman we brought back had the desire to play piano. Never touched an instrument before or wanted to. Now she's a professional musician."

Oh, the horror. Chinese food and piano. How did those beleaguered individuals find the courage to survive? But instead, and before he could stop himself to consider:

"Has anyone ever come back as another person?"

This question prompted Dr. Zuniga's expeditious return to her chair. The helium leaked from her ears and her eyebrows settled to a normal position on her face while she added more notes. Andrew cringed and chewed the inside of his cheek.

Stupid. Stupid. Why can't you just shut up, Andrew? No, Natalie. Natalie. Shut up, Natalie. But then, why should you? They ripped out your brain and crusted it with Shake 'n Bake. What further damage can they really do?

"In a way that's what brings us here – your recovery plan." Brigman turned his attention to Andrew. "Whatever the cause of changes in the individual's brain, the question is posed – how much is too much? At what point is a patient too different from their previous identity? Natalie Keller died a year and a half ago. We don't yet know if your reanimated brain has the amount of substance – the behavior, the memory, the character – that makes you her, and not someone else."

The breath he was about to exhale abruptly lodged in his throat, and a few seconds passed before he could speak.

"If I'm not Natalie, who am I?"

"Technically, you're no one."

He laughed. "That's ridiculous."

Whoever I am, I am someone. You can't just be nothing.

"Is it? Consider if I was reanimated to discover I'd lost my medical knowledge. Would it be right to practice as a doctor? And what if I lost all memory of my family? Would it be fair to continue to be responsible for them and financially support strangers? Am I entitled to my assets, my legal obligations? It's extremely unlikely with how advanced our neurosuspension techniques are, but the most remote possibility still requires an answer."

"And for that reason," Tweed supplemented, "per section 42–2, and in accordance with United States law, 'A legal conservatorship will be established between reanimated individuals and a court appointed conservator. The conservatorship will remain in place for no less than six months following the date of reanimation, whereupon the conservator may grant the conservatee full benefits and entitlements in assimilation of the previously held identity. The conservator retains the right to pass full conservatorship to the CryoLife corporation at request and upon return of the conservatee to the facility at—'"

"Wait, wait. *Conservatorship?*" Andrew's breathing now came quickly, and he felt his heart hammering his chest. He saw Robert touch his wrist, but barely felt it and didn't bother to start counting before snatching his hand away. "Granting? Passing? I'm not a child. I'm not mentally incapacitated. And I'm no one's property."

"Certainly not, ma'am," Tweed said. "And we can understand how this is upsetting for you; however, in the eyes of the law, Natalie Keller is dead. Until we can verify who you are, you don't have a permanent identity. These processes and regulations have been established for your protection."

"I can manage my own assets and make my own decisions!"

Robert's patronizing laughter caused a small stream of butane to escape and meet with a spark.

"Natalie, Natalie." He reached over and patted Andrew's hand. "Since when have you ever managed anything beyond the grocery list?" Robert chuckled. "Don't worry, hon. I'll be taking care of everything like always."

The disparity inside his head was overwhelming. He felt furious and insulted to be virtually stripped of his rights. But—

This was Natalie's life. This was my life. She—I—we ... Whatever. We wanted this. We liked this.

Natalie didn't have to worry about income, bills, or property. Was her name listed on the house? Their bank account? Andrew had no idea. She'd been complacent in being told by Robert that all was well. She worked at the school, cleaned the house, and took care of the children. He gave her an allowance for groceries, clothing, and spending money. Everything else Robert handled. So really, as Natalie, Andrew had no reason to be upset about life carrying on "like always."

But I don't want that. The new me. I want to be independent and have control over my life. I—

"It's just necessary for you to temporarily have a guardian who can legally represent you, act as your healthcare proxy, and manage your assets." The psychiatrist broke into Andrew's thoughts and he looked over at her distorted smile. "In a few short days you'll be going home with your husband and little boy. Before you have time to think about it, the six months will be over and it'll be like nothing ever happened."

"Just another perfect, happy reunification. Thanks to CryoLife," Brigman added.

Perfect. Happy. He was trying. How many seconds had he allowed Robert's hand to be on him just now? But it wasn't working. Things weren't happy. Not while he felt this way. Things also weren't perfect. And how long would it be before Robert found that out?

Andrew tipped his head to Robert without taking his eyes from the head doctor. "Unless he finds something wrong with me and returns me to you? Unless he finds a nick in the paint or some other mistake you people—"

For the first time, Andrew saw Brigman's fake congeniality swept away by coldness. The doctor's brow furrowed, his mouth tight and pinched. "We do not—"

"Mrs. Keller, you're understandably confusing that portion of the agreement." Zuniga crossed her ankles and nodded. "It's nothing negative, but another clause designed to protect you. Should the conservator determine that an individual doesn't meet the criteria for granting the previous identity, rather than abandon you in this in-between stage, you'll simply return to our facility until the conservatorship expires."

"And then?"

"We'd grant you a different identity and send you on your way."

The balloon woman made an interesting point.

So I can try this out and make an honest effort like I promised myself I would. Once I'm off the meds, I pick up where Natalie—I left off. It may not seem like things will be great, but they could be.

Andrew looked at the floor. It was short, rough carpet and not the Pollock-ish tile from the hallway, but that was okay.

Worst case scenario and I just can't pull it off, I come back here and get a new identity. Not that I want that. At least I can trust Robert. And not that it really even is an option since these meds have me on a constant acid trip. I'll get over it once they leave me alone.

Andrew lifted his head and looked carefully between Robert and the head doctor. "Okay."

Dr. Brigman's broad smile returned. "Good. Now it won't all be fun and games. There are still CryoLife regulations you'll need to comply with following your release from the Center, including the continuation of your medication."

His chest tightened. "All the medication?"

"The medication is critical," Zuniga said. "It's a specific immunosuppressant that only licensed distributors are equipped to handle."

Breathe. An immunosuppressant is fine. That wouldn't cause these feelings. They've got me on something else I'll stop taking, I'm sure of it.

"Of course, if you have the slightest concern, feel free to contact us right away, and we'll take care of it." The doctor nodded to Robert. "Part of our complete, lifetime support system for you both."

"Really superior." Robert removed his hand from Andrew's, leaving it moist and sticky. "It's unfortunate that more organizations don't operate this way."

Andrew rubbed his palm along his thigh to relieve the clamminess. He curled his hand around the wheelchair's armrest. *You're Natalie. You're Natalie.*

"Was there anything else we could answer for you?" Brigman asked.

Robert seemed barely able to contain himself. "Dr. Zuniga, you mentioned Natalie will be able to come home in a *few* days. Can you be more specific?"

There was that sick feeling in the pit of Andrew's stomach – the nausea that ended all thoughts.

"With the progress your wife is making, I'd anticipate she'll be ready to leave about a week from today," the doctor answered.

Robert stood and unlocked the brakes of Andrew's wheelchair before catching Brigman's extended hand. "So next pizza Thursday?"

The man laughed and gave his hand an extra pump. "Yes, sir. Next pizza Thursday."

Andrew swung his gaze to the ceiling before closing his eyes. *What the fuck.*

Chapter 5

"It's not that bad, Nat."

To say the previous day's meeting had left a bad taste in his wife's mouth was an understatement. She'd been aloof before, but now she calculated every move made as if actively resisting some invisible force. The slight connotation between uncertainty and caution.

"Easy for you to say it's not bad." Natalie stared out her room's window. "Did you die? Did you have your rights handed over to someone else?"

"You're acting as if I'm going to lock you up." Robert squeezed her hand. "You know me better than that. I won't prevent you from doing anything you want. I'm just going to take care of you."

"What about the regulations? Besides the medication bullshit?"

You'll get used to the combativeness. Maybe don't think of it that way. Quirky. Yes, the only unpleasant side effect from a procedure that brought her back from the dead is that she's quirky. No big deal.

"You can't leave the state without approval. You can't own or operate firearms. Hon, about the only thing that'll impact you, is you aren't eligible for employment, and you have to retake the driving test. Unless you want to be a world traveling gun salesman, it'll be like before."

"I can't have a job?"

The lobby contained the same ugly splatter tile Natalie had been captivated by the day before. He studied it and considered how to answer her question without causing upset or inviting more negativity.

"You have to have an identity to be considered a person. Only people can have jobs," she muttered for him.

Robert wasn't necessarily unhappy that she wouldn't be working. Before the accident, she'd been about to return to her teaching job after Michael, and he'd been planning to talk to her about not going back. She loved the art stuff, but their family was the first priority.

"I like the idea of you being at home." He curled a piece of her hair behind her ear. "Especially after what happened, Simon needs you. And, Nat, nothing can replace Michael, but we could have another. You could dedicate yourself to being a mom."

Having his family together and safe in one place – coming home to a cozy house full of children, laughter, and love – was not only ideal, but critical. Everything again within his control, and this entire CryoLife, reanimation, assimilation mess would be forgotten.

"Should I get you another blanket?" he asked when she shuddered. "The air is high in here. I can have them turn it off."

"It's fine."

Robert took off his jacket and tucked it around her shoulders. She resumed looking out the window, avoiding his eyes. Her features seemed to contract, as if she were trying to block out her surroundings, or keep them inside.

"Is something bothering you, Nat? What else is on your mind?"

The tightness in her face eased some, dialing back from the pained expression to one of just anxiety.

"They mentioned a deductible had to be paid. I can't imagine it was cheap. If you're still dealing with that, how will we get by without me working?"

Was that it? Had she been so worried about money? But it made sense in a way – family came first for Natalie, and she needed to know that she and Simon would still be taken care of.

You never need to doubt that, ever.

"I have everything handled. Don't worry about it."

"How much did you pay?"

"It doesn't matter."

"Yes, it does. How much was it?" She gave him a sharp glance.

I guess this could make sense too. Robert smiled. They had so much in common, and vanity was on the short list of shameful qualities that drew them together. Without being spoken aloud, he knew they individually always felt they were better than other people. *You want to know how much better, how much more valuable.*

"Two million dollars."

Her eyes grew wide and she gave no answer.

"I sold the house, my parents sold their house, and half the business. Plus the life insurance, damages from the accident, and a loan. I would've begged for it, I would've stolen it. For an amount a hundred times that. I would've done anything to get you back, Nat."

When Natalie met his stare, her chin trembled, and Robert felt confused. Did she want it to be more? Should he have lied and said it was a higher amount?

"I'm not worth it, Robert."

"You're alive, and there isn't a price that can be placed on that."

His sacrifices past and future were well spent. Her every movement brought him pleasure. He watched her inhale, closing her eyes. The sun washed over her complexion and her hair shone like bundles of curling gold. CryoLife had returned her with the wear of life lifted. His perfect, perfect Natalie. It was a miracle.

Her voice quivered. "I'll try to be deserving of your love, Robert."

"That's silly. It's not about deserving, and you have nothing to prove." He chuckled, though the professed indebtedness had a shiny feel to it.

"I have to prove to you I'm the same person. But I'm different. I feel different."

"Nat, what we've been through is horrible. People change when things happen to them." He smoothed his thumb under her eye, pushing her tears aside. "When I got that second call telling me it was no longer necessary to meet the ambulance at the hospital, I became a different person. Now I know how it is to lose everything, and I'm going to think about that second call for the rest of my life. I'll never take you or Simon for granted again."

"You never took them for granted."

Robert wondered if Natalie felt he hadn't appreciated her. Could this be where the trouble originated? Why had she said "them," referring to the children? But how she felt before didn't matter. Only the future was relevant. Still, he should've told her a higher price for the deductible.

"I always thought you'd be there. Until you weren't. I don't expect you to be the same. We'll be closer and better people for this."

He was hoping she'd give him a glowing smile – the one where she showed her teeth and her dark eyes gleamed. But his valiant convictions earned him only a slight curve of her mouth.

"You're a good man, Robert. Too good."

It wasn't what he wanted to hear, but he was sure that'd come eventually.

*

The next day, Robert decided he'd kept Simon from his mother long enough. But when he broached the idea of a visit, he was disappointed with Natalie's reaction.

"Do you think that's wise, Robert?"

"Don't worry about those right wing nutjobs outside, hon. We'll only use the east entrance through the hospital."

"No, it's this place. He's a little boy."

"Don't tell him that."

"But he is. I don't think it's a good idea. A little boy shouldn't be in a place like this."

"A little boy shouldn't be without his mother for over a year. You have no idea how much he misses you."

She didn't, and not due to reluctance to tell her. Simon had only been discussed when Robert initiated it, and Natalie always changed the subject. He'd come to the conclusion that she avoided talking about their son because she missed him too much. She didn't ask about Michael either.

When he'd walked into her room that morning, she'd held the family portrait from her side table. He stood in silence, watching her trace a finger around the image of herself. It'd been their last photo – she'd been pregnant with Michael.

Was she thinking about the empty crib he'd disassembled? Picturing the small clothes and toys? He'd wept over Michael's blankets while he was packing them into a cardboard box, holding them to his face and breathing in the scent of the boy he'd barely known, but loved so much.

It occurred to Robert that no one had actually told Natalie that Michael was dead. Except for his side comment that their child wasn't replaceable, but maybe she'd missed that. Again, not that she'd asked. Did she want to know anything? If he'd suffered? Or what happened to his body? Perhaps that was part of what continued to trouble her. He'd had the opportunity to work through his grief, but for her this was fresh.

"Hon, you know Michael's gone, don't you?" Robert had slid into his chair.

She set the portrait on her lap. Her eyes were bleary.

"Yes." Natalie whispered.

"Do you want to know anything else?"

"No."

"Do you want to talk about it?"

"No."

After sitting in silence looking at the picture together, he'd mentioned Simon. And despite her protests, he'd worn her down.

"Don't worry." He kissed her forehead before leaving for the night. "He'll forgive everything. He wants his mother back."

*

"Mom, look who's here to see you." Robert opened the door and nudged Simon in.

Natalie smoothed her hair. The action made Robert smile – it was fast and even. They were working on her ability to walk, and the progress was amazing.

Only five more days. Five.

Shaking, Simon glanced up from his shoes. And when he saw her – complete and looking like she might've if they were at home and he'd interrupted her reading in bed – he dropped the flowers he'd been carrying. He rushed to his mother, and like he had in Robert's dream, jumped into the bed. Straddling her waist, he hugged her neck, colliding with such momentum that she coughed.

Robert thought it must've been the shock of seeing him in general that caused Natalie's hesitation to hold him. She glanced to Robert. When he nodded, she tentatively folded her arms around their son.

"Mom." Simon leaned back and cupped his hands around her neck.

Again, Natalie looked to Robert, who shrugged and sat in his chair.

"Mom, where's your scars? I saw the man in the white coat cut off your head." He lifted her hair and tried to see around her neck. "How'd he sew it on again so you don't have scars?"

"Maybe you only thought you saw that, Simon." Natalie looked into his eyes.

"No, I did."

"Then where are my scars? Remember when you fell on the sidewalk and cut your cheek? You have a scar from that, so how could I not have scars if my head had been cut off?"

Robert smiled. He saw the gears turning in Simon's head as he considered the argument.

"But it was so real, Mom."

"Sometimes dreams can be very real."

Simon pulled his legs to her side, and laced his arms around her neck. He hummed and curled his fingers in her hair. Natalie fidgeted and couldn't find the right position to place her hands.

"I think someone brought a gift for you," Robert said.

Simon sat up and pulled a small jar from his pocket. "You'll like this, Mom!" He pressed it into her hand.

The jar contained leaves and gray insects balanced on the sides.

"I caught them yesterday in the park! They were under this big rock!" Simon held his arms open to indicate the massive size, before seizing her in a tight cuddle. "You'll hunt bugs with me, won't you? I'll show you the rock in the park."

Natalie passed the jar to Robert, and after another nonverbal prompt from him, she wrapped her arms around the boy.

"Yes, I will." Her eyes went to Robert for reassurance.

"Dad said you weren't coming home today, but you will tomorrow?"

Robert touched his shoulder. "Mom can come home in a few days."

Simon straightened his back and pressed his lips close to Natalie's ear to whisper. "You can come home before then. But home isn't the same place anymore. It's on Third Street on the first floor of the blue building."

"Thank you, but your dad is right." Her face pinched. "Don't I need to be completely better to go bug hunting?"

"We could do other things. Or nothing. Can't you be in bed at home like you are here? Dad said he'd protect us, but we have to be together." He hugged her with a fierce grip. "Who protects you when he's with me?"

"Didn't you see those nurses? They wouldn't let anything happen to me." Natalie patted him on the head in a mechanical motion, her hand flat and stiff.

"They're not Dad. Only Dad can protect you. And me. I can too."

She chewed the corner of her lower lip and drew back in hesitation before speaking.

"I'm sorry, Simon. But you're going to have to be patient."

Robert expected him to launch into the uncontrollable weeping that accompanied the night terrors. Would he have to drag him out of the room? Have Brigman sedate him so he wouldn't rip her apart when they tried to make him leave?

But Simon closed his eyes and nuzzled his cheek to Natalie's shoulder. "Please don't stay away much longer, Mom. I miss you."

Her frame grew more rigid. After a long break, she replied. "So, how's school?"

Robert rubbed his chin. It was an odd response. No "I miss you too" or "I love you"? What was wrong with her?

It's not her fault. You've got to keep that in mind.

Natalie's sudden awkwardness, resistance, and anger were things he was sure he could become accustomed to, now that the CryoLife doctors had given him a reason for her behavior. The "tissue alteration," as Brigman had called it, was worth having her back.

If you're changed from this, it doesn't matter. You're still you. He watched Natalie's face. Was she aware of the changes in herself? *If you are different, maybe you'll try to fix or control these behaviors.*

And as he'd assured Natalie before, Simon didn't care. He forgave his mother's strange, distant actions.

"School's good," Simon whispered, winding the ends of her hair around his fingers. "But don't talk. Be warm, Mom." He hummed louder. "Just be warm."

Robert wasn't concerned with the request. He knew Simon wasn't referring to Natalie's lack of affection. Coldness was death to him. He'd rather have her slightly imperfect, but there. And he now knew she wasn't gone forever. She wasn't dead. She was warm. And this was supreme.

We can get used to this, Simon. It's still her.

The rare times Robert had had a peaceful sleep in the past year stuck out in his mind. And never had he slept as well as the day he saw his wife open her eyes. It'd been a new door opening. A back door, into the past. Joy and hope pumped out the misery and loneliness. The emotions had been draining and when he got home his bones gave way beneath him, and he sank into a dreamless sleep.

So he understood how Simon could let the release power him off. His fingers slipped from her hair, and he melted into his mother. Natalie looked petrified.

"He's only asleep, Nat."

"I know he's asleep." She looked at him before swallowing and turning her eyes to Robert. "I'm sorry, but I can't do this. I can't do this to you, or him."

"What are you talking about?" He placed his hand on hers, but she pulled away. "Is this about the warm comment? He's not talking about how you're acting. Don't you remember when his hamster died? He asked why it was cold."

It was one of his favorite memories. He'd been dozing when he heard the voice on the opposite bedside. Natalie's arm had unfolded from his chest as she turned with a yawn.

"What is it, baby?"

"Scooter won't move. Why's he cold, Mom?"

Robert pictured Simon holding out the stiff rodent, but he'd kept his eyes closed. How were dead hamsters disposed of? It'd clog the toilet, and they didn't take the trash for another week. Maybe he'd throw it over the fence with a pair of tongs and let the neighbor's cat have it.

"Oh, Simon, I'm sorry, sweetheart, but he's dead." Her arm moved as she petted either the hamster or the boy.

"What's dead?"

"Dead is where your body can't work anymore. It's sick, or hurt, or old. The parts don't work together right."

"What happens to you then?"

"You leave. You can't stay in something that doesn't work anymore."

"Where do you go?"

"I don't know, baby," Natalie had said it in such a genuine tone that it didn't sound like a cop out. "You go wherever you're supposed to go."

"But where's that?"

"You know when you get there." Her body leaned farther from Robert. "Set him on the nightstand, love, and come here."

The mattress creaked as Simon crawled into bed.

"I don't like being cold."

"Neither do I." She pulled the blanket around the two of them.

"That's how I knew something was wrong with Scooter. When he's sleeping, I poke him and he's warm. When you're cold, is it almost dead? Does it mean you're becoming dead?"

"No. It means you need a cuddle with someone who loves you. Don't think so much, baby. You're not going to die."

"Are you going to die? Is Dad going to die?"

"Not for a very long time. Don't worry about it."

Their son's fears had been soothed, and it hadn't been long before Robert heard their rhythmic breathing. He turned on his back and folded his arms under his head.

Perfection.

He'd glanced at Natalie's hair falling across the pillow. He could tell she had Simon in her arms, her cheek to his head. There wasn't a single thing out of place. His family. His life. He had everything he ever wanted.

I created this. I built this.

And now he was going to regain it. Minus the dead rodent on the nightstand.

"Yes, I remember." The Natalie in the hospital bed brought him back from the frequently visited memory. "It's not about that. I'm different. I—"

"Does it look like it matters to him that you're a little different?"

"It's not a little different." She sighed. "There's something wrong, and I can't hide that from you."

"It's an adjustment, I'll give you that. But you'll feel more normal when you're home."

Robert put aside the half concocted thought of her wanting to leave them. This was Natalie. And she'd always been afraid of disappointing him. Her goal in life was to be the perfect wife and mother, and she was panicking because she felt she was falling short. Which she was, but he could deal with her deficiencies.

And shortages could be temporary anyway. Perhaps she hadn't considered that. "You don't know you can't get better."

Natalie lowered her eyes to the floor.

"You said you'd never prevent me from doing what I want. Even during the next six months when you own me, in essence."

"I don't *own* you. I'm your guardian. There's a difference." He motioned to Simon. "I'm Simon's guardian too, and look,

I let him out of the dungeon occasionally." The joke met with a blank stare. "Nat, I'm kidding. I'd never force you to do anything."

"You feel like that now. You bought me. You probably have a receipt for me."

He squeezed her shoulder. "I paid for a group of doctors to bring you back to us. I paid for them to perform a service. I don't own the product. I don't give a fuck what the law says I technically have, or can do."

Robert expected this to draw a positive reaction. She wanted to know she was valuable, but also that he didn't think of her as an object, right?

"And if I try and it doesn't work, will you let me go?"

Robert took off his glasses. He rubbed his eyebrows with his thumb and pointer finger. He couldn't rationalize this as being part of her new eccentricity and be okay with it. Why was she being this morbid? *Let it go.* No matter how uncomfortable this new reality currently was, she could be dead. With that tamed, what else mattered and why were they wasting time being upset about it?

"Natalie, I'll say it again – I won't prevent you from doing anything. If you wanted me to turn the conservatorship to CryoLife so you could be someone else, I would." He slid his glasses back on. "But don't give up on yourself. Please try."

Her eyes drew inward but she put her cheek to the top of Simon's head.

"I'll try, but I wanted to make sure there was an out."

"There's always an out. Even in the most difficult situations."

And Robert smiled. He'd won. As usual.

Chapter 6

Natalie was released on schedule. And the hiccups in between were so minor that Robert paid them no mind. Again she changed after the troubling conversation during Simon's visit.

She seemed complacent. And while it wasn't her normal self, it was closer than any version before. Robert believed it was more due to him and Simon encouraging her to work harder at recovery, and less because of the medication she was on. Most of the time.

With the target date of release in sight, the CryoLife staff were amiable about transitioning his wife's care. A couple of days before she left, Dr. Zuniga reviewed with him the medications Natalie was taking.

"It's been such a traumatic event for you and your son, Mr. Keller. And it's been almost as bad for Mrs. Keller."

"I know." Robert nodded.

"After reanimation, individuals have a tendency to become depressed. Or possibly aggressive."

It was good to have that out in the open. "Yes, I noticed she gets riled quicker than she used to."

"A normal part of adjusting, I assure you," Zuniga said. "So based on our continued talks, we'll make recommendations of medication to help her assimilate."

Robert hadn't been sure how he felt about this at first.

"You said recommendations?"

"Yes. If we think a new medication or dosage would be effective, as her conservator you'll need to approve. We try to make it easy for you by only providing our medication to a licensed distributor so her immunosuppressant medication can be combined on site with everything else. The end result is that she'll only have to take one pill." Zuniga had tipped her glasses and looked at Robert. "Technically, Mr. Keller, you don't need to worry her about what's in the medication."

And the psychiatrist had shown him the document detailing what CryoLife was giving Natalie. The complicated medications didn't have the friendly names advertised on television. But Zuniga explained what each was, and how they worked together to help his wife.

She also mentioned alternatives they could try if Natalie became too listless, or developed facial tics. The level of control made him feel better. Characteristic of the entire CryoLife operation, he didn't get the sense of being a pawn. He was a player. And not even "a player." *The* player. Natalie had relied on him to make decisions for the last ten years, and she could continue to do so.

"You'll need to sign for the prescription yourself for the first couple weeks. We don't allow them to handle their own medication until they're in the right habits to continue independently." Dr. Zuniga pushed a document across the table.

Robert glanced at the pharmacy's address on the paper. He knew the place.

"And, Mr. Keller, be sure to tell me if you have problems. Specifically, the interaction with the pharmacy. As I said, CryoLife only works with certain distributors, and we have high standards of quality and service."

"We've had prescriptions filled there before. I don't remember having any issues."

"And I don't expect you to have any. I just want you to know that we're here for you." The doctor touched his arm. "We want to make the transition home as smooth as possible, so if there's anything more we can do, please don't hesitate to ask."

*

The ankle monitor had been the biggest upset for Natalie. Maybe they'd had the misfortune of catching her as the last dose of medication was wearing off. Her anxiety had shot through the roof.

"What was that about you not owning me, Robert? About this arrangement not being a prison?" Natalie paced her room like a caged animal. Since she'd regained the ability to walk, she was constantly in nervous motion.

"It's important for your safety."

"For *your* safety, you mean. The safety of your investment."

"Hon, we need to make sure you're okay. If something happened to you, if you had a reaction to your medication, we'd need to be able to find you."

She raised her palms to her forehead, squinting her eyes shut. Her shoulders quivered as she brought in loud, ragged breaths.

Robert exchanged a look with Dr. Brigman, who stood in the doorway holding the black ankle monitor. The doctor mouthed, "It's okay" before clearing his throat.

"Mrs. Keller, it's—"

Natalie spun on her heels and dropped her arms. Unlike Robert had thought, she wasn't crying, but her words came fast and panicked. "I just want to be alone sometimes. I need to be alone. I need to think. By myself. Alone."

"And you can still do that, Mrs. Keller." Brigman stepped farther into the room. "We don't have someone watching your every move. Why would we do that?"

She eyed the device in the man's hands as he approached. Robert saw her tense when he got within arm's length, but Brigman must have seen it too. Instead of proceeding, he sidestepped to the hospital bed.

"It's standard procedure, and I promise it comes off after two weeks." Brigman patted the mattress. "Come along, I can't allow you to go home without it, Mrs. Keller. You want to go home, don't you?"

Still, Natalie remained frozen.

I'm going to have to grab her and hold her down, I guess. Robert sighed. He didn't prefer having to be rough with her, but this game was wasting everyone's time.

Though he thought her stare had been fixated on the ankle monitor, at his slight movement toward her, she flinched. And he found that no further advance was necessary as she backed closer to the bed while eyeing him.

"That's it, have a seat." The doctor stood, waiting until Natalie sat before he knelt. He rolled the right cuff of her jeans. "Mrs. Keller, did your husband tell you that my son used to be a patient here also?"

She shook her head, the anxious breaths continuing as Brigman slid the black strap around her ankle.

"He liked to be alone and think too. And nothing could stop him from doing it, especially not an ankle monitor."

The doctor locked the strap in place and pressed the rivets around it tightly. When he stood, he took a keychain from his pocket. "What do you think about?"

After clearing her throat Natalie answered in a wavering voice, which made it seem like another question. "Art?"

Brigman hit a button on the keychain. A green light illuminated on the ankle monitor's housing, and there was a sharp beep. "He'd probably say the same. All sorts of silly things." He laughed and looked to Robert. "A word with—"

"Dr. Brigman." Even though Natalie had cut him off, she seemed to fumble for her next words. "Besides your son, you'd mentioned two other patients. The Chinese food man and the musician. Is there a way I could reach out to them?"

"Why would you want to do that?" The corners of Brigman's mouth twitched slightly, but he maintained his smile.

"Someone to talk to who understands."

"Well, Mrs. Keller, you have resources that are much, much better than that. All of our CryoLife affiliated doctors and therapists are happy to talk with you, and we know more 'how it is' than anyone, due to treating the thousands of patients before you." He turned toward Robert. "We don't encourage contact with other patients due to privacy, and truly there isn't a need. They're just normal people restarting their lives. It'd be like having a support group for people who just came back from Hawaiian vacations."

While Natalie focused on the floor, Robert nodded. "That makes sense. If she wants to talk, we'll make sure to set something up with the staff here."

"Excellent," Brigman said. "And may I also have a word with you privately, Mr. Keller?"

Robert tried to catch Natalie's eye, but she didn't look up. "You'll be okay, Nat?"

He paused for a response that didn't come before shutting the door and walking down the hall to where Brigman waited.

"Doctor, I apologize. I have no idea what's gotten into her."

"Mr. Keller, there's no need. This is part of working toward the goal of a complete assimilation. I understand that firsthand." The doctor smiled. "I am going to recommend we overlap her medication more though. Maybe move it to four or five times a day instead of two. And increase the neuroleptics."

"To help the anxiety?"

"Correct, but that's not what I want to talk to you about," Brigman said. "You remember when we chatted that day in my office? How I said I'd care for you like family?"

"Yes."

"Well, I meant it. And even more wholeheartedly in your case. See, you remind me a lot of myself. You're so devoted to your family, Mr. Keller. A loving husband and role model to your son. Protector, provider, caretaker."

Robert remained silent. Yes, he was all these things.

"You and I are the same kind of person. We take ownership and accountability of those around us. We stand for the virtuous qualities so many of today's men are lacking. We're leaders of the finest degree."

Robert still didn't reply.

"So, based on my own personal experience, not on anything professional, I want to offer some advice before you go."

The doctor clapped his hand against Robert's shoulder.

"This is your hour. This is your time to lead. You can see that your wife is struggling. My son had the same type of challenges. It's completely normal, but at no other time in her life will Natalie need you as much as she does now. You can't forget your position."

"My position?" Robert shrugged off Brigman's touch.

"Yes. Protector, provider, caretaker. If she's having difficulty finding her place in the world, you'll need to show it to her."

Robert turned his eyes to the wall, before looking at him.

"Did your son not find his place, and is that why you only keep a picture of him when he was a child?"

"Unfortunately, Mr. Keller, I was too dewy-eyed at having him back to hold the reins properly. To teach him, like he should've been taught. I failed him, and I regret it every day. I don't want the same to happen to you."

Robert found he couldn't avoid the question. "You talk about him in the past tense. What happened to him? Did he die?"

"No, but he might as well be dead." Dr. Brigman sighed. "Don't let unconditional love divert you from truly supporting your wife. You must lead with absolute authority." His smile returned as he took Robert's arm and steered him to Natalie's room. "I want to see you happy."

They stopped before the closed door.

"We are the builders of our own worlds. We are the masters of the universe. And we must stick together."

Robert didn't need the advice, but it was true nonetheless. While Natalie was still coping with the trauma, as soon as she fell into the routine of being a wife and mother, a firm hand wouldn't be necessary. It was nice though, to have someone who understood and cared enough about him to provide off-record suggestions.

"Thanks for your help, Doctor."

"A pleasure. Let us know if you need anything. And best of luck."

Robert put his hand on the doorknob.

"One more thing, Mr. Keller." The doctor caught his eyes. "Keeping the ankle monitor on for two weeks is our requirement. But that doesn't mean you can't use it in future. You don't have to return it. It's included." Dr. Brigman tossed the keychain to Robert with a wink. "Part of the lifetime support system."

Before he could respond, the doctor strode down the hall and turned the corner.

*

And then the day Robert had dreamed of finally arrived. He pushed her wheelchair toward the eastside door. There was one brief stop at the nurse's desk to sign out. Then they were free. She was free!

Natalie had been groggier since the ankle monitor incident. He assumed it was a result of Brigman increasing the neuroleptics, whatever those were. But after talking with Dr. Zuniga, he'd decided to let the current dosage go a week. In the meantime, he would be lenient with her.

He knelt by her wheelchair and held out a clipboard and pen. It took her several seconds to find his eye contact.

"Nat, this is a breakdown of the regulations. You need to sign that you understand them."

She didn't respond.

"Hon, you need to sign this document so I can take you home. Do you want me to read the list to you?"

Natalie shut her eyes and reopened them. She shook her head and turned to the clipboard, holding out her hand for the pen. It was a series of difficult movements, as if her joints were made of wood.

Robert stayed beside her, watching her sluggishly read the list. He didn't care if she read it, but there was a nurse hovering to ensure she did.

"You took her temperature?" he asked. "No fever?"

"Yes, sir." The nurse replied. "Minutes ago, and it was normal."

Normal. Normal is so excellent.

Robert turned his attention to Natalie. When she arrived at the signature line her hand tightened on the pen. She pressed it to the paper and he held the clipboard steady.

But then he had to stop the pen in motion.

"Nat, you just need to sign your name." Robert put a hand to her forehead. He looked at the nurse. "Check her temperature again, please."

Natalie breathed deeply. It was like she was coming out of a daze. "What?"

The nurse showed him the thermometer.

Normal.

"It's the medication then." Robert nodded to the nurse, who returned the gesture.

Natalie looked back at the clipboard and blinked.

"Not a problem. Let's cross this out." Robert guided her hand to the scrawl on the page.

And? And what? He considered asking her. But if she was too delirious to even sign her name, the chance that she'd be able to provide an answer wasn't worth the breath in asking. It didn't matter anyway.

He moved her hand to scratch out the writing with the pen. "There we go. Now sign your name, and we'll go home."

But just in case, he kept his hand on hers and helped her write it.

Chapter 7

Home. As Simon said, it was the first floor of a blue complex on Third Street. A two-bedroom in an okayish college neighborhood. It wasn't bad, but a substantial downgrade from the house they'd had before.

That one had been three thousand square feet. New red bricks and gray shingles. Four bedrooms, three baths. An open living and dining room. A kitchen with stainless steel appliances, granite countertops, and an island.

But it'd gone on the block. Sold quickly to the highest buyer for the noblest purpose:

To bring me back.

And whenever a line formed outside the single bathroom, or they hit elbows turning in the tiny kitchen, Andrew was reminded that despite his efforts, he continued to fall short of Robert's expectations.

Not that Robert said much. He did comment on things and offer corrections, but his remarks were mostly in reference to un-Natalieish behavior. He hadn't complained about their cramped living quarters.

Through a heavy mist, Andrew remembered standing beside Robert as he'd unlocked the apartment door the first time:

"It's smaller than the old house, but it's still nice as long as you keep it clean." Robert sounded like he was shouting up from the bottom of a well. Everyone had been sounding that way.

Andrew didn't respond. Along with the strange voice tones, speaking had taken significant effort. Even his thoughts came in fragments.

Robert pushed open the door and waited for him to step inside. Instead, he felt rooted outside the threshold.

"Go on, Nat."

Yes, go on. This is your home now. You live here with your husband and son. Your name is Natalie. You—

From within the apartment, an elephant stampede followed by a roar:

"Mooommm!"

And the choice of whether to enter the apartment or not ended. The eight-year-old attached himself and sucked Andrew in.

A whirlpool. Quicksand. A black hole.

The door closed and locked behind him, and his internment began.

Stop. You're being dramatic. It's been a week and things are better. You aren't in such a fog anymore. Things sound more normal now. You can speak fluidly again, and there's—

A knock at the bathroom door. "Are you almost ready, hon?"

"Yes."

But he had no idea. Robert had asked twice, and while some things had improved Andrew was still struggling to master a vital element of the Natalie role. That evening, for the thousandth time, he was trying to do what she'd done every day for twenty-seven years – fix her hair and makeup.

No exaggeration. She probably did it in her crib. I swear to fucking—

A sharp intake of breath as he poked himself with the pencil again. The whites of his eyes were red from repeat stabbings.

You're too close to the mirror. Back up. You can do this.

He leaned over the fake marble sink with his face only an inch from the mirror, but he hated to back up. That was the worst part. This close, it was a piece. Only a cheek. Just a lip. A single bloodshot eye that seemed impervious to repeat puncture wounds. And these individual parts could belong to anyone. Male or female. Natalie or Andrew. It was scattered Cubism.

When he pulled back, the sections came together in the face of a stranger. And whenever he'd tried to apply the makeup, they took the form of something worse – a lie.

Not this time. This time, I'm going to do it. I'll get it right. Andrew set down the pencil and felt for the eyeshadow brush without changing proximity to the reflection of his eye. *You want to get it right. You're tired of fucking up.*

That's really all Andrew had been doing since he'd been pulled into this vortex. And he felt sure that Robert's patience was wearing thin.

"What are you doing?" Robert had asked two days ago.

Andrew had been sitting at the dining room table when Robert came home from work. It had been a rare, peaceful afternoon where as long as Andrew stayed within Simon's line of sight and made no sudden movements, the boy let up from mauling him and watched television.

"Looking." One of Natalie's art magazines was in front of him and he'd extended the centerfold. Three white panels connected by thick swoops of black brushstrokes. Smaller rivulets branched off from the main tributaries and paint spacklings formed hundreds of action points. The movement of the painting changed at every angle.

A black ribbon unraveled and fraying. A drop of dye slowly spreading through a glass of water. If a ballerina's slippers were dipped in ink.

It was one of the most interesting paintings Andrew had ever seen. He turned the page so Robert could see.

"It looks like a dirty restaurant table."

"It's called *June Celebration*."

"Celebration for baboons at a zoo maybe." Robert looked around the room. "How long have you spent on this?"

"Only a couple of hours or so. But Simon is fine and everything's clean."

"Is it?"

Andrew nodded. He'd been very careful in cleaning the apartment to Robert's specifications, even wiping down the ceiling fan blades. And he knew Robert didn't understand his fascination with painting, but maybe if Andrew explained it in a different way.

"It's actually a lot bigger than this." He raised his voice as Robert walked into the kitchen. "It's seven feet tall. So in person, to stand in front of just a part ..."

Andrew trailed off when Robert returned with a single cotton swab. He shuffled his chair forward as Robert reached behind him and wiped the tip along the ledge of the electrical outlet cover. Robert briefly inspected the dust particles that clung to the cotton wad before dropping it on the centerfold with a frown.

"Natalie, you obviously have more important things to do than waste time on chimp paintings."

He's right. In front of the bathroom mirror, Andrew tried to push back the remembered hurt. He needed to concentrate on the makeup. This is why he kept failing. Robert wasn't being mean by reminding him that he was focused on the wrong things.

You're Natalie. And you like art, but you need to put more effort into being Natalie. That's what you're doing now. You're making yourself look nice for your husband. We'll go out. It'll be fun. Good to see other people. And they'll call you Natalie, and say how much they've missed you, and compliment your hair. That's when it'll click. You'll finally feel home.

He was pretty sure Robert felt this way as well. That's what this "welcome home" party was about. After a few days adjusting to life outside the Cryobiotic Treatment Center, it was time to reunite with the other people who'd been feeling Natalie's absence for the past year and a half.

"What if they don't like me?" Andrew had asked earlier in the week.

"These aren't a bunch of new people." Robert laughed. "They're our friends. Zack and Evie, Marty and Imogene, David and Maryann. Don't worry, Clark and Shelly will be there too. And Barbara, Stuart, Rosemarie—"

"That's too many people. Way too many people."

"We're not having it here, hon. I rented a space at the SpringHill."

"No, that's too many people for me, Robert. To be around."

"But you know everyone."

This assurance didn't help. He'd rather have Robert drag in random hobos off the street. Andrew imagined walking into a room full of people who felt they knew him. They'd look at him and see the Natalie they'd loved for years. Her face would spawn memories of past adventures, heartbreaking moments, and exciting journeys. And Andrew knew the stories, but that's all they were to him.

"It'll be like the summer barbeques we used to have, except you can take it easy."

Robert had leased a venue. He'd reserved a catering service. And he'd hired an actor to impersonate his wife.

What a fucking show.

But the SpringHill space was theirs for four hours, and the shiny metal buffet tables would move on to their next party. The performer Robert had traded two million dollars for was permanent.

He deserves to parade her— you around. He paid for you.

But so many people. Looking. Expecting. Judging.

It was an odd feeling to only be able to worry a certain amount. In the Center, he'd begin an uneasy thought path and start racing up a staircase without end. But since the haziness that surrounded his release had cleared, there was no more escalation. He knew he should be glad the anxiety had capped, but he wasn't. It was like trying to dive into only the reflection of a pool.

Judging. Judging. JUDGING. And crack – right into the glass when he'd thought he had six feet of chlorinated space.

The lack of frantic anxiety didn't solve the problem.

"It's still, still too many people." Andrew had folded his arms. He clutched his elbows and paced. Robert's eyes followed him, his eyebrow raised and lips pursed to the right side of his mouth. But Andrew couldn't stop. This is what he did now. Pace. Walk for hours in circles around the apartment.

"Okay, okay. Calm down, Nat. I can shorten the guest list. How many people would you feel comfortable with?"

None. This wouldn't be an acceptable reply.

Or have as many as you want, but can you take me out first? Get an apple corer and slam it over my head, gather this skin, and take that with you. Or give it to someone else. But in addition to not being a satisfactory answer, Robert would promptly report this response to the CryoLife therapist. And not that they could do anything but ask him stupid questions and stare at him, but—

Andrew paused and glanced at Robert. *I have enough people who stare at me.* He kept pacing.

"Eight people?" Robert ventured. "Six people?"

Yes, this is good. You work it down yourself.

"Four?" A longer hesitation. "Nat, you at least need to see Clark and Shelly. They've been dying to see you for—"

"Fine. Fine." Andrew walked toward the short hall.

"For only two people I guess I don't need to rent—"

He cut Robert off by shutting the bedroom door. He quickly made his way to the living room and circled the tan couch, his favorite place.

Two people. Only two people. Two people.

But that discussion had happened days ago. And now meeting Clark and Shelly felt as intimidating as Robert unleashing a clown car of Natalie critics.

I'll try. I'm going to try. It won't be bad.

Another knock at the bathroom door, and this time Robert also turned the locked knob. "Are you okay?"

No.

"Yes."

"What's going on?"

The inner turmoil of feeling like a fraud. Guilt and shame pulling me under and drowning me in a dark abyss. I'm going to die at the bottom of a dank hole without having any idea who I am. A complete identity and existential crisis.

"Hairspray," Andrew said.

"Okay, but we're going to be late."

He closed his eyes and took a breath, digging the ends of his fingernails into the rubbery caulk that framed the sink.

Pull back. And maybe this time, the pieces will come together. You won't see Figure dans un Fauteuil. You'll see yourself.

With his eyes still shut, Andrew took two steps back. The corner of the towel rack bumped his shoulder, and he rubbed the polyester fabric of the dress Robert had selected between two fingers. He opened his eyes and looked into the mirror.

Tears ran down a poorly contoured face, ugly dark trails plowing through roughly caked layers of foundation. He put his hands to his eyes, and when he pulled them away he inadvertently wiped clods of the greasy mascara into the dress's fabric. Andrew twisted his fingers in the gnarled blond hair and hid his face in his forearms. He leaned forward and sobbed.

It wasn't Natalie.

It wasn't Andrew.

It's a whore! That's what you are!

"Natalie? Are you okay?"

He lowered his arms and glared at the image in the mirror. *You're a two-million-dollar window dressing!*

"Natalie, open this door."

No matter how hard you try to be her, you're not. You can't do anything right. You're a pathetic excuse for her!

The door shook as Robert banged it.

I want to be me. And I don't know who that is. But this, this thing! Andrew seized the soap dish and heaved it against the mirror. The fragile bowl shattered, showering slivers of porcelain onto the counter. *You're not me! You are a whore!*

Two minutes later, the door left its hinges and slammed to the bathroom tiles inches from where Andrew crouched in a ball near the bathtub.

"Natalie. Natalie, what's wrong? Are you okay?"

Robert tried to pull his arms and unfurl him from the constricted position.

"Are you sick? Are you hurt? Natalie, talk to me."

Andrew wanted to shove him away, to shout in his face.

A forward dive off the springboard in tight tuck position:

Stop! Stop calling me that!

Somersault.

Just stop! I'm not Natalie!

Somersault.

I'm me!

Somersault.

I'm—

The crown of his head crashed into thick tempered glass instead of the pool water. He could go no further.

Robert released Andrew's shoulder when he stopped shaking.

"Natalie, what's wrong?"

I don't know who I am.

But he couldn't admit that he was an imposter while Robert raked his vision across every inch of the body, looking for something to be wrong. His cognitive dissonance wasn't a trail of dirt Natalie's husband could hone in on with a cotton swab.

"Hairspray."

Robert leaned back on his knees and his brow furrowed. "Hairspray? You're uncontrollably sobbing and breaking things over hairspray?"

What would Natalie say? Could he glue some scraps of her together and form an adequate particle board response?

One that wouldn't reveal the angst or the lies? One that *sounded* like her and would satisfy Robert? Natalie, Natalie …

"I want to be perfect for you."

The answer met each and every criteria, including not being a lie. His first triumph as Natalie. And as a bonus, Robert postponed the "welcome home" party with Clark and Shelly for another day.

Chapter 8

Shelly wasn't bad. She'd been Natalie's best friend since middle school, and Andrew remembered how they'd had slumber parties and written boys' names in bubble-printed script on notebook covers. They'd been an inseparable pair – crying at weddings, cooing over babies, comforting each other in the hardship of jobs, loss of parents, and a million other crises. Shelly reminded him of Natalie, and Natalie wouldn't have been bad either if he hadn't been expected to perform as her.

"See, I told him. Or rather, I told Clark to tell him, 'Natty's not going to want some big party. When you had your back surgery last spring, would you have wanted me to invite a hundred people over to poke at you, Clark? Would you?'" Shelly took a sip from her water glass before continuing. "She can come over for the afternoon, nothing fancy. But they never listen."

I listen. Or I think I do. I listen, I watch, I try to learn. But none of it does any good.

The day following the hairspray incident Robert had been reluctant to go to work, but their financial situation had forced the issue. He'd taken Andrew's temperature, made his skin shiver by kissing his cheek, and then was out the door.

It was a godsend that Andrew's routine allowed him some moments of being alone. Besides Robert's hovering, when Simon was around, the child was insufferably clingy and wanted only to be with him at all times. And just "being warm" had ceased to be acceptable.

Only that morning, Simon had made the increasingly common demand:

"Talk."

"About what?" Andrew had been standing in front of the kitchen counter again, drifting through an art magazine and Simon was on the floor near his feet.

"I don't care. Just say stuff."

"Can't we be quiet for a while?"

"No. I want to hear your voice." Simon yanked his pant leg. "Say stuff."

Andrew had sighed. He closed the cover and turned on the kitchen sink. "I am turning on the kitchen sink. I've turned on the hot water, not the cold water. It takes the water a few seconds to become hot. I pick up the dish washing liquid. It's an orange color but doesn't smell like oranges. I ..."

This is my life. Narrating my actions like I'm basting a fucking turkey on television.

But weekdays he received a reprieve when Simon went to school and Robert was at work. It was then that he spent his solitary time on three activities – he paced, looked out the bay window, and cleaned the apartment (ensuring that all outlet covers were properly dusted now). His tasks were usually uneventful; however, a few days ago he'd stumbled across a stash of discs hidden in the closet.

Expecting to have uncovered Robert's year-and-a-half substitute for Natalie, he'd been interested to find the real her. Two dozen discs worth. A boxed set. Some special things like Christmases and birthdays, but also mundane snippets – planting a tulip bed, frosting a cake, washing the dog.

The Natalie Files.

And perhaps, where the "welcome home" party idea had failed, these instructional videos would be the key. Andrew would learn to be Natalie by listening and watching her firsthand. They were a boring legion of cherished memories, but after three days of review, he'd made it through them a handful of times.

The results of his efforts were still dismal. When Natalie sat in a chair, she was right at the edge, primed to take off. She kept her shoulders rolled back and her posture straight. In approximately eighty-five percent of the sitting shots, her ankles were crossed and her hands rested in her lap.

Yet here you are. Fucking up repeatedly. You can't clean right. You can't do makeup or hair. You can't take care of the kid. Even something as simple as sitting in a chair you fail at. You held that pose for a good five minutes.

At Shelly's kitchen table, Andrew was slouching in his seat with his legs stretched out and his arms hanging at his sides. Had Shelly noticed? She was looking at him strangely.

He corrected his position to full-Natalie. For good measure, he threw in another classic Natalie move – the stir-her-icewater-clockwise-twice-then-tap-her-spoon-on-the-rim. For no good reason.

Stir. Stir. Tap.

And a lap full of water.

"Here, let me get you a towel." Shelly pushed back her chair, and Andrew watched her waddle out of the room.

When she was gone, he folded his arms on the table and stared into the spilled water. He thought about crying. There was no makeup to run today. He'd piled that garbage onto Natalie's vanity in the bedroom.

Never again. Never.

"Oh, dear. Natty, it's okay." Shelly had returned and thrust a towel at him. "It's just water, and you're not wearing one of your good dresses."

Those he'd given up too. He'd found an oversized sweatshirt and loose jeans shoved in the dresser drawer. But unlike the Natalie videos, he'd searched for these clothes.

The Natalie Files. Season four, disc eleven, episode two – the scene opens on Natalie painting a wall. Nothing art-like. Just a plain, boring wall. She has her back to the camera, running a painter's pole along a sheet of drywall.

Cameraman sneaks closer. The foam roller swishes. Low humming. She can't hear him because of the earbuds. He reaches out a hand and grabs her shoulder. She screams.

"Rob! You jerk! Get over—"

In his first session of watching The Natalie Files, Andrew had stopped the frame as Natalie laughed and swung the paint roller toward the cameraman. He skipped back to the opening and watched it again.

"Rob! You—"

Reverse. Watch again.

"Rob—"

Reverse. Watch again. And again. And again. Andrew knew it was her, but somehow it felt better to look at her this way. Easier. He wasn't sure why at first, but this section didn't fill him with shame. It didn't make his insides crinkle like the rest of The Natalie Files. And while he didn't feel *good* about it, he felt okay.

Until you turn your face.

As he played the sequence for the umpteenth time, Andrew pressed his palm on the screen to cover Natalie's head.

And there was only a person with a painter's pole. Not Natalie. Not a woman. For the first time, maybe, *possibly* he saw a glimmer of himself.

I need to find that sweatshirt and those pants.

Andrew knew they had to be there. Robert seemed to have kept everything Natalie had breathed on. Somewhere in the apartment, there was probably a bag of tissues she'd used to blow her nose.

When he'd found his prize, it'd been wonderful. He hadn't dared to look in a mirror, but he'd thrown on the outfit and thought about the video. How these amazing clothes masked the ugliness of Natalie's body. She'd been proud of those wads of fat on her chest and around her hips, but these attributes had been hidden by the divine baggy sweatshirt and jeans. He felt better. Not completely home, but maybe on the porch outside.

I'll never take them off.

Remembering this elevated his stomach from where it'd sunk. Andrew sat up in the chair – proper Natalie position – and looked at Shelly.

"Remember that time you spilled grape juice on your silver blouse at my Christmas party?" Shelly chuckled.

Natalie had mourned that garment like she'd lost a piece of her soul.

"Yeah."

"I'm surprised at the new outfit." She gestured toward him. "Does Rob know you left the house that way?"

"Yeah."

He hadn't been pleased, but he had to know – Andrew was still tagged with the ankle monitor. But although there'd been that twitch under Robert's eye, he hadn't verbally complained. He'd suggested something else, but on meeting resistance, dropped the matter.

Maybe because I managed to do the stir-her-icewater-clockwise-twice-then-tap-her-spoon-on-the-rim perfectly this morning.

"Hmm." Shelly narrowed her eyes, the corners of her mouth tipping up. "So you're wearing it to be comfortable, are you?"

"Yeah." It wasn't perfect, but God, it felt more like *him* than Natalie's other clothes.

"So is there something you're not telling me?"

He'd been paying attention to her before, but now his focus magnified.

She knew. Shelly knew something was wrong.

But, of course, you'd see it! Andrew felt a sparkling exhilaration. *You were her best friend. You knew her longer than Robert, and you were closer to her than he or Simon ever was. You saw right through this game, through this false skin! You see the real me, not—*

"Wipe that smile off your face. You're an animal, you know that? An animal. How long have you been awake? A month?" Shelly was on her feet squealing. "I'm so happy for you and I'm so excited I can barely stand it! Do you know when you're due yet?"

He couldn't see it, but he felt the color drain from his face.

"I realize I broke our pact by this one being another boy, but this couldn't be more perfect!" She put a hand to both his shoulders and pressed her forehead to his. "Concentrate, Natty. Focus. Girl. Girl. Gir—"

"No!"

In pushing away from her, Andrew fell out of the chair. He scrambled to his feet and took several steps back.

The thought of sex as a woman nauseated him, and the knowledge of what it could lead to made him ill. He sensed the sickness coming on now, as cold shivers ran through the body and his breaths came rapidly.

When Robert had mentioned having another child in the Center, it seemed like Andrew had a mini-seizure. His mind frazzled and blanked out. When he returned, his stomach threatened to jump ship. He'd managed to release enough revulsion with a shudder to keep from exploding, but he'd detoxed for days, the poison of the idea leaking from his pores.

Is that what this is? I'm having a seizure. I'm having a stroke. I'm dying. I'm dying. I'm—

"Natalie, calm down." Shelly approached him, but he couldn't move. She hugged him, and smoothed his messy hair. "I'm sorry. It's too soon after Michael. I didn't mean to be so insensitive."

A reply didn't come to mind. There were no thoughts as she removed an arm and pushed him toward the table. Shelly righted the chair with her free hand.

"Sit, Natty. Talk to me." She eased into her own chair, and Andrew felt her watching him.

What's wrong with you? Andrew wanted to scream. *There are countless examples. The Natalie Files. Season four, disc three, episode twelve. Season six, disc one, episode seven. Season two, disc five—*

Natalie loved her children. Hours of film proved she'd wanted to be a mother. God, how many episodes was she pregnant? And like one of those fake sitcom women, she wasn't miserable. Robert liked the plan of Natalie being a stay-at-home mom. Natalie *loved* the idea.

And I can't even talk to Simon. I don't know what to say to him. He deserves to be loved by a mother but ... I can't even take care of myself, let alone someone else. *I don't know how and I don't want to know.*

"Do you want me to call Rob for you?" Shelly touched his hand.

"No."

It wasn't Robert. It wasn't any man. Consensual or not had no impact. It was all a violation. Of the physical body, but also of something more vital.

I am not this body. I'm a prisoner inside it. No amount of studying those videos can bring us together.

The tense white space of *Beta nu*. Diagonal asymmetrical lines framing an empty canvas. He'd found the painting in one of Natalie's books and it'd struck him more emotionally than *June Celebration*. Of course he hadn't been stupid enough to try showing it to Robert.

This is me. I am blank. Andrew had bent the book's spine and held the page to his chest. *Pinned into place. I'm trapped.*

But the imprisonment could be worse.

The real me, forced into that position …

Makeup and clothes were one thing. The Natalie way of sitting, walking, holding a fork. They were external actions he could perform – like washing dirty dishes behind rubber gloves. But sex and conceiving a child reached the person locked within Natalie's skin. It'd be a desecration of his soul.

"It's not the same as with Michael, but do you remember when I had the miscarriage before Carter?" Shelly's voice went up an octave, but Andrew couldn't look at her. "I wouldn't let Clark touch me for weeks. I mean, if it resulted in death, what was the point?"

I would die. I can barely tolerate Robert's touch now. He'd stopped trying to increase his tolerance by elongating the counting sessions. Fifteen seconds was all Robert got, and even that was a stretch sometimes.

"You had to tell me, probably a thousand times, that it wasn't my fault before I finally believed you. So, honey, here's number one with nine hundred and ninety-nine more to go: Michael's death was not your fault."

It's not my fault. I can't help what happened. That Natalie died and CryoLife gave her brain damage. I can't help that I exist instead of her and that I can't do the things she used to do. It's not my fault I can't be her. The surface, the foundation is different. And I can do some things, like dust electrical outlet covers, but the deeper parts of Natalie – how she loved Simon and wanted to be a mother, I can't mimic or make those qualities my own and—

"It's not my fault," Andrew whispered.

"That's right, it's not."

All I can do is manage what I have. I have this feeling I can't ignore. I may be trapped, but maybe I'm not empty. Something fills me. It's my strongest, deepest sense – I am not a woman.

Andrew smiled at Shelly. And though the alarm in his head went off, warning him that he was slouching, he ignored it. Full-Natalie chair position was so fucking uncomfortable.

Chapter 9

Andrew's daily activities dropped by one when, a couple mornings later, the urge to pace the apartment vanished. He walked to the couch, but didn't feel compelled to circle it twenty-five times before Robert got out of the shower. Instead, he wanted to sleep.

He woke when he felt Robert's hand on his forehead. But unlike previous times where Robert's touch made him jump, he could barely keep his eyes open.

1 Mississippi. 2 Mississi …

Robert shook him awake. "Are you sick, Nat?"

"No, I'm tired."

"Simon, get the thermometer."

Andrew's eyelids parted a crack to see Simon standing next to Robert beside the couch. Upon catching his stare, Simon's upper lip trembled and tears flowed from his eyes.

"Mom's going to die! She's going to diiieee!" He pulled his hair with his fists. "Mooommm!"

Two weeks of suffocation by Simon – his near-constant presence, conscripted food show host narration, and the endless demands for attention – were beginning to overshadow the pity Andrew felt for him. Yes, he was clearly traumatized, but Andrew was tired of chronicling everything with a 50-pound weight clutching his leg and Simon screaming if he paused for breath. And the behaviors only seemed to be getting worse, as only the day before, Simon had insisted on following Andrew into the bathroom.

"Stay out here."

"No, I want to be with you."

Simon had pressed against the reattached bathroom door, trying to prevent it from closing.

"I'll be in here for three minutes."

"That's too long. Let me come."

"No." But he hesitated. As the circumstance wasn't Andrew's fault, it also wasn't Simon's. Maybe he could compromise. "I'll talk to you the entire time."

"That's not good enough. I need to see you too." The boy tried to bump the door open.

"No. Stay here." Andrew pushed back, the resistance despite his concession beginning to anger him. Not just with Simon, but also with Robert, who'd been of no support regarding Simon's actions.

Isn't the right to a solitary piss written somewhere? Or does that get looped in with the fucking conservatorship too? Do I need to ask permission to take a piss? Make sure that's okay with everyone and that my time isn't better spent wiping down lightbulbs?

Simon curled his fingers around the door and continued to push in. "Please don't lock me out, Mom."

He couldn't decide which name was worse. "Natalie" or "Mom." Probably the latter. While it wasn't spirit-defiling sex, it scraped the same area with a garden rake. Not enough to slam a small boy's fingers in a door, but it made the action tempting.

"I said no!"

"Please, Mom. Pllleeeease don't leave me!" Simon wailed.

Andrew eased off the door, pulling it back slightly. Immediately the child's mouth closed. And his fingers retracted.

Andrew slammed the door in his face and turned the lock. Outside in the hall, an eruption of epic proportions broke loose.

He had paced a small circle while Simon shrieked and inflicted every manner of violence to the other side of the bathroom door. At some point, Andrew had fallen asleep to the sound of the boy's weeping.

"Natalie!"

He woke to hear Robert again pulling the pins from the bathroom door hinges. Before he'd gotten to his feet to unlock it, the door was off. Like a suction tube, Simon immediately latched onto him.

"Mooommm! Mooommm!"

Andrew tried to pry him off, but he slunk to the floor and went limp, clutching his ankles as he bawled.

"What's the matter with you, Natalie?" Robert demanded.

"I just wanted to go to the bathroom by—"

"Look at the door! Look at him!"

There were large gouges in the bathroom door. Various pans were scattered in the hall and a broken flower pot lay at Robert's feet. The door panel was also stained with red streaks, and when Andrew glanced at the human ball and chain, he realized the child had tried clawing the door open with his fingernails.

Yes, there needs to be boundaries but I should've talked to him. I could've done that and maybe he wouldn't have completely flipped out.

"Robert, all I wanted was three minutes to myself in—"

"Then you come back in three minutes! You don't leave him out here to try and tear the door down for three hours! What if someone had called the police?"

Surely the police would understand wanting to take a shit without an audience. Can't you even try to understand my view at all?

But Robert had been angry. More than Andrew had seen him before, as either himself or Natalie. He breathed in quickly, letting out tiny bursts of steam to keep from erupting.

"I'm sorry, Robert, I didn't mean to."

Please don't hurt me. I could've handled it better. He annoys the fuck out of me, but I didn't mean for this to happen. Please, please don't hurt me.

Did the entreaty come through on his face? Robert released a long sigh, his shoulders easing.

"Nat, if you can't handle him, you need to call me." He'd knelt and smoothed the child's hair. "He's been through a lot."

So have I.

Now, lying back on the couch, Andrew shut his eyes to block out the crying parasite.

I do feel like shit because of what happened and because you're stuck with me. You'd be better off being raised by a fucking dingo. We've both been through a lot. But I'm sorry, I'm just so drained from you.

"Mom's not going to die, Simon," Robert said. "Be a good boy and go get the thermometer."

The sniveling trailed away.

"I'll call my mom to come get him, and I'll take you to the ER."

Ah, Robert's mother. Andrew had spoken less than two words to her since he'd been released. While she'd never been very warm with Natalie either, the woman now made it a priority to stay a healthy yard away from him. The cryogenic reanimation idea was still uncomfortable for some, and Andrew was pretty sure Robert's mother regarded him as a type of unnatural monster.

Which I feel like regularly anyway, so it doesn't matter. She's still one of my favorite people in that she gives me a break from Simon.

But if the reprieve was conditional on an ER visit—

"I'm not sick, Robert. I'm tired."

"We can't be too careful." The whimpering returned, and Andrew felt the plastic cap pressed into his ear. "Ninety-eight, three."

"See."

"Headache? Chills? Congestion? Muscle—"

"No, I'm tired."

"We'll still go to the ER to be sure."

"No. Just let me sleep. Take him to your mother's and let me rest."

Robert paused briefly. "I'll call you every hour on the hour to make sure you're okay." Andrew opened his eyes and watched him lead a reluctant Simon away. "Simon, you'll go to Grandma's house today."

"But Mom—"

"Will be here when you get back. Grab your bag."

*

The exhaustion faded at almost ten in the morning, just in time for Andrew's other daily activity. He went to the bay window and pulled aside the heavy drape.

Across the street, a large Spanish colonial bustled with mid-morning energy. He thought it was probably a frat house due to the droves of college-aged men who came and went through its doors. And since his visit with Shelly, the goings-on at the house had become more than a distraction. The certain revelation that he wasn't female had caused him to start thinking.

Maybe this could be me.

He got a better feeling watching the young men exiting the house – laughing and punching each other in the shoulder – than he had in The Natalie Files. It was more inspiring than the sweatshirt and jeans had been. The idea of being one of them captivated his afternoons and the solid lines of *Beta nu* felt less like insurmountable barriers.

His cell phone buzzed. He dug it out of his sweatshirt pocket and answered without checking the number: "Ninety-eight, four."

"When did you take it?"

"Two minutes ago."

"Any other symptoms?"

"No, I was tired. I feel a lot better, and you can stop calling." Andrew squinted to make out one of the faces in an upstairs bedroom of the frat house.

"You really feel better, Nat?"

"Yes."

Silence.

"I'll call you at eleven. I love you."

"You too."

He ended the call, tossed the phone over on the couch, and dreamed.

I'll look kind of like him. With the thin face and short blond hair. But I'll dress like that one. Or him.

Andrew was grateful for the baggy sweatshirt and jeans, but that's not what these young men wore.

I'll wear dark ties and tan khakis. Polos and suits. Cargo shorts and ribbed shirts without sleeves. I'll put a button-up shirt under a sweater and let the collar branch open.

The man he'd spotted in the window walked out the door and down the porch steps. He took them two at a time, swinging a red bag over his shoulder. As he strolled across the sidewalk, he shoved a hand in his pocket, and Andrew marveled at how crisp the pleats were in the back of his shirt.

You know, there's nothing that prevents you from dressing like that now, Andrew.

He thought of the one neutral sequence in The Natalie Files, freezing the image in his mind. As if it were a paper doll, he visualized the young man's shirt in place of the fleece fabric. A pair of pin-stripe slacks overlaid the jeans, and the painter's pole was the red bag.

Perfect.

And it had to be a sign that Simon was gone and he had hours to try on Robert's clothes and maybe, finally feel at home in the body.

Andrew let the drape fall and made his way to the bedroom. He folded back the closet doors and pushed Natalie's clothes to the side. He trailed his fingers down the stiff sleeve of one of Robert's cotton shirts.

This could be mine.

He selected a blue button-up and unpinned a pair of Robert's slacks, which he put on first.

He pulled the straight slacks up on his legs. The waistband was tight around his hips, but by bucking his knees together he was able to get the slacks zipped.

The shirt sleeves were long, the cuffs coming over his fingertips, but that wasn't a problem. He'd seen his neighbors roll their shirtsleeves to the elbows, and he probably would've done that even if the sleeves hadn't been long. He thought the trick looked cool and relaxed. Like he was walking along a beach and couldn't be bothered by something as trivial as rolling down his sleeves.

He buttoned the shirt starting at the collar as he'd seen Robert do. And when finished, he pushed the ends into the snug waistband of the slacks. He didn't know how to tie it, but he looped a darker blue tie around his neck and let the fat end dangle to get the effect.

And he was ready.

Almost ready.

In trying to be Natalie he'd looked in that damn mirror so many times that he knew it'd spoil everything. So he approached Natalie's vanity from the side and draped a pillowcase over the top of the mirror to hide his face.

And *now* he was ready.

Andrew stepped in front of the mirror just as he had before the makeup incident. He opened his eyes and looked for the first time at the body.

It wasn't Natalie.

It wasn't Andrew.

It was a woman wedged into a man's clothing.

The slacks were so tight around his thighs they looked like they were bursting at the seams. The crotch strained to encase his hips and stretched to where it was painfully apparent he was missing a penis. The pockets puckered, the inner lining poking out of them.

The shirt was horrible too. He didn't look cool and relaxed. The fabric around his armpits hung like wings, and the lower half pooled at his waist, making him look bloated. The proportions of the shirt were off – the pocket on the right side was far lower than it should've been, with the bottom only five inches above his waistline. And they were there too – those God-awful tumors sticking out of him, pushing the fabric of the shirt out so it dropped like a fucking tent after pulling over the highest peak.

Andrew staggered away from the mirror and tore the clothes from the body. In a fit of tears, he ripped the shirt apart, buttons flying across the room. He pulled off the slacks and threw them into the mirror, the force causing it to tip unsteadily.

The whole body shivered as he put his customary outfit back on. He tried to catch his breath as he marinated in the oversized sweatshirt and jeans. These clothes were safe, and he tried to concentrate on that golden frame of The Natalie Files when they'd worked their magic in hiding the feminine features underneath. But he couldn't focus.

Another dive. Andrew approached the platform.

It's hopeless. Hopeless. Hopeless. Hopeless!

A handstand with his front facing the pool. He could see it. He could smell it. He knew the water was real this time.

I'll never find my way, and there's no purpose to any of this shit!

Launch and somersault.

I can't be Natalie. I've tried, and I can't do it. I can't even fake being her. How am I supposed to go on for the next forty or fifty years living this lie? I can't survive her! I can't!

Somersault.

I feel like I'm Andrew, but I obviously can't be him either. I'm a freak! I'll always be stuck in this body unable to be free.

Beta nu's lines pushing tighter and tighter together.

Half twist.

There is no escape! I should call it quits. Right now. Right the fuck—

Human skull direct to pavement at thirty-five miles an hour accomplished exactly what one might imagine – it stopped Andrew mid-thought.

He gathered the ruined clothes, carried them to the dumpster, and returned to the couch to wait for Robert's eleven o'clock call.

Chapter 10

When he'd first seen the woman sashay into his pharmacy, he remembered thinking that in another place and time he would've been attracted to her.

I'd have been all over that, was his exact thought.

She'd worn a skirt above her knee, and a sleeveless silk blouse that revealed the ivory skin of her neck and upper chest. Her fine facial features had been perfectly accentuated, and her golden hair curled thick and luxurious around her shoulders.

He'd pictured himself with his friends, elbowing each other in the ribs.

"Now that is a Georgia peach."

And she'd held the hand of a small boy, who pushed open the door for her. In the crook of her other arm, she'd supported the handle of a car seat. He would've liked that too. Once upon a time, he'd wanted to be a father.

Where were you when I was straight? Jesus Christ.

It'd been difficult to keep his bitter thoughts in check and concentrate on filling the prescription for her baby. It wasn't fair.

It wasn't right. But which of the many injustices was he referring to by "it"?

That something I deserved to have can parade itself before me and there's not a damn thing I can do about it. I guess I could put up a sign: No service to attractive women with babies. I'd have much more room without that feminine product shelf. I could put in an air hockey table. Or a skee ball game.

But he'd somewhat worked through the hostility by the time the woman returned after an absence of over a year. His thoughts didn't immediately jump to dreams of gender segregating his pharmacy, maybe since he could tell that something about her was off. Significantly off.

She came in with the same boy, which sealed her identity, otherwise it might've remained a puzzle. She wore large jeans and a baggy hooded sweatshirt, her blond hair tied in a messy ponytail. There was no makeup on her face, and her eyes were dull with dark circles underneath.

What the fuck ran over you?

He watched from behind the counter as she went to the drop-off window. Before, she'd had a way of walking that could make a person dizzy if they were only looking at her feet. She balanced on her high heels and took tiny, carefully placed steps as if she were a fairy dancing from flower to flower. Now she was a giant. If there'd been a miniature city in her path, she would've crushed it under her boots.

After the technician advised her to take a seat, she tromped to the bench on the side wall. When she sat, she absorbed twice the space a woman of her size normally would. With her legs open and her arms on the back of the bench, she looked defeated, as if she'd run a marathon and finished in last place.

And not once had she looked at the boy.

Before, the woman hadn't taken her eyes off him, and she'd treated the baby in the car seat with such a tender affection it made him wistfully sick inside.

The boy was inspecting shelves of candy in another aisle. But he was out of her sight, which the woman who'd come in before never would've allowed. She'd struck him before as one of those leeching mothers, who'd be first in line for a man-sized child carrier. She would strap him to her body and carry him in a papoose until he was thirty, if he'd let her.

The child crowed after finding his selection.

"Mom!"

He looked around the corner of the aisle. She didn't respond.

"Mom! Mom!"

Still nothing. She was awake, but wasn't focusing on anything.

"Mom! Mom! Mom!"

The boy at last took the candy and went to her. He sat on the bench, pulled his legs up, and snuggled close. She didn't acknowledge his presence.

"Ma'am?"

Her prescription was ready.

"Ma'am?"

And it appeared the same apathetic scenario was about to replay.

He was intrigued, and stepped from behind the counter.

"Hello, ma'am?" The technician accompanied the call with a wave.

"I'll take it from here, Barty." He nudged the young man at the register aside and took the medication bag. It was stapled shut, but a name was printed on the front. He recognized the prescription, having put it together himself. Previously it'd been signed for by a man who looked equally miserable.

And unless she was the new delivery person, things had become more interesting.

For the past few weeks, he'd been combining quite the CryoLife cocktail for a Mrs. Natalie Keller.

Not out of the ordinary. Just your usual chemical steamroll.

"Excuse me, Mrs. Keller," he said.

There was no response. But he was too curious to waste further time.

"Hey, you." He clapped his hands together. "Get your ass off my bench and come get your pills!"

That caught her attention. She turned and glared at him. He responded with a smile.

The boy stared at him with wide eyes and clutched his mother's arm.

"Stay here." She pried his hand off.

When she walked toward the counter, the idea crossed his mind to imitate the distinct way she moved. It was comical, like a person trying to inflate with every step. Or Godzilla. But he relinquished the desire. It might be in poor taste for someone he wasn't acquainted with, even if it'd be hilarious.

She stopped in front of the register and looked him up and down, as if sizing him for a fight. Her face grew red and the way in which she'd set her jaw made it look broader. She ground her teeth, her hands clenched in fists.

"Like what you see, doll?" He winked at her when she met his eyes after examining his body for perhaps the third time.

She sucked a breath in through her nose, and he wondered if she was going to jump over the counter at him. Wouldn't that be funny to tell the guys? Attacked by a homeless-looking woman.

But she didn't lunge for him. She composed herself and held out her hand for the bag.

"Ah, ah." He corrected with a tick of his finger. "ID, please."

She gave a loud huff and pulled a wallet from her pocket. He watched her fumble it open and thumb through various cards. Last time, she'd worn a purple purse on one shoulder. When she came to the counter, she hadn't looked like she wanted to maim him. She'd unzipped the purse and flipped through numerous cards with the tips of her long, shapely fingernails. She'd held out her insurance card with a smile.

Now, though his palm was open to receive the ID, she slapped it on the counter.

"You have hands. You pick it up," she snapped.

He retrieved the card. There was the picture of her, looking less grungy with a fake smile. He skimmed her other information before checking the bottom corner.

CRYO. And a five-digit number.

0-3-8-7-7.

"Thank you, Natalie." He offered the card back coolly between two fingers.

She jerked it away and stuffed it into her wallet as he switched the medication bag from his right hand to his left. When she looked at him again, he'd extended his hand.

"I'm Oz. Like the wizard. Only real, and more handsome," he said.

"I'm married."

"Not happily."

"Give me my pills, jackass."

Oz hugged his shoulders, giving an exaggerated shiver.

"Ooo, cold, doll. Cold. It's eighty fucking degrees outside, but it's freezing in here!"

"I want my medication." Natalie raised her voice. "If you won't give me my fucking pills, I'll go elsewhere!"

"I doubt that." He handed her the bag, which she snatched away.

Natalie turned and walked toward the door. The boy, still terrified but forgotten, sped after her.

"I think you'll come see me again!"

He laughed when she flipped him off through the glass door.

Chapter 11

Andrew hated that fucking thing in the pharmacy.

That's what he is. A thing.

There were so many people to hate in the shit circumstance he was bound to endure. Overprotective and always disappointed Robert. Traumatized Simon whose extreme neediness caused him to alternate between immense guilt and frustration. Plastic CryoLife doctors and therapists that couldn't be trusted. Even ever-pregnant, good-intentioned Shelly who wouldn't stop calling him.

The anger wasn't biased toward specific individuals either. Random strangers also incited Andrew's rage. He wanted to break the fingers of every man who held the door for him. Who invented the women's restroom? He felt like a pervert going in there. Fuck that gender segregating dickhead too.

And words were awful. The old world, "polite" phrases with "lady" in them that men said to be charming? Words like "pretty" and "beautiful" and "lovely," which had a definite feminine feel and context?

But the pharmacist combined it all. He was everything and had everything Andrew wanted, and he'd barely been able to control himself.

Be glad that all I can do is jump off the diving board – that the rage I could be feeling is stopped. I don't know why that is, but you should be grateful for it.

The first thing he'd hated about Oz was his appearance. Not the command or clapping his hands at him as if he were a dog. He hated how Oz looked and his clothes.

"Hey, you, get your ass off my bench and come get your pills!"

Asshole.

Andrew had scraped the Simon-barnacle off and approached the counter. He'd planned to retrieve the medication with a roll of his eyes and ask Robert to start getting it again. He hated leaving the apartment and hadn't wanted to pick it up.

"You should get out more anyway, Nat," Robert had said after he'd protested. "You've had your ankle monitor off for two days. I thought for sure you'd be spending all your time with Shelly since you don't even have to ask my permission."

Monitor or not your authorization is still required, oh great Conservator. God forbid you lose track of my whereabouts for an hour.

"I'd rather stay home and it's on your way to work. Can't you get it, Robert?"

"No. I really want you to get out of the house. It will help you feel better. If you're nervous about being alone, ask Shelly to go with you. Then maybe you two can do lunch afterward."

Why is spending two hours looking at a painting a waste, but the same amount of time swilling iced tea with Shelly is considered well spent? But calling Robert out on double standard bullshit resulted in the annoyed expression that made Andrew worry. *Since you can essentially do whatever you want with me. I have no rights after all.*

"I'll go alone."

"And I want you to call me when you leave. It should take you ten minutes to walk there, so I'll also expect a call when you get home."

And track your slightest sniffle. Time occurring, note any contributing environmental conditions, and duration of sniff. Document in triplicate. Yellow copy to you. Pink to the CDC. White to keep.

"Fine."

The pharmacist's rudeness was actually a stroke of luck since it provided Andrew with an excuse to not pick up the medication in future.

I may have to fill out sniffle incident reports, but Robert won't tolerate someone being an ass to me. Think about that. Just pick up the meds, roll your eyes, and walk straight on out.

But then Andrew looked the man over.

He wore his white coat open and relaxed. Under it, a fitted light green shirt was buttoned across his flat chest. A pistachio colored tie with thick black stripes was knotted a couple inches below his Adam's apple to accommodate the undone top button. The shirt was tucked into black slacks that hit his hips at the right spot. His pockets didn't bulge or bubble. His slacks fell straight in a perfect cut, their uncuffed ends covering the top of his shoelaces and breaking around the ankle.

And there was his face. The defined jaw and tan skin. How his sandy brown hair was mussed, but every loose strand still seemed perfectly arranged. A curved, black barbell pierced his left eyebrow. Though he was clean shaven, there was stubble on his neck. A formula in delicate black letters was inked beneath his right earlobe – $N^c H^k (X,Z) = H^k$ – and disappeared under the collar of his green shirt.

But worst was the confidence about him. The way he grinned and leaned against the counter. He was cool and contented, a man at ease within his own body. He never thought about how he moved. How he walked. How he breathed. How he spoke. He floated through the world – bold, handsome, and secure in his masculinity. Debonair. Charming. Perfect.

Looking at this man who dressed how he wanted to dress, looked how he wanted to look, acted like he wanted to act, caused a high-octane rush through Andrew's body.

It threatened to pump through him again as he thought about the incident in the pharmacy days later. Robert had already left for work, and thankfully Simon had started his summer sport program. Or something. He hadn't seen him since yesterday, but wherever he was it had to be better than being at home.

It's a relief to have one less burr on my ass, even if I did figure out a method to deal with him. Don't think about the pharmacist anymore. It'll upset you, and it's almost ten.

But he wasn't sure he'd be able to focus on the frat boys with that son-of-a-bitch still hovering in his mind.

Andrew remembered that before Oz had spoken further, he wanted to lunge across the counter and dig his fingernails into the man's face. He wanted to rip the clothes from his body, pick up the cash register, and dash his head in. He'd pictured hammering the corner into his skull, the pharmacist's brains slopping into his face in a pink gummy ooze. He could taste the blood.

"Like what you see, doll?"

Andrew had been screaming inside his head, his hands twitching to peel sections of flesh from Oz's face. Fortunately, the same old dive sequence performed itself and Andrew maintained self-control as he hit the barrier.

But barely. Only barely.

The man who introduced himself as "Oz. Like the wizard. Only real, and more handsome" hadn't comprehended that he could've said anything and not made Andrew as angry as he had by just existing. By looking how he did.

When Andrew returned home that day, the fury had abated. But he needed to be alone, desperately. He was overwhelmed. Robert had been at work, but the boy was still there, ever lurking. Ever demanding in his desperate need for security.

"Mom. Talk."

Simon looked over the couch as Andrew stood in the kitchen, manic to the level of shaking.

"Mom. Talk. Now."

If he didn't start speaking, the boy would rush into the room and degenerate into a sobbing mass around his ankles.

"I am putting away the dishes. I've picked up a fork. I'm putting the fork away now." In his anxiety, Andrew had jerked open the medicine drawer rather than the silverware drawer. The motion was delivered with such force that a round bottle rolled forward from behind a box of bandages.

Benadryl.

"Mom, you stopped talking. Talk."

"I am wondering if we have strawberries and yogurt."

One super special strawberry smoothie later, Andrew might as well have been alone in the apartment.

With the picture of Oz looming in his mind, he'd shut himself in the closet and curled into a ball.

That will never be me. I'm stuck in this body, in this house, with these people who'll never know who I am. Who don't even want to know. And if I leave, it'll always be the same. I'll never be at peace with myself. I'll never be free.

He rocked in the fetal position, the legs of Robert's hanging pants bouncing against his forehead.

Andrew had attempted to forget how he'd looked in Robert's clothes. Since that awful day he'd spent hours in front of the mirror wearing his sweatshirt and jeans, trying to overwrite the horrible reflection.

He hadn't been able to replace it though. And after seeing how handsome and comfortable Oz looked in his own skin … Andrew compared him to the image of himself in Robert's clothes and sank into the deepest despair he'd yet experienced.

There was no hope for him. Even if he asked Robert to keep his promise and pass the conservatorship to CryoLife. If he started a new life as Andrew and managed to survive, he'd never be like this man. Only in his own head would he be whole, and what good did that do? No one could see the man he was. They'd see a woman in men's clothing. A freak.

Andrew had leaned his head against the closet wall.

He made a beautiful woman. Natalie had worn modern, sexy things that embraced her curves. He'd seen it in The Natalie Files and pictures. He remembered wearing them. He remembered how she'd been proud of her body. Natalie felt like she'd been a trophy wife and more attractive than other women.

I can't do it. I can't go back down the path of trying to fill her shoes.

But if he stayed in Natalie's identity, he wasn't a freak. Even if he continued to wear sweatshirts to hide everything, not brush the hair, or do the makeup. He was safe. Unkempt and raggedy, but safe. Depressed, but safe. And he'd endured it so far.

If I can't take it or hide it anymore at some point ... If there are no more outs or options. Then I'll do it. I'll deliver myself. No fucking dive will stop me. Andrew had swallowed the lump in his throat. *But today isn't that day.*

He'd crawled out of the closet and adjusted his sweatshirt.

And I'll never go back to that pharmacy. I'll kill that man if I see him. I'll kill him.

Back in the present, his cell phone alarm alerted him to the time. Ten o'clock. His fantasy life was about to hit its peak as the young men went off to class, or came home from their hangovers.

Andrew clenched his teeth and shook Oz from his head. *I won't let you ruin this for me. They're impossible dreams, but they're all I have.*

He knelt in front of the bay window and drew aside a portion of the drape.

"What the fuck?"

Andrew fell backward and the curtain closed. He caught himself on his hands, and his wrists stung from the impact. His clear view to the Spanish colonial was obstructed by something on the windowsill.

He sat on his knees again and cautiously peeled back the corner to find the object still there.

It was a small four-ounce jar sealed by a navy blue lid. The jar was filled to its wide neck with a green-tinted liquid. And in the middle, suspended in the ooze, was a tiny gray brain. Two eyeballs floated in front of the miniature organ.

Andrew let the drape cover the jar. He must be dreaming. He'd had one of those deep sleeps that'd become normal, and he was in the process of waking.

But on a third peek out the window, the brain and its two cloudy orbs literally stared back at him.

He looked across the street and studied the house, searching for the face of the prankster. The house's occupants had obviously discovered his routine of watching them, and this was some joke. But no one darted their head around a corner to laugh, or pay the blue apartment complex any mind. The frat house stirred with its normal movement as if nothing had happened.

Natalie would've fainted. She would've woken up crying and fainted again at the sight of the brain. But Andrew opened the window and brought the jar into the house.

It was cool around the outside, and he could see the tiny wrinkles and veins on the brain's exterior. When he looked underneath the jar, the organ bobbed with its tethered eyes as if to say hello.

There were no markings of where or who it might've come from. Not even an indication as to the type of brain.

It'd have to be a small animal. Maybe a dog? No, smaller than that. A rodent. A mouse or a gerbil brain.

Who would be going around cutting out gerbil brains, other than college students? Maybe for an anatomy course of some kind, and this joke really was an elevated form of burning dog shit on the porch. Yet there was no one from across the street watching the scene of the crime.

Andrew reexamined the object, searching for a clue. But there was nothing.

He shut the window and set the jar on the coffee table. He sat on the floor and looked into its droopy eyes.

He imagined paramedics freeing the trapped mouse from the vehicle and laying its limp body on a stretcher.

"Our technician jumps into action. We provisionally connect the body with a machine to continue circulation and

oxygen while the blood is replaced with a stabilizer reducing freezing damage. We then extract the brain. It's kept in storage and cooled by liquid nitrogen."

And here was the end result.

This is me.

The sparkwheel in his head spun. This brain wasn't a random, weird prank. It was personal.

This is ME. Small sparks, but the wheel wasn't quite hitting concurrent with the ignition yet.

Who would do something so cruel? Robert liked to sneak up and scare Natalie, but he'd never make fun of her. And he'd been occasionally critical of Andrew's many failings, but this type of dig was beyond him.

And that's what this is. Ridiculing me, insulting me!

Simon was too immature to have done it. Shelly wouldn't – she felt Andrew was still angry with her since their last conversation, so she wouldn't chance further irritating the situation by teasing—

In his brain the steel wire struck the flint as the lighter's gas valve released. A flame shot from the end.

The pharmacist.

He had to be the one. He knew from preparing the medication. He knew from the damn number on the ID. And he'd gotten the address from the ID as well.

How dare you?

Andrew saw the room bathed in red. All he'd been through, all the pain he'd endured and would be forced to continue enduring. Trapped in this body. Forever imprisoned.

And here was the pharmacist. Not only living and enjoying his freedom, but reaching through the bars and poking Andrew with a stick.

Jab. Oz was probably hooting about it. *Jab. Jab.* Having a hearty laugh about his suffering. *Jab. Jab. Jab.*

It crossed his mind to call Robert. To call the police.

No. I don't need them. Fuck your stupid conservatorship, Robert. I don't need anyone. He stood and snatched the jar from the table. Grabbing Natalie's purse from the hook by the door, he stuffed the jar inside. *If you're going to laugh at me, you're going to do it to my face, you motherfucker!*

He marched outside the apartment, slamming the door behind him.

Andrew wasn't sure how he was going to kill Oz only armed with a mouse brain, purple purse, and house key, but he was damn well going to try.

Chapter 12

Oz was in the back of the pharmacy arranging medication at the top of a high shelf.

In how many ways can a pharmacist organize twelve different brands of dick steroids in eight places on a shelf? He moved three bottles to the left and brought a box forward. *There is an answer. Somehow. Somewhere buried. Maybe—*

He almost fell off the ladder when a technician burst through the door.

"Boss man, that lady who gave you the finger wants to see you."

"Which one?" Oz looked at him.

"There was more than one?"

"You only work here part time, Barty." He gave a wide smile. There'd been only one.

"She looks like she rolled out of a dumpster."

"Oh, that one. I knew she'd come see me again. Is she alone?" Not that he was afraid of the man who'd previously signed for Natalie Keller's medication. On the contrary, he felt pretty sorry for him.

If a pharmacist should offer one of his bottles of dick steroids to a supremely unhappy man who obviously needs to get some, then how many ways could aforementioned pharmacist organize his remaining—

"Alone and mad as hell."

"Show her back then."

"You better get off that ladder."

It was sound advice, and Oz backed down the rungs. Before Barty turned to leave, he loosened his tie and pulled it over his neck.

"Hang it on the doorknob. And don't poison anyone while I'm occupied."

The technician swaggered out with a laugh.

When Natalie entered, she slammed the door shut violently. She looked in the same disheveled state, except she seemed to be breathing fire and wore her purple purse.

"What a completely unexpected surprise. Mrs. Natalie Keller! To what do I owe the pleasure?" Oz held out his hand.

She jerked the purse to her front and dug out a familiar small jar.

"What the fuck is this?"

"That's a rat brain floating in a jar of alcohol."

"I know it's a rat brain in a jar of alcohol!"

"Well, if you knew what it was, why did you ask me?"

"I want to know why you put it on my windowsill this morning!"

Natalie slammed the jar on a table. The gray brain inside hit the lid and bobbled around – tendrils of brain matter spinning like the inside of a snow globe. He was glad he'd come off the ladder.

"Don't break it. It's special."

She stood glaring at him. The same rage contorted her face as it had days ago, and he wondered if he'd finally gone too far.

This bag lady was about to go crazy. She'd chuck the rat brain at him and try to tackle him to the floor. He'd have to restrain her while Barty called the police. They'd haul her away screaming, but at least they'd probably hose her down at the station.

So attack me, doll. You could use a bath.

To his surprise, Natalie pulled herself together.

"You're a fucking freak. Leave me alone, or I'll call the cops." She turned to go.

"Oh, we're all freaks, doll. They made us that way."

Oz knew he'd hooked her when she stopped. He picked up the jar and held it to his eye, looking at the back of her sweatshirt through the murky alcohol.

"I didn't extract this rat brain. A friend of mine did. Nicest guy you'd ever meet. Sunshine lodged in his ass. Squeamish of his own puke. And then, bam!" He returned the jar to the table and clapped his hands together. "Tractor trailer rolls his car off a viaduct. Three years later he wakes up and is fixated on death and dead things. Scraping them off the side of the road, pulling out their organs. It consumes him. He's a freak. Though more tolerable, in my opinion."

Natalie glanced over her shoulder.

"He gave me that rat brain to remind me of better days. I thought it might remind you of them too. We brains in jars."

When she fully turned, she examined him again, but without the same furious intensity. Her eyes picked him apart before meeting his gaze.

"What do you want?"

"I'm not in league with those CryoLife fucks. I don't want anything, I just remember you from before. You came in here two years ago with this revolting stench of happiness. You polluted my fucking pharmacy for days with your reek of perfection. And now look at you." Oz motioned to her with his hand. "You look like that woman's miserable younger sister. You don't give a shit about yourself, or that kid. You're not you. And you know it."

"I do care about him, I—"

"Save it for someone who buys it. You feel guilty. You feel obligated. You don't want to see him run over by a train, but you aren't kissing the ground he walks on like you were before."

Natalie averted her eyes.

"It's not your fault. They did this to you. You don't have to feel bad. Well, you do have to feel bad. It doesn't get better." Oz pulled out his wallet and retrieved a business card. "But, you don't have to feel like a freak alone."

He placed the card on the table. Taking a pen from the pocket of his white coat, he wrote a pair of lines on the back, only stopping once to flex his hand and relieve the writer's cramp. He handed the card out to her.

"I have friends like us. We meet to talk, be ourselves for a while, and be pissed about what happened to us. We play snooker, get drunk, and occasionally smoke some weed."

"I'm not interested."

"You're never going to get through this if you don't have an outlet. Look at yourself." He traded the pen in his pocket for a cigarette. He lit up without hesitation.

"I may not be the one who gets to decide if you're the same person, but I'm not blind. You're failing, and you're going to continue to fail. And then where will Billy, or Johnny, or Yhatzee, or whatever the fuck his name is, be? And where will the hubby be?" He dashed a small crumbling of ash on the table corner. "Take the card and think about it."

She picked up the card and looked at the name of the bar, date, and time he'd written. Then she turned it over.

"Osborne."

"That's the first name my parents gave me, the name I had for twenty-one years. Then I died, and when I came back, I decided to call myself Oz. I'm that fucking creative." He breathed smoke into the air in waves. "And what should I call you, doll?"

"Not doll." She placed the card in her pocket and turned to the door.

"One more thing," Oz added. "This isn't a family support group. Don't bring little Tommy or the hubster. And it's not a CryoLife rim job party either, so your conservator or other CryoLife tools aren't welcome."

"Is CryoLife aware of your get-togethers? They told me—"

"If they aren't, I'd prefer to keep it that way. And if they are …" He ground the cigarette butt into the table and held his chin in his hand. "Well, I don't give a fuck."

There was silence before she put her hand to the door.

"Don't flick your cigarette into those oxygen tanks, and stay away from my apartment."

Oz laughed as she left. She was a welcome addition to his group, even if she hadn't accepted his rat brain.

Chapter 13

"I'm telling you, brother, she's going to come." Oz curved his hand over the side of the billiard table, his fingertips touching the green baize. He shook the stiffness from his left hand and slid the cue shaft through the loop of his first finger. "And you're gonna like her."

"I like everything that's dead. Or was once dead."

"That you do, my friend, that you do. You depraved … twisted …" He broke eye contact with his opponent to give the cue a quick stroke, trailing off to see if his aim had been true. But he'd created a sidespin that only served to line up Santino's next move. "Fuck!"

"You make it way too easy, Oz. You'd do better if you kept your mouth shut and concentrated. At snooker, and at everything else. You know the best way to improve accuracy, don't you? You shorten the distance between the balls, and …"

Something so easy, calculated in a millisecond ten years ago.

His friend banked a shot that potted two balls before giving him a wicked grin. "Get bigger balls."

Oz pulled a cigarette pack from his back pocket. It was brand new, and breaking its seal made a satisfying, crisp sound. "My considerable talents are wasted on this tedious game. Tinks, tag in for me."

He thrust his cue into the hands of a small man with coiled hair who'd been watching the game before tilting his head to light a cigarette.

"Beat that son-of-a-bitch into the ground."

Santino moved to another end of the table, ducking his head around a high-hanging pendant light. He pulled a blue cue chalk from the pocket of his cardigan sweater and nodded toward a distant table. "Go huff in your corner and wait for your mystery woman. Slowly killing yourself."

"It feels spectacular." Oz inhaled deeply and sauntered to a round table set with drinks.

He sat with his back to the wall and leaned his chair on two legs, propping his feet on the table. Folding his hands behind his head, he surveyed the bar.

Oz was confident Natalie would come since she'd been interested enough to seek him out about the rat brain.

If someone leaving you animal organs in jars only pissed you off, you'd go to the cops first. You wouldn't find the person to ask why.

Natalie had also thought it through and realized that having requested her identification, he would've read her address. He liked clever people. He considered his friends in their group to be clever and inquisitive. They weren't intimidated enough to be complacent, but were cognizant that nothing could be done to improve their situation.

Except to become one of those fucking drones who forgives and forgets. Too afraid to confront the reality of the situation, he'd brought more than one person into the group only to have them concede and slink back into their holes. These were the people CryoLife liked best. The ones that ended up in their positive testimonials and on their brochures.

But I don't forgive, and I'll never forget what they did to me. Oz thought of arranging the medication on his shelf and of the pool table. Such simple, simple things. He drove the dying butt into an ash tray and lit another. *I'll never forget what he did to me.*

His nerves felt calmer after the new cigarette was half spent, and he watched his friends at the billiard table. They were good men. Like he used to be.

"Where are your friends? Or was this another stupid trick?"

Oz nearly lost his balance when Natalie appeared next to him. "They're playing snooker."

"Why aren't you playing?"

"They like to have some sport out of the game. It's not fun when I take every shot and clear the table before they get a chance. I'm a considerate person, you see." He brought all four legs of his chair to the ground and slid out the seat to his right for her. "I pull chairs out for fair ladies, I leave extraordinarily thoughtful gifts for them, I invite them to raucous, glittering parties ..."

Natalie scowled and pushed the chair back into place. She removed her own on the opposite side of the table and sat with a grimace.

Oz smiled and waved his hand for service. "What's your poison?"

"I don't drink."

"Oh, that's right. Holly Housewife. No place for booze in our quaint world, is there?"

He didn't know for sure that she was a housewife, but as loudly as her current look screamed "dumpster hobo," the vibe of pre-reanimated Natalie had been "professional snot wiper."

Oz turned to the waitress. "Another gin for me and a club soda for my friend."

"I can order for myself," she said sharply. "Just water with lemon."

"Water. With lemon. And don't forget the lemon," he repeated to the waitress, who walked away. "What a housewife thing to order. Watching your figure? Master doesn't want a chubby wife?"

"If you're going to push my buttons, I'll leave."

Oz tapped his cigarette ash into the tray. "Sometimes we have to laugh at these beasts we've become so they don't consume us."

"I'm not a beast."

"But you feel like one. And that's what matters."

Natalie said nothing and there was silence until the waitress set the drinks on the table.

"So, what excuse did you give your master in order to get out of the house? Quilting bee? Book club? Carving Jesus statues out of butter?"

"I told Robert I was having dinner with a friend. And he's not my master."

"Oh, yes, he is. You have 'Property Of' written all over your forehead."

"I'm free to go anywhere or do anything."

"Then why didn't you tell him you were meeting a guy in a bar? A guy who left a rat brain on your windowsill?"

Oz took a sip of his gin and watched her squeeze the lemon. She didn't milk the edges of the rind together gently. She crushed the wedge between her thumb and forefinger – popping three seeds into the water. She clawed the rest out with her finger before they fell to the bottom. It made him smile. Delicate people irritated him.

"Here's why you didn't tell him: Master would've said, 'Oh no, Honey Bunny Stinky Poo. I don't think that's a good idea. I need you to stay home, make bread, and hold still while I tank you up with fifty more fucking brats.'"

"Enough!" Natalie slammed her fist on the table.

"Wow, chill. Chill."

Santino stood behind Natalie's chair. He placed a large hand on her shoulder, which appeared to startle her. When she looked at him, he gave a wide smile and removed the hand.

"Don't let Oz rile you. He zeros in on every vulnerable spot and tries to pick you clean. He's like a vulture with sonar."

Oz felt moderately guilty. He liked to antagonize people, but not make them genuinely upset. Many in their situation were miserable, but so wrapped up in trying not to be wretched, they needed a shove. Not to be pushed over the edge, but to feel they were about to be. Hitting their pressure points was a stark reality check. And he wasn't about to apologize for being the one who regularly gave it. Instead, he used his thumb and first finger from both hands to form two circles which he held in front of his eyes.

"Caw! Caw!" He laughed.

"See?" The man offered Natalie his hand. "I'm Santino. Keeper of the peace, and apologist for the Grade A jackass you see before you. My services are ever in high demand."

She smiled and gave her hand to him.

There was a time I could make a woman smile – when I wanted to make them smile. But even if he was no longer interested in pretty women, there was something about Natalie that he liked. And this mysterious quality made him want to kick Santino under the table for trying to be a charming dickhead.

"And I'm Tinks." The man with wired hair offered his hand, which she also accepted.

You didn't take my hand either time I offered it to you ...

They waited for her own introduction but after only receiving silence, the two men sat on either side of her.

"Not a problem. We know how it is." Santino gestured for a waitress. "I remember being intimidated myself."

Natalie shook her head. "I'm not scared of you."

"Scared and intimidated are two different things. And I didn't mean of me, or any of us." He folded his fingertips on the table to form a triangle. "Realizing you're not alone isn't daunting?"

"I knew there had to be others. That I had to be walking past them."

"But as you realized that, can you honestly say your next thought wasn't, 'but they're not like me.'"

She gave a slow smile in response, and again Oz wanted to slug his friend.

"I'm sure there may be some ex-patients out there who genuinely believe their lives were saved by the reanimation process. But we are the proof that CryoLife ruins as many people as they get right." Santino placed his glass on a coaster. "There may not be much we can do except to support each other in not feeling so alone in this world, but that does help. Sometimes anyway."

Truer words have yet to be spoken.

The sentiments appeared to resonate with Natalie as she looked up from her ice water. "Will you tell me what happened to you, Santino?"

"Of course."

Chapter 14

"So before, since the *before* always influences understanding the *now* – you know the clean cut, conservative, choir-boy type? That was me. My father was an assistant pastor, and I was engaged to the girl who'd sat three church pews behind me my entire life." Santino leaned back in his chair and closed his eyes. "I thought she was the most beautiful girl in the world. She had green eyes and cinnamon colored hair that—"

"That smelled like roses and sunshine and the diarrhea that drips out Cupid's ass." Oz lit another cigarette. "Get on with it already."

Why do you have to be such a fucking asshole?

Andrew gave Oz the glare that Santino didn't. Many things had aroused his curiosity, and driven him to lie about going out with Shelly in order to attend tonight's gathering. While the scent of Santino's presumably ex-fiancée's hair wasn't something he cared about, perhaps it'd help to "*not feel so alone in this world.*"

"I didn't see it coming. The semi swiped me and rolled my car above the rail." Santino made a shoving pantomime with his hand. "I remember feeling weightless – held into place by the seatbelt, but my back off the seat. I heard metal crunch and everything went black.

"I was reanimated three years later, and God's honest truth – I felt exactly the same. I walked out singing the praises of CryoLife. And I was their most loyal, ardent supporter for most of the drive home." Santino paused before continuing. "Are you familiar with Daffin Park?"

"Sure." Andrew pictured the park's rows of oak tree lined allées. Natalie had taken her children there.

"If you continue on Liberty, my folks live a quarter mile down the road. But there's a stop sign right across from the park. We're at that sign and I'd been leaning out the window. I look at the gutter, and there it is: a cat. Now, I'd seen dozens of dead cats before, but this one—"

Dead cat? Without turning his head, Andrew glanced at Oz and Tinks. Neither of them reacted, so perhaps he'd misheard.

"That cat was gorgeous. It was lying on its side – fresh. Pink and red intestines had rolled out onto the asphalt like sausage links. And its mouth was open, caught in this last agonizing yowl. I could see its teeth and tongue, and its glazed eyes." Santino shivered, but smiled. "I had to have it. To touch it. To take out its organs and arrange them on a table. There was a drive to do it. It had to be done. *Had to happen.*"

Andrew wasn't sure he had any "drives." Maybe the pacing, except that had gone away. He liked watching the frat house across the street as part of his daily routine, but he wasn't compelled to do it. There was art. From Jackson Pollack floor tiles to the Matisse-ish looking lights over the billiards table. He couldn't help but see that everywhere though, so it wasn't the same.

"I knew it sounded crazy and I had to let my father drive on. But God, I thought about that cat the entire day. I couldn't concentrate. All I could see was maggots destroying it before I could get back. Or a crow pulling it into the park where I'd never find it. The thought of losing it twisted my heart to pieces. So as soon as the house went quiet for the night, I unlatched my window to get it."

"Didn't the alarm go off when you left? The ankle monitor?" Andrew asked. Before his own had been removed, he'd thought about testing its limits, but never had. It was such a relief to have it gone, even if he still hadn't ventured any farther than the pharmacy before tonight.

"Yes, but I didn't care. I had to have that cat. This was the plan:" He leaned his elbows on the table. "I was going to secure it, hide it in the garage, and then go out for them to find me. By then I'd be taking a stroll, having innocently forgotten about the perimeter boundaries.

"So I have a pair of tongs and my mother's turkey roaster under one arm. When the ankle monitor started beeping, I ran faster. And the cat was still there! I can't tell you how ecstatic I was."

Oz pulled a new cigarette from his pack. "Over-the-moon like a limpdick discovering an empty park bench. Piss-in-your-pants excited like a starving trash man jumping on a Christmas—"

"Do you want to tell this story?" Santino snapped.

"You clearly said you couldn't describe how ecstatic you were. For the convenience of our guest, I was merely providing examples to convey your level of enthusiasm. Picking up where you fall short in most things. As usual. And despite this heatwave." He pushed his lighter into the pocket of his jeans and winked at Andrew. "You're welcome, doll."

It grated him to be called that, but in a different way than "Natalie," "Mom," or other pet names. Maybe because he now knew that in some hidden way, Oz was like him. Even before Santino's assertions of them being evidence of CryoLife mistakes, Oz's word for them – freaks – had been one Andrew had used to describe himself often. And "freak" wasn't "I've been reanimated and enjoy Western movies." Freak was serious. Freak had profound, disturbing flaws.

Something had to be wrong with Oz. He didn't look it, but he couldn't be a perfect specimen. There had to be something.

And when I find out what your secret is, I'm going to relish in it. I'll reduce your pain to one word and throw it in your face. See how you like the jabs, you fucking asshole.

"Silence from the peanut gallery moving forward would be much appreciated." Santino turned his attention back to Andrew. "I take the tongs and fit it around the cat's head. I lift it to go in the turkey roaster, and its guts start falling out around me. It was magnificent – these spiraling ribbons on my shoes. And the smell was perfume. There's this sweet spot of death where it's a sour, teeming smell of life! Of microbes living and feeding! And this cat was curving into ambrosia."

He inhaled deeply as if reliving it, and Andrew tried to keep the disgust from his face.

"I got as much into the roaster as I could before running back. And every other part of the plan went off perfectly. You've probably discovered this by now, but in most cases people are so glad to have you back they overlook a lot of things."

How true that is. Andrew frequently wavered as to whether Robert's delusions were to his benefit or not. Sometimes it felt like it might be best to call it quits and return to CryoLife for the next five months. But would they really grant him a new identity? All he knew about Brigman and Zuniga were their exaggerated smiles and patronizing verbiage. The level of overcompensating didn't bode well for their actual honesty.

"But that wasn't the end of it. The obsession started taking over every aspect of my life and nine months later, I was busted. You recall me mentioning my fiancée?" Santino glanced at Oz. "The one with the hair that smelled like watery cherub feces?"

Oz removed his cigarette and they exchanged a smile. "Some people leave a lasting impression."

"She calls me hysterical saying they're going to have to put her cat Fluffy down because it's old and in pain. And what am I thinking? This is literally, the best thing ever."

"Why?" Andrew asked.

"I'd never taken apart an animal that hadn't been hit by a car. God, do you know how hard it is to find a dead cat that's not putrefied in Georgia? If it's been baking for too long, it's a soup in there. It's like splitting open a water balloon. One pop and it's done. Hardly satisfying."

So many things I'll never regard the same way – road kill, water balloons, the Sistine Madonna.

"I'd never been so excited in my life – which is a finite measurement not requiring creative elaboration. I went with my fiancée to the veterinarian's office and held her in my arms as the cat slipped away.

"After it's gone, she asks what's going to be done with Fluffy's body. The guy says how they cremate, and my fiancée is upset about this. 'How could they burn Fluffy.' So I suggest taking the cat home and giving it a funeral. Putting its body in a box with catnip or something. She loves this idea. And then the situation gets better.

"On the way home, she says, 'I can't bear to see her, Santino. Will you put her in the box with the pillow and her bell? I don't want to look at her cold and lifeless.' More bawling. But I'm just ..." He held his hands in the air.

"Handel Hallelujah chorus! I had no idea how I was going to put it back together."

And there goes The Messiah.

"I waited until my fiancée fell asleep before going to the garage. I take Fluffy out and lay her on the workbench. I turn on the overhead lamp, unsheathe the scalpel, and, guys, I'm telling you. That first split on an animal that wasn't crushed to death ... To see the organs poke through the seam like budding flowers. Or then when you—"

"Santino. No one else gets a jones off this shit."

While Andrew didn't have Natalie's extreme sensitivity, he'd been feeling that weight near the back of his mouth that came before a gag. For the first time, Oz's interruption had been welcome.

He turned from Santino and made eye contact with him.

Oz had brown eyes. They were a warm, caramel color, and his pupils were easily discernible from his irises, unlike some brown eyes Andrew had seen, including his own. In contrast to the rest of Oz, the eyes could belong to anyone – a man or a woman. As a result, they were much less painful to look at than the rest of him.

Unfortunately, as he was across the table Andrew couldn't utilize the makeup-Cubism technique. Maybe that was a good thing. He caught Oz's smile, which seemed genuine. For the first time since meeting him, the man had done something without the motivation being an attempt at shock value, cockiness, or drawing attention to himself. It'd just been nice.

So Andrew smiled back at him before returning to Santino.

"True, it's not for everyone. Long, beautiful story short is that my fiancée walked in on me dissecting her beloved pet cat. She'd had that cat since it was a kitten – which, by the way, are not great. There isn't enough of them."

"Cutting up a kitten is like jacking it in the shower. Works in a jam, but not the real McCoy," Oz offered.

This comment didn't merit a smile.

"You could put it that way," Santino answered as if agreeing about the weather. "But she never wanted to speak to me again and blew my secret in the open. Fortunately, my parents were still under the 'my son is alive, it's a miracle' spell. They thought I wanted to change my career plans to be a veterinarian. Which I did, but only for access to fresh animals.

"Before you ask, I've never hastened the death of any poor creature for my own pleasure. I don't need to. There are plenty in my line of work. And I can keep pieces I especially like. The brain Oz gave you, that was a good one."

Santino leaned across the table and took an olive Tinks had discarded on his napkin.

"It was a difficult extraction. You see, the rat skull is relatively weak." He removed the tiny plastic sword that'd skewered the olive and held it above the fruit's flesh. "If you press too hard to split it open—"

"Santino!"

Oz's reprimand pushed Santino out of his trance, and he dropped the miniature sword.

"My apologies. I can get carried away." He flushed and rubbed the back of his neck.

Andrew swallowed and looked away from the nearly bisected olive. "You seem happy about it. You have a way to do what you want, and you're not hurting anybody."

"But it's nothing the me before the CryoLife procedure would've done. If it hadn't been for that, I'd be a computer analyst with a wife and family. Now, think about me having dinner with a girl. She asks what my hobbies are and I say, 'I love dissecting animals. Keeping their various parts in jars on my shelves.' How does that sound?"

"But it's not dangerous. You're not dangerous. And it's only animals, too. That's not so bad."

"People aren't exactly the same, no."

"He's also a necrophile." Although Oz hadn't raised his voice, it felt like he'd shouted it into a cave. The last word boomed off the walls and echoed back. "Know what that is, doll?"

Andrew tucked his hands behind his elbows and waited for Santino to refute Oz's assertion. But the man's only response was to toss back the remainder of his Sazerac and motion for another.

"Oh, my God." Andrew felt his cheeks go numb.

"Once you've been dead, it could be said that developing a taste for them follows logic."

"Shut up, Oz." Santino gave him a glare and then fished the lemon peel out of his glass. His voice was thick with shame as he spoke. "My unnatural behavior is the result of brain damage caused by the CryoLife reanimation. I was a normal man before that procedure." He dared to look at Andrew, his face red. "Dear, I never had these feelings before they did this to me."

"But if you ever decide to kill yourself, do it draped across his porch in some sexy lingerie."

"Oz!" Santino slammed his glass on the table, and some of the brown liquid sloshed over the rim. "Put your fucking filter on, or I'll do it for you!"

"Lighten up." Oz tilted his chair again. "No one's judging you here, brother." He took the cigarette from his mouth. "This is a judgment free zone. We're all broken. We're all monsters. You're with your own kind."

"I may be a sick man, but what I do doesn't hurt anyone. The animals or people."

Andrew studied Santino as an awkward silence unfolded. Though there wasn't the same rage and jealousy as he had when looking at Oz, there'd still been some level of envy. For his short hair, his glasses, his height. The way his hands were large like Robert's, but the fingers were slender. For the damn sweater with shank buttons that fit him so well. Even the bantering friendship he had with Oz was appealing.

You can't be this. Look at you. You can't be this thing. You can't be—

His thoughts ceased.

This is what people see when they look at you, Andrew. They see a normal woman. They assume you must do normal things. Not that you would go telling the world your secret, but they decide before you'd have the chance. They tell you what you are from a glimpse. You hate that. Yet here you are, doing the exact same thing to someone else.

It'd always felt like there was a distinct difference between feeling guilt and shame. For Andrew, guilt had the action feel of "I've done something wrong" whereas shame was more a state of being, a condition. "I, as a human being, am wrong."

I am. And I'm sorry.

"It's not against federal law. Only a state law in Georgia." Oz tapped his cigarette on the ash tray. "It's a felony in Alabama. And in Florida. So we have to go to South Carolina for him to get his kicks, in case he gets caught. I was fine with take out or delivery, but we always have to dine in. It's such a boring drive."

"You go with him? You help him?" Andrew wasn't sure what to make of this. What kind of a person—

"Why wouldn't I? It's not my scene, but he's my friend. And I'm the one with the connections." He smirked. "It may not be illegal, but about any way he could get a body is. Unless you know the right people to get you an all-access pass. Then it's a buffet."

"Oz, just stop." Santino covered his face with his hand.

"You people. Holy fuck. This is what you are now. No reason to be ashamed of it." Oz threw back the gin in his glass and set it on the table empty. "So you like a cold one? Who gives a shit? It's who you are, thanks to that fucking procedure."

I'm wrong. But you're a jerk.

"It's not your fault." Oz added. "This is what you are."

"And what are you, besides a fucking asshole?" Where Andrew had scooted away from Santino, he moved his chair back and unfolded his arms.

"Between a fucking asshole and a shitting asshole, I'll take the former."

As much as Andrew hated Oz, his chest tightened with yearning to be this man. He wanted to cleave him into pieces and collapse in a puddle of pathetic crying.

Oz tipped his chair back on two legs, crossing his ankles on the table. He was wearing a red polo and dark jeans. Without his pharmacist's coat, Andrew could see how well formed his upper arms were, and how he sported numerous tattoos and tribal bands.

"But in answer to your real question, I'm the best." He pulled the cigarette from his lips. "And hence, the last."

You look so perfect on the outside. Andrew glared at him. *You'd better be feeling the same disemboweling, burning pain I am. If there's any justice in the world, something had better be tearing you apart inside.*

Chapter 15

"Like Santino, well, like most people I've met, for me it was a car accident," Tinks began.

Tinks's voice broke the intense, angry stare Natalie had trained on Oz. Usually, he didn't mind feeling conspicuous, but something about the way she examined him made him feel less in the spotlight and more on the operating table.

She coughed. "That's how it was for me too. I suppose there aren't a lot of ways a young person dies, but their brain could remain in good condition for the procedure."

"I've thought the same. I also find most people don't have the sense they're dying. They are unconscious, or think they're going to pull through. But I was devastated. I knew I wasn't going to make it."

You and me both, brother. Those terrifying, precious moments of realization before it comes. Life is pieced together. Solved, whether you like it or not.

"It was at night, and I'd taken a hairpin turn too sharp. Suddenly, I'm on my back in the mud and I couldn't feel my body from the waist down. I wasn't in pain or anything. Only shocked.

"The paramedics got there before I registered what'd happened. They were leaning over me with these twisted looks – like they were so disgusted that their entire face was shrinking. One guy turns around and is retching, while another one falls to his knees beside me.

"I can't see it, but I feel that he's pressing something into my hand. I run my fingers along these individual beads, and when I close my fist I feel the edges of the cross in my palm. And that's when I knew I was going to die."

At twenty-one, you think you're going to live forever. Shit happens to other people, not to you. You're invincible with plenty of time. Oz looked across the table at Natalie. She glanced at him before returning to Tinks. *You lived longer the first time than any of us did.*

He wondered what it was like to make it to twenty-five intact. Without having one's insides scooped out, dreams stolen, and existence made meaningless.

If I'd reached twenty-five, things would be different. Even if that fucker still brought me back. With more time being … complete. I could've changed the world.

"The paramedic starts praying – Sacred Heart of Jesus, reparation for my sins, assist in my last agony, commend my soul. All that good stuff."

"I take it you're not religious?" Natalie asked.

Tinks briefly lowered his eyes to his napkin. "What *is* God if He allowed this to happen to us? And if He *is* and stood by watching, why should I commend anything to Him? Why should I give a fuck what He thinks of my sins?" When there was no reply after several uncomfortable seconds, he chuckled and continued. "But, in retrospect I guess even if there was a rosary in the middle, someone was at least holding my hand.

"Not that I was terribly compliant. I was screaming at him to shut the fuck up. I wasn't ready to die yet. But he kept praying until this voice interrupts him mid-beseechment. Tells him to back the fuck off and save the religious shit for another day. I thought it was an angel – this shape in white near my head. And it assured me that I was going to live. That's the last thing I remember before waking.

"And there was no peaceful respite where I thought things were normal. I knew something was wrong right away."

Oz remembered the emptiness – the restart of the mind due to a push of Zolpidem. Unlike the others, he'd anticipated that something would be different. A shift in brain cells that could change everything. But any modification would be okay as long as one factor remained untouched.

In the blank space he dug for it. He'd been scrambling, panicking before Brigman read the required statement. Searching desperately. But his soul had been forever mutilated. The gift was gone.

Nothing. Just nothing—

Again Oz almost fell out of his chair. This time Santino had kicked one of the legs. He opened his eyes, but no one else had seen anything. Santino shook his head at him.

I wasn't asleep. I heard everything. Tinks asked if she liked music. Natalie answered "who doesn't?" Then he snorted at the irony. Blah, blah, blah.

"I heard music," Tinks said. "Faint at first, like someone a room away. It was classical music, and whoever played it favored one particular piece. It was on a continuous loop. Every time I came out of the sedation, it was there. And the longer I was awake, the louder the sound grew.

"In a week it went from elevator music to the decibel of a brass band. Since I couldn't talk, the CryoLife staff only knew

I was upset, but not why. And I thought I was going insane. They only had to stop the music."

A rank-2 intonation temperament plotted on a Grassmannian space. Tiny arrows shooting off from a bowed plane. This is music. And it meant something once.

"So the first thing I say when I can finally speak is to tell them to have that motherfucker down the hall shut off his radio or whatever. They look at me with these confused expressions, and it hits me: I was hearing music no one else could. It was entirely in my head."

Natalie shifted in her chair and folded a corner of her napkin. "Like an earworm?"

"Maybe an earworm on steroids. It's maddening for the constant repetition, and painful from the volume. When was the last time you broke your teeth from grinding them over an earworm? I've had more dental surgeries because of a piece of classical music than I can count. And that's not the worst that's happened."

"Can't they fix it?"

"Oh, they tried. But they don't know as much about the brain as they say. They're still trying to fix me." Tinks turned. "How many times have they switched my meds, Oz?"

"A dozen in the past four years. Minimum," he answered.

"Meds make it lower. So I can think, and talk in a normal voice, and sleep. Actually, once it quieted the first time, I thought maybe it was a gift. You're familiar with the story of the woman who came back and wanted to play piano?"

Natalie nodded.

He still tells the same fucking lies.

Oz tipped his chair down and leaned across the table. "There's no woman who became a musical genius. She doesn't exist. It's a fucking fable Brigman tells to keep you hopeful

141

they haven't completely fucked you. Keep you looking for something good in the monster they've turned you into."

"How do you know she isn't real?"

"Oh, I know. I know."

Possibly due to being four gins in, Oz knew he may have given something away. He tried to look fierce enough that she wouldn't question further. And she didn't.

"He's right," Santino said. "Beyond what they tell you in the Center, no one has ever heard of this musical protégé."

"But at the time, I was unaware of this," Tinks continued. "The music hadn't gone away, but the medication made it more like a gnat buzzing in my head. So I started the path to fulfill my musical destiny. I was hearing the piano, so that's where I began."

"You said it's a specific piece?"

"Yes."

"I'm just curious – would I know it?"

"It's very recognizable." Tinks moved the tip of his finger around the rim of his martini glass. "But whatever your damage is, I'm sure you might understand – giving it a name aloud is sometimes too difficult. Most times, in fact."

These men were Oz's best friends, but there were times where he didn't understand either of them. However, he could always be depended on to bring clarity to a situation or force a person to face—

Once more Santino gave his chair a swift kick. But what stopped Oz from still revealing the internal concert's name was less Santino's non-verbal threat and more the way Natalie looked at Tinks. She gave him a smile similar to the one she'd given Oz earlier. The one that'd caused an unexpected lightness in his chest and made him question what he liked so much about her. And when he no longer cared for the smiles of women, why did this matter to him?

"I understand how that is," she said.

"Thank you." Tinks returned the smile. "Anyway, since that was the instrument in my head, I sat at the piano and waited for inspiration. But nothing came. The keys were as foreign to me as ever, and even after I enlisted a tutor, I had no hope.

"Months of trying go by. And not only on the piano, but everything else. I couldn't master simple scales. The music in my head frustrated the ability to separate the instrument I was trying to play with what I was hearing. It had a life of its own, like it wanted to compete. The louder I played, the louder it'd grow itself. So I'd never forget it was in control of me. And you'd think it'd become something I'd get used to. Like people who live near waterfalls and can't hear them. But it's not the same."

"But you said you're on medication. Doesn't that help?"

"The pills keep it low, but it only works so long."

"And then what happens?"

"It erupts. I get crazy when the meds fail and it comes back full force. I forget that my ears have nothing to do with it. The last time I took a Phillips head, set it in the canal, grabbed a hammer, and the next thing I know, I'm waking up in a hospital bed. Again." Tinks turned his head so Natalie could see the ear. It looked normal except for scar tissue inside.

"They can fix ears. They can't fix brains. And I can't guarantee I won't cut my own head off or blow myself up trying to do it on my own."

"I don't think I could do anything like that."

"Self-mutilation? When I'm thinking clearly, hammering a screwdriver into my head even surprises me."

"Well, yes," Natalie said. "But also suicide. I don't want to kill myself."

"Yet." Oz tapped more ash into his tray.

He hadn't meant the remark the way he usually did when he allowed thoughts to spew unfiltered from his head. He was searching for a specific reaction from Natalie. She lowered her eyes and stared into the half empty glass of water.

I knew it. You have that look. You're not suffering enough. Yet. But it's beginning to sink in as a viable option.

"So tell us about you," Santino said. "How is it in your new reality?"

Santino and Tinks leaned in, while Oz remained in his kicked-back position. He knew she wouldn't tell right now; it didn't matter how much of their souls they'd exposed.

"What about your fearless leader?" Natalie looked across the table at Oz.

"Fearless leader, eh? I like that," he mused. "Fearless leader."

He did have a knack for bringing people together, if only from his knowledge of people's medication, and lack of hesitation to say just about anything. He also had a habit of cultivating networks in odd places based on his side hobby of pot distribution. He'd brought every person into their band of brothers, so he could be cast as a leader in that aspect. But once they were in the clan, there was no leadership. There wasn't a location to lead anyone to.

"Yes. What about you? What happened to you?"

"I died."

"That much I worked out. But the circumstances? Was it a car accident?"

"No. I wasted away like a withering flower. A snowflake on the cheek of a child. A fresh pile of dog shit on a hot summer's day." He folded his arms behind his head. "My breath escaping me like a playful autumn leaf out of grasp, or the aforementioned shit leaving the ass of the dog. Drowning in my own lungs like a … well, like a person is apt to do if they can't swim and happen to find themselves in such an unfortunate predicament."

"And how are you different? I assume your so called 'humor' has been constant." Natalie rolled her eyes.

"No, I used to be quite boring."

"I think it's unlikely you'd refer to yourself as a beast if all you became was interesting."

"I won't bog you down with another sob story."

He pushed the cigarette stub into his ash tray. At certain portions in the tragedies of the others, his two friends had turned away, or beaten around the bush. But that wasn't him. He faced everything head on and kept steady eye contact with her alone.

Oz slid the second to last cigarette from his pack and lit the new one. "I'm a fag. A big one."

He grinned and waited for a response.

"You shouldn't call yourself that."

Natalie had taken the bait. It was too easy. If only he could line up snooker balls this well.

Or remember how to do it. But don't think about that. Concentrate on what you still have control over.

"I reserve the right to call myself whatever I choose. Be it 'fag', 'big fag', or 'incomparable specimen of masculine splendor.' It's my call."

He was ready for a good fight. A war of taunts volleyed until she forgot whatever curiosity she might've had. It'd conclude with her surrender. He was too difficult to bother with and she'd never re-ask him anything about his past. His secrets would be safe.

The only person who'd broken this defense had been Santino. It'd taken months, and several, several gins. But once the wall had been surmounted, Santino had never challenged Oz again. And that'd been years ago. He doubted Santino remembered.

He gave no indication of being wiser. So despite the single successful invasion, Oz considered the strategy effective.

"It's all about the shock value with you, isn't it?" Natalie looked at him blankly.

Yes, it's sleight of hand. When I'm juggling swords, or eating fire, you don't notice anything else about me.

But though she apprehended his motives, she didn't question further. To his disappointment, she pushed back her chair and stood.

"Perhaps next time, guys." Natalie held out her hand first to Tinks, then to Santino. She made no effort to extend the courtesy to Oz.

"The hubby and kiddies alarm going off? It's too late to make supper." Oz felt cold as Santino released her hand. "I suppose you could get a start on packing love notes in with their fucking pudding cups."

"You're married? And you have kids?" Tinks's lips parted in shock.

Natalie looked at the ground and nodded.

"Whatever you're going through, my friend, I'm sorry." Santino touched her shoulder. She flinched but didn't move away. "We can see how your burden weighs on you. And I'm sure it's made heavier if you feel you're hurting people who care about you."

The sentiment had her eyes glossy with tears, and Oz wondered if no one had ever said they were sorry for what'd happened to her. Was it possible she might not have told her secret to her husband? What was the first thing said when a person found out something bad happened to you? They apologized. Had she been living this long without feeling the gratification from someone genuinely apologizing about a fucked up circumstance?

"Thanks, Santino." Natalie swallowed the emotion. "You're a good guy. You all are good guys."

She even looked at Oz, and his stomach fluttered. It'd been a long time since he'd been called a good guy.

"I'll come back."

He watched her as she left – her hands hidden in the large pocket of her sweatshirt. She walked with her shoulders back in straight steps without swaying her hips. His brain hummed until the door closed behind her. Then he was normal. Somewhat.

"Oz, I think you may've found a kindred spirit," Santino said when their eyes met.

"What do you mean?"

"I think you know what I mean."

Oz considered it. Sure, it was possible she'd reawakened preferring women. It might explain why she'd gone from a high-maintenance, feminine woman to one who wore her greasy hair pulled back and dressed in baggy clothes. But she didn't fit the profile of a butch lesbian either. Furthermore, he'd never been much of a lesbian enthusiast, but he liked Natalie. He felt drawn to her, as he hadn't been to anything else in a long time.

"Nah, it's not that. But there's definitely something."

Chapter 16

Whatever else happened to be going on at work or home, Robert always made it a top priority to keep his appointments with Dr. Zuniga. It'd been explained that until the psychiatrist felt Natalie was stable, weekly medication management sessions were critical.

"Shouldn't my wife come to these?" He'd first asked.

"That's not necessary, Mr. Keller," Zuniga said over the phone.

"Why not? She's the one taking the medication."

"We actually find that the most helpful information for medication control is derived from the conservator's observations." The smile in her voice made Robert feel more comfortable. "Dr. Brigman mentioned that you and Natalie are art aficionados?"

"That's Nat's thing, not mine." He didn't understand the stuff in the least. How could she spend so much time gawking at garbage? That magazine page she'd shown him really did look like a fecal-smeared wall in a monkey house.

"Well, I'll make the analogy anyway and hope the meaning comes across. I regard viewpoints on med management like looking at just a small corner of a painting versus taking a step back and seeing the entire canvas. Based on her perspective, Natalie is only capable of looking at that tiny piece, while you are able to provide us a full outlook. The more complete the picture, the better decisions can be made. Does that make sense?"

"Certainly." Really wasn't Natalie herself the painting? Thinking of it that way, she wouldn't be able to provide much valuable input.

"Consequently, come by yourself and feel free to speak openly as you might with a friend, Mr. Keller. Or may I call you Robert?"

"Sure, Robert is fine."

So once a week, and unknowingly to Natalie, Robert detoured to the Cryobiotic Treatment Center to speak with Dr. Zuniga. And it really was similar to visiting with a friend, for more reasons than the casualness. The doctor listened to him and provided explanations for Natalie's strange behavior. She was also supportive of Robert's actions, siding with him in most things.

For example, she had agreed that the "welcome home" party had been a great plan. Natalie needed to show an interest in something social, and a big get-together at the SpringHill was an event she previously would've loved. The only thing better than having lots of friends around was being the center of everyone's attention.

Her birthday is her favorite holiday. And she has more people over for those stupid candle and makeup parties. I don't get it.

After her fit had resulted in him popping the pins from the bathroom door to get to her, her reaction made more sense. He was irked by having to cancel his carefully constructed and non-refundable arrangements, but that she was so upset over wanting to be perfect for him wrenched his heart. It reminded him of how she used to be.

Robert hadn't needed Zuniga's insight to solve that incident, but she'd given him the needed reassurance regarding Natalie's next stunt.

"So how did this week go?" The doctor had crossed her legs and leaned back in her chair. "Were you able to make any headway in arranging a smaller social setting?"

"I was. She finally agreed to go over to Shelly's house."

"That's wonderful to hear."

"Well, yes and no." Robert relaxed into her office couch and removed his glasses. He felt his left cheek flinch as he cleaned the lenses. "You should've seen what she was wearing."

Two days ago he'd done a double take when Natalie marched out the door in a grubby sweatshirt and jeans. Had she forgotten to look in the mirror?

"Are you sure you want to wear that, hon?" Robert had asked. "Won't you and Shelly probably go out shopping or to lunch?"

"I'm not staying that long."

He'd laughed. "Sure you will. I'll come home at seven and you'll still be over there." He unlocked the car, but remained blocking the passenger door. "Which is fine. You can go downtown and get one of those kiwi pickle seaweed face things you like."

"I don't think so. I'll probably be an hour. Maybe."

Natalie had approached the car, and he inspected her from head to toe. She'd tied her golden hair in a ratty ponytail. Her face was clean, but it was bland without anything on it. And those clothes ... was that a paint stain on the sweatshirt? The ends of the jeans were ragged and threads trailed off the back.

"Nat, are you sure you don't want to change your clothes?"

"I like these. They're comfortable."

"Where did you get them? I don't remember buying those for you."

"I found them in her dresser. *My* dresser."

It had happened once or twice that she'd referred to herself in the third person, but Robert didn't think much of it. How many times did he call himself "Dad" when talking to Simon? "Dad's going outside." "Don't use those papers, those are Dad's."

Robert had sighed and stepped away from the car door. "Okay, but if you do decide to go out, have Shelly drop you by the apartment to change, or borrow something of hers."

You could run into anyone downtown.

When he'd gone to see Dr. Zuniga, she'd picked up a manila folder. Flipping back a page, she skimmed over some writing before shutting the cover. "And did she keep to that timetable? I remember you saying how close she is to Shelly."

"When I got home from work, she'd been there as if she'd never left."

"Still the same clothes?"

"Nothing about her changed. She was still wearing that ugly sweatshirt."

"Do you think maybe they had a disagreement? Perhaps that's why she came home early and they didn't go shopping?"

Despite the worrisome situation, Robert smiled. It was a relief to have someone think the same way he did. With how Natalie was acting, he occasionally second-guessed his thought patterns. But he couldn't be irrational if the psychiatrist drew the same conclusions.

"I considered that. But I've been checking her cell phone and they can't be fighting for Shelly to call as much as she does. She's calling at least three times a day."

"You're going through Natalie's phone without her knowledge?"

"Yes." He slid his glasses on and studied the doctor. "Do you have a problem with that?"

"No, it's your right as conservator to monitor her communication, it's your duty as husband to protect your family. How can you do that without transparency?"

That's right. I can't be sure everything is okay unless I know everything.

"And as for the clothing, it's fantastic that you're not only positively cheering her on, but being so understanding of the situation," Zuniga continued. "But these things take time, Robert. Natalie is still readjusting."

Robert watched as the psychiatrist opened the lid of her laptop. She talked to him as she typed.

"What I'm going to do is update her medication slightly. We'll try something different to ease the anxiety and help her build more confidence."

Good, yes. Something different.

＊

It helped Robert to have Dr. Zuniga as a sounding board, but the good doctor never lost sight of the main purpose for their sessions: Natalie's welfare. Her first question at their next meeting was straight to the point. "How have things been since we removed the Haloperidol?"

"Better," Robert said, although he hated lying to anyone. He sunk into her couch and returned her smile, trying his best to hide the reality.

"Robert." She pulled her glasses down an inch. "I can't help you or Natalie if you're not truthful with me."

"I mean, at first it was better. There was an incident earlier in the week before I picked up the new prescription."

"Do you want to tell me about that?"

Part of him did and part of him didn't. Was it really a good idea to describe how Natalie had locked Simon out of the bathroom for three hours?

Robert remembered how he'd come home and Simon had been on the ground, hugging his knees. It was as if he hadn't heard the front door unlock. He sat there, the sticky blood from the ends of his broken fingernails staining his pants.

What about the dead hamster? The care you took in explaining that his pet was dead, and then pulling him into bed with you? Comforting him. Assuring him that everything would be all right. Robert had folded his arms around their son and the boy had just continued to rock, not even acknowledging his presence. *What did you do in there for three hours? Plug your ears while he screamed and tried to get to you? He's just a traumatized little boy.*

But was there any merit in revealing to the doctor such a substantial, disturbing shortcoming in Natalie's recent mothering skills?

"No. It happened on the Haldol anyway." Robert shrugged. "Since she's started the updated medication I've noticed a difference."

"A positive difference?"

"Well, the pacing stopped."

"That's good, I know it was irritating you." Dr. Zuniga scribbled down a note.

"I don't understand anxiousness. It's a waste of time and energy."

The psychiatrist nodded. "Any other effects?"

"She's tired a lot. Sometimes she seems barely awake and she misplaces things."

"Such as?"

"I found her cell phone in the freezer and a box of cereal in Simon's sock drawer. Little things which really aren't a big deal. And her hands tremble sometimes. None of her other behaviors have stopped. She still won't do her hair or makeup." He gave a bitter chuckle. "You know what occurred to me yesterday? My wife is gorgeous, absolutely gorgeous. But when I came home from work and saw her in that baggy sweatshirt, I didn't see Natalie. I saw my overweight high school gym instructor."

"She's putting on a few pounds?"

"No, she's the same as ever. But you'd never tell with how she dresses now. She hardly even looks like a woman."

Zuniga spoke slower, obviously narrating the remarks she was adding to Natalie's file. "Still. Appears to be. Confidence. And image. Issues." She raised her pen. "Got it. Anything else?"

Robert had to think a moment before responding. "Well, she seems to have a little more patience with Simon. That's positive, I guess."

This time, he must've done a better job in not revealing that there was more to the story, since the psychiatrist smiled and opened her laptop.

"That's very good, yes. If you don't mind, Robert, just give me a minute to enter these updates into the database."

As she typed, Robert's thoughts drifted to the unabridged events that made him question the validity of Natalie's newfound tolerance with Simon.

Where before their son had been so clingy, now he was relaxed. Every night when Robert had come home from work, he'd found Simon asleep on the couch. He'd wake and eat, only to go right back to sleep, and his moments of consciousness were usually spent half-lidded.

"Why've you been so sleepy lately, big guy?" Robert had tucked him in the night before. "You and your mom been having all kinds of adventures?"

"No." He yawned. "We went to the medicine place the other day."

"Yeah, you told me about that one. But what did you two do today?"

"Nothin'. Had strawberry smoothies. Watched TV."

And the boy was gone. Robert kissed his forehead and left the door open a crack.

He'd walked down the short hall and into the kitchen. The dish drainer beside the sink was full of clean dishes. It was Natalie's job to put them away, but it wasn't worth waking her. She was on the couch asleep and the length of time it took for her to move past the grogginess and become useful verged on the ridiculous.

Robert stretched his arms above his head, popping both his shoulders, and took a handful of forks from the drainer. He'd pulled open the silverware drawer and noticed a pill bottle sitting in the organizer.

Again with this? That evening he'd found a toothbrush in the closet, a stick of butter on top of the television, and a pillowcase over her vanity mirror.

He removed the bottle.

Benadryl. A niggling suspicion in the back of his mind. *Strawberry smoothies.*

Robert had opened the child-proof cap and looked inside. There were only ten pink tablets left.

The small kitchen was joined to the living room, only separated by a counter bar with three stools. He looked over at Natalie sleeping on the couch.

Are you drugging our child to avoid dealing with him? To shut him up?

He considered his options. Should he wake her up and confront her? There was always the possibility it wasn't true. He didn't ration Benadryl. Maybe there'd been only ten tablets for a long time.

I could prove it for sure. Toss these in the sink and see if she buys a new bottle tomorrow. But no, that won't prove anything. What if she needs it tomorrow? Of course she'll buy a new bottle.

He was almost certain, and that was good enough.

Technically, this isn't that bad. She's not poisoning him. Benadryl is harmless, and maybe if he does calm down, she'll love him again. He can be overwhelming, and she's still adjusting. Remember what Dr. Zuniga said about how good you are that you're so understanding.

But still, his son was being drugged. He couldn't allow it to continue.

Robert waited for the psychiatrist to finish typing before he spoke.

"I was thinking though, with regard to Simon. Even if Natalie has been more patient lately, maybe she needs to be alone first, right?"

"I apologize, Robert. Can you elaborate?"

"I don't know if you're a mother, but it really is a full-time job. And it's like she just 'came back to work' after being away for more than a year. I thought it might help if I gave her a break. Start her at part-time and work from there."

"So what are you suggesting?" Dr. Zuniga picked up her pen.

"Nothing. There is no suggestion because I've already done it." He cleared his throat. "I'm having Simon stay at my mother's house for a while. Unless you think that's a bad idea."

Usually Robert preferred when the doctor agreed with him, but in this instance he hoped she might not.

It'd been difficult to explain to Simon and hard to see him go away. He hadn't confronted Natalie about the drugging or consulted her in his decision. He'd packed Simon's bag and drove him over while she was asleep.

I want my son back. He locked his jaw and ground his teeth to keep back the tears. *Tell me it's a shit idea. I'll pick him up tonight and find some other way to solve this drugging business. I want my family to be complete. I—*

"I think that's an excellent plan." The psychiatrist gave him her usual warm smile. "Limiting her stressors will help her focus on effectively acclimating to the situation. And you're so selfless in putting Natalie's needs before your own happiness."

Yes, I am. He nodded at her, still not trusting himself to speak. *Nothing is more important than Natalie, and once she has the wife part down, Simon can come home. It's only a slight delay. Better than her being dead or at the Center.*

"I guarantee, Robert, you've made the absolute best decision for your family. And it may be painful right now, but you won't regret it when everything falls into place."

After a few more seconds he relaxed enough to swallow and speak. "Thank you."

Between the two of us we can't be wrong.

*

Proof of Robert's wise decision making had come only days after Simon was gone and before his next medication management appointment:

"Robert, Shelly invited me to go to dinner with her. Can I go?"

He could've applauded. Thank God, Natalie *wanted* to

go out. This was a sign that it'd been a combination of the medication and pressure causing the odd behavior. Now she was turning around.

"You don't need to ask me, Nat. Would you like me to drive you?"

"No, I'll walk. I just wanted to make sure it's okay."

"I don't mind you going out with Shell."

Even if there hadn't been an impact from their previous visit, Shelly was a positive influence on Natalie.

She'll be a good mentor in getting back into the swing of things. She takes great care of the house, of the kids, of Clark. Yes, this is excellent. Very—

Natalie walked down the hall in the sweatshirt and jeans, her hair in a tangled ponytail.

"Don't you want to wear something nicer for dinner? Fix your hair?"

"No, I like this."

At least it was dark outside.

"Call me if you want a ride home, okay? Love you."

"Okay."

Robert had waited up for her, eager to see if Shelly had been able to work any magic. Especially since she'd been gone for hours. He'd hoped his wife would swing into the room – beautiful and happy, shopping bags in hand with exciting adventures to tell.

But Natalie came back tired and quiet. She wore the same shabby clothes and her hair was still a mess. Yet, she did walk through the door with a smile on her face.

I'll take it, Shell. It's something.

And he couldn't wait to share this good news with Dr. Zuniga.

Chapter 17

Oz was many things, but patient wasn't one of them. Though Natalie had said she'd return, the next gathering wasn't for a couple weeks. She didn't need her prescription filled for another two weeks either. So he faced a minimum of fourteen days until he saw her.

How could she expect me to wait that long?

He sat in his car outside her apartment building two days later. The building was within walking distance from his pharmacy, but he decided a skulking pedestrian looked more suspicious.

The more he thought about Natalie, the more curious he'd become. And not only about the secret she was keeping. It could be no more horrible or shocking than what'd happened to Santino or Tinks. Or him. What bothered him was why he wanted to see her. Why did he think about her in the middle of the night? Even before the CryoLife procedure a woman had never enthralled him enough to prevent sleep.

Only one thing had that impact. We used to stay awake long, long into the night. He sighed and closed his eyes.

But it's better to pretend that it didn't exist. It's not like it will ever come back anyway.

Still, despite the effort to shove the idea aside, the parallel had occurred to him last night. Natalie had caused his midnight thinking sessions to return.

Oz had been lying awake thinking about her before he realized he was lying awake thinking about her. If that was possible. Which it must've been, since it'd happened. He stared at the ceiling of his bedroom, his arms folded behind his head. And an image of Natalie flooded into his mind.

When Natalie had materialized at his side in the bar, the atmosphere in that familiar place changed. With the dark sweatshirt and jeans three sizes too large her silhouette looked like a brick turned on its end. That blond hair, pulled back with unruly strands struggling to escape. He knew her features were exactly as they had been. CryoLife didn't make those kinds of mistakes. But something wasn't the same about how she set her jaw. About how her face moved. Even if she'd been wearing the short skirt and low cut blouse, there was a rough quality to her.

And as he thought of her, he was shocked to find he felt the itch. Not for a woman, a man, or whatever androgynous thing she was trying to be, but he felt the itch in his fingers for a problem to solve. And unlike the snippets that came into his thoughts at regular intervals throughout the day, Natalie was a problem he knew he was capable of solving.

So last night, still lying in bed, he'd chewed his lower lip, and wondered about the location of his cigarette pack. He needed to chill out. The pot was downstairs and so was the gin. He'd laced his fingers together and stretched his palms to relieve the strain before turning and creeping his hand across the night stand until he found it. Cigarettes were his preference anyway.

What did I do before you, hmm? Oz took a deep drag and collapsed into his pillows. *Maybe I could've solved it with you to help me think. That's the only good thing about this fucked up mess. It brought us together.*

As he relaxed, Natalie again came before his eyes.

And now there's you ...

He hadn't felt this way about anything since before his death. This magic spark that danced around a problem. It gave every equation an aura meant to grab his attention. And though he hesitated to crack the door on contemplating a closer comparison, the darkness and nicotine made him bold.

Something needed to be understood, tamed, and made beautifully simple. What was behind the ratty hair, the baggy clothes, the dismal eyes? It was like a group of variables floated around her. What did they mean? What did she mean? If he dragged her into the abstract world to test her, to find a place where she'd fit, or make a new place for her to fit ... What would he find? When the hidden meanings were solved out, what was left? What was the answer?

My new problem ... Where would I start with you? How would I create a proof for you?

It'd sent a shiver down his spine, and he knew there was no turning back.

It wasn't his fault that something about her had impacted him. So today he didn't necessarily feel weird as he waited until after nine before getting out of his car and walking to her door. He wanted to know more about this hold she had on him. Because of her, he'd felt a flicker of who he used to be ten years ago. He'd seen the illusive flash and it must be understood.

He pressed the bell twice.

When Natalie opened the door, she didn't appear happy to see him, but also not unhappy.

"What are you doing here, Oz?"

"I thought we could hang out."

"I told you I'd come to the next thing."

"But before then. You seem … lonely," he ventured. "I thought you could use company. Are you going to invite me in?"

"No, I'm not alone."

"Do you have a secret lover that slips in after the hubster leaves? Kids don't bother me."

"How do you know Robert's gone? Have you been watching the apartment?" The prospect appeared to make her nervous. He saw the door quiver as if she were about to shut it.

"I have better things to do than watch your apartment. I pay attention, that's all."

No measure of relief crossed her face. Oz sighed and continued to explain.

"You only just started picking up your own meds. I checked my database of who'd been signing for them before, and Robert Keller has signed for pickup every time at approximately nine in the morning. So he must've been stopping on his way to work." Was she impressed by his sleuthing? "We are creatures of habit. And why else would someone be awake at this ungodly hour, except if one had to work?"

"Did you close your pharmacy so you could bother me then?"

"I'm the proprietor. That doesn't mean I work 24/7. And are you happy? I'm not stalking you, I notice patterns. It's one of my old habits. Perceiving patterns. Putting them together."

"Patterns that become apparent when you pull records from a confidential database."

"Signing for medication pickup isn't private. The contents of the medication are. But I won't admit to reviewing that data. No matter how interesting the information may be."

CryoLife wasn't forthcoming about its mysterious blends. It was unique for every person, and the mix changed depending on the psychiatric sessions, routine medical tests, and taste of the particular owner. There was also the difficulty of explaining to someone they were being forced to ingest psychotropic drugs. If patients thought they were being given only immunosupressants to prevent organ rejection, it was easy to ensure they took the medication religiously, extra nuggets and all. But was Natalie intelligent enough to have guessed that she was being slipped other things? And having thrown out the tempting bait of how useful he could be, would—

"You know what's in the medication?" Her hold on the door relaxed. If he wanted, he could've pushed his way in.

"I mix their witch's brew in my backroom."

They were both silent.

"Come on, it's freezing out here."

"It's eighty degrees, Oz."

"How do you know I don't have brain damage to my hypothalamus? I could be going into hypothermia."

Natalie opened the door.

"Thanks. It's not like I'm going to rape you. Even your hubby isn't my type."

Oz stepped inside the apartment and made a show of rubbing his biceps as he looked around.

It could've been cozy – it was small and well furnished, but didn't feel comfortable. He didn't know if it was the way objects were placed, or the objects themselves. It also could've been the feelings radiating from Natalie that coated the place.

It was as if the walls buzzed with stress. The apartment and every stick of furniture in it was nervous. There were even a couple frames draped in tan pillow cases on the walls – one by the door and one beside a family portrait. He wondered what the concealed pictures contained, or if the apartment had begun to hide from itself.

Against his inclination, he plopped back on the couch. He was too intrigued to let a vibrating apartment dissuade him. And he trusted his ability to make himself at home wherever he was.

"So this is where you live, huh?" Oz asked as she shut the door.

"For now."

"Thinking of running away, are you?"

"No. But Robert wants to buy another house by the end of the year."

Natalie sat on the edge of a couch opposite him. Her back was straight and her shoulders prim. In stark contrast, after lacing his fingers together to stretch the tension from his palms, he'd relaxed into the cushions and tucked his arms over the back of the couch. He'd been considering putting his feet up on the coffee table.

I'm more chill in your place than you are.

"He had to sell the old one for the deductible."

Oz was pleasantly taken aback at the volunteering of this information. She hadn't had to tell him. This knowledge added another level of understanding to how unhappy she was. Did her husband rub it in? Did the kids?

Exponentiation. Original guilt repeatedly multiplied by itself. Raised higher and higher to the power of all the fucked up assholes around you.

He guessed that Robert was like the other people who opted in to CryoLife – doing so without considering the liability clause.

The company couldn't get away with not disclosing that their procedure changed people. They downplayed it, but they admitted the risk. In a font the size of ant shit. But it was there.

And Natalie could partially blame herself for making the decision without looking into it more; however, with her out of the picture, it was the responsibility of Robert to claim the service "benefit" or not. The program hadn't been established for people of modest means. With the changes in her, was her husband regretting his purchase?

"So, it's indentured servitude then."

She shrugged. It was so riveting, like how it'd been in the old world. Plugging things in and seeing how they reacted. What should he try next, since she appeared ready to play? Or too defeated to fight.

"But you said, 'He had to sell the house.' The key phrase is 'had to,' doll." Oz leaned forward. "He didn't 'have to' do anything. Nobody forced his hand. And you can't be held accountable for his decisions. I mean, you were dead at the time."

"He felt he had to."

"Again, how can you be responsible for his feelings? He's an adult person."

"He loves me. Or loved."

"What part of that is your fault?"

He sank back into the couch and kicked his feet up on the coffee table. She didn't reproach him.

"Sorry, but you're not that beguiling. I'm proof of that. You can't make anyone love you. They choose to do that, and you have to let them make their choices and own their mistakes."

"But this isn't a situation you understand, Oz." Natalie sighed, her shoulders sinking further. "It's not that clean cut. He was distraught and grieving. He wanted to do the right thing."

"Being upset isn't an excuse for making poor decisions. And I don't mean to blast the guy for being 'noble'. How long were you out though? It couldn't have been much more than a year based on the elapse between when I first saw you, and when you came in to get your meds last week."

"Sixteen months."

"Do you know how long it takes them to construct a body? Approximately nine months. So, if you were only out for sixteen, he had that money in six. They won't do a damn thing until every drop is paid. And how long are they required to keep your brain in storage before they toss you out?"

"Five years."

"So why would he go into financial hardship instead of being more responsible? In five years he could've come up with it – saving, and I'm sure with the fundraising bullshit, but he could've done it. He picked the timeline, that's not your bad."

"He wanted me back. I told you, he loved me."

"But I say again, how can you possibly blame yourself for that? Look, doll, you think this is complicated, but it's not. Listen, do you see him anywhere? Is he here right now?"

She raised an eyebrow. "No, he left for work."

"So you aren't connected. You aren't the same body and mind. You're two separate individuals. Simply put: There's the you compartment, and there's the Robert compartment." Oz put out one fist and then the other.

"You leave his feelings, his decisions, his weird erotic fantasies in his compartment. They may affect you sometimes, but they're not yours." Satisfied in having made his point, he dropped eye contact to fish his cigarette pack out of his pocket. "Let the man own his decisions. If he has buyer's remorse, he has only himself to blame. Don't be such a selfish bitch."

He didn't know if she was comforted by his sentiments. Genuinely, he was trying to make her feel better. As no one had apologized to her for the circumstance besides Santino, he doubted she'd spoken of her unhappiness to anyone. He knew you couldn't talk to or trust those CryoLife therapists. They were representatives of CryoLife, eager to quiet criticisms with pills.

And if she'd mentioned how she was feeling, no one would dare make the assertion that Robert had been irresponsible. No one would explain that she had to separate herself from him, let alone encourage her to do it. They were CryoLife. They brought families together. Everything was fluffy bunnies and unicorns shooting rainbows out their asses. Any good psychiatrist would've told her she wasn't accountable for Robert, but a CryoLife psychiatrist thrived on making a person feel vulnerable, dependent, and indebted.

"You can't smoke in here, Oz," Natalie said, but she smiled.

"You're a cigarette Nazi, eh?"

"I couldn't care less what you do, but if you smoke, Robert will know someone has been here."

"Will he dangle you from the ceiling in chains? Whipping your naked skin with a riding crop to punish you for opening the door?"

"I don't want to talk to him about it. If he thinks I have new friends, he'll want to meet them."

He was touched to be classified as a friend. It was plural, so it included Santino and Tinks, but it also meant she appreciated what he'd said.

"I'll meet him. I'm a nice guy."

"He won't think you're nice."

From the family picture that hung on the wall, which included the pre-reanimated Natalie, Robert looked straight laced. A pleasant but reserved man. The kind who always wore a shirt and tie and carried two ballpoint pens in his pocket. Would Robert not like him because he was gay? His tattoos and piercings? His chain smoking? The drinking and growing weed in his basement? He wouldn't be fond of all these characteristics, but what she was probably referring to was his big mouth. It was a good thing Oz didn't care what Robert thought of him.

"If I can't smoke here, we can't stay here. I'm beyond not admitting I need them. Pack the kid, and let's go."

"What makes you think I'm going anywhere with you?" Natalie didn't move.

"You're depressed and need to get out of this prison. You've got Big Brother watching your every move." He motioned to the portrait as he stood, returning the lighter and pack to his pocket. The unlit cigarette still dangled from his lips. "For real, I don't care about bringing the kid. Let's get the fuck out."

"Simon isn't here."

"I meant the baby. You can bring him. Or her. Whatever it is."

"What baby?"

"You came into the pharmacy with a car seat two years ago. The way you were kissing at it made me think you were trying to suck its face off, or get it to eat out of your mouth like a fucking bird."

"It died in the accident."

Oz paused, searching her face.

"Well, I'd offer my condolences if you were upset, but it appears you've healed up decently."

"I've had a while to get used to it. Of course, I'm sad." The skin around her eyes tensed. "I mean, a baby died."

"So do rhododendron plants. 'What baby?' 'It died.' 'A baby.' You don't need to worry about me judging you. My best friend fucks dead people. My other friend hammers tools into his head. Yeah, it's sad when anything dies, even rhododendron plants. But if you felt connected to the kid, you wouldn't refer to it that way." Oz took out his keys and, hooking his finger in the ring, swung them around. "As it is, I lied. I was hoping you'd have stuck it in a daycare. Let's go."

"I'm not going with you, Oz."

He thought she might initially refuse, which was why he'd prepared a backup plan. To work through these types of problems one had to stay a step ahead. Know the rules and where to move next.

"Even for these?" He presented a small orange bottle and shook it, producing the sound of pills ricocheting off the insides.

"What are those?"

"Unlaced pills. The pure stuff, without the fun CryoLife additives they put in to keep you a fucking drone."

Her eyes widened.

"But I can't in good conscience give them to you unless I'm sure you don't need the bonuses. And I won't know that without spending more time with you." He pocketed the bottle. "I'm a professional, doll."

"Tell me what they're putting in the medication."

"I can't think and not smoke at the same time. I'll tell you everything in the car." He could see her hesitate. "Really, what else do you have to do today, and more poignantly, what do you have to lose?"

The sharp realization broke the dam.

"I have to be home by three when Robert gets back. It's his one early day."

As Natalie dug through a basket near the entrance, Oz glanced at the covered picture by the door.

What are you hiding? He only briefly hesitated invading her privacy. *Let's face it, I have the restraint of a two-year-old.*

He pulled at a corner of the pillowcase tucked around the frame and the covering dropped to the floor. His initial uncertainty at seeing his own reflection turned to shame.

"Are you Jewish?"

"No, why?" She brought a set of keys from the basket and faced him. He gestured to the uncovered mirror.

Oz was relieved he hadn't disrupted a Shiva for the sake of his impulsiveness, but his confusion returned. He felt her watching him as he ran his gaze along the mirror's gilded frame.

"I wouldn't say it's an ugly mirror. Maybe gaudy in comparison to the rest of your décor." He picked up the pillowcase and folded it over his arm. "Not that a tan pillowcase goes better, but whatever you prefer."

"I prefer to go, if we're going to." Natalie took the pillowcase and tossed it onto the coffee table. She held open the door. "Go."

He considered launching himself back onto her couch and badgering her further about the covered mirror. There was something more to it – her body language told him there was.

But you'll tell me when you're ready. If I haven't figured you out first. Oz strode through the door and pushed his hands in his pockets. His fingers went directly to his lighter. *Who are you kidding? It's not the fairness of allowing her to be comfortable. It's that you can't wait another five minutes for a cigarette.*

Chapter 18

"Where are we going?" Andrew asked as they approached the car parked on the street.

While he took wide steps to try and keep pace with Oz, the man quickened his stride at the grass strip that separated the sidewalk and curb.

Don't open the door. Don't open the door. Don't—

Oz jogged around the front and held out the passenger side for him.

"It's a surprise," he said.

What are you doing, Andrew? Getting into a car with someone who's practically a stranger and that you can barely stand? He stayed with his hand to the door and watched Oz circle the car. *Though he was nice to me in there. His version of nice.*

Oz's blunt opinions about Robert and the situation had made him feel better. It wasn't just that he felt heard, but he had the sense of someone *wanting to hear.* Yes, the other guys at the bar had been anxious for him to reveal his secret, but they hadn't been concerned about him. He'd been a curiosity among curiosities. Oz sought him out because he "seemed lonely." And he listened carefully enough to pick out subtle things Andrew hadn't meant to let slip.

"If I'm going to get you home in time to change the kid's diapers, you need to get in the car."

Finding out about the pills. That's the reason you're going. And you'll try not to kill him. No promises, but you'll make an honest effort. Andrew closed the car door and buckled his seatbelt.

Oz started the engine. He pulled out his lighter, but then paused. "Am I allowed to have a cigarette in my own car? Or do I have to suck on this fucking thing all day?"

"If you smoke, you have to have me home by two, so I can wash my clothes and shower." If Robert discovered … Well, he didn't exactly know what Robert would do. He'd cleaned the outlet covers and lightbulbs. Scrubbed the grout around the bathtub with a toothbrush. Wiped down the inside of the vents. Could he go out with a friend if he'd done all that? Being social had clearly been approved over artistic pursuits.

"Not a friend who smokes," Robert would probably say, since cigarette smoke couldn't be allowed to pollute his wife.

Oz pulled out of the parking space, and the car sped down the street.

"You're such a fucking nun," he mumbled as he held his lighter to the cigarette.

"So, are you going to tell me what's in the medication, or was this a stupid game?"

"Listen to you. This is twice you've accused me of lying to get you alone. First with the group, and now again. If I wanted to get you alone, I clearly don't need to lie. I didn't lie to get you to let me into your apartment, did I?"

"You said it was cold outside."

"If you believed me, that's your fault. It's eighty degrees."

"Tell me then, if you intend to."

Oz veered the car to the left and checked behind his shoulder to merge onto the highway. "A little of this, a dash of that. Depends on your psychiatric sessions. Depends on what your master wants."

"What do you mean?"

"If you're too depressed, or too manic. Too angry, not angry enough. Want too much sex, don't want any. You name it, they have a pill for it. And they change your personal mix often." Oz looked from the road to meet his eyes. "Since you've been released, they've changed your medication three times."

Three times?

"They probably thought the last combo wasn't working, so they're trying something else. Do you feel more tired than you did weeks ago? More run down? Maybe cloudy in the head? And from time to time you get a tremor in your hands? That's the new meds."

Andrew pushed his hands in his pockets.

"But I was told if I didn't take them the body would reject my brain and I'd die. Or is that not true either?"

"No, that's true. It's necessary to keep everything simpatico. But it's also a good opportunity to pump you full of anything else that suits their fancy, and ensure you keep taking it like a fucking mule."

"But what else am I supposed to do, if I need a part of it?"

"You were supposed to get in the car with me. Which you did." Oz took one hand off the wheel and slipped the pill bottle from his pocket. He tossed it to him. "Here you go. I'm a man of my word."

Andrew opened the lid and emptied some capsules into his palm. They identical to the ones he'd been taking since the beginning.

"Now, that's not the immunosuppressants without all the shit. But it's a downgrade from the other cocktail."

"You said they were unlaced."

"Slightly unlaced would've been a better term." He tapped his cigarette ash on the window frame. "What they have you on is highly addictive. If I cut you off cold, you'd have withdrawal symptoms they'd identify."

"Withdrawal symptoms?"

"Sure. People trade this shit in back alleys. If I gave you the straight immunosuppressants, you'd be manic. You wouldn't be able to sleep. You could start having seizures. And then what kind of responsible healthcare provider would I be?"

Andrew felt Oz looking at him, but he studied the medication, his hands shaking.

"The ticket is to step off gradually so we don't cause problems that would prompt them to put you on more meds. It'll take a bit to wean you off them. Length of time depends on how you feel."

Hitting the reflection of the pool instead of the water. Is this where it came from? Is this what caused it? These pills constructed a barrier inside him. A blockade to self-expression. He wasn't stupid enough to not have supposed before that it was a possibility, but to have it confirmed …

"They can't make me take something against my will!" He dropped the pills into the bottle and closed it. "They can't do this!"

"Wrong-o. They can make you do whatever. There isn't even a 'make you'. It's 'you do.' Or have you forgotten that you're a piece of furniture?" Oz flicked his cigarette outside the car.

"Robert wouldn't stand for it."

Natalie hadn't taken medication. She hadn't needed drugs to be perfect. When Robert found out that CryoLife was secretly contaminating—

"Newsflash, doll, Robert allows it. Whenever they recommend a change to your meds he has to sign on the dotted line. And not only is he the reason they *can* do it, he's *why* they do it. To try and keep him happy with you. How does it feel to be a juiced up organ grinder monkey?" Oz brought out his lighter again.

The flame rose from both the literal lighter and the figurative one Andrew saw in his head.

"He doesn't own me! No one owns me!"

"Yes he does. He paid for you. And when you buy a chair, you can do whatever you want with it. You can sand it, paint it, or break its legs off and use them to fuck yourself." He removed his cigarette and glanced at Andrew. "I don't know which metaphor I prefer. The chair or the monkey. How about we combine the two images – a lap-dancing grinder monkey."

How could Robert betray him? He knew he'd fallen short of Natalie but for God's sake he could've offed himself days ago. And did it matter that he was still alive from guilt and not love? Robert didn't know that. Yet he'd still—

"Dance, pretty monkey girl."

Andrew had trusted Robert. Even though Robert didn't understand him, and there'd been times when he'd been scared of him, he'd felt secure that Robert would never hurt Natalie. So as long as he wore her skin, he—

"Keep on dancin'. Shake that ass."

What to do? What to do? Not that his world had been completely safe before, but now there was no protection. None at—

"Go on and get those quarters. Boom, boom—"

"Shut up! Will you shut up?"

"Aw, yelling at me won't get another dollar in your G-string or a banana in your—"

Andrew turned to Oz. "I'm warning you." He said his next words in slow, separate sentences. "Right. Now. Stop it."

They were at a traffic signal. Depending on how awful Oz's snarky response was, Andrew would lunge across the middle console, tear his face off, and then exit the vehicle. He had no idea where he was, but he didn't care. He had a feeling he might as well unbuckle his seatbelt.

"I bet it was your aggression that caused them to put you on the antipsychotics when you were released."

The car continued on. "Antipsychotics? I'm not psychotic!"

"I know. But would your master be pleased if he lost control of you? And how does an angry, volatile patient reflect on CryoLife? All asses must be covered, doll. This isn't some nude beach."

"Am I on them now? You didn't say antipsychotics earlier."

"I didn't say it because you aren't on them anymore. Remember how you felt when you first got out? Jittery and restless?"

The pacing.

"And I'll tell you what else – Tinks was put on the same meds after he rammed that screwdriver in his ear. They prescribed him ten milligrams. You they gave eight. How does that make you feel? The guy who drives tools into his head only got two milligrams more than you. Congrats."

He thought of the meeting at the Center – Brigman's fake smiles, Zuniga's balloon expressions, and Tweed's blank stares. Robert aside, these were people he should've been able to trust.

"It's just necessary for you to temporarily have a guardian who can legally represent you, act as your healthcare proxy, and manage your assets," Zuniga had said.

Bullshit. Prescribing him antipsychotics so Robert could keep a tighter hold of him was a clear abuse of the so-called conservatorship. And if they'd done this, how could he even consider ending the façade with Robert and going back to them?

I truly am alone in the world. There is no one I can trust. Nowhere I can go. The pressure of tears built, but he shoved them back. He was not going to cry in front of this motherfucking ass—

"Hey." Oz had reached over and nudged his shoulder. Andrew turned his head to find him smiling. The nice smile, not the cocky one. "It'll be okay."

He cleared his throat. "Oh, yeah? Well, what am I supposed to do then?"

"I told you, you were supposed to get in the car." The man winked at him. "And the rest will work out. You have friends, remember?"

Friends.

And even if it didn't put him completely at ease, Andrew still smiled. The group of misfits and their vulgar, yet rather endearing, captain were better than nothing and might be of use to him.

Chapter 19

"If you're tired, you can sleep. I know how your meds are – no need to keep up pretenses," Oz said. "We're still thirty minutes out anyway."

"From where?"

"You'll see."

Natalie rested. Oz knew it was partly the medication, but he also chose to believe she felt secure with him. He liked that feeling. He was rough around the edges, and sometimes couldn't help the things he said, but he was a person who could be counted on.

Pretty fucked that I'm your knight in shining armor.

But although he blamed Robert, in the end it was CryoLife. And especially Brigman.

That fucker. You'll do anything to keep your precious company from going under. From admitting that you can be wrong. That you have been wrong.

He imagined the doctor guiding Robert's hand in authorizing the psychotropic drugs. Robert was a sheep. What idiot didn't check shit out? With the information easily accessible, there was no excuse. Brigman was the puppet master, the perverted Victor Frankenstein desperately trying to keep his reputation untarnished. Robert was just a lazy douche bag. Oz would never have allowed them to give Natalie drugs he hadn't researched himself first.

Now you're thinking like you're in love with the girl, Oz. Which you aren't. You like men. Nice, solid men. Though not too solid – still somewhat pliable.

It'd crossed his mind last night that perhaps the attraction to her was partly sexual. A physical desire could be the explanation to the problem. Maybe the part of his brain that'd been affected was healing. He knew brain tissue didn't regenerate, but he'd spent some time online looking at naked women to test the argument. It'd done nothing but swamp his computer with grotesque pictures and bore him. So while he knew he was still gay, the pull toward her remained. Another independent variable had been creeping into the theory however.

Maybe I forget you're a woman. You wear those hoodies and baggy pants. You could be a long haired man out of the corner of my eye. And if you were ... Damn, it wouldn't be a good idea for you to be alone with me.

Not that he'd ever hurt or take advantage of anyone under any circumstance; the end goal was being helpful. That's why he'd gone to pharmacy school. This new mission didn't compare to what had been his pre-CryoLife purpose, but being a pharmacist positioned him to impact the chain CryoLife held on unknowing patients. And while he couldn't help anyone who didn't use his pharmacy, or people who didn't want to be helped, releasing those who yearned for freedom and offering companionship to the other wounded gave him a sense of meaning. It didn't excite him, but it made him a tad less insignificant.

And I can be useful in other ways.

Marijuana distribution opened a vast network of contacts and put a variety of services at his disposal. It was a much better currency than money, which had a cold, slimy feel when it came to the transfer. Pot relaxed people and made them happy.

So on that front, I'm in the happiness trade.

If there wasn't something Oz could do for a friend himself, someone out there would give him the plug-in for a baggy of basement-grown joy. They'd do it with a loyalty unmatched and a willingness to go the extra mile.

Even delivery and pick-up. He grinned. Santino had been his biggest triumph – the most compelling evidence of how handy he could be and why Natalie should trust him.

Santino always explained his situation to others by leading with the cat story, including when he'd first revealed it to Oz. It had taken many rounds to break him down enough to admit his death interest extended beyond animals. He refused to elaborate about the way in which he was intrigued by a human cadaver, and what he'd do with one. But who knew? Perhaps he wasn't quite sure himself. Maybe he needed that chance to find out.

Only weeks after Santino revealed this fascination to him, one of Oz's young, female acquaintances from school had overdosed on prescription meds. So without Santino's knowledge and for only a few bags of Master Kush, Oz secured the first body. Or, as he'd introduced her – a "gesture between friends."

"You've got to be fucking kidding me," Santino had said.

Oz shut the steel doors to the back room of his pharmacy and turned on the light. In the center of the room was a table. On the table was a sheet. And under the sheet was a body. It was covered entirely, except for one shapely hand.

"The right kind of green can buy anything." Oz chuckled.

"What've you done? Who is she?"

"You mean who *was* she? Finding an 'is she' would've been a lot less trouble for me." Oz sparked his lighter and lit a cigarette.

Santino had a wonderful look of shock on his face. "Fine," his voice cracked. "Who was she?"

"Does it matter? A previous colleague of mine who decided to make a premature exit. As such, I was able to procure you an opportunity to … figure yourself out." Oz ran his hand along the table while he walked to a shelf. "And, since you refuse to enlighten me as to your purposes, I also took the liberty of putting together some goodies for you."

Oz removed two gift bags from the shelf, which he then sat on the center table, next to what appeared to be the body's head. The first bag read "Happy Birthday" in garish, vivid colors and glitter sprinkled over the counter as he pulled neon tissue paper from the top in flourishes.

"For option one, I have some carefully selected items." He took objects from the bag and placed them on the table as he named them. "Here's a knife. And a fork. Salt. Pepper—"

"Jesus Christ!"

"It makes no difference to me if you bless your food. I'm nondenominational."

"I'm not a cannibal."

"I don't care if you are. You can do what you like. It's not as if she's going to mind."

"But you were her friend."

"No, I was an acquaintance, and we shared similar interests. But even if she had been, we of all people know that what matters is here." Oz had tapped his forehead. "Once this cuts out, you're a bag of decomposing flesh. So who gives a shit? No one is going to miss a finger, ear, or whatever the most succulent part is. That's outside my expertise."

"I'm not going to eat her. I'm not going to do anything to her."

"Then you're a fucking idiot. Because she's right here."

Oz turned toward Santino and leaned against the table. He took the cigarette from his lips and blew a trail of smoke before meeting his friend's eyes.

"If it's within the scope of your ability to have what you want, why shouldn't you reach out and take it? Whatever it is." He put his hand atop the rigid one resting on the table and squeezed it with a smile. "You want her. I know you do."

Santino's gaze flitted between Oz, the body, and the floor as he shuffled his feet.

"Do you want something in return?"

"No. Call her a gesture between friends."

And Santino had smiled back.

Oz flicked his dying cigarette to the floor and flattened it with his heel before pulling out another.

"Good. I was going to be gravely disappointed if you hadn't accepted this token of my friendship."

"Thank you."

"I mean, I could get in a lot of trouble for this. I put my heart, my soul, my very body on the line for you."

"I said, 'thank you.'"

"It's kind of unprofessional of me to keep expired—"

"Oz," Santino cut him off. "I'm sure you spent hours thinking of witty statements, but—"

"Say no more, you're right in assuming Cinderella will be missed shortly. I got her particularly fresh." He checked his watch and took two steps toward his friend. "No one will bother you here; it's a secure room. Be done by three. And clean up after. This is a place of business."

He walked toward the door, enjoying the last drags he'd have on his cigarette, since he only permitted himself to smoke in the back.

"Oz, what's in the other bag?"

Oz had looked over his shoulder, his hand on the steel door. The other bag was a grotesque shade of bright blue with a yellow menorah and dreidel on one side.

"Well, I thought if one's partner wasn't exactly enthusiastic …" He trailed off with a smile. "I left some cigarettes in there for you."

"I don't smoke."

"Pity. It's quite enjoyable." Oz pushed open the door.

From then on, they'd confided in each other their dark secrets. He had a deeper bond with Santino than he'd ever had with anyone. They had a strong, admittedly strange, connection – both hating themselves, but liking each other partially since they had that in common. There'd been many tears, many drinks, and many bodies.

"Where are we?" Natalie woke as he put the car in park.

"The gun range outside Pooler." Oz cut the engine and grinned at her. "Have you ever fired a gun, doll? You'll love it. It's exactly what you need."

Chapter 20

The long concrete building was isolated on a rise, and a town was sprinkled several hundred yards away. There weren't other cars in the parking lot, although the end of a dirty blue pickup truck was visible on the side.

"Oz, I'm still under the conservatorship guidelines. I can't fire a gun."

"Neither can I." He dug his wallet from his back pocket. "No, you assumed right. I did assim to my original identity. Ten years ago. But, as you can see, they never take the mark off you. You're branded for life."

He flicked out his driver's license and she took it. Her eyes went straight to the corner.

"'CRYO-00038-P.'"

"That's a composite number. Yours is prime. Did you know that?"

"What's the 'P' for?"

"'P' for permanent. I have a permanent identity."

"But I thought when you assim everything goes back to normal?" A shadow crawled across her face as she returned his ID.

"The conservatorship goes away, but once they give you brain damage, they don't trust you anymore. And we're not a protected minority. It's your scarlet letter. There are jobs you'll never get and privileges you'll never enjoy. One of those being that no one will sell you a gun, or let you handle one."

"What if you assim to another identity? It won't go away then?"

"Nope. Not that I've ever known anyone who has."

Oz kicked the car door open and stepped out. He intended to be a gentleman and circle the vehicle to open her door, but by the time he closed his own, an additional bang sounded.

"Then what are we doing here?" Natalie looked at him over the roof.

"We're in the South. And no matter how many fucking gun laws there are, there will always be a coot who'll give a gun to a man with blood on his hands. Nuthin's more important than that there second amendment," he said, the last sentence caked in a stereotypical deep Southern accent. "One of those coots happens to be a friend of mine."

Before locking the car, Oz walked around and popped the trunk. He lifted the gray flap that covered his spare tire, and took out a plastic sandwich bag filled with crushed green leaves.

"Is that pot?" She put her hand to her mouth.

"No, it's parsley. Come on, Holly Housewife."

He heard her fast footsteps on the pavement as he walked toward the building.

"Don't call me that." Natalie glared.

"Prove to me you're otherwise then."

"I'm not doing drugs with you, Oz."

"This isn't for you," he scoffed.

Oz pushed the door open and they stepped inside. The lighting was dim, the atmosphere humid. A counter stood unmanned a couple yards from the front door, the top striped and encased in bullet-proof glass with a sliding window in the middle. To the right was a closed door, and within the booth to the left, another door sat open a crack, through which came the sound of a television.

He stepped to the counter and hit the top of the nickel call bell repeatedly.

"Red! Red, you son-of-a-bitch!" Oz yelled as he struck the bell. "How do you expect to do any business when you're not watching your fucking shop?"

"I'm coming! I'm coming!" A gruff voice hollered. "Lay off the bell!"

The television's volume lowered, and a heavyset man bumbled out the door. He looked cross at first, but on recognizing who it was, his face brightened.

"Oz, you piece of shit," Red said, the latter half crooned as an endearment. He opened the sliding window and leaned out.

"If I left the front of my pharmacy without anyone watching it I'd be robbed blind. My cough drops, my tissues, my birthday cards …"

"And what are they going to steal here? They can take their pick, the three-year-old *Life*, or the *Family Circle*. No one comes here for anything in front of the counter."

"I'm also not here to sample your fine literature selection. We need to shoot a few rounds. Blow off steam." Oz took Natalie's arm and guided her forward. She tensed at his touch, but didn't pull away.

"Are you sure you're talking about guns?" The man's greasy eyes rolled over her.

Oz felt the muscle in her arm stiffen. Her brows drew together and her glance darted toward the exit. An unfamiliar tightness squeezed his chest. Red wouldn't harm her, but he had the urge to place himself between them.

"You're a sick fuck, Red."

"I mean, are you …" He swiveled his shoulders, looking between the two of them. "Fixed?"

"No. If anyone in the room needs to worry, it's you." Oz patted Natalie's arm. "But I don't go for fat lards in wife beaters that are three sizes too small. So you're both safe."

"If I were, which I'm not, I wouldn't be after a tattooed little fucker like you."

"Something tells me my other advantages might outweigh the ink to sway you."

Letting Natalie go, Oz brought the sandwich bag into view. He shook it and the wads bounced into each other. Red wiped his hands on his thighs before holding them out. Oz tossed him the bag and he caught it, his cheeks rosy and glowing.

"That's my boy." Red bounced the bag in his hand and looked to Natalie. "No offense to you, sweetie, but if he ever gets tired of this man thing, he's going to marry my daughter."

"Where is she anyway? She blew off my get-together at the bar. I was heartbroken."

"She's in Africa picking bugs out of an Ethiopian's eyes. She comes home in a few weeks."

"I suppose that's a reasonable excuse for missing my party. Someone has to groom them." Oz turned to Natalie. "She's one of our other friends you didn't have the opportunity to meet."

"Oh, she's like you, is she? And what did those bastards do to her?" Red asked.

"Made her want nothing more than to hold a semi-automatic. So now that you have what you want, set us up so we can make that a reality."

Red put aside his pot bag and pulled a set of keys from his pocket. When he bent under the counter, the sweatpants he wore retreated approximately five inches down his backside.

"Red, we can see your nasty fucking cleavage, and there's a lady present." He caught Natalie's grimace after his statement.

"The sooner you tell me what you want, the sooner I'll come up."

"Give me my usual, and the .22 for my friend."

"Yours or mine?"

"Mine. And three clips for the .22. We're on a tight schedule."

When he surfaced for air, Red placed two handguns and the clips on the table. He also removed two sets of large headphones and glasses with orange tinted lenses from the wall. He garnished the pile by adding a tiny plastic bag that contained four earplugs. As he slid the gear toward them, he gave a sharp look to Natalie.

"Has she ever fired a gun before, Oz?"

"I'm going to show her. Don't worry yourself about it, old man. Take the cannabis into your hole, and string yourself out to *I Love Lucy*. I'll ring you when we're done. Open your fucking door."

Oz knew he could've convinced Red to leave them alone without the offering of weed, but any time he supplied Red with drugs, he worked deeper into the man's good graces. "It's your favorite, Red. Skunk Special."

Red's eyes grew brighter, and he curved a fat hand under the counter to press a button. "Don't shoot each other's kneecaps off, and if you decide to fuck her, mop up, huh?"

The chink of a bolt sliding came from the door in front of the booth. Red swiped his weed and lumbered into the left room. The door closed except for a crack, and the television volume cranked up. Oz turned to Natalie and jerked his thumb toward Red's room.

"That's Red."

"Are you waiting for me to say he's nice?"

"He is nice. You don't need to say it. He stores my stuff so, if they ever raided my house, they couldn't get me on anything."

"No greenhouse in your basement?" She folded her arms.

"Are we forgetting that I'm a licensed pharmacist, doll?" He put his hand to his chest as if offended. "That could've been a prescription. The poor man might have glaucoma. And out of the goodness of my heart, I drove out here to deliver the only thing that brings him relief from his pain."

Riotous laughter came from behind the door, and an oily herb and blue cheese smell leaked from the room.

"Such pain," Natalie said.

Oz gave a sly smile as he picked up the smaller handgun. He handed it to her pointed downrange. "This is Caroline." He took the larger. "And this is Rio."

"You name your guns?"

"You name your kids. And these don't shit on me." He moved to stand beside her. "Keep your finger outside the trigger guard. The first thing you always do is make sure she's not loaded. Remove the clip, and pull the slide back to check the chamber."

He demonstrated and watched as she mimicked the action.

"Good." Oz substituted Rio for a pair of glasses from the counter. He guided them onto her face before retrieving the gun.

"Keep the barrel pointed down, and follow me."

He curved his stiff right hand around the clips, pocketed the earplugs, and looped the two pairs of muffs over his arm.

His arms full, he kicked the door open and caught the edge with his shoulder to hold it for her. She walked through with her arms in front and the gun barrel pointed straight to the floor as if it might explode.

"Relax." Oz allowed the door to shut behind them.

The shooting range was a long gray corridor with sections separated by short spans of cinderblock walls. It opened into a wide back expanse where dozens of targets hung from clips suspended by sliding rods in the ceiling. Oz stopped at the seventh section and set the headphones on the floor. He put his own orange-tinted glasses on, nudging her to turn toward the swinging targets.

"Watch carefully. You've got to know how to hold and aim her so you're confident when you fire."

It was forty-five minutes before Natalie took her first shot.

Oz showed her how to hold the gun and steady it while keeping her thumbs clear of the hammer. He guided her in aligning the front and rear sights, and coached her in controlling her breathing.

During the lesson she grew more relaxed. Natalie was a good student, paying attention to everything he said and responding to his praise. It made him more curious about how things were for her at home. What did she do in that apartment? Veg? Wait for the kid and Robert to come home and keep pretending everything was okay? Her enthusiasm indicated a thirst for new experiences. Whatever else was going on, boredom wasn't helping.

You're one lucky bitch that I found you. And I'm going to figure you out.

As Oz instructed her, there was also the familiar gratification of being the expert – having the full command of knowledge and sharing it. Though he'd never touched a gun before he'd been reanimated, the feeling of mastery was the same. Bits of this dormant satisfaction came through at times – when he helped Santino and Tinks, discovered another person to bring into their group, or found new ways to annoy CryoLife, but teaching Natalie how to fire a gun gave him an unusually close sense of being at home with himself.

When she made an attempt at a firing stance, she held her shoulders squared and her pelvis straight. It was near perfect. Natalie was smooth and poised. She didn't have to be coaxed to grip the gun. Her hands curled around it with ease and steadiness. And when he corrected her elbow into the slight obtuse angle, he noticed again how hard her jaw line was.

I remember you being all curves before. All soft. Oz had been startled. He thought about the family portrait hanging on her apartment wall. *You do look the same but … there's just something more edged about you.*

And he liked it.

"Pull the slide!" He shouted so Natalie could hear above the earplugs and headphones they wore. "Place your clip in the chamber. She holds ten rounds, but don't shoot them all off at once. You've got to know how the follow-through feels."

He stepped back. With the bagginess of her sweatshirt, it was easiest to see her breaths by watching her shoulders move. They were thin shoulders that she usually kept in an upward, tight position. But she pushed them down before clicking the safety off. She moved her finger onto the trigger and squeezed it with a bold conviction. He couldn't help but feel proud.

She wasn't frightened by the shot either, and kept her position. Without releasing the trigger, she turned her head to him. When he looked down the range, he could see the bullet had hit the target. It was close to being in the outermost circle.

"Great job. Go for another." Oz gave her the okay symbol.

Natalie took the rest of the shots from the magazine slowly, looking to him for reassurance after each. On the next clip, she didn't require his approval. He didn't mind as he'd never been the type to demand obsequiousness. But with her propensity to react in this way, he wondered how controlling Robert was.

She went through each bullet in the same steady fashion. Number twenty cut through the third black circle, and she set Caroline on the narrow counter, slipping the headphones around her neck.

"Did you see that, Oz?" Natalie pulled out her earplugs and sweat gathered on her brow.

"I saw." He brought his voice to a normal level. "You did good, doll. Here, last clip." He offered the magazine. "Make it anyone you want."

"Anyone I want?"

"I didn't bring you here for target practice. You've got to get this pain out of you." Oz put the clip in her open hand. "Take down whatever motherfucker you want. Let it out."

He watched her consider as he put his muffs on. The decision didn't appear difficult.

How many times have I envisioned Brigman at the other end while I'm putting round after round into his chest? And fuck brooding how the old me could've used an arctangent and calculated the right angles to ensure every shot nailed him in the face. Fuck calm. Nothing will ever bring my gift back, but, God, it feels good to take him down. Take him down, Natalie. Take down whoever you feel did this to you.

After repositioning her ear protection, she moved back the slide, ejected the old clip, and shoved the magazine into the chamber. She held the gun, and unlike the first twenty shots, she didn't align her sights. Her breaths were unsteady and she fired without care to aim.

Chapter 21

Andrew saw everything laid out before him – not one specific person, but the entire fucking month of interactions with people rolled by on a conveyor belt. And as he climbed the rungs of the springboard, he knew he was going to hit the water for the first time in weeks.

Because I'm late taking those motherfucking drugs that are strangling me. He imagined Robert and Simon. Brigman, Zuniga, and Tweed. Shelly. Those people who only wanted Natalie. *I may not be worth much, but I deserve a chance.*

But he'd been betrayed – suffocated by people who were supposed to love him unconditionally. Or at least love Natalie.

He saw her too. Standing at the back of the gun range by the hanging target. In those hip-hugging, low-cut, flower-printed dresses Robert liked. She tossed the blond hair over her shoulder and brought her hand to her face. With her palm upward and long fingernails pointed in his direction, she pursed her lips and blew him a kiss.

"I am the only acceptable version." Natalie had a high pitched, sing-song voice. She always sounded like she was talking to a child. "There'll never be room for any less, any more, or any different."

His hands shook as he held the gun. He wanted to aim at her. It was her fault for existing. Her fault for dying. Her fault for being this thing he couldn't conform to. But he couldn't shoot her.

They never gave you a chance either. Not if I've been drugged since the get-go. You're just the fucking scale.

So was it the fault of the people who'd created the Natalie unit of measure? Those who had the specific expectations and tried to enforce them? He wanted the situation and his pain to be their fault. It felt like it should be.

Or you, maybe it's you.

Oz had continuously needled him with both his words and appearance, but the man had also put himself in a vulnerable position. He hadn't had to reveal anything about the drugs. Andrew could run to Robert or CryoLife with the information. Oz had taken the risk with nothing to gain.

But he was still there. Still that slap in the fucking face every time Andrew looked at him and took a bitter inventory.

How you act. The way you speak. The things you do. Giving me a heads up on the pills and showing me how to shoot a gun doesn't erase that.

He considered flipping to the left and training the gun on Oz's chest.

You're so comfortable in your masculinity that you wear a pink shirt? You probably have purple and yellow shirts too. You wore that to spite me. I know you did.

Oz was unarmed, having apparently only asked that sleaze-ball Red for an additional gun to instruct. Andrew could get away with it. Destroy that pink shirt with bullet holes and blood, and then never have to deal with this image of the impossible dream.

As Andrew's pointer finger curled around the gun's trigger, his feet left the diving board.

But no, no. It's not Oz. If I can't shoot Natalie, I can't shoot him either – literally or figuratively. He's another scale, like she is. There's the thing everyone says I should be, and then there's what I want to be. And I hate you both at times, but I can't fully blame either of you.

Who was it then?

You.

He focused near the target on a familiar figure, but one with many faces.

Somersault – the painted whore in the mirror with running makeup, trying desperately to be Natalie.

Somersault – the grubby looking androgynous thing at Shelly's kitchen table, struggling to find a middle ground.

Somersault – the woman with her rolls squeezed into a man's clothing as a pathetic attempt to see Andrew.

It's your fault. It's your fault for stepping onto either scale in the first place.

Twist.

For allowing yourself to be measured by anyone. For recognizing their power to measure you.

Twist.

You weak, disgusting piece of shit! I hate you!

And he hit the water.

I hate me for what I've done to myself.

Andrew grit his teeth and felt hot tears streaking his face as he pumped ten rounds down the expanse.

Only half his shots hit the target. When they were spent, he clapped Caroline on the counter. His hands cupped his forehead, and he dug his palms into his eyes.

It's not fair. It's just not fair.

Andrew picked up the gun and threw her to the floor. Next he seized Oz's gun. Since it was empty he chucked it against the booth's cinderblocks.

There was nothing more.

But I need something. Anything!

He grasped the shoddy counter and wrenched it off the wall, the muscles in his arms burning from the effort. He launched the piece of wood as far as he could across the range, smashing it into dozens of fragments.

And then he collapsed, crying. As usual, he was completely alone.

He stretched his arms in front of himself and banged his fist on the concrete. The sharp pain from the impact reverberated through his arm, but it felt good. It was an ache outside the darkness that was devouring his soul.

No thoughts came as he wound down and swam toward the sun's reflection in the pool. He pulled himself up and clutched his legs to his chest, burying his face in his knees.

Andrew kept his eyes shut and tried to picture the lifeless body of this thing he'd become – a gob of pulp on the floor of the gun range. The red that leaked from the torn flesh broke that empty white pool that had been his self-image of *Beta nu*.

Curled tight on the concrete in the thick black outline with layered blues – I am Picasso's Blue Nude. *I'm outcast. I have nothing to gain or to lose. I'm exposed and stripped of everything but the feeling of being irretrievably lost …*

When the crying was almost gone, a hand touched his shoulder. But Andrew was too exhausted to tense as he normally would've, especially having forgotten that though he felt alone, he wasn't.

He turned his head to see that Oz had knelt beside him. His mouth had a gentleness to it – neither a frown nor smile – and the tension in his face was concentrated in his eyebrows as he looked at Andrew.

"Tell me who you really are," he said.

Though he'd heard the stories of the others and recognized that Oz had taken him under his wing and wouldn't betray him to CryoLife, there was still hesitation in telling him. In saying it to anyone. He hated himself for the attempts to be what he wasn't but, once it was said aloud, there was no going back. Admitting his identity put him at the mercy of another person's reaction for the first time. Anything could happen.

But what does it matter anyway? Whatever the result, I can't be more alone. Someone might as well know. Why not you?

He let the control slip from his fingers and allowed himself to float on the surface of the water.

"My name is Andrew. I'm really a man."

*

They'd left the gun range in a daze and without saying a word to each other. Andrew wasn't sure what he'd expected after putting his secret into the air, but he hadn't predicted the response would be absolute silence. Even having been around Oz for such a short time, he recognized how unusual it was for him to have nothing to say. He saw patterns, knew what was coming, and kept a move ahead. Two moves ahead, or three.

Maybe that's part of it. Andrew watched Oz gather the guns and gear and a corkscrew twisted into his stomach.

How far away am I from where I want to be, that you're this shocked?

If Oz couldn't see it enough to put together a verbal response, would anyone be able to?

This was a bad idea. Bad. Oz walked out to the main entry without waiting for him. *He's forgotten I'm here. See what you've done? This is what happens. There's no place for Andrew in the world. You're worse than a curiosity among curiosities – you're invisible as everything except Natalie.*

Andrew trailed after Oz before he could be left behind. Even if Oz no longer wanted anything to do with him, the least he could do was take him home. What would Robert say if Andrew had to call for a ride home from a gun range?

Now you're completely fucked. "You have friends," my ass. There's no choice but to go back to that apartment and pretend nothing happened. Your mind will stay free until you run out of the clean pills Oz gave you, and then you'll be imprisoned again. If Robert has to come get you, he'll tell CryoLife and maybe they'll lock you in further with the antipsychotics.

Red had stumbled out of his Skunk Special fumigated room with bloodshot eyes after Oz rang the call bell only twice. He leaned unsteadily over the counter, dragging the equipment toward him with both arms. The pile fell on the floor with a clatter.

"Oops." Red stared past the two of them before concentrating on Oz. "Hey, you're smart. Come in here and fix my TV. There's so many people on it, and they keep talking to me."

"Call your provider." Oz's voice was mellow, as if he weren't fully present.

"They couldn't troubleshoot a peanut butter and jelly sandwich. Heeeeyyyy, do you have one of those? I could eat a peanut butter and jelly sandwich as big as a house." He knocked on the glass encasing the booth several loud times. "Hey, hey, I bet, together, me and you, we could make a house *with* peanut butter and—"

"Maybe next time."

Oz turned and walked toward the door.

Fuck you. You're taking me home. Andrew followed.

"Where are we going to take a shit in our peanut butter and jelly house, Oz? Where? Whhheeere?"

Red's cries ended as the glass door closed behind them. Andrew quickened his pace and pulled open the passenger door. He had his seatbelt buckled before Oz settled into the driver's seat.

At last Oz spoke without turning to him. "It's past three. You should call your ... your ..."

Master? Hubby? Hubster? Any of the asinine—

"Robert. You should call your Robert." Oz started the engine and backed out of the space.

"And tell him what?"

"That you'll be late." His hands shook.

I should've shot you.

Andrew pulled out his cell phone and swiped across the screen to unlock it.

Eight missed calls from Robert. Multiple texts:

WHERE ARE YOU?

PLEASE ANSWER YOUR PHONE.

NEED TO KNOW WHERE YOU ARE.

CALL ME. NOW.

He's probably regretting taking that damn monitor off me. But, hey, who needs an ankle monitor when you have me on antipsychotics? Andrew took a breath. *Calm down. You can't let the anger come across. Until you plan what you're going to do, you need him.*

Robert answered on the first ring. "Natalie, where are you? Why didn't you answer your phone? Or my texts? I've been—"

"I'm sorry. I went out."

"Why? With who? I called Shelly, and she didn't answer either." His sentences were punctuated with panicked breaths.

"We didn't have cell service." Thank God Shelly hadn't answered. And he'd patch that lie after Robert calmed the fuck down.

"You couldn't have phoned or texted before you lost service? Or left a note to tell me where you'd gone?"

"I'm sorry. It was last minute, and we got distracted. I didn't mean to make you worry."

"It's okay." Robert sighed. "Are you having a good time, hon?"

Until revealing my secret identity backfired in my face.

"Yeah."

"When are you coming home?"

"Soon."

"If you want to stay out with Shelly that's fine, Nat. I was just worried about you."

"Okay."

"Will you text me if you'll be late?"

"Yeah."

"All right then. Have fun." The smile returned to his voice. "I love you."

"You too, Robert. Bye."

And now you can resume jacking off to The Natalie Files and dreaming of CryoLife finally crafting the right behavior modification drug to bring her back.

Oz's eyes were focused on the road and his hands gripped the steering wheel at the precise ten-two position. Before he'd driven with only his right hand at the wheel's bottom, his left either holding a cigarette or sailing in the air outside the window.

I'm glad I didn't tell your friends. They'd have been this way too. But I wish I knew what your flaw is. I may not be able to do much, but I'd use it to strike at you in any way I could.

Andrew went back to his phone, opened an empty text message, and tapped a quick note to Shelly:

ROBERT CALLED YOU. I HAD MY PHONE OFF AND HE WAS WORRIED. ALL IS GOOD. NO NEED TO CALL.

That should take care of it, and if not … Well, he'd deal with that problem when and if it became one. There was enough to worry—

"I think I forgot my lighter," Oz said.

"Because no other lighters exist on the entire fucking planet." Andrew reached over to the console and pushed the car's cigarette lighter into its socket. "Why don't you say something useful? You never seemed to have the capability of shutting up before—"

Abruptly, Oz swung two lanes to the right and peeled off the next exit despite still being miles from Savannah. He said nothing as he accelerated down the ramp.

Andrew's heart raced.

I misjudged him. I was completely wrong, completely off.

He was hypervigilant to the looks people gave him. Men like Oz's friend Red honed their gaze, trying to see past the sweatshirt and pick out his shape. Even Santino and Tinks had eyed him. But for all his button pushing, Oz had never made him feel vulnerable. Andrew had never felt like, if they were alone, Oz would try anything.

The car turned into an empty parking lot of a convenience store.

And here it is. He's going to come at me, try to rape me. Andrew seized the door handle as Oz pulled into a spot. *Run for it. Run. This is your only chance to escape. Run!*

But his hand refused to obey, and he remained numb in the passenger seat.

"I'm so sorry."

Andrew looked at him. Oz's voice had been ragged with emotion, and his hold on the door handle eased. "Sorry? For what?"

"For being such a jackass to you. The housewife comments. The woman comments. I went too far. I didn't know the circumstance, but it wasn't right." Oz swallowed before continuing. "And I'm sorry for you. I mean, fuck, I can't imagine. I have losses too, but I'm still a man. I can't picture being in another body. Being seen like you are, treated like you must be. You must feel trapped."

Trapped. Beta nu. *Yes, that's exactly it.*

"And so alone."

Complete rejection of the Blue Nude.

Andrew fully released the door handle and turned toward him.

"You believe me then?"

"Of course I believe you, Andrew."

Andrew. Not said at random. For the first time directed at him. The release of joy that was *June Celebration.* Repeated, flowing movement without boundaries. Just elation undiluted by any additional color. And the other paintings somewhat faded into the background.

Andrew. Andrew. Andrew. It replayed in his head and every time he heard it, a blast valve pulled on a hot air balloon. He felt himself lifted higher and higher.

Or maybe the opposite. The balloon basket sinks lower until it lands. Oz's caramel eyes locked on his, and there was no doubt to whom he was speaking. *Finally, I'm grounded. Andrew. That's my name. That's who I am.*

He felt the tears building in his eyes.

"No one has ever called me by my real name before," Andrew said.

Oz smiled before breaking their stare. "I like it. I think it suits you."

It does. It'd felt right in his head before, but hearing it in another person's voice ... "Natalie" was a swift punch to the stomach. Hearing his real name pulled something in the center of his chest, like unfolding a well-worn accordion.

"So is he demanding your expeditious return? Or do you want to grab a drink, Andrew?"

Andrew. Dripping honey. *I'm glad I didn't shoot you.*

"Yeah, a drink would be good."

Chapter 22

They found themselves at a restaurant fifteen miles off the exit.

"Robert doesn't need me," Andrew said. "Both he and Simon are as miserable as I am, but no one will admit it."

"A two-million-dollar mistake is difficult to concede making. I assume they don't know?"

"No one does. Except you."

Oz looked across the table at Andrew. It was so clear now. He saw it. He couldn't believe he hadn't seen it before. That Robert didn't see it. Or the kid.

And Brigman's an ass, but he's not an idiot. How did he miss this?

The covered mirror also made sense. There were those who didn't see, and those who didn't *want* to see. Who couldn't bear to see.

But I do now. And everything is balanced and equal, as it should be.

Oz had made no effort to open the car or restaurant door for Andrew. He didn't pull out his chair. Unlike what he'd done at the bar, he also didn't try to order for him. And he could tell that, although they were small tokens, these things were momentous to his friend. But then the waiter …

"Something to drink for you, ma'am?"

"Clean your lenses. Man." Oz pointed to himself. He pointed to Andrew. "Man." He then waved toward the waiter and shrugged. "And who the fuck knows."

The "man" looked to the floor and apologized. He took the order of water with lemon and made a beeline to the kitchen.

"Oz, thank you, but it's okay. I'm aware of how I look, and there's no reason to make anyone feel uncomfortable."

"Sometimes people need to feel uncomfortable. It's good for them. And you could be a man. There are long-haired men. There are feminine looking men. No one's going to pull your jeans down and do a dick check. They're not even going to ask for your ID since you don't drink booze."

"I'm used to it. I mean it's uncomfortable, but—"

"I thought there wasn't a reason to make anyone feel uncomfortable."

They traded a smile and sat in silence until their drinks arrived. Oz drained half his gin right away.

"You're not going to be able to drive."

"When one is out with a friend who doesn't drink, one takes advantage of it."

"I don't like to drive since the accident." Andrew dropped an ice cube from his spoon into the water. "I got my license in case of an emergency, but I prefer that someone else drive."

Oz finished the glass, the pressure in his head beginning to build. "Then we're going to be here a long time. I'm having at least three more. But I'm sure you have a lot to say. Over a month of silent torment. And I'm all ears."

He closed his eyes and stretched, folding his arms behind his head. The alcohol coated his stomach, the heat rising into his chest and shoulders. He prepared to listen to another saga of hardship and loss. An additional horror story to add to the CryoLife collection. A new and welcome diversion from himself.

"Actually, with that scene back there, the crying and telling someone the truth, I don't want to think or talk about it."

"Shall we discuss the weather, then? About how it's eighty degrees, but if anyone tells you it's freezing, you believe them? You're one gullible son-of-a-bitch."

"Let's talk about you."

When Oz opened his eyes, it took him a second to focus on Andrew's face.

"I told you my secret. You tell me yours."

"I did. I was straight. I woke up and I'm gay. It's not as fanciful as what you heard from Santino and Tinks, but that's it."

Despite having another gin set in front of him, Oz crossed his arms and his relaxation disappeared.

"But you're lying."

Andrew looked between him and the full glass of gin.

Clever, my friend. I'm predictable when it comes to my addictions. He lifted the glass. "There's no reason for you to distrust me. I've been nothing but honest with you. I've told you things that would ruin me, in fact."

"You don't seem upset about being gay."

"It's been ten years. I used to be distraught about it." Oz took a swallow of the gin.

It was an underhanded move, but in his fuzzy desperation, it was the only thing he could think of. Andrew was mounting an assault on the hallowed citadel, and he had to throw out every possible defense.

"When you walked into my pharmacy two years ago wearing that tight ass skirt and low cut blouse, I was still upset about it. I didn't give you the friendliest reception because I wanted to want to jump your bones desperately." He smiled to finish the act. "Sooo desperately."

Andrew's skin paled, but he was undeterred. "There's something else."

"You don't know me. You've seen me three fucking times."

"You're defensive and vague. You don't beat around the bush about anything. But when I asked in the bar, you spout a bunch of shit and change the subject." Andrew counted the reasons on his fingers. "How do you know so much about what they do? Why do you care about people like me, Santino, and Tinks, if you aren't broken too?"

When Oz weighed the decision, his brain sloshed from side to side within his skull. The only person with whom he'd gone into detail about what had happened to him was Santino. But he knew Santino wouldn't laugh or judge him. And they'd been friends for months before he'd been cornered into revealing everything.

Is there anything to lose? Giving in when this inebriated would be easier than trying to fight.

But the main reason Oz didn't want to talk about it was just that – he didn't want to talk about it. He avoided thinking about it. Thinking about thinking about it was too much.

"You lost something. Tell me what it was and how you died. All of it."

I suppose I can compromise. I can tell you how I died. But only that.

"I was twenty-one. In my prime. Up until then, it'd been school and school and more school. But I finally had the whole world ahead of me and could dedicate myself to what I wanted to do."

"What was—"

"I'd been feeling weak in my arms and hands for a couple months, but I was working a lot. Running myself ragged." Oz gave a micropause, like checking for a reflex. But Andrew didn't interrupt.

Good, very good.

"I'd come back to my house and crash for twenty minutes before I'd be awake thinking. Always thinking … Until there was one night that I came home, put my key in the lock, and couldn't turn it."

Oz raised his hand, pinching his thumb and pointer finger together and turning his wrist. "A half hour struggling with this motion. I had my other hand holding my fingers around the key in position, wrenching my entire arm to the right. I looked like a moron, but I couldn't get it. Ultimately, I woke my neighbor for help.

"Told the guy I'd been drinking and was too intoxicated to do it myself. But I didn't drink then. I was such a Puritan. No smoking. No pot. No tattoos. No guns. Nothing fun. Boring, like I said. So if anyone can break you of this water with lemon shit, it's me."

Andrew folded his arms. "Go on."

"That night it jumped out at me that whenever I did anything requiring my hands, I was clenching them into fists or flexing them to release tension."

He tossed back a good portion of the gin. "Did I stop wearing button-ups because it was hard to do the buttons? No, I stopped wearing button-ups when I stopped wearing ties. But I'd stopped wearing ties since I got tired of not being able to get that Windsor knot right until the twentieth time. I'd attributed it all to sleep deprivation.

"The next morning, this stuff starts adding to the key and tie thing. Suddenly I was hyper aware of the weakness in my hands. Like, why was it difficult to squeeze toothpaste onto the brush? Were they making toothpaste thicker?" He glanced across the table. It was so difficult to maintain a lighthearted appearance. "How do you open a gallon of milk? One with the twisty top."

"Like everyone else I suppose. Twisting?"

"With the ends of your fingers right? You curve your thumb around the plastic ridges, pressure to the side of your pointer finger, and turn. Simple. Here's how I would do it:" Oz covered his glass with his right hand and put his left on top. "Palm on the lid, and use the other hand to turn the entire hand. A concentrated effort, but easier than a milk carton, that's for sure. I figure – I'm a strange guy in general and do weird shit all the time. Why would I open milk like other people?"

"If you told me you'd built a Rube Goldberg machine to open your milk, I'd probably believe you," Andrew said.

"That would've been a fantastic idea. Band wrench welded to gerbil wheel, powered by radioactive rodent with super strength. It's too bad the patent office isn't open this late."

"A tragedy. But anyway—"

"Of nuclear holocaust, last-chip-in the-bag, Pompeii-ish proportions."

"Moving on, please."

"Besides my preoccupation of thought, it was your normal morning. I was able to do what I needed and get out to my car okay. Where the key episode repeated. And I couldn't very well have my neighbor start my fucking car for me. So after an hour of trying, I gave up and made the call."

"Who did you—" Andrew rolled his eyes. "No, no stop playing around and tell me."

"So that process by which humans, chinchillas, and dolphins make other humans, chinchillas, and dolphins? The whole insert tab A to slot B? I called my tab A."

"Your father?"

"I prefer to term him as the piece of shit whose motile gametes infiltrated my mother during a specific biological timeframe. But that doesn't fit well on a coffee mug or a tie tack."

Andrew shifted in his seat. "I'm sorry?"

"Why?" He shrugged. "I'm not. He's not. I'm not what he wanted in a son, and he's not what I wanted in a sperm donor. We haven't been on speaking terms for years, and it's better that way."

"But back then, when you were in trouble, he was the first one you called."

"He was useful in that particular situation. Like a tire jack, or a piece of toilet paper. I needed a doctor and he got me in to see a specialist without the red tape. Needless to say, the diagnosis wasn't good."

Oz set down another empty glass and flexed his hand before picking up the next. "However, the old man wasn't concerned. Why? CryoLife. It didn't matter how much time I had. They'd bring me back. The disease could keep returning and they'd continue to rebuild me. I was practically immortal, as long as I didn't damage my brain.

"He tells me: 'Let's do it now, Osborne. Save you two years of decline. I'm sure, if I look through my files, there's a judge who owes me. We'll do it right away once we have the court order.'"

"Why would a court order have been necessary?" Andrew asked.

"CryoLife rides the fine murder line as it is. They've been able to get away with starting brain extraction within that period of being declared 'imminently dead,' remember? Axing me two years early would be too much, even for them. Unless you petition the state. But he needn't have gone through the trouble of creating a plan. I told him to go fuck himself."

Oz ran his fingertip around the rim of a new glass. It was a juggling game. He could tell Andrew was confused by why he'd make such a decision if he didn't know more about CryoLife at the time. He chose his words with care.

"See, I was working on something really important to me. I thought I'd have time to finish it. And then I didn't care what happened. That's the good thing about this disease – it spares my brain until the last. So I could keep working. And I knew I could finish it. I knew I could ..." He trailed off, gritting his teeth. With his inhibitions lowered, he was saying what he didn't want to think about.

"What were you working on?"

"It's not important."

"You said it was 'really important.' What was it?"

"It doesn't matter!" Oz snapped. He took another drink and held the alcohol in his mouth until his eyes watered. The stringent, acrid burn felt good. He swallowed it when the inside of his cheeks went numb and took a breath. "I'm sorry, but it isn't relevant anymore."

Andrew didn't press further, and Oz hurried to continue his story.

"My father was pissed. Eventually though, he throws his hands in the air and says, 'Fine, go through hell for two years. No one wants to die. When you're staring down the barrel, you'll change your mind, Osborne.'

"But I was sure I wouldn't. Not only would I have my project complete, but I'd never been supportive of CryoLife. Him calling my life's work garbage, and me saying the same to him was one of our primary disagreements." He met Andrew's expression with a slow smile. His friend's eyebrows had risen and there was a look of knowing in his face. "Yes, you've got it. An unlucky connection for me, but a fortunate one for all of you."

"Why is that?"

"I've been able to get away with pretty much anything. And as long as I'm alive, I can and will continue to meddle with his plans, which benefits my friends. But I wasn't a fan before I became one of his freakish creations either."

"Were you one of the protesters? Are you still?"

"No, those scripture-licking dick holsters have the right answer, but their theorems are bullshit. CryoLife doesn't play God. They play with nature," Oz said. "I mean, humans have survived for what, 200,000 years? We have highly developed brains, opposable thumbs, hard-shelled tacos, and it's a product of evolution. Some people die and aren't meant to pass their DNA to the next generation.

"Natural selection is a good thing – weeding out bad attributes and weakness is necessary. If our ancestors had possessed the ability to save the dip wads that were eaten because they couldn't walk on two legs, allowing those people to breed instead of die, we might still be slithering."

Andrew accepted another glass of water from the waiter. "That seems harsh."

"Go watch a lion take down a zebra on the nature channel. Life is harsh. Only in our species do we spend copious amounts of energy trying to force people to survive, and it's going to ruin us. I should be dead. You should be dead. And yeah, it's fucked when young people die. I wasn't looking forward to death. But if that's what the universe had in store for me, who was I to question?"

"Well, your father obviously didn't take 'no' for an answer."

"But I tried to block him – before I couldn't write any longer, I signed an advanced directive refusing attempts to resuscitate or reanimate. He hit the fucking roof. It was awesome."

"I don't mean to piss you off, but if he didn't want you to die, isn't that proof that he cared about you?" Andrew asked.

"He didn't so much 'not want me to die' as he 'wanted to keep me alive.' There's a subtle difference between the two. He'd built that CryoLife niche for himself, a reputation he wanted to pass to me. He knew I would've achieved more than he ever could. I was so smart, Andrew, so intelligent ..." The words caught and he had to push through the tightness in his chest. "But I didn't want it. And it didn't matter how successful I was. I wasn't a doctor, so it wasn't good enough. He never gave up hope that I'd come around though."

"You don't seem like him. I don't think you could do what he does. No offense."

"None taken."

Andrew folded a corner of his napkin, smoothing the crease with the side of his thumb. "You're too honest. And there's something artificial about him. He's nice, but it's like a heavy glaze to coat something instead of compliment it."

"Yes, he's a sugar-crusted shit rag. When his beloved company isn't on the line, that coating melts away. I wasn't brokenhearted when he cut off communication. I concentrated on what I was doing. My project was crucial. It needed all my time.

"As hard as I was working before, I worked harder. When I couldn't write anymore, I henpecked at the computer. When I couldn't do that, students wrote for me on dry erase boards so I could look at the data and think. That's how I thought best. Something tangible before my eyes, to come back to. I could spin off in a thousand directions. Off into my world, while having an anchor in reality."

Oz closed his eyes. He was trudging through thick, gelatinous sludge and thoughts were slowed in having to wrench each footstep from the sucking mud.

"Not being able to pace bothered me at first, since that helped me muddle through ideas. But while I could move the tips of my fingers, I ran the motorized wheelchair back and forth until the batteries ran down. Of course, my time was running down as well.

"I was able to live alone but I had an aide who came by to help me. One morning I felt like someone was sitting on my chest. It was terrifying. I couldn't have picked up the phone to call 911. I had to lie there for hours until my aide found me."

He tried to hide a shudder. The level of alcohol he'd consumed made the feeling of the weight almost real.

"I'm lying there, struggling for every breath, and the old man's words go through my mind. I imagine the shotgun barrel as having supplanted the hand of a clock ticking toward my face. As it took a strong turn in my direction, I thought about CryoLife.

"It would've been simple, right? Call the douche bag and have him get a court order. Totally possible that in a month, I could be receiving anesthesia for brain extraction, instead of for inserting the trach. Nine months later, I could have all the time in the world with a disease free body that wouldn't abandon me."

"I'm sure that's what a lot of people would think," Andrew said. "You're only human."

"Meaning I'm also capable of evaluating choices and not making stupid decisions based on fear. Which I didn't. It occurred to me that the dick wad was waiting for me to cave. He probably had the judge on speed dial, attorney on retainer, and the court order drafted. I wouldn't have put it past him to have the body itself in the works. That's how little he believed in me. So when my aide came, I wouldn't let her call him. Dumb whore still made me go to the hospital."

"If you couldn't breathe, that was probably a good decision."

"I had work to do. There wasn't time for that shit." Oz pushed another empty highball glass to the table edge. "They put me on HFT though."

"HFT?"

"High Flow Therapy – nasal oxygen delivery. Keeps the airways open. I could still talk, and therefore work. Which I did. With the barrel ticking in my ears and the doctors bitching at me to consider options."

"They wanted you to do CryoLife too? I didn't think they were allowed to offer that route."

"No, HFT isn't a permanent solution. It's beneficial to come off it before it stops working altogether. They wanted me to choose between the trach, another type of ventilator, or start hospice." His hands shook as he held his new glass.

"I'm sorry."

"Don't be. Like all of us, I would've rather lived a long, boring life with my original parts, including brain function, undamaged. But how often does preference enter into life? It doesn't. You take what you're given and shut the fuck up about it. Though in hindsight, I should've made a choice. Since I refused to, the doctors called my father.

"He shows up unannounced in my classroom. Instead of 'Hello' he greets me with 'You look like shit. One might say imminently dead.' So I know what's coming. And here's where he tries his polished turd bedside manner with me for the first time in twenty-two years."

Oz extended the thumb and index finger of both his hands. "Picture this: He kneels to be at my eye level. Really creaks it to the floor as if he's an eighty-year-old man on the verge of death himself – makes a big show of it. He's got the egotistical lines ironed out of his face so he looks like this sweet gray-haired grandfather that builds dollhouses and whittles on the fucking porch. Very amusing."

Oz tried to smile, but the result felt cracked and unstable. "He says to me, in a *Gone with the Wind* soliloquy dramatic voice: 'This isn't about me. It's not about my glory or pride. It's about you. I admire your convictions, but let me help you live, Osborne.'"

"What did you say?" Andrew asked.

"Nothing. He knew I wasn't buying his shit, so he pulls a lower move by bringing my project into it. He gestures to my dry erase board behind him."

Oz closed his eyes and saw the board. The giant space had been filled from corner to corner and top to bottom. To cram more writing into the highest margins, a student had been using a step stool. There'd been more black and red writing than white space ... When he reopened his eyes, the restaurant teetered, and it took a moment for him to refocus on Andrew.

"He starts into another fake-ass speech. 'It can be about your *thing*,' he says, since he never bothered to remember what it was called. But he goes on: 'God knows who else besides you understands what you're doing, but if you can't do it for yourself, do it for your project.' The man then fishes through the cobwebs of his tear ducts and makes his eyes glassy. I'm telling you, he was going for an Oscar."

"Maybe he truthfully was—"

"All he's ever cared about is building and maintaining his company. No matter how disappointed he was in me, how would it look if the so-called medical genius behind CryoLife let his son die? Unlike his regular patients, I knew the real him for two decades and saw straight through his shit. And I was pissed that he'd tried to manipulate me by mentioning the project. That was sacrosanct. So I reiterated that he could go fuck himself, which caused the veneer to crumble.

"He stands up, easy cheese, and his face folds back into those obnoxious superiority wrinkles. He starts to bargain with me. 'Come home, get the trach, keep working, and we'll hold off doing the extraction until the end.' Blah, blah, blah. To which I respond that I was going to finish my life's work and die with dignity. That I'd rather have maggots eat out my brain, put my head under a car tire, et cetera. Until amid my list of preferences to CryoLife, he lost his temper.

"He had the folder with my advanced directive in his hand. He bent it in half and hit me across the face with it."

Oz kept his eyes focused on the tabletop. It'd been ten years. It wasn't the same skin he had now. But the burn on his cheek felt genuine.

How long did you want to do that? How good did it feel to strike your son in a wheelchair when he couldn't hit you back? I bet you wanted to do it again, you son-of-a-bitch. You probably still jack off to the power surge.

"Oz, are you okay?"

He looked at Andrew and made a conscious effort to relax. His posture had been so rigid it ached in easing the tightness.

"I'm fine." Another attempted smile ended in him shaking his head. "Anyway, so after he hits me and calls me a fucking idiot he motions to my board and tells me 'All this fucking shit you've wasted your life on is going to die right along with you.' Then he storms out.

218

"When the HFT stopped working a week later it felt like I just went to sleep. I woke in a hospital room with a tube down my throat, and a ventilator forcing my lungs to function. Pretty much a blinking corpse – more machine than man."

"But you'd finished your project, even if your life was over?"

Oz felt his throat constrict and he coughed. "That project was my life. They were both over. If I'd known what the final piece was, there was no way to convey it. So when that asshole shows, though he's a dick and reminds me that I'd suffered for no purpose, I'm almost happy to see him. Because he offers me another chance to make my existence not a complete waste.

"To be honest, I might've given in," he continued. "But then he tears my advanced directive in two and brings in that half-attorney, half-rectal thermometer, Tweed. He tells me that the document isn't legally binding and is only my *preference of care,* which he doesn't give a shit about. Says as my healthcare proxy that he's 'calling the shots.' But he *promises* to bring me back whole."

Oz knew he was talking too loud, but he didn't care. The emotion choked him and it felt like waking with someone sitting on his chest again.

"I wanted my life back so I could finish what gave it meaning. But do you know what happened, Andrew?" Oz released the glass as his fingers curled into his palms with a disjointed motion. "I woke up, and it was gone. I couldn't do anything, as if I'd done nothing before. Like a fucking slate wiped clean. Gone."

Chapter 23

Andrew's thoughts at the bar days ago rose in his mind:

You'd better be feeling the same disemboweling, burning pain I am. If there's any justice in the world, something had better be tearing you apart inside.

From just looking into his eyes, he'd seen Oz's suffering. No amount of alcohol, continuous evasion attempts, or shock-value comments could hide the devastation. The debilitating illness, fights with his father, and the loss of his talent and life's purpose – whatever it was.

During the ankle monitor placement when Brigman had asked him what he thought about, Andrew had answered "art" because he couldn't say "feeling like a man." The doctor had responded that his son thought about the same. Was Oz's board full of pictures or drawings? His project some fresco in dry erase marker? Maybe.

Despite a decade having passed, the loss still caused Oz to disintegrate. He was torn apart and more vulnerable than Andrew felt, even under the hungry, searching eyes of men. Oz folded his arms on the table, burying his face in them as sobs shook his body. To Andrew it seemed like he curled into himself. He grew smaller and smaller, pressurizing and constricting into a coiled spring, his frame tightening with every breath.

And it was similar to Andrew's experience on the floor of the gun range, only now he felt removed. He looked on the *Blue Nude* as Picasso had painted her to be seen – from a higher perspective, the model's face hidden in despair but her body contorted in painful grief.

I am not alone. I'm in two places at once. Two states. We both are.

But the morbid companionship was swiftly eclipsed by the current situation.

Before him was a man who may have looked how he wanted to look and acted like he wanted to act, but Oz was broken and devastated. There were pieces of him missing, and his heart ached for them. Worse still, it was a permanent desire, ever destined to be unfulfilled. He wanted so much to have his life back.

Andrew felt the same. There was no value in him as Andrew. As Natalie, he'd had a purpose. He'd been one complete person. It was an awful, confusing paradox – he hated the things he wanted to do, but he hated stopping himself from doing them. Robert could be controlling, and Simon's paranoia overwhelmed him, but weren't those attributes a result of Andrew? He didn't remember Natalie's family being this way with her. So they were good people. Given the chance, would he rewind and sink back into Natalie? Forgetting everything that'd happened and erasing Andrew? Absolutely.

But neither he nor Oz would get a chance to reverse. Their past lives and identities had been stolen from them. Sold for cheating death. They hadn't been ready to die, and had so much to live for.

What was there to live for now?

We are Blue Nude *fused with Schrödinger's cat. We are alive and we are dead.*

They were new people born into old shells with twenty odd years of baggage and obligations. They were filled with memories of previous passions, hopes, and dreams – none of which could be enjoyed any longer. CryoLife had handed them back as a jumble of broken shards. It didn't matter that it was well intentioned. Yet no one else could understand. If they told the doctors, the media, or yelled it from the rooftops, what would people say?

They'd say shit like: "At least you're alive." "Calm down, it's not that big of deal." "You'll be okay. It's okay." Even though we aren't alive – we're in pieces. And it will never be okay.

The statements were infected bandages people slapped over their wounds to shut them up. Had Oz heard them before? Maybe it was best not to say anything.

So instead, Andrew leaned over the table and placed his hand on Oz's head. His hair was shaggy and soft. Andrew wished he had hair like this. It was light enough that it didn't show the gray hairs he must have. He reviewed the timeline in his head – Oz must be what, thirty-two? Thirty-three, maybe?

He tried to convey thoughts of comfort as he combed Oz's hair through the tips of his fingers. He saw Oz's shoulders tense as if he were waiting for him to say something.

But Andrew knew there was nothing he could say to make the situation less horrible. He couldn't give Oz his life back or recover whatever ability he mourned. The best any of them could do in this new world was to gather what they were given and try to put together a new life, he supposed. That's what he had to do. Daily.

But maybe that road is easier by being surrounded with people who loved you. For your faults, for the things you used to be but now aren't, and the things you weren't but now are. Recognition and acceptance for your current identity. Acknowledging the Blue Nude *within the soul.*

Oz hadn't spoken magical words to him when he'd been sobbing on the floor of the shooting range. And despite how wonderful it felt to hear his name, nothing had been said which erased his pain entirely. But Andrew had felt some of the burden lifted. Why did he feel less of a weight?

And then he knew.

He curled his fingertips in Oz's hair. "Oz, I'm here."

Someone else being there who understood and didn't judge. What had fallen away was bearing it alone. He'd turned to see another person, nudging him aside to take a corner of the world. And it made a huge difference. To both of them.

Oz lifted his head. Andrew took his hand back, but in withdrawing it, he hesitated and turned it over, instead placing it to Oz's cheek. He caressed it, feeling the softness of his skin beneath his knuckles.

He wasn't sure why he made the tender gesture. He hated when Robert touched him, and maybe Oz had been counting the seconds of their contact too. But touch could be a way to convey care or concern when one wasn't being constantly oppressed by it. Smoothing Oz's cheek felt like the right thing to do. Maybe it was a silent apology for wanting to bash his brains in with the cash register, tear his face off on multiple occasions, or for almost shooting him earlier that afternoon.

Something changed in Oz's eyes when he brought his hand back – the distinct wild spark in them melted. Andrew felt different when they were in that stare. It made him nervous, like his stomach was about to drop. He tucked his hands under the table and glanced away.

Oz cleared his throat. "Do you know what the Hodge conjecture is?"

"No, I don't."

"It says that de Rham cohomology classes are sums of Poincaré duals of the homology classes of subvarieties. Do you know what that means?"

I don't know what those things are individually, let alone what they mean together.

"And do you know what cohomology is? Or algebraic topology? Or differential topology?"

"No, Oz."

"Neither do I, but I did once." He held his pointer finger a hair's width above his thumb. "And I was this close to an argument disproving it."

Oz barely spoke above a whisper. "There was a time when it came so easily. When I pulled proofs out of the air and mathematics flowed into and out of my lungs like oxygen. But when I returned from death, I was left empty. Again, I couldn't breathe. And I've been in a state of perpetual suffocation since then." He took a breath. "Now, if you ask me to multiply two digit numbers, I need a calculator."

Math? Really? Andrew felt disappointed. *But I guess it's respectable. It's not being a contractor. It's not being a homemaker like Shelly.*

"So you were a mathematician?" Andrew asked.

"I was an artist."

"An artist?" Math was the least creative thing out there – every problem was solved. It was repetition drills and learning rules, not freedom and art. Distinct, finite values rather than interpretations and the flowing movement of emotions.

"Mathematics is art. It's not sitting around, punching numbers into calculators. It's thinking great thoughts." Oz broke their shared look and turned his eyes to the ceiling. As upset as he'd been before, a grin spread across his face.

"It's pulling together the right patterns to explain the world, and make it make sense! It's taking an unsolvable problem and battling it! Throwing argument after argument at it, and forcing it to align or surrender! It's seeing what no one else sees, roping it together, and bringing it down to create simplicity and understanding from chaos. You drag things into the abstract world where anything is possible. It's an empty canvas, and you just create. It's art."

Andrew supposed it was possible he'd misjudged the medium. His knowledge of mathematics didn't extend into these ranges Oz was talking about, so maybe there was an intersection where math became an art form.

I guess if all the art I'd ever seen was limited to coloring books and paint by numbers maybe I wouldn't think much of it.

Even if he didn't get the concept, that was beside the point. It mattered to Oz. And maybe there was more in common with the two passions than he'd perceived. Oz seemed to be as enthusiastic about his mathematics as Andrew was about abstract art.

I see it everywhere I go. Could it be like that for you and numbers?

"I was an art teacher," Andrew said. "Only high school."

"Were you? That's why you understand. Or did they take that from you?"

"No, I'm fine."

"Do you draw or paint or ..."

"No."

She didn't really make it herself, and neither do I. That was such a small part. Being an artist can't be taught.

When Natalie had to instruct students to create, drawing with the grid method was the route she took. Take a transparency that'd been printed with a grid and tape it over a photo.

"Then go square by square," she'd told her students. "You focus on one small bit at a time so you only draw what you actually see, not what you *think* you see."

This was art for her. There was only room for the reality. But what was special about just making a copy of something else?

He thought of the photographs hanging on the wall in the apartment. What did that really capture? Nothing underneath three smiling faces even though there was always something deeper.

But abstract is more than just an image. It's every angle of a subject. Motion, personality, feelings and bringing to life the fourth dimension. It makes more sense than anything else.

"I preferred teaching history and theory. Analyzing paintings, interpreting them."

"Any particular movement?"

Andrew leaned in and smiled. "It's funny; I don't like what I did before. I hated covering everything but the realists. Courbet. Manet. Corot. That's Greek to you, I'm sure."

It'd been Greek to Robert, who probably didn't even realize art had movements. He remembered even saintly Natalie being irked at times with his attitude. Robert thought of art as a cute hobby of Natalie's, like she spent all day gluing feathers and pipe cleaners to pine cones.

But art was never something insignificant. And it's fucked up that she could have a more fascinating discussion with a sophomore than her own husband.

It might be nice to have an intelligent friend to talk about art with.

"Boring, but not Greek." Oz bit his lower lip. "I mean boring in the best sense of the word. The way basic math is boring."

"It's refreshing to have someone to talk to about it, even if you think it's boring."

"Art itself isn't boring. Just anything practical or useful is boring as shit."

"I used to like the things that looked like what they were supposed to be. And I didn't understand anything else. I'd think, 'Anyone could do that. So where's the skill? Who gives a fuck about panels of color or cubism?'"

"I heard the same things about so many mathematical theorems. The Euler line, the Schoenflies theorem. People don't understand the divinity in simple expression and distilling something's essence."

Distilling something's essence. The phrase was golden. Oz did get it.

"Now I don't have much feeling from other types outside abstract," Andrew said. "When I woke – and you know how the emptiness is – I went in my mind to the Rothko Chapel. I could lose myself in that world."

"That's exactly what true mathematics is. It's a world of abstraction. Expression unlike any other. The creation of beings, of worlds, of universes without limitations. It's having everything you've ever wanted. Reality being born, and folding in on itself to be born again at my command."

Have I ever seen someone this passionate about anything? While he felt a deeply personal connection to many paintings, Andrew could imagine Oz launching out of his chair and slamming into the ceiling, or talking so fast he'd forget to breathe and pass out. Part of it could be the alcohol, but it was very curious.

And with the options being to stay out later and hear more about a subject he wasn't particularly fascinated with, or return to the apartment for more of the Natalie game:

Andrew pushed his half-full glass of water across the table. "Tell me more."

Chapter 24

No one had ever asked Oz to keep talking about mathematics. Even gentlemanly and sensitive Santino hadn't prompted him to continue. He hadn't been rude, and tried to appear interested, though he wasn't. However, Oz wasn't able to discern indifference from Andrew's face. So he talked.

It was possibly the first time in ten years that he fully felt alive. Though he'd attempted to move on after the reanimation and find a new purpose, pharmacology didn't excite him. He didn't love it. He didn't live for it. And there was always the nagging ache that he'd been meant for greater things. He'd been given this gift, but was wasting his life on something else. He'd tried and failed multiple times to restore it, but he still felt awful. His current existence was a lie. He was purposeless. Vacant. And the brightness that once surrounded him had dimmed.

But for the first time Oz had been compelled to tell someone, not out of the extreme duress under which he'd revealed it to Santino in order to preserve their friendship. He'd wanted Andrew to hear what he'd loved and lost.

His expectation of Andrew's reaction had never extended to the possibility of a prompt to speak on about the subject. He expected that, like most people, there'd be the strange look and pacifying statement before moving on to their opinion of more interesting things. Or he could laugh, or scoff. Or think Oz was stupid. Andrew would compare the loss to the situation of Santino or Tinks. To his own unfortunate circumstance. And he'd say something like:

"You fucking bastard. Your best friend has sex with corpses. Your other friend has such intense attacks of pain, he tries to split open his skull. I'm a man trapped in a woman's body at the mercy of a controlling husband. And you can't do math? Who wants to do math? No one! What a fucking waste of time! Waste of energy, waste of life! Math is what you're so upset about? Jesus Christ, Osborne!"

Halfway through the anticipated diatribe, Andrew's voice had transformed into that of Brigman's. His father would say, and had said, those last things. With a twist of his upper lip, as if he'd driven past a tire fire: *"You want to be a what? You got a degree in what? You're giving a lecture on what?"*

Putting aside that I'm your son and any decent parent would be proud of their child, as a scientist for you to have zero respect for a mathematician makes no sense to me.

"Math is fine. I have nothing against it," Brigman had said before Oz had even been diagnosed. "But you aren't solving real problems. What you're doing has no real impact—"

"No real impact? If disproven, it changes the definition of basic topology. Differentiable manifolds, the sequence of abelian—"

"Which does what for the world? While you were fiddling with your equations in the pursuit of nothing, do you know what I accomplished today?"

"You got your dick out of the vacuum hose without—"

"Five people, Osborne." He'd held up his hand. "I saved five lives today with the technology I developed. And once we branch off into creating full bodies for cryonic neurosuspension instead of individual organs, I'll save more. I gave ninety years of life to an infant. So ask me again why redefining algebra is meaningless. You might as well be cleaning elephant pens at the circus for the good you're doing."

"Who has time for elephant shit when there's so much of yours to clean?"

"At least you'd have something to show for the time you waste."

Andrew's response hadn't been either the worst case, or the politely disinterested scenario. His tone hadn't made the profession sound stupid, and his smile had given Oz a pleasant queasy feeling. And then to prompt him to continue talking? To not turn the conversation to himself? Oz felt that spark. The match burst into flame.

But as swiftly as it was lit, it blew out.

He stopped mid-sentence, the shadow falling across him. He'd only been talking for half an hour.

"Oz, are you okay?"

"I don't have anything else to say."

It flooded back. The bitterness, the pain, the resentment. And adding to it, there was shame. Ten years ago, he could've lectured for weeks on the intricate nuances he understood. Now, he was tapped dry in thirty minutes. He had a captive audience, but no material. And his heart sank.

He couldn't elaborate on things he no longer comprehended. There were concepts he couldn't give an outline on. For some theories and equations, he only knew their dear, sweet names and nothing more. Except that he'd loved them.

"You're tired. And you haven't thought about this for a long time. You can continue when you've had a chance to—"

"There is no 'chance to'. This is how it'll always be. You can't repair brain cells." Oz fought back more emotion as he looked at Andrew. "Hardy said, 'A mathematical proof should resemble a simple and clear-cut constellation, not a scattered cluster in the Milky Way.' I was creating the heavens, and now I don't even have a telescope. I'm thousands of feet below the surface of the fucking earth. It'll never make enough sense for me to say more than what I've already said."

He crossed his arms and buried his face in them again.

I can talk about how amazing it is. About the magic in the abstract world. I can remember something I'll never be able to do. This is why Santino didn't press me and why I ignore it. I try to forget that I ever loved to do anything.

He wasn't going to cry anymore. His brain had been saturated with gin and squeezed over a kitchen sink like a sponge.

The table shifted as Andrew leaned over, and Oz felt a hand on his hair.

"It seems we all come out the other side different. Not necessarily bad. Just different. And I think you could find something that inspires as much passion out of you as the Hodge conjecture, if you weren't too scared to look for it."

The pain was still there, but it became like condensation on the outside of a glass. Oz could've lifted his head. His conscience told him to, but he rarely listened to anyone, including himself. Instead he remained motionless, his eyes heavy but open in the shadows of his folded arms.

Oz concentrated on feeling locks of his hair being lifted and then returned by the nimble fingers that'd curled around the gun, pushed the glass of water toward him, and caressed his cheek with such care.

You can't buy this. Well, I suppose you could. But if you're paying for love, you might as well get the full Monty. And would it feel this compassionate?

With his reserves coasting on fumes, Oz almost allowed himself to wonder …

He lifted his head sharply, knocking Andrew's hand away.

"It's late; we need to get you home." The momentum caught up to him, and he winced. "There's no way I'm driving anywhere."

"I can take a cab."

"I have something better."

He dug his cell phone out and made a few swipes on the screen. The phone rang only twice before Santino answered.

"For God's sake, do you know what time it is, Oz? I am right in the middle—"

"Can you put that shit in the freezer and take a cab to the restaurant on 33rd? I've had too much to drink and need someone to drive my car."

Oz covered his eyes. His head was killing him. But he also wanted to avoid looking at Andrew and Santino was protesting.

"Yes, I'm aware of how old I am, that I should set limits, be responsible, and blah, blah, blah. You're such a fucking old woman."

"Oz, we could share a cab. It's—"

He cut Andrew off with a wave of his hand.

"No, I'm not alone," he said into the cell. "So why don't you stop being a dick and get over here? You're embarrassing me in front of our friend." He grinned and let his hand drop. "Our special guest last Friday."

In less than ten minutes, Santino rapped his knuckles against the driver's side window. Despite the startling noise, Oz didn't have time to steady himself before his friend opened the door that'd been supporting him. He fell out onto the pavement, smacking his head on the asphalt.

"What the hell, you motherfucker!"

"You really are drunk, aren't you?" Santino nudged Oz with the tip of his shoe. "Are you dead? Again?"

"You wish." He rubbed the side of his head, already feeling a lump.

"You're not my type. Not pretty enough." Santino ducked his head into the car. "It's a pleasure to see you. I hope he didn't cause much trouble. Did you run into him and were kind enough to babysit until I could retrieve him?"

"We've been together all day." Oz got to his feet and scowled as he dropped his keys into Santino's open palm. "Drive, asshole."

He slugged into the back and draped himself across the entire seat. The ceiling spun, the dome light bouncing like a pin ball. He closed his eyes to keep from being ill. Two car doors slammed, and there was the ribbing of hard plastic as Santino adjusted the driver's seat. The car engine started. Two seatbelts clicked.

"Seatbelt, Oz."

"Go fuck yourself." He gave the accompanying hand signal in what he hoped was Santino's direction.

"So where are we headed, hmm? I assume you don't plan on staying and scraping him off the bathroom floor at eleven in the morning? I'll make sure he doesn't drown in a puddle of his own vomit."

"You can start going west on eighty-five," Andrew replied, and Oz sensed an anxiety in his voice that hadn't been present for a while.

To think, you used to be more relaxed with him than with me. I win after all. No one is as fucking slick as I am.

Oz lifted his head and brought back his leg with the intention of kicking the driver's seat. He lost balance and missed horribly. Pain radiated through the bottom of his foot from the collision with the door.

"How many did he have?"

"Six or seven."

"Miracle he's conscious. It's a toss up – which organ will commit suicide first?"

"I'm right here," Oz groaned. "Don't talk about me like I'm not present."

"His liver from the drinking, or his lungs from the smoking?"

"I'm right here, Santino," he said it louder.

"He's intent on destroying himself."

"I'm right fucking here!"

"At least he had enough sense not to put anyone else in danger. That's oddly thoughtful of him."

Oz gave up. Santino was going to ignore him until they were alone. It was punishment for compelling his friend to leave his lab.

"So, you don't like to drive? I didn't either after the accident and it took me years. Tinks is the same way. Perfectly normal."

Chapter 25

Andrew hadn't expected to find the apartment dark and silent when he arrived home. Robert would turn on the lamp and reveal himself sitting on the couch. Waiting and demanding an explanation for the lateness of the hour, the cigarette smell in his hair, and scent of gun powder on his hands; things he didn't yet have a lie for.

But the living room was empty. Andrew snuck down the hallway and pressed his ear to the bedroom door. He heard slow and steady breaths. Simon's door was cracked a foot, but when he peered inside, the boy's room was empty. Everything was as if he'd never left.

He had left though. And Andrew's world had turned upside down since he'd last been within the confines of the apartment. The walls felt more stifling than ever.

With the utmost care for stealth, Andrew shut the bathroom door and turned on the light. It was blinding, and he rubbed his eyes with one hand, while turning the shower handle with the other. He'd wash away the evidence and tell Robert that time had gotten away from him and Shelly.

Until I think of a better solution, I need you.

He turned his back to the mirror as he always did when undressing. The only good thing that'd come from trying on Robert's clothes had been the discovery of hiding mirrors with pillowcases. It'd become part of his daily routine to throw a pillowcase over every fucking mirror in the apartment as soon as Robert left in the morning.

But I can't continue living this way. Tonight clinches it. Something has to be done, and you can't be too afraid or intimidated to slip into the lie. Remember how it was when he called you by your name. You could leave behind this squalid apartment and have that. You could be free.

Andrew stepped out of the shower and tied the wet hair into a nub at the back of his head. After shutting off the bathroom light, he crept across the hallway.

When he pushed the bedroom door open, he expected Robert to rise like a vampire.

"Where have you been? I need to know exactly where you were. When was the last time you took your temperature? Are you feeling okay?"

Yes, no thanks to the antipsychotic drugs you have me on.

It'd be hard to withold that information and his anger. But Andrew lied to Robert constantly. He deceived him by existing and going through the motions. Heaping lies atop lies.

So it will just be balancing one more banana peel atop the towering can of garbage. And really, this one I don't feel guilty about. Because I doubt you feel the slightest bit of remorse for drugging me. After all, it wasn't about the grocery list, so why would you even waste the time talking to me about it? Fuck you, Robert.

But despite the deception, there was that damn conservatorship. He couldn't afford to lose what little support he had from Robert. Yet.

Robert didn't appear to wake as Andrew slid into bed. He lay on his back, close to the edge and away from Robert's sleeping body. Why was he even worried? Robert had been taking sleeping pills since Natalie's death. If he was asleep, jackhammers in the room couldn't wake him.

Andrew found a good position with his arms behind his head and settled into his thoughts. There was a lot to consider. First thing, the medication.

He'd left the pill bottle in the pocket of his jeans, now in the hamper. Since he was the only one who did laundry, he was sure of its security. He'd take care of it in the morning. Would Oz come by tomorrow too? Be on the doorstep and—

Robert turned and folded his arm around Andrew's chest. His voice was groggy, and his arm leaden with sleep. The touch made Andrew tense. The inner countdown started.

1 Mississippi. 2 Mississippi.

"Did you have a good time with Shelly, love? You must've to be so late. I missed you."

Robert's tenderness ebbed Andrew's fury over the medication and shifted back some of the guilt.

Lying to me wouldn't be an issue if I were Natalie. And even if that's not my fault, it's not yours either. It's just a fucked up circumstance all around, and you deserve someone who missed you too.

"You should spend more time with your friends. They make you happy." Robert drew him closer and placed a kiss on his temple. Andrew fought the desire to move away and brought his arms to his sides.

7 Mississippi. 8 Mississippi.

"I worry about you," Robert said.

"There's no need for you to worry."

"Mmm, that's right." He yawned. "You're here."

11 Mississippi. 12 Mississippi.

It was Robert's breath near his ear, his face on the pillow next to him. But Andrew thought of Oz, and an idea began to form in his brain ...

"Are you okay, Nat?"

The counting stopped as the name hit square in the chest. This again. This. AGAIN. He didn't want to respond, but he had to.

"Yes. Go to sleep."

"Wake me if you need anything." Robert squeezed him close, nuzzling his cheek.

Andrew felt claustrophobic. It was too much. Whatever Mississippi he'd be on now, enough was enough.

"Robert, you're suffocating me."

"I'm sorry. Good night, Nat. Love you."

He took reminders better when he was half asleep. Robert retracted his arm and turned, his breaths quickly becoming steady. Andrew shuddered.

Would it be the same if you were a woman? If I was whole, and it was a woman snuggled close to me? Is that what I want?

The image of lying next to a woman with her arm around him crossed Andrew's mind. He tossed it out. But he shivered again when he substituted the woman for a man other than Robert. They made him equally uncomfortable.

Andrew brought his arms back under his head and tried to relax. He closed his eyes, unafraid he'd fall asleep. He felt more awake than he had in a long time.

Now what was that before the walls started closing in ...

The idea shone like a pearl in the darkness.

Oz. He knew Andrew's secret. He appeared to be understanding and supportive. And Oz cared about him. Andrew wasn't sure he was ready to think about how much.

The way Oz had looked at him in the restaurant? He hadn't looked at Tinks that way. Or even Santino, and it was evident how close they were. Especially if he developed deeper feelings, Oz wouldn't let him be on the streets if he chose to leave Robert. His usefulness could extend beyond supplying unlaced medication. Maybe he didn't have only two choices – enduring with Robert or gambling on CryoLife's integrity. Oz could be the answer he was looking for. The escape route.

I do feel safer with him than Robert. And it's been almost eight hours since I thought about killing him. That's a pretty good stretch. He's amusing, and I didn't mind being with him. Could I be happy with Oz? Could he be happy with me?

If Oz treated Andrew like another man, it had to be better than suffocation with Robert. And God only knew what could happen if the conservatorship passed to CryoLife. Hadn't Oz said something earlier about not knowing anyone who hadn't assimilated to their original identity? Was that because his network included everyone under the sun except for those who'd chosen to revoke? Or did CryoLife just not allow those people to exist?

Look at what they've been able to do with Robert in control. I'm flawed, but at least he's interested in keeping me alive.

Perhaps Oz wasn't just *an* option. He was the *only* option. For life and sanity.

And maybe even peace.

Andrew knew there were things that could be done to bring the body more in line with how he saw himself. Besides being a pharmacist Oz interacted with all manners of individuals. Was there an exact agreement about how often Red was supplied with drugs? How many bags of pot did he trade for access to a dead body in South Carolina? How many ounces would he have to give to a doctor? It was an exhilarating thought to consider being able to change.

But that idea brought up what should be the highest priority question:

If I got everything I wanted – my identity as a man validated, the body I want, the life I want – would I want to be with Oz? Or am I willing to lead him on to get out of this prison? I don't want another situation where I can barely tolerate who I'm with.

As he did on so many other nights, Andrew lay still and closed his eyes. He imagined that he was how he saw himself in his mind. And not the emotional representations of *Beta nu*, *Blue Nude*, or *June Celebration*. But how he'd actually physically appear.

Short blond hair framed his face, and his brown eyes were so dark they sometimes looked black. He wasn't muscular, but his chest was strong. And flat. His waist didn't taper in – it formed one solid trunk to his narrow hips. And below his hips, he wasn't missing his penis. It was there, instead of an empty space of nothingness and shame. He saw himself possibly as a runner, his thighs slabs of muscle curled around his bones, his calves lean and taut. Wholeness. Perfection.

He sighed.

So, if I'm this person, and it's Oz over there instead of Robert, how do I feel about that? If he does the exact same thing – turns and drapes his arm across my chest, kisses my temple. What is that like? How do I feel about him pulling me close? Am I counting the seconds of contact via Southern states? Am I claustrophobic?

He opened his eyes and lifted his head to look around. The walls weren't wavering and pulling toward him. The ceiling wasn't crumbling, and the bed wasn't rolling on the ocean. He didn't panic, as he sometimes did when he thought about Robert touching him.

And unlike only minutes earlier, when he'd pictured himself with a random woman and a different man, he didn't feel discomfort. This puzzled him until he realized that the others were faceless, nameless.

And I'm not just my body, so there has to be something more for everyone else. We're not a flat painting. There is depth to who we are. If Oz was the same person, I'd be okay with him being this close to me.

But neutrality wasn't good enough. Did he want this closeness? He laid his head on the pillow.

Oz says he missed me. Did I miss him?

Andrew's next couple heart beats came too close together.

Truthfully, he missed Oz now and hoped he was okay.

When Santino had dropped him off at the apartment, Oz had been passed out. Andrew had been alarmed when there'd been no response to his goodbye.

"Is he okay?"

Santino turned his head to the back seat. "Yes. I'm astounded it didn't happen sooner with as much as you say he had."

"Are you sure? He's not moving."

"He's not going to feel much like moving tomorrow either, I'd wager."

"Couldn't he have alcohol poisoning?" Andrew's previous life as Natalie had been innocent and sheltered. Smoking and drinking were new to him. How much did it take for alcohol poisoning to set in? He had no idea.

"He could have a lot of things."

"Shouldn't you check?"

But he hadn't received an answer. And it'd taken Andrew several seconds before he sensed that Santino was staring at him. Unlike what he expected, when he met Santino's gaze it wasn't leering. Santino's glasses rested halfway down the bridge of his nose, and he looked at Andrew over the frames.

"I'm just worried about him." Andrew had shrugged.

Santino delayed his slow response and studied Andrew's face. "I'm sure he'd appreciate your concern; however, he'll be fine. I'll take good care of him. I always do when he gets like this."

Andrew turned the car door handle and unbuckled his seatbelt. He pushed the door open and was about to step out, when he turned and gave a final glance to the back seat.

Oz lay curled on his right side, his arm tucked under his head. His sandy hair fell across his forehead, and he looked like he was asleep.

"Please be careful." Santino had touched Andrew's arm, startling him.

"Careful?" Andrew pulled away and got out of the car.

"Careful yourself. And careful with him."

"Why? He seems harmless."

"He is, but I didn't say 'careful of'. I said 'careful with.'"

Andrew stopped, his hand on the car door as they regarded each other.

Man with a Pipe. Even though Santino had no pipe. But his perceptive expression, and the feel from him was the same. Like he was waiting for Andrew to elaborate, to admit.

But Andrew just shut the door. He didn't know if there was anything to confess. He still wasn't sure, and that was a problem.

But I can admit that I miss him. I wonder what he's doing. He's probably asleep.

He swept these thoughts from his head. One could miss many things or people. People who were only close friends. He had to concentrate on figuring out if Oz fell in that category, or somewhere else.

So we're lying here and he has me pulled close. The room isn't collapsing. Andrew tried to begin where he'd left off.

What about his breath near my ear? It would smell like pine trees and cigarettes. And it'd taste like that too.

He had no interest in smoking, or drinking gin, but there was something about this combination of vapors passing through Oz's lips that drew him in. If Robert's breath was switched for this fragrance, instead of its refrigerator and toothpaste smell, it would disgust him. No, pine trees and cigarettes were uniquely Oz. It was the person behind the breath.

If Oz says to me, "Good night, Andrew. Love you." What do I say? Do I say it back, genuinely meaning it? Or do I say nothing, and hope he goes to sleep and leaves me alone?

He stared at the ceiling, replaying the sound of Oz saying his name.

"Andrew. Andrew. Andrew."

Undeniably amazing. But imagining the last part in Oz's voice:

Good night, Andrew. Love you.

There were still four sturdy walls surrounding him, but that wasn't good enough. Feeling "not uncomfortable" wasn't love.

Does it need to be love? I'm fond of him. And how he could help me. Maybe I could be happy with him.

He looked toward Robert's back.

I'd rather have him than you. But is it because I'd be choosing him, instead of having him forced on me? He'd be my equal. He's intelligent. He's useful. He hasn't lied to me like you have, and I feel safer around him. Andrew turned his head to stare at the ceiling.

Safe is something. It's not the same as peace or happiness, but Oz is the type of person that if he loved me, he'd keep me safe. And I could get used to that. Maybe he'd care about the real me. About who I am instead of who he'd want me to be. Maybe I could love him. I do love it when he says my name.

And Andrew fell asleep, thinking of smoke curling through an evergreen forest, and listening to the sweet record of his spoken name.

Chapter 26

Oz wasn't scraped off the bathroom floor the next morning, though he felt like he had been. He woke in a bed, fully clothed and dehydrated with a stabbing pain running through his skull. The blinding light coming through the window roused him and indicated that he wasn't in his own bedroom.

I'd never leave the shades open when it's going to be this bad. He rolled on his side, away from the window, curling his knees toward his chest.

Why was there such a cruel thing as light? What good was it to anyone? Why couldn't people move through darkness with bat sonar? Not that random screeching to elicit object vibration would be better for a hangover, but why did it have to be so fucking bright?

He kept his eyes closed and tried to breathe without moving his face. The end of the previous night was a blur. After he'd entered the restaurant with Andrew, everything had a cloudy haze. He knew he'd caved and disclosed everything, becoming a blubbering, emotional mess. The odor and grease of weakness clung to his clothes and saturated his skin.

But there'd been that man … That man who twenty-four hours before he'd regarded as a woman. A beguiling woman who'd made him so curious that he'd forced their worlds to collide.

It was easy to switch to considering him a man. And not because it simplified things for Oz. On the contrary, he had a feeling things wouldn't be simple for a long time.

It could only be such an effortless change with it being true. Despite the feminine face and long blond hair, there was a masculine feel to Andrew. At his most tender, he radiated strong, powerful tones.

A red warning light in Oz's head flashed, but he allowed himself to remember the fingertips curling around his hair to convey he wasn't alone.

Andrew might've touched anyone in this way. Robert, the boy, anyone. But then their eyes had met, and Andrew's hand had withdrawn. It'd moved to Oz's cheek, his knuckles grazing it while they looked at each other. And he'd known that touch was for him alone. The touch and whatever was behind it.

"You could find something that inspires as much passion out of you …"

The cautionary light became a shrieking alarm, and Oz pitched onto his back. His head pounded and his eyes seemed like they were made of wood. He blinked, and felt splinters driving into the back of his lids.

What the fuck do you think you're doing, Oz? He squeezed his hands into fists and reopened them slowly before rubbing them over his face. *I'm not going to think about this. It's too much and too complicated. I can't handle complicated anymore. Mathematics, people, or feelings.*

Oz took a breath. *I'm going downstairs to kick Santino in the balls for leaving the fucking shades open. He did it on purpose.*

With this resolution, he pulled himself out of bed and straggled down to the kitchen.

Santino sat at his table, a cup of coffee in his hand, and a newspaper concealing his face.

"Good morning, Sunshine. Or Mr. Seven Gins. Whichever may be weighing more heavily upon you. I imagine they both are." Santino didn't lower his paper, but the sly smile appeared in his voice.

"You're an asshole."

"And you interrupted me last night."

"You didn't have to answer the phone."

"Yes, I did. It was you. You'd put aside whatever or whoever you were doing to take a call from me. Of course, I wouldn't be calling drunk off my ass and needing a designated driver."

"You're right. You're not that interesting." Oz slid into the opposite seat and stared at the back of the newspaper. The headlines ran together.

"What exactly were you doing last night?" Santino set his paper down. "You looked like someone gutted you. Much like you do now actually."

"That's how I feel. My head, anyway."

"Coffee's there. I'm your rescuer, not your servant."

He walked to the counter as Santino raised the newspaper and turned a page. Thank God, he'd dropped it. Oz sighed and the coffee steam breathed over his face, easing the ache in his eyes.

"What were you doing with her?"

He knew Santino had raised the paper to hear that audible relief before continuing. It was like leaving the shades open or talking about him like he wasn't there.

But the construction of the sentence didn't escape him. He stirred his coffee cup, keeping his back to Santino to avoid revealing the slow smile he couldn't stop.

"Her who?"

"You know who. That woman you brought last Friday. What were you doing with her, alone and drunk?"

Andrew hadn't told him. Oz felt a wave of satisfaction in their shared secret. Should he say something? It'd be difficult to pretend not to know, especially with Santino. And it'd be hard for him to talk about Andrew like he wasn't Andrew. He'd feel guilty, even if it was done to preserve Andrew's privacy. Perhaps it could be avoided though.

"We spent the day together. We had dinner. I got a little drunk."

"It's not unlike you to get a 'little drunk'."

Oz smiled before crossing to the table. *Success.*

"But why did you spend the day, and have dinner, with a woman?"

Failure.

"We're friends."

"I find it hard to believe that her husband would allow her to be out with a single man."

"A single gay man."

Santino lowered the paper and met his eyes. He was silent and seemed to be waiting for an explanation.

Though Oz wiped his face of emotion, his mind clicked through the frames beginning with Santino's arrival. They were bleary, and he'd eventually passed out. But with his guard eroded by alcohol and vulnerability, had he unintentionally let something slip of his confused feelings? Was that why his friend eyed him with such a look of skepticism? A knot formed in Oz's stomach.

"I don't care what you are." Santino lifted his mug. "You should always be careful about being alone with a married woman, but there's more on the line in this situation. Her husband has absolute authority."

"He gave his permission. He said to stay out late if we were having a good time."

"We? As in his wife and a single man? Did he specifically say, 'Yes, dear, you can stay out all night with another man. No, I haven't met him, and you're an attractive woman. Yes, have as much alcohol as you want. Lower your inhibitions.' He didn't say that. He didn't know. Admit it."

"He knew. He just thought I was a woman."

"I can see why." Santino snorted. "But you're playing a dangerous game. The husband could've carted her straight to CryoLife when you dropped her off."

"He wouldn't. I've seen him. He's too much of a fucking pussy. He wears a fucking pocket protector. He'd shit his pants if I cracked my knuckles in his direction."

"But this isn't about you versus him. He may not pick a fight with you, but think about what he could do to her. It's still not something you should mess with. If you push him enough to drag her into the Center, there'll be nothing you can do." Santino gave Oz a narrowed look. "She's his property. Don't jeopardize whatever freedom she has. Don't joyride in his car. She belongs to him. Not to herself. And not to you."

Oz considered the truth to Santino's words. He felt that Robert had far too much pride to return Andrew's conservatorship to CryoLife, but there was no telling what happened behind the closed door of the apartment, or what could happen. He thought of what he, himself, had said to Andrew yesterday:

"When you buy a chair, you can do whatever you want with it. You can sand it, paint it, or break its legs off and use them to fuck yourself."

For the next few months, Andrew was Robert's chair. He was Robert's car. He was Robert's lap dancing grinder monkey. He was just Robert's.

"Property Of."

Robert didn't give the impression of being physically violent, or cruel, but anything could be simmering under the surface. Andrew had said he was miserable. He'd paid two million dollars into the recreation of his perfect family.

Oz knew the type of woman Robert had expected to get back. They came into his pharmacy. Busy soccer moms buying lotion infused tissues for snotty noses and sex lube for their husband's dicks. They spent hours curling their hair and applying makeup before sliding into tight fitting capri pants that emphasized wide, child bearing hips.

When they came to the counter to pick up their happy pills and looked at him, they saw only his shaggy hair, his pierced eyebrow, and the tattoos that crawled up his neck and across his knuckles. They hoped that precious baby Tommy or Timmy wouldn't be such a freak show. They took their tissues, lube, and Prozac home to quaint houses where they put on Betty Crocker aprons and waved feather dusters. When these women dreamed, it was of minivans that stretched for blocks with children filling every seat.

This was what Robert wanted and what he'd paid for. But he'd received Andrew. He hadn't gotten a tom-boy, a masculine woman, or a lesbian. Andrew was a man. And since Oz had become close to the situation, a gnawing fear took the edge off any humor.

Robert was going to discover the truth. The outrage and pain that'd made Andrew fire the gun in that way before lashing out at everything he could put his hands on? That anger couldn't be contained permanently, and especially when uncapped from the emotion-stunting drugs. When Robert found out, what he may be inclined to do, and what he was capable of doing were two separate things.

Oz pictured Andrew's eyes. *If you belonged to me, I couldn't keep you. I'd let you have your freedom. I couldn't see you unhappy. Even if you wanted to be someone else or stay out with another man.* He allowed himself to feel that touch to his cheek, and his chivalrous thoughts halted. *Or would I?*

If he didn't know what he'd do in that situation, how could he intuit what Robert might do?

Santino's words repeated in his head.

"She belongs to him. Not to herself. And not to you."

Unless Robert did get fed up enough to turn the conservatorship over to the Center. Then Andrew would belong to CryoLife. It would take a lot to move Robert to that action. Would the disclosure of Andrew's gender identity do it? Could even his association with Oz taint the Natalie dream beyond what could be repaired in Robert's eyes?

He had to be more careful in his actions and thoughts. It was for the best to put this foolishness from his mind. Andrew's survival depended on it.

"Good man," Santino said, as if Oz had spoken the resolution aloud. He shook his newspaper out and held it in front of his face again. "So, tell me what you did on your date."

"It was nothing. We went to the shooting range."

"Romance at its finest. How's Red?"

"Happy to see me. And the pot."

"In reverse order. And Sue?"

"She's pulling tape worms out of peoples' asses in Somalia or some shit."

"It's a shame your companion didn't get the chance to meet her. Sometimes women relate easier to women." Santino didn't appear to catch the smirk that crossed Oz's face. "What did you do after that?"

"We had dinner. I got carried away with the alcohol. You came and saved the day, for which I am eternally grateful."

"As you should be. So you picked her up, shot off guns, and had a steak? That's it?"

"Prime rib. But yes."

Santino lowered and folded his newspaper, taking off his glasses and laying them on top. He closed his eyes and rubbed his eyebrows with the fingers of his left hand.

"Why do you lie to me, Oz?"

"I'm not lying."

"Omitting the full truth is the same thing."

"Do you expect a play by play? An account of every instant?"

"I expect a reason for why you looked so upset last night." Santino gave him a pained look, the skin above his cheeks wrinkled in concern. "I was worried about you. You looked like you'd been dragged across town lashed to someone's bumper. And you're never like that. I have to work so hard to chip away a sediment of the layers you encase yourself in. And you've never let it out. Ever."

"So, you're jealous?"

"I'm not jealous." He scowled. "You're such a narcissist. I care about you, you were reached and—"

Oz made himself chuckle.

Santino struck his open palm against the table. The coffee cups clattered.

"Will you stop with the head games? I want a straight fucking answer!"

He paused before proceeding with cautious innocence. "We talked, brother. We talked about serious shit, and I let it get to me."

"What kind of 'serious shit'?"

"I said what happened."

"'You told her about how you died?'" Santino's face eased. "In detail?"

"Yes."

"About your father?"

"Yes."

"And about the Hodge conjecture?" He raised an eyebrow.

"I didn't mean to, but yes."

Oz was touched that Santino had remembered what the problem was called. It hadn't been discussed since the initial reveal, but his friend had cared enough to commit the project's name to memory. It was more than his father had been able to do in twenty years.

"You're not able to separate those three things. They're too entwined for you to tell one without the others. Especially when you've got gin as a vehicle."

"I know. It was stupid."

"It wasn't stupid. You must trust her," Santino said without bitterness or envy. "How did she react? What did she say?"

He took a breath. "'I'm here.'"

"'I'm here?'"

"What's wrong with that?"

"Nothing. Just an odd response. I mean, she was there."

"But that's what I wanted to hear." Oz felt the phantom hand caressing his cheek, and his skin flushed.

You knew that. You knew exactly what I needed.

"Oz."

He blinked and refocused on Santino. The look of skepticism had returned.

"She let you in on her secret, didn't she? And I was wrong. She's not a lesbian."

"I told you that wasn't true from the beginning."

"Then what is she? If she's not a lesbian, then you're putting her at more risk if the husband finds you hanging around."

Though he didn't think it was his place to divulge someone else's secret, for the sake of his friendship with Santino, Oz had to. Eventually it was going to come into the open and, when it did, his friend could act shocked.

"What is she?" Santino asked.

"She is a he."

"She is a he? As in, she is a man?" He narrowed his eyes. "Are you sure you don't just want her to be a man? That's awfully convenient for you, isn't it?"

"Straight men are all convenience for me. You have bells on your necks and 'Thank you, come again' signs on your asses," Oz snarled. "Very convenient."

"Is she a straight man?"

"Yes."

"Did she say that? She's married to a man."

"Who's under the assumption that he's married to a woman. Can you get off my ass and think about how difficult this is for him?"

"For the husband?"

"No, fuck him. For Andrew."

"Andrew, eh?"

Santino unfolded his glasses and slid them onto his nose. He then turned to Oz with a stern expression.

"I don't care if he's gay or straight, Oz. If he's a man, then you need to take a good look at yourself and stop whatever it is you're doing. Keep it platonic, even in your head, or you'll destroy him."

"We're just friends."

"No, *we* are just friends. I'm not blind. And you'd better get yourself under control, because other people aren't either." Santino picked up his coffee mug and took a swallow.

"And get the fuck out of my house. You're late for work."

Chapter 27

Oz heeded Santino's advice for almost two weeks and didn't seek Andrew out.

He tried to focus on his business. There were hundreds of things to prepare and compute in preparation for tax time. It was a good opportunity to get shit out of the way and avoid burning the midnight oil in April.

Taxes weren't anything like the mathematics he loved. It was gathering data and punching it into the computer. And when in the end, it was a spreadsheet calculating everything, it wasn't math, even the boring kind. But it distracted him and sort of kept away the worrying.

Menial tasks hadn't ended his midnight thinking sessions about Andrew. But as the days went on, and the intensity of that gin-soaked night faded, Oz considered that the separation could be positive. He didn't plan on staying away forever, but it was good to distance himself and rebuild his wall.

It also gave him time to question how much of what he thought had happened had actually happened. He'd been so inundated with alcohol; he couldn't be sure of every detail. The words he'd used to tell Andrew about his death and the Hodge conjecture failed him. It was possible he'd made an idiot of himself. And if he'd deteriorated into the sobbing fit he remembered, it wasn't possible, it was true.

But had Oz only projected how he'd wanted Andrew to respond, constructing some elaborate fantasy? Had Andrew really touched his hair or caressed his cheek?

"You could find something that inspires as much passion out of you ..." Had Andrew said that? If he had, was Oz reading too much into things?

And on top of the whole mess, he couldn't ignore the fact that Andrew had been coming off the medication. He'd missed three doses. Quitting the drugs sometimes did stranger things than starting or staying on them. Who knew if he'd meant what he said, if he'd said it. What he'd done, if he'd done it. Would he even remember anything?

Ultimately, Oz decided on a timeline and a plan.

The next gathering at the bar had been five days away when he came to a decision. If Andrew didn't come, then Oz would go to the apartment out of concern that he hadn't been to the bar.

As for the plan, he was going to put aside whatever had happened at the restaurant. He'd forget about it and pretend the evening had ended when Andrew revealed his secret. It wouldn't be fair to hold Andrew responsible for statements or actions he may not have been able to control.

Oz felt he'd successfully reconstructed his shield. He was cool and collected. He was prepared to let everything roll off his back like he always did. There'd be no awkwardness on his side. Not a single noteworthy thing had happened after the gun range. And Andrew was a friend. Nothing more.

But he crossed the days off his calendar with stiffening slowness. He wondered. He worried. And as he thought to admit he was missing Andrew, he went back to work. The empty feeling usually disappeared in a pit of numbers.

"Boss man."

He was in the zone, blocking out everything else.

"Boss man."

Oz dashed in another five numbers using the ten-key pad. Things were better today – all cylinders firing properly, and he hadn't had to stop typing once. He was about to go to the next column when Barty kicked his chair.

"I said, 'Boss man!'"

He spun to face the technician who'd intruded into his office.

"What is it, Barty? Can't you see I'm fucking busy?"

"That lady you fought with a while ago is out here wanting to see you."

"Take a message like a good secretary." Oz tapped the papers he'd been working from to form a neat stack.

"I told her you weren't available. She said you'd make time for her."

"She said I'd make time for her?"

He'd forgotten. No one saw what he did. No one knew what he knew. They shared a secret.

"Her exact words were, 'If he knows what's good for him, he'll make time for me.' She must have liked what you gave her before, boss." The young man winked.

"Our sign does say 'Come again,' doesn't it?" Oz grinned and stuffed his hands into his pockets. "Let her in. But tell her first that I make no time for a woman."

"They make time for you."

"They rearrange their lives, put their kidneys on the black market, sell their first born children, and then they hope."

The technician left, closing the door behind him. Oz fought the impulse to pace and calm his nerves. If Andrew came in and saw him pacing, what would he think? So he stayed in his chair, his hands shaking in his pockets.

Get a grip, Oz. You're calm. You're collected. He took a breath and tried to control the slow exhale. *You're the coolest motherfucker there has ever been. And it could be anyone. You fight with a lot of people. You love fighting with people. How ridiculous will you feel being nervous if it's not him? You feel stupid enough being nervous that it might be.*

He turned to the computer screen so he could appear occupied. He saw the door open and, in the reflection of the screen, Andrew entered his office.

"So you don't make time for a woman?"

"I'll make time for a woman when there isn't a single man left on the planet. And maybe not then. There might be sheep. And there's always Santino."

"There'd be me."

"No, in this apocalyptic universe, you'd be annihilated with the rest of them. Struck down by a meteor, sucked into a black hole, crushed by a whale on a beach … The great tragedy of our time. Unless you're a sheep. Are you a sheep?"

"I'm not a sheep."

Oz spun his chair and coughed into the crook of his elbow. When he looked at Andrew, he knew it'd happened. It'd grown dimmer, but it returned with strong magnitude and enveloped him. He felt the hand caressing his hair, the touch on his cheek. With great effort, he shoved it back. No. He was cool. The coolest motherfucker there'd ever been.

"That's good. I'm not a vegetarian." Oz folded his arms behind his head in his standby position. "So how are ya, brother?"

But he could already tell. The wilted tiredness in Andrew's eyes was gone, and he stood with his shoulders back, his posture straight. What horrible things these drugs did to people who didn't need them.

"I feel great. Well, not great, but much improved. I can think straight."

"That's always a plus."

"I wanted to thank you."

"The pleasure is entirely mine."

"And I wanted to ask for your help."

"Oh?" He cocked his head. "Pray tell, how can I assist you, good sir? And you can sit down. Move that shit over there, to that other shit over there."

Andrew transported six large file folders from the second seat in the room. When the chair was empty, his guest moved it within a yard from him. He sat and leaned forward, as if about to disclose something confidential and dangerous.

"I want to cut my hair."

"I have many skills. Barbering isn't one of them, unless you want to be bald. I could manage that."

"No, I thought you might know someone who'd do it."

He was confused until he remembered their gun conversation, when his friend had found out that the CryoLife tag was never removed. And he laughed.

"I meant they'll deny you privileges like selling you a gun, approving a credit card, or moving to Taiwan. Anyone will cut your hair. They won't ask for your ID. Now if you wanted a tattoo, that's something we'd have to go underground for."

"I just want my hair cut. And I know I can have it cut, that no one could stop me. It's not that."

"Then what is it?"

"I need someone to, or a place where they won't … Do you know of someone who will cut it not like a woman?"

"You mean will they cut it like a sheep? I'm not sure that'd be right for the shape of your face."

"Will they cut it like a man?"

"It's business, Andrew. Pay them, and they'll do whatever you want." Oz noticed how he smiled when his name was used, and it was so much brighter when not on a delay from the medication.

But as quick as the smile was to appear, it was also fast to fade. "I worry, they'll take one look at me and they'll cut it short, but not like a man's haircut."

"I don't understand."

"I pay more attention to these things, I realize." He sighed. "But there's a huge difference between short hair for a woman and for a man. And I don't want to look like Natalie with some pixie cut or short in front and long in back. I'm not worried that they'll refuse me service, only that they'll botch it."

"In which case, you get it cut shorter by someone else."

"And if they fuck it up too?"

"Then we'll shave you bald and I'll try to not cut your ear off. Of course, there are no guarantees, but I'll give it my best shot."

"I want it done right. So will you come with me?"

"Do you need me to hold your hand? It doesn't hurt to have your hair cut. It's a bunch of dead cells."

But he wanted to go.

"To help me decide what to have done. To support me."

"You ask the gay man to help with your makeover? How stereotypical is that?"

"No, I'm asking my friend because I trust him. I'm willing to admit this is scary for me." Andrew put his hand on Oz's knee. "You make me feel safe."

Assimilation

His mouth went dry, and it took him some seconds to collect himself.

"Well, you might have horrible taste." He mustered a chuckle. "If you go alone, you might get a crew cut. Not that it matters, but does Robert know?"

"No. I'm my own master, and I'll do what I want." Andrew withdrew his hand and folded his arms. "If you'd told me that no one would cut it, I'd have done it myself. I hate it."

"It's not that bad." Oz recognized why Andrew wanted the hair gone, but if he was going for a more masculine look, there were other areas he would've recommended starting with. Was it his place to point them out though? Probably not. Only if the opportunity presented itself.

"But it's not what I see in my head. When I think about what I'd look like if you turned me inside out and saw who I really am."

It was an idea Oz had never considered, but he supposed it made sense. People didn't spend their entire lives in front of mirrors. Somewhere in the mind existed a mental image of how one looked. He looked how he thought he should.

"What does the real you look like?"

Andrew averted his eyes, swallowed, and then looked at Oz. "That's not something I want to talk about. It's sufficient to say I don't have long hair. I want it cut off. Today."

Oz had more than a mild curiosity about what Andrew wanted to see in those mirrors he covered. But he decided to drop the subject.

"And I don't care what Robert might say. If he shits his pants when he sees it, he can clean it himself."

Oz remembered his conversation with Santino, and that cautionary voice in his ear:

"Think about what he could do to her."

But it was hair. Hair grew back. How much of a risk could it be? He couldn't see Robert having a conniption about a haircut. He didn't know Robert, but really? A haircut?

"Let's get going then." Oz bounded up from his chair and walked to the door. Before opening it he removed his white coat, sliding each arm out in a swift motion. As he hung it on the wall hook, he turned back. Their eyes met, and his shoulders tingled.

"What? Do I have something on me?" He coasted a hand through his hair, pushing the other in his pocket.

Chapter 28

Andrew had woken with the hair, hating it from the beginning. It wasn't his hair, or Natalie's. It was CryoLife grown hair, and having it chopped off was far from a loss. What'd kept him from going alone was precisely what he'd told Oz – he'd been afraid of what a stylist would do. If he pointed to a picture of a man's cut, he'd walk out looking like a butch lesbian. In many ways, short women's styles were worse than the long hair. One ill-placed snip of the scissors, and he could appear to be one of those perky athletic women so assertive in their femininity they didn't need a swath of hair.

And there were also the mirrors. Salons were rooms of mirrors he couldn't cover. Every reflection cast back the things he hated about himself. He'd walked in behind Oz, shaking and with his eyes to the floor. The tiles weren't miniature drip paintings, just a creamy tan—

"Patrice, you lazy ass whore!"

"Oz, you filthy motherfucker!"

A sandwich bag transfer. Did Oz use actual money for anything?

"This is my friend, Andrew. Take good care of *him*. *He's* tired of looking like a dirty hippie."

Andrew added the emphasis in his head. It sounded fantastic. Much better than those other—

Oz had placed his hands on his shoulders and gave him a shove forward. He stumbled and looked up. A large woman in a blue apron was gave him a sly grin.

"Friend, eh?"

"If he were more than a friend, I'd have grabbed his ass, not his shoulders." Oz walked past both of them and slumped into a barber chair. He spun in it a handful of times before stopping the motion with the chair facing the mirror. In that position, he attempted to tilt the chair back. "Your chairs aren't adjustable enough, and they're too damn close to the counter for me to put my feet up. How do you expect anyone to relax?"

"This isn't a lounge. It's a business." She turned to Andrew, and her smile drooped. "I don't mean to offend you, honey, but how old are you?"

"I don't rape children, Patrice."

Settle down. This isn't a bad thing. She didn't ask if you were a man. She sees a male. That's how Oz has been referring to you. You don't look twenty-eight, but that's okay. As long as she sees a man, who cares how old you look?

"I wasn't talking to you. I was talking to your friend. And don't you dare light that cigarette. I have customers allergic to—"

"Then get a move on. That's high quality dro I gave you. And what have you given me? An uncomfortable chair and a disturbing view of your ass. Work, woman."

Patrice snatched a fistful of curlers from the top of a rolling trolley and threw them at him.

It'd be nice to be like this. To be confident and have close friends that you could pick on and talk trash with.

"Have a seat over here." She'd walked behind the chair next to Oz and beckoned to Andrew. "What are you thinking you'd like?"

The question he'd been dreading. What to say? "A man's haircut?" Would she look at him funny? He could just say "a haircut," but there was that nagging feeling that he should specify—

"He wants it short, like your husband's—"

"Here's a book for you to look through some pictures—"

"God, Patrice. Do you keep picture books of it? I thought this was a business, not a—"

"If you don't like any of those, I've got books of others right—"

"Seriously? You've got a library of dick pics? He's straight. But you can pass them over here if you—"

"Will you shut up?" Patrice snapped. "Let the man talk and put away that cigarette before I throw you out!"

Andrew looked up from the book she'd set in his lap. Oz said nothing, but smiled as he removed his cigarette. In his pattern-seeing, problem-solving way, had he calculated antagonizing his friend to elicit this response?

"Let the man talk." How wonderful to be rightly acknowledged. *Did you provoke her on purpose because you knew it'd be meaningful to me?*

Like he'd read his mind, Oz winked at him before resuming a slow spin in his chair.

"What do you think, hmm? Maybe this one would go well with the shape of your face." Patrice's long nail ticked on top a photo, but Andrew didn't look away from Oz.

With his head tipped back his bangs fluttered away from his forehead in motion with the chair. Though he'd complained of the discomfort, he looked perfectly at ease. One leg was crossed over the other, and the cigarette he'd been ordered to put away peeped out from the pocket of his blue button-up. His left arm hung loose over the chair's side, while his right was tucked under his neck. He'd rolled his sleeves over his elbows, as Andrew had sought to do with Robert's shirt. But on Oz it looked perfect.

Everything about you is perfect.

Andrew had been evaluating his options and had arrived at two choices. He could stick it out with Robert and see where things were when the six-month conservatorship expired, or he could tell Robert the truth and remain with to CryoLife for the duration of his sentence. Yes, going back to CryoLife was a risk, but the idea of them killing him seemed somewhat irrational in the light of day. So Oz didn't know anyone who hadn't assimilated. That had just been a side comment and it proved nothing. CryoLife was an established corporation, not the fucking mob. They couldn't just make people disappear.

But whatever he decided to do, either way, when it came time to strike out on his own, he'd need help. And from the look on Oz's face at the pharmacy, Andrew knew he'd probably receive any assistance he asked for.

And perhaps I could reciprocate. I'm more open to loving you than Robert. At least I like to look at you.

Robert wore slacks and button-ups too, sometimes rolling the sleeves. There was a different energy Oz brought to his style though. The way Robert moved caused a cotton shirt to look like a heavy, canvas material. Oz had a carefree vibrancy that made everything around him seem effortless. Having moved past the jealousy, he was so much easier to be around.

"Or how about this one? If you want to look older, this might be a good option. Or something similar to this would be low maintenance. You tell me, Andrew."

He turned to Patrice. "Whatever you think. Just short, like he said."

She picked a rubber band from the trolley and tied it around Andrew's hair. "My husband used to have long hair actually, until I made him cut it."

"She likes most things short. That's why they're such a good match," Oz said.

"Now I don't mind long hair, but when I met him it was just this ratted nasty mess. Why I even took a second look at him I have no idea." The stylist guided her scissors through the ponytail. "But that's how it is. Love and nonsense. Makes you see past the many, many flaws."

"I'm sure he feels the same way about your many, many flaws. Or he would, if he could see past your—"

Patrice chucked a spray bottle at him. "Next time, I'll throw the scissors. And not at your chest, either." With one final cut, Andrew felt a sudden lightness at the back of his head. "There you go, honey. That'll be the worst of it."

Patrice handed the mantle of golden hair to him and he petted it with ginger fingertips. Natalie had spent over an hour styling her hair in the morning – curling then brushing it to loosen the tight tresses into flowing waves. She'd loved it and been proud of it.

Like growing hair is some accomplishment. I guess maybe for you it was. You didn't do much of anything besides look good for Robert. There's more to me than strands of dead cells.

Andrew smiled and turned to Oz, holding the band of hair in triumph like a decapitated head.

269

"Are you going to keep it?" Oz asked. "Let Robert keen over it?"

"No." Andrew pressed the hair into the stylist's hand. "Donate it, or throw it in the garbage. I don't care. Get rid of it."

"Sure thing. We're almost done." Patrice tossed the severed ponytail onto the counter, removing her scissors again. She glanced at Oz. "Who's Robert? I swear to God, Oz, if some parent comes in screaming at me—"

"Relax, I told you he's not a minor."

"If I get hassle ..." She looked in the mirror, smoothing two sections of hair at Andrew's temples with her fingertips. "You can take your weed and shove it up your ass."

"That'd be an interesting high, I suppose."

"Hands free."

"And hands not otherwise occupied are free to hold a cigarette. Hint, hint."

"If you want to smoke and can't wait three more goddamn minutes, go do it outside."

Andrew watched from the mirror as Oz stopped spinning in the chair and stood. Unlike what he'd anticipated, he didn't feel any panic at the idea of being left alone in the salon. When Oz looked at him, he smiled to indicate that he was okay.

"Wants and needs are two different things." Oz took the cigarette from his pocket and walked to the door.

"You *need* a nicotine patch."

"I'll never surrender. Ever."

The bell on the door jingled as it closed.

Patrice picked up a bottle and sprayed a fine mist over Andrew's hair before continuing to cut. "I take it you're new to being around him?"

"What makes you say that?"

"You're not obnoxious yet." She grinned. "I'm kidding. He's a great guy. I don't know what I'd do without him. Lean your head forward." Patrice took a pair of clippers from the trolley and turned them on. "The marijuana isn't for me. My father has liver cancer, and Wifi Kush helps him sleep. Oz doesn't charge an arm and a leg for it."

"You trade him with haircuts?"

"This is the first time he's asked for something."

"Maybe you really should let him smoke in here then."

The stylist wiped a towel over the back of his neck. "See, you're learning."

Learning. Another plus of going the Oz route. It was kind of like spying on the frat house across the street and imagining being among them. If Andrew hung around Oz enough, he could learn to be like him. Oz had taught Andrew how to fire a gun, perhaps he'd teach him how to be confident. Or Andrew could study him closely in order to pull bits and pieces of him to mimic. Like The Natalie Files. Only The Oz Files weren't as awkward to watch, and the show hadn't been canceled yet.

"There you go, honey. What do you think?"

He refocused on the mirror.

It wasn't Natalie.

It was almost Andrew.

Almost. If he looked at only the face, ignoring the baggy sweatshirt that the real Andrew would never wear. The curve of his cheek was still rounder than he'd like, and his skin was too smooth, but the hair made a difference.

True to what he'd hoped, Patrice had cut it in a traditional men's style. Closer at the back and on the sides, and just a touch longer on top. It was squared in a straight line on either side of his forehead, the edge rounding down his temple.

"Too long? Too short? Not that much can be done about the latter."

"It's perfect."

"That's what I like to hear."

Andrew could see her off to the side, squeezing a drop of paste onto her fingertips, but he couldn't take his concentration fully away from the mirror.

There I am. Halfway. Maybe seventy percent. Closer than I've ever been before.

For the absolute joy of seeing his own reflection instead of a stranger's, he wanted to cry. But he held it in. He was sure that sobbing over a haircut wasn't something Oz would do.

Chapter 29

Outside the building, Andrew shook his head, running his fingers through the short hair. It was incredible. So freeing. Almost better than hearing his name for the first time.

I have two things. The name and the hair.

Fuck CryoLife, fuck Robert. He could run a dozen laps around the parking lot.

"My head feels lighter!"

"You look like you need to take a piss." Oz leaned against the side of the car and tipped his head to light another cigarette.

"It was this noose choking me. The back of my neck feels cold." The warm breeze felt arctic – as if menthol had been slathered over his skin. Was this similar to the sensation of shaving? Maybe he'd try it.

"Speaking of the cold." Oz took a drag and released the smoke in a slow exhale. "Do you know where we live?"

"Where we live?"

"Where we are currently. It's not a trick question – just answer."

"53rd Street. Savannah. Georgia. United States. The world. The—"

"You were good the first few in." Oz coughed. "And what month is it?"

"Has the smoking cut off the oxygen to your brain? It's August, Oz."

"Oh, I'm fully aware. But I thought you might not grasp that we live in a southern climate where the average temperature in August easily exceeds ninety degrees. It's ninety-two today. That kind of heat fries eggs on sidewalks and bakes poodles in their sleep."

"Point?"

Oz took the cigarette from his lips, and made a sweeping gesture. "You look like you're off to go snow tubing in Finland."

Andrew froze. Off in the distance of his mind, the diving board flickered into view.

"Look, brother, I know why you do it. But you don't have to."

"No, I really do."

When he looked at Oz, it was almost like seeing him for the first time. All the jealousy and anger rushed back. He didn't feel the desire to emulate him, because here Oz was throwing himself in his face again.

Andrew answered in a low whisper: "I'll get home on my own."

He walked away, fists at his sides. The springboard disappeared.

You wouldn't lose control in public. Not when you're sober anyway. Hating you doesn't mean I still don't want to be you. It's part of the reason I hate you. And how dare you remind me that it won't matter what people call me, how I cut my hair, or how I'll try to mime you – I'll never be you.

"Don't be so fucking dramatic, Andrew," Oz shouted.

It's not dramatic. For all your knowledge, you don't understand a single fucking thing. I don't care what you've been through, it's not the same.

"I'm trying to help you!"

Help me? How can you help me when your presence is offensive to me? You can't trade bags of weed with random people and help me. Nothing can, but even if it could:

Andrew spun around. "I don't want your fucking help!"

But shouting a single sentence wasn't enough. The diving board illuminated, and he made a mad dash toward it as he charged back to Oz. Fuck what anyone else would do. He was Andrew. And he wanted to rip Oz to pieces.

And fuck somersaults or twists or any of that bullshit. He jumped and hit the water.

Andrew stopped inches from where Oz stood near the car.

"Why would you want to help me? Do you feel sorry for me?" He grabbed the cigarette from his lips and threw it to the ground. He crushed it into the asphalt with his heel before jabbing a finger into Oz's face. "Poor, stupid Andrew. Stuck in the body of a woman. Here, toss a bag of pot to someone and make him feel like he's not hopeless. Give him a bone. You're one of those perfect, beautiful people who should take pity on us. It's the cross you bear, association and charity toward freaks!"

"That's not—"

"You have no idea what it's like to be me! You have no fucking idea how it is to be trapped in this body! Do you think I want to look like this? Do you?"

"I—"

"Shut the fuck up! You want to hear something else you don't know?" Andrew's body shook as he yelled. "You don't know what it's like to be me, and be around you! To look at you and see what I'll never have! To see your face and watch you move!"

He seized Oz's shirt.

"Did you have to think about putting this on? Did you worry about how it'd make you look? No, you didn't! You threw it on and walked out the door! You knew that whatever you wore, it'd fit perfectly! No one would think you're a freak! You don't have to try to do anything! You're always young and handsome and masculine, no matter what you wear!"

He let go of the fabric, but made a sharp motion at Oz as he backed off.

"Do you think any of this would fit me? That I'd look anything like you? Anything like how I feel inside? I hate your fucking shirts! I hate your fucking pants! I hate how you're confident and how you're so comfortable in your own skin! You're a walking reminder of everything I want! And I hate you for it!"

Oz stared at Andrew and said nothing for what seemed minutes. It was probably a good thing as the screaming had left Andrew lightheaded. He considered turning and stalking away, but kept still, his vision reined in on Oz's eyes. And for those first few seconds of silence, they contained an emotion he hadn't previously seen.

The expression was similar to when Oz had spoken of the loss of his mathematical ability. Except he'd told his story to others before and knew what words to say and at which points he was liable to break down. That loss had also happened a decade ago, so while the pain was still vivid, a paper-thin layer of skin had covered it.

But this was a fresh hurt for which there were no immediate words. The shock of being maliciously and unexpectedly wounded.

Did even your father come out and admit he hated you?

The thought caused Andrew to feel slightly guilty, though not enough to apologize for the outburst. Then Oz's injured look snapped away, the control and cockiness re-emerging. Instead of relief, the resilience irritated Andrew.

I wish I could let shit roll off so easily. God, I hate you.

"I can't help how I look either," Oz said. "Even if my appearance pisses you off, it's all I have to work with. I can't change myself to make you feel better. And if I could, I wouldn't." He took a step toward Andrew. "Maybe you need to look at me and get a fucking grip. Stop pining over wanting to be me, and do something about yourself. That's why I brought it up. Not so you'd fly into a fucking fit. I wanted to help you."

"You want to help?" Andrew asked. "You want to back your car over me, so they'll cut out my brain again and put it in a man's body? They'd freezer burn another part, and I'd feel like a woman."

"Or a sheep."

The comment was like flicking a pebble into a pond, and Andrew felt the pressure ease.

That's it, you need to remember yourself. Remember the plan. You don't know what could happen, and you'd like to think you won't need his help, but you might.

And were he to chart out the time since waking in the Cryobiotic Treatment Center, despite the rock bottom lows, the period since meeting Oz had been filled with better moments. If he could manage to tolerate him, this wasn't a wise bridge to burn.

"I'd prefer not to back over you with the car. In addition to the sheep potential, you know that sound when a bug hits the windshield, and it pops apart?" Oz shivered and smiled, though it was tense at the corners of his mouth. "I think if I ran you over, it'd make a sound like that, and that freaks the fuck out of me. It'd totally ruin my day."

Maybe things will be better now that you've heard how I feel. Your head was too far up your ass to put it together on your own.

"What can you do?" Andrew asked.

"Get in the car."

Red stored his guns, Patrice gave a haircut, and mysterious people provided cadavers for Santino in bartering for Oz's services. All Andrew had ever been asked in exchange was to "get in the car."

He circled the car, pulled open the passenger door, and climbed into the front seat. Oz continued to lean against the driver's side. The familiar ache in his chest resurfaced as Andrew watched him pull the cigarette pack from his pocket.

Can nothing rattle you?

He thought of how Oz must look to anyone walking by – a handsome young man casually smoking a cigarette outside his car. The exact combination of ordinary and distinction made him only stand out for the right reasons. Oz purposefully, yet easily, sparkled just enough around the edges to be special.

You're too smooth. Years of practice wouldn't bring me halfway to being as cool as you. If someone yelled at me how I yelled at you, there's no way I'd recover immediately to—

Something sounded like it hit the car on the driver's side. Andrew had been daydreaming and not fully focused on Oz, but he didn't seem to have broken his collected stance. His arm had moved, but it was probably from taking out another cigarette.

Chapter 30

Oz had tried to forget what happened earlier, but he couldn't. Every time he looked at Andrew, he heard it in his brain. Even though Andrew had divulged the episode of trying on Robert's clothes during the car ride, which brought his ferocity into closer perspective, Oz didn't feel better.

He could see from Andrew's viewpoint how it might appear he took aspects of his life for granted. It'd never occurred to him to cherish the simple things Andrew referred to. Who, aside from someone in Andrew's situation, would?

Oz didn't think about the clothes he wore. He kept outfits in a rotation. He could go home, count the hangers and pinpoint the shirt he'd wear two weeks from now. It wasn't worth the effort to select something every morning.

How much time did Andrew put in? Painstakingly finding sweatshirts that hung decently and jeans that made him look like a gangbanger but hid the curves. Feeling like a boy in oversized clothes, or a monk in a robe.

Oz avoided mirrors too, but for a different reason. He had no use for them. Andrew was right: he liked how he looked.

He was aware he'd be "young and handsome and masculine," so why bother crooning in a mirror? He rushed a comb through his hair, pulled on the clothes of the day, and was out the door in less than ten minutes. How long did Andrew spend agonizing? Wishing to be seen as who he was?

Yet, while the reason for his anger and jealousy was understandable, it wasn't fair that Andrew placed blame. The acrimony stung him, but Oz remembered his own words days ago:

"You aren't connected. You're two separate individuals. You leave his feelings, his decisions, his weird erotic fantasies in his compartment. They may affect you sometimes, but they're not yours."

As often as he replayed the mantra though, following right behind:

"You're a walking reminder of everything I want! And I hate you for it!"

So while the things at the restaurant that night had been done and said, they hadn't been real. Oz had read too much into it, and he had no one to blame but himself. He'd failed again at solving something he thought he'd understood. And it wouldn't have hurt so much had he not invested or hoped.

As he'd leaned on his car smoking, he'd been able to relax. His breathing had grown steadier, though his chest felt like someone had opened it and used a melon baller to scrape out his insides. When he was raw and bleeding, they'd packed the cavity with sulfuric acid and lye. It ate its way through his back, and he felt he was about to be bisected.

"I hate you!"

His hand had formed a fist before he registered it, and he'd swung his arm forward then back into the frame of the car. The hit could be heard across the parking lot, but he didn't think Andrew had noticed. He hadn't said anything when he'd gotten in the car to drive.

Oz's hurt improved when they entered the athletic store. Being able to play the instructor and having the upper hand helped.

"This is a rash guard, and that's a lower body rash guard." Oz had taken a sleeveless shirt and pair of shorts from a rack. "They're made of spandex and nylon – surfers use them to protect from abrasion." He tossed the clothing to Andrew along with a t-shirt and basketball shorts. "Tuck the top into the bottom, and then put on the other clothes."

As Oz knew they would, the rash guards made a world of difference. A previous weed connection had been a transsexual man who'd told him about this trick. It was especially useful in that it was innocuous. If anyone found the rash guards, there was nothing incriminating about a piece of unisex clothing that could be purchased at any store. Though the customer had moved on, Oz had remembered the technique; he thought it was terribly smart and resourceful, and he liked things like that.

He'd watched Andrew admiring himself in the mirror – stretching the t-shirt across his chest, pulling the fabric in a roll at his back, and Oz knew this was significant. He hadn't looked at his body in a full-length mirror since the Robert-clothing incident.

But all Oz could think about was what Andrew had said to him:

"You're a walking reminder of everything I want! And I hate you for it!"

The uneasiness again got better at the department store. He selected items of the right size and shape, since Andrew didn't yet understand proportions in men's clothing and body types.

Although Robert was a larger man, the clothes he wore were form-fitting and clung to his frame. Natalie's body wasn't fat, but it clearly belonged to a woman. The issue Andrew had was cramming feminine distributions into Robert's Saran Wrap shirts and nut-hugging slacks.

Oz had plopped himself in a waiting room chair and at one point, Andrew approached him like a dog with a tennis ball, a tie in his hand.

"Will you? I don't know how. And I want you to teach me."

Oz obliged. He looped the tie around Andrew's collar and performed the folds and twists of a single Windsor knot. He felt the heat from Andrew's throat as he cinched it.

"Leave the top button open. It's better that way." He stopped from unbuttoning it for him and stepped back to his chair.

He looked at Andrew's reflection in the mirror, watching as he undid the top button. With the help of the rash guards, he was wearing a normal man's clothes. And with the short hair, he passed okay, despite the softness in his face. Not for a man in his late twenties, but for a young boy who hadn't fully grown out of childhood. And he seemed ecstatic about it.

The happiness hurt Oz more. He turned away, wishing he could smoke in the store. Fuck other people's right to clean air. And that's when he remembered the cigarette Andrew had taken from him and smashed into the ground.

"You owe me a cigarette. That one you crushed during your tantrum wasn't half done, you fucking punk. It's wasteful." Oz was unable to keep the biting tinge from his voice. "There are nicotine addicted children in China who would've loved to have that."

"You shouldn't smoke, anyway. It's bad for you."

"Oh, yes? I had no idea. None whatsoever. Thank you for bringing this riveting news to my attention. We should go to the papers with this. Sound the alarm. Everyone must be made aware. No one has any fucking idea that smoking is bad for you."

"Santino is right. Between the alcohol and cigarettes, you're intent on destroying yourself."

"No, between the alcohol, cigarettes, weed, fast driving, and daily swims in shark invested waters, I'm intent on destroying myself."

"You should stop smoking. And drinking." Andrew loosened the tie, removing it from the stiff collar. "You said you didn't before the procedure. Is that something else that changed?"

"No. I didn't come back needing to suck down smoke and booze. I choose to do those things of my own volition, and I enjoy them very much, thank you."

"Why?"

"Well, Water With Lemon, precisely because I didn't do them before. Do you know how much it pisses my father off? That fucker was, and continues to be, fond of reminding me how he built this body. He'd tell me, 'I made you. I built you. I constructed you. And you're perfect.' Yeah, bringing me back was about me and my work. About him only wanting me to live. Not about his pride."

There was more he could say, but he wasn't sure how agreeable he felt revealing anything else to somebody who hated him.

"So, I started smoking. And drinking. And getting pierced. And getting tattoos. My father so loved his perfect creation." Their eyes met in the mirror. "I'm going to destroy it."

Andrew turned to face him, his brow furrowed. They stared at each other before he walked into the dressing room. Without saying anything.

That was your fucking chance. If you wanted to apologize, if you wanted to let it be known that you care about me, and not just what I can do for you. There was your window. You could've fucking done anything! But you walk away?

When Andrew returned, it was impossible for him to not feel Oz's anger.

As they drove back, tension suffused the inside of the car, making the air thick and foggy. He'd burned through his first cigarette pack and half the extra pack in the glove box, but it wasn't helping. He struggled in taking himself down a couple notches to avoid driving like a maniac, but the pressure continuously built.

"Oz."

He hit the brake sharply for a red light.

"Oz." Andrew turned toward him, but Oz stared at the traffic signal. "I don't want you to destroy yourself."

"Oh, no, huh?" He tapped his cigarette ash on the window. "I'd think it'd be a boon for you. You can't look at me when I'm dead, can you?"

"Technically, when you're dead, I could still look at you."

"If I have myself cremated, would that accommodate you then? Or would it bother you to look at my ashes too? Maybe I could vaporize myself. Or climb into a barrel of acid."

Go ahead. Try again. I dare you.

"Oz, I'm sorry."

"Are you sorry because you mean you're sorry, or because I helped you, and now you feel like an asshole?"

"I mean that I'm sorry. Can you pull over? You're scaring me."

Part of Oz wanted to drive faster. But while he picked on people for sport, and felt he'd been treated with unfair cruelty, it wasn't right to terrorize Andrew. Damn his conscience. Why wasn't the filter on his actions as open as it was with his words?

He pulled into a parking lot and turned the engine off. Andrew's hand touched his arm.

"I want you to know, I meant everything I said earlier."

I feel a ton better already.

"I'm a miserable person, Oz. I'm envious of you and sometimes my jealousy gets the better of me. I shouldn't have blasted you like that. If I was going to tell you how I felt, it shouldn't have been in anger. And I'm sorry."

Oz looked out the windshield in silence.

"But this is my problem, not yours. And I want to get over it. I like being around you. I like you. A lot." Andrew squeezed his arm. "You don't want to hear this, but I do think you're perfect. Whoever built us doesn't matter. We lost a lot through this whole mess, but I think we need to move on. Forget about everything. Your father, the Hodge conjecture, Robert, Simon, Natalie. Fuck it, and let's go."

"What are you talking about?"

"I don't think I can live this lie anymore. I may not be able to make it the next few months pretending with Robert."

"What do you mean? What are you going to do?"

"I mean, I'm going to try to stick it out until this conservatorship garbage expires, but maybe it'd be best if I went to CryoLife. I'd have the peace of mind—"

"No, you can't. Why would you do that?" Oz's mind raced. He tamped it down.

"They'd probably put me on the meds, but the whole bit about how they'll grant me my real identity after the conservatorship, and then when they let me go—"

"What makes you think they'd let you go? Or worse – look what they've already done to you. You think going to them will give you a better result? Out here you can have some freedom, and I'll keep control of your meds so they don't slip you extra shit. If you return to them, you'll be at square one. And I'm telling you the God's honest truth – for all the crazy people I know, I've never met anyone who's gone back to CryoLife."

"Just because you haven't met anyone doesn't mean they don't exist."

"I also haven't met Santa Claus, but I doubt he'll be wedging his fat ass down my chimney any time soon. At least, I wouldn't risk my life on it."

Could Andrew really be so stupid? As controlling as Robert might be, he was better than CryoLife.

How many times have I known someone even thinking about going back? And then one day, they're just gone. As if they hadn't existed in the first place. And they never return.

If Andrew really wanted to die, he should just shoot himself in the face now. Then there would be something to find.

"Okay, I'll wait out the conservatorship and then I'll leave."

"Where are you going to go?"

"I thought I'd go with you."

"With me?" Andrew nodded in response. "Well, I do have a spare room. You could take care of my basement greenhouse and ant farm. I only have one bathroom, though. Santino would have a larger space to offer you. I'm sure you'd be welcome."

"I don't want to live with Santino. I want to be with you, if you'll have me."

Oz had allowed his mind to race again – cars jetting at 200 miles an hour. Until they suddenly stopped, brakes screeching and hot trails of rubber burning off onto the track. There was the sound of twisted metal as his thoughts collided and he wondered if he'd heard Andrew correctly. If he had, was he understanding him? He was tired of suppositions.

"What does that mean, Andrew?"

"It means whatever you think it means."

"You're saying this to a man. You, who are also a man, are saying this to a gay man."

"I know who I'm saying it to."

Oz's throat felt dry. "What's wrong with Robert then?"

"I don't feel the same way about him. He'd never see me as anyone but Natalie."

"If he could, would you stay with him?"

"No."

"Because he's not gay?"

"He's not you, Oz." Andrew's fingers stroked his arm lightly, and Oz wished it'd been a short sleeved day.

"You make me feel safe, and cared about, but you don't suffocate me. You're independent and don't desperately need me. Robert makes me feel like I'm a fucking inflatable life raft." Andrew shook his head. "You're intelligent and clever. You make me laugh; you make me forget about how bad I feel. And I—"

"Wait, wait, wait." Oz pulled back his arm. "I make you forget about how bad you feel? Less than three hours ago, you were shouting at me in a parking lot, saying you hated me because I remind you of everything you want."

"I apologized for that, and I explained what was behind it. I'm not allowed to get upset?"

Oz studied Andrew carefully, trying to tease out whatever was behind the dark eyes. Freedom was a strong motivation. Incentive enough to elicit deception? Even unintentional dishonesty? It was possible. But he couldn't – he wouldn't – allow himself to be set up. No one had ever captivated him as much as Andrew, but he wanted the real deal. Anything else would be unbearable.

"No, you can be upset, but I'm allowed to be confused by you going from one end of the spectrum to the other so quickly. It's not only your feelings on the line. It makes sense for me to be cautious," Oz said. "I think it makes sense for *you* to be cautious as well. You're still figuring yourself out, and I get that. You shouldn't tie yourself into anything."

"I know what I'm doing." Andrew turned. "But if I misread that you have any interest, you don't need to take some noble high ground. Just tell me."

Maybe he'd pushed it too far.

"No, no. You didn't misread. But isn't it like you taking steps toward assimilating to the right identity? You need to value yourself enough to not sell out." He placed his hand to his own chest. "I am not *your* life preserver. If you want an escape, you have one. Whether we're friends or anything more. You don't have to buy my help with your love. The only price of my assistance is the pleasure of your company."

Oz was glad when Andrew faced him with a smile. "Thank you for not taking advantage of me."

He wasn't sure how to interpret that reaction. Was this a veiled way of admitting the professed feelings had been disingenuous? Who knew? But he was probably reading too much into things.

"Likewise."

He started the car engine and checked behind his shoulder to back out. When Andrew placed his hand on his arm, it surprised him.

"I did miss you the last few days, when you weren't around. It wasn't something I wanted to do, I'll admit. But I found myself thinking about you often," Andrew said.

"And how much you desperately hate me?" He chuckled and returned to checking the rearview mirror. Andrew withdrew his hand as he moved his arm to dig out his cigarette pack. "And my shirts? My pants? My flashlight keychain? My—"

His stomach flipped as Andrew lightly brushed the side of his face with two fingers. "About how soft your cheek was."

Oz felt like his mind was stuttering, and as he hardly ever did, he struggled to find a response. Ultimately he laughed. Humor was the best strategy for distraction. For others, and for himself. If he concentrated too much on Andrew's statement, his general lack of control could lead anywhere.

"Nice try, but I share my moisturizing secrets with no one."

Chapter 31

"You seem agitated today, Robert."

"I suppose that could be a word for it. Yes, I'm agitated."
He glanced over at Dr. Zuniga behind her desk and pulled out
his cell phone. Sitting on the edge of the couch in her office,
he tapped his foot as he slid his finger across the phone screen.
"Very agitated."

"Do you want to tell me why?"

"With your impressive degrees, I'm sure you've heard the
phrase of a picture being worth a thousand words. Why tell
you, when I can show you." Robert stood and dropped the
phone in her hand. He folded his arms. "Look at that."

The lack of shock on her face irritated him further.

"A picture of Natalie asleep?"

Technically, it was. She had her right cheek on the pillow
and her arm shoved underneath it. But that wasn't the problem.

"Look at her," he demanded.

"I am. I apologize, Robert. I'm afraid I'm not seeing what—"

"The hair. Look at what she's done to her hair." Robert
returned to the couch. "I came home three days ago to her

290

whistling in the kitchen. I walk in excited that finally she's turned a corner. And this is what I find. She hacked it off. All of it."

Was it odd that he was so devastated about Natalie's hair? He couldn't deny that he was. She'd always had beautiful, long golden hair. Granted, she'd been tying it back and it'd often been greasy and ratty, but it had been there. Once or twice he'd seen her with it down, and it made his skin tingle. Before the accident, he loved to run his fingers through her hair. He'd sit with her head in his lap and lose himself in caressing it.

"And where is it now? Where? At the bottom of a trash can with gum and banana peels?"

"Did she say why she cut it?" Zuniga asked.

"She said it was hers and she was tired of it. I don't understand. There was this time, Doctor, when she went to get her hair done, and they cut off four inches instead of two. Four." He held up his fingers. "It was still past her shoulders, but she cried for a solid week."

"This was before the accident?"

"It's always before the accident. And how could she do this? I thought she needed my written approval to make changes to her body."

"For permanent changes, yes. But we can't stop someone from getting a haircut, Robert. You couldn't have stopped her from that before."

"She wouldn't have done it before. My Natalie would've never changed herself in any way I didn't like."

"Maybe she thought you'd like the new hair. Did she ask if you did?"

"No, she didn't seem to care." Robert chuckled to release some pressure. "And that's not all. I couldn't get a picture of her in her new clothes."

"You'd said before she's been wearing sweatshirts and baggy pants, not her normal attire?"

"Oh, it's worse. Much worse. She's taken to wearing this spandex undershirt underneath men's shirts – polos and dress shirts. I asked her about it, and she says the undershirt is designed for athletes and she wants to take up running."

"Well, that sounds like the old Natalie, doesn't it?" Dr. Zuniga slid Robert's cell phone across the desk. "She wants to stay in shape for you."

"She knows I don't like that."

"What's not to like?"

"A beautiful woman jogging along the side of the road. People looking at her. It's not safe, and she shouldn't be doing that."

"Robert, in no way am I meaning to upset you further, but don't you think you're being extreme here? Women go running, and there are many beautiful women with short—"

"It may appear extreme to other people, but it's not to us. These are things we were on the same page about. There are specific things and roles Natalie and I agreed on."

"She promised you that she'd never cut her hair?" Zuniga raised an eyebrow.

"She promised that she would invest in herself for me." He leaned forward. "She doesn't have to look at herself every day. I do. If she wanted me to grow my hair out or stop shaving, I'd do it for her."

"But this isn't permanent. Perhaps she was—"

"No, no that doesn't help. Why she did it doesn't change that it's done." Robert leaned his elbows on his knees and covered his eyes with his palms.

It'd been awful to see Natalie so disfigured. And he knew that, yes, the hair and body were hers, but he was still affected. Didn't she care about him anymore?

Before she did anything new, she always consulted me. Like Brigman said – that's my role: protector, provider, and caretaker. She's not just changing her image, she's challenging my position. And that's not Natalie.

"Robert, I understand why this is so upsetting – that hair is a symbol of your wife, and you connect it strongly with a person you love."

"Yes, that's right." He leaned back on the Chesterfield sofa and closed his eyes. It was nice to be understood. Natalie used to understand him – used to anticipate his every feeling and thought. Almost like they were the same person.

"I think she's acting out. It's like a teenager getting a nose piercing. After a trauma I see many of them regress to an immature state. Think of it like going through puberty."

"Puberty?"

"As awkward as it sounds, you need to be her guide through this. That's one of the main reasons the conservatorship is established. They need structure and control. You need to step in, like a father figure."

"A father figure?" But he didn't want Natalie to be his daughter. She was supposed to be his wife. The mother of his child. "She's twenty-eight. We're married and have a son. It's not my responsibility to raise her."

"That may have been the wrong phrase, I apologize. She needs your guidance. Again, she's been through a substantial trauma. You don't think what Natalie experienced would make her consider her life and question herself? Remember how you told me when you found out about the accident?"

That day had started like an ordinary morning. He'd been at work adding notes to a remodel bid.

And the first phone call came at 10:23am.

"Mr. Keller, your wife and children have been involved in a serious vehicular accident. We need you to meet the ambulance at Savannah General—"

Had he responded? He couldn't remember. He hadn't heard anything else. He'd been gone. Out the door and speeding down the highway, the tachometer redlining and redlining.

What had been going through his mind was his family. *Natalie. Simon. Michael. My wife and children. My wife and my little boys.*

I've never felt my role more strongly than right then. Protector, provider, and caretaker.

And if that car would move fast enough, if he kept pushing his thoughts toward them—

The second call came at 11:04am.

"Mr. Keller, I apologize, sir, but if you can meet one of our officers at the police station that would be best."

"What about the ambulance? The hospital? Is my family okay and I can pick them up?"

Robert would somehow gather all three of them into his arms. He'd hold them close and never let them go. The world was a horrible, unsafe place. Its only light came from his wife and his babies.

"It's just no longer necessary for you to be at the hospital."

On the freeway he'd almost caused a pileup by coming to a complete stop in his lane. The brakes squealed and his car fishtailed. Horns blared and cars swerved. But he didn't care.

"Who's dead?" Robert whispered.

"I'm sorry, sir. What was that?"

"Who's dead?" The words came through clenched teeth, and with each sentence they were louder. "Which one of them? All of them?"

"Mr. Keller, please come to the police station."

He threw his phone across the car. It bounced off the passenger window and into the seat. He folded his arms over his steering wheel and sobbed. He'd lost everything.

In Dr. Zuniga's office, Robert looked away from her and rubbed his temple with two fingers. "Yes. It was the darkest day of my life."

"That didn't change you?" she asked.

"It did. I told Natalie it did. And that I'd never take her or Simon for granted."

"So let me ask you, Robert. While I can empathize with how upset you are about Natalie cutting her hair and wearing different clothes, would you rather have her with short hair or not at all?"

He'd confided a lot to Dr. Zuniga. Many of his feelings as well as the happenings at home, albeit usually a condensed version. But he hadn't told anyone of the wicked thoughts that'd played through his head after he'd pulled himself together to drive on to the police station:

God, if there is a God. Please don't take my wife from me. If you leave me anyone, leave me her. We can have other children, but I can't replace Natalie.

And he'd never reveal to anyone how on walking into the building and seeing only Simon, his heart had broken again. He'd held the boy to his chest and cried into his hair, partially because his son had been the survivor and not Natalie.

The guilt over recalling this calmed his anger. "You're right. She's alive. And it will grow back."

"That's right." Dr. Zuniga smiled and nodded.

"But I don't want her to do anything else. Anything. What if she comes home with a tattoo next?"

"I assure you, Robert, that won't happen. She can't permanently change her body without your authorization."

The doctor wrote a note on a separate sheet of paper before handing it to him. "This medication adjustment I'm recommending should help quiet her mind so she can concentrate more on recovery, less on adolescent distractions."

He glanced at the paper. It looked like the others – a list of medications, with a place for him to sign at the bottom. He signed as he always did. This suggestion seemed especially fitting.

"Yes, that's the problem. Her mind isn't quiet enough. Like it used to be." Robert passed the paper to Zuniga. "Is there anything else that can be done? That I can be doing?"

"It's a delicate process." She tucked the paper inside a file folder. "But continuing to engage in old activities and interaction with others will help reinforce her role. Is she still seeing her friend Shelly?"

"She's gone out with her nearly every day."

"Well, that's good. Didn't you say she seems better after being with her?"

"Yes, not like her old self, but she is happier."

"I'd encourage her to keep spending time with Shelly. Perhaps you can also integrate the family aspect by having Natalie invite Shelly and her husband over, or the four of you going on a date."

"That's a good idea."

"And if you get the chance, you might consider pulling Shelly aside and talking to her. Perhaps she could provide some insight regarding anything Natalie is struggling with specifically." Zuniga flipped through pages of the folder. "I'll be honest, Robert, she's not very open with our doctors. Very reserved when it comes to discussing her feelings."

"She can be shy and doesn't like to cause trouble or feel she's inconveniencing anyone. I'll talk to her about being more honest. Has she said anything about Simon?"

"Not that I'm seeing here."

Robert looked at the floor. Their son had been gone for over two weeks and not once had Natalie asked where he was or when he was coming back.

The school bus stopped not five feet from our mailbox. She'd wait at the curb for him, and was as excited for him to come home as he was.

"I still think having Simon stay with your mother was the best course of action," Dr. Zuniga said. "Even if it's unusual that Natalie hasn't asked about him, keep in mind the original reasons behind it. Motherhood is a huge responsibility, and she needs to become accustomed to that aspect of her life, but a slow reintroduction would be more effective. Didn't you say Shelly has children?"

"Yes. Three boys and one on the way. She's a good role model for Natalie."

"I agree. And I'd definitely push for Shelly to involve the children in activities. We also can't forget that your wife is grieving. That could be another reason she's having a difficult time reattaching to Simon. Does she talk to you about Michael? She doesn't mention him in sessions either."

"No. She hasn't asked about him."

A shelf hung on the wall in the living room upon which, among family pictures, sat a white box. On top of the box was a sculpture of a winged angel kneeling beside the small bed of an infant. The angel's head was tilted to the right as she looked at the sleeping child's face.

Robert had chosen that particular urn for Michael because the angel reminded him of how he'd seen Natalie look so tenderly at the baby. But he was unsure if Natalie knew it was an urn. He'd never ordered a plaque for the front as he wanted her to decide what to engrave on it. A poem or couplet? There was a variety of symbol selections – doves, hearts, footprints. But she ignored it.

Do you know he's there? he'd wondered many, many times.

"It's probably painful for her, Robert, but here's another opportunity to use Shelly to your advantage. Ask her to talk to Natalie about it. She might be willing to open up with her friend and start exploring her grief."

"I don't want to put Michael away, but maybe I should."

"She eventually needs to move on and nudges to start working through the loss will help her get there."

Robert briefly hesitated. He chewed the corner of his lower lip before meeting Dr. Zuniga's kind eyes.

"I've often thought that another baby would help. Natalie was happy after Simon and Michael. And she likes the art and other stuff, but she seemed to get more fulfillment from being a mother than anything else."

"And that could be what she needs, sure. But you'll want to be cautious in your approach. She's still hurting, remember."

"So am I. She was dead for sixteen months, and I hurt that entire time," Robert said. "I've hurt longer than she has."

"That's true. Think of it this way – you're more experienced with the pain and therefore more equipped to help her through it. It goes back to the same solution. The hair, the clothes, the lack of expressing her grief: You know what's best and you need to use your strength in supporting and guiding your family forward." Zuniga stood behind her desk. His phone was still at the corner and she handed it to him with a smile. "You have your goals and a path to achieve them."

No matter how upset he came in, Robert always left Zuniga's sessions feeling better about himself. As usual, the CryoLife staff were beyond wonderful, and she was right.

He had his path:

I'll try to remain neutral and patient. I'll keep reinforcing the desirable behaviors. I'll reach out to Shelly and get her working with me.

His goals:

I want Natalie acting how she used to – caring for me and our children as a wife should. We're her main priority and she ought to have an enthusiastic objective to grow and nurture our family. I want my family back.

If part of that accomplishment included a Natalie with short hair, he supposed he could tolerate it.

Chapter 32

The vacuum existence with Robert and Simon had nearly driven Andrew insane, and it puzzled him as to why Natalie would've wanted to stay home. He supposed that was all right for people like Shelly. It just wasn't for him – he wanted new experiences. However, having been fortunate enough to find this outlet in spending time with Oz, he was struck by the realization of being in another routine.

He'd seen Oz every day for the past two weeks, and usually Santino and Tinks as well. When Robert left for the office, he'd first rush through the meaningless house chores. After that, he'd walk to the pharmacy.

If Oz didn't need to work, they'd cruise around. Oz was interested in museums, music, and theater – what Robert saw as a waste. He continued to introduce Andrew to things and offbeat places he wouldn't have considered. The "underground" tattoo parlor he'd spoken of, bizarre flea markets, bars with secret backrooms. And every door always seemed open to him.

Someday maybe they'll open for me too.

Frequently they also made the drive to Pooler and the gun range. Since Red had been told about Andrew's identity, he'd stopped leering and become almost loveable in a sleazy, foul-smelling way. It was great having one more person acknowledge him, so Andrew had shifted to sharing Oz's opinion. Red was nice.

But should Oz happen to be working, Andrew would remain at the pharmacy. He'd pull over a crate in the back room, or the other chair in the office to watch Oz work, which was amusing. And when Oz could break away from what he was doing, they'd talk. Unlike Robert, who was only open to discussing a limited number of topics, Oz could talk about pretty much anything, including art. So while Andrew still wasn't sure if he could reciprocate Oz's feelings, being around him was a refreshing change from home.

"So, did you talk to Shelly about her, Clark, and the kids coming over for dinner?" Robert had asked him last night.

He'd been hounding Andrew about this idea for the past two weeks. Suddenly, Robert wanted everyone to get together. It made Andrew's skin crawl – he hadn't seen Shelly since their initial meeting, though he periodically texted her trivial shit. As his alibi, she was worth investing a text every now and then.

"This apartment is too small to entertain anyone."

"I told you, I'm fine if they'd prefer their house, or we could meet somewhere else. We could take the kids to that pizza place with the ball pit."

Let's see – intelligent conversations with a man who doesn't treat me like a subordinate, or shrieking children in a pool of plastic balls. Decisions, decisions.

"I don't think it will work, Robert."

"Why not?"

"Shelly's uncomfortable."

"With what? With me? I've known her for—"

"No." Andrew shook his head. "She's super pregnant. She's ready to crap out her kid any day—"

"Crap out her kid?" Robert's brow furrowed.

"Well, that's what it is."

"Is that how you view having Simon? Having Michael? Crapping them out?"

He shrugged. *Shitting them out? Backwards vomiting them out? Flushing—*

"It's concerning to me that you feel that way," Robert said. "What does Shelly say when you talk about her 'crapping out' her child?"

"We don't talk about that. Robert, try to be understanding."

"I am *more* than understanding."

"No, you're not. Shelly can't even sit comfortably. She feels ugly, and she's cranky. She doesn't want to drag her screaming kids to a pizza place to shoot the shit with you for two hours. She's not feeling well."

"She's well enough to go out with you alone. Every day." He folded his arms and drummed his fingers on his bicep. "For more than two hour stretches."

"It's not as bad in the afternoon or early evening."

"So you can schedule something during those times then."

If Robert kept pressing, Andrew knew he'd have to alter his current schedule with Oz. This thought made him aware that he'd jumped from the pretending-to-be-Natalie routine to a new one. Unlike the last time though, he felt driven to keep what he had, as well as further resentment toward Robert for trying to take it away.

"Robert, Shelly is my friend. You have your own friends."

"You don't think Clark is my friend?"

"Then go have a beer with him alone. Why do you need me with you?"

"I don't need you with me, I want you with me."

"And I don't want to put my friend in an uncomfortable situation, so will you stop?" Andrew walked toward the hallway.

"Simon would probably like to go, Nat. He likes Shelly's boys. He—"

"We're not pulling him out of baseball camp for pizza and a ball pit."

And I'm not giving up my escape because you have a jones for Shelly. Andrew grabbed his keys from the basket by the door. *Why you'd have one I have no idea. She's a fucking cow.*

"I'm going out. Not sure when I'll be back," he called.

"Okay. I love—"

Andrew shut the front door.

*

"You should be more careful." Santino's eyes watched him across the billiard table.

Part two of the new schedule was a visit to the bar after the pharmacy closed. Santino and Tinks were often there, and they were teaching him to play snooker. Andrew loved feeling like "one of the guys." He liked being with Oz, although the feeling of uncertainty still shadowed their time alone together. But acceptance among a group of other men? This was the recognition he'd dreamed about while spying on the frat house.

Andrew changed the position of his cue to target a different red ball. He looked over at Santino. "This one?"

"Careful in the game you're playing with Robert, not snooker. What are you going to do when he finds out?"

"He's not going to. His head's too far up his own ass." Andrew struck the cue ball. As expected, it lightly grazed a red ball, hit the side, and aligned multiple promising shots for Tinks. "Goddamn it."

"No worries." Oz switched his cue to the opposite hand and took a cigarette from his pocket. "He needs all the help he can get, don't you?"

Tinks tucked a cue chalk in his pocket and approached the table. "Keep telling yourself that." He squeezed his eyes tight shut before opening them and shaking his head. "Whatever makes you feel better."

"So you pop off with something stupid like, 'Go have a beer with Clark alone.' What would you do if Robert walked through these doors right now?" Santino asked. "Nothing is stopping him."

"He doesn't drink."

"And neither do you. And neither did Natalie. So why would Natalie say 'Go have a beer with Clark.' You don't think that's suspicious?" He took a drink from his glass and replaced it on a nearby table. "You're letting Oz get too much into your head, which is dangerous. Notice how much alcohol is required for me to tolerate his presence."

"There's an idea. Let's get Robert drunk. Or high." Oz appeared to place zero concentration into his next shot. He braced his fingertips on the side of the pool table and stretched his hand. "We'll make him a special White Widow pie. That'd be fun. And put some Strawberry Diesel in the kid's smoothies. He'll be taking a piss in a litter box."

Andrew still hadn't accepted the offer of alcohol or drugs, though he'd thought about it. But his abstinence was proof of how cautious he really was being, despite what Santino thought.

"You could easily be taking a lot less risks." Santino moved the spider rest in front of a red ball to reach the cue ball. "For example, you could cover your ass by giving him his pizza party."

"You don't understand. That'd be unbearable."

"If man can climb Annapurna and live to tell the tale, I'm confident you can leave Fat Bandit's Pizza Shack with your limbs intact. Most of them anyway." He seemed to put as little focus into the shot as Oz did, yet he potted a pink followed by another red. "And then Robert will back off for a while."

"Maybe we should give you the weed instead." Oz smiled. "Chill you out so you can deal with them."

Andrew fucked up another shot. Why was he even trying? "No. I can't do it."

"You could at least spend some time with Shelly. What if Robert calls her and starts asking questions? He finds out you haven't seen her in weeks, and there goes your alibi. What then? How do you explain where you've been going?"

"Petting ducklings at the park? Those puny bitches won't rat me out if they know what's good for them."

"Yes, you think you're both hilarious, but you aren't this stupid." Santino came around the table and leaned in closer to Andrew, lowering his voice. "Do you understand what a conservatorship means? You don't have more than the most basic rights. If you push him too much, he'll pack you up and leave. He'll take you to CryoLife. He could make you disappear. And no amount of humor can save you."

It was a sobering thought, and Andrew knew Santino was right. Robert could burst through the doors of the bar, drag him out, and lock him up. He had full control. As much as Andrew didn't want to relinquish the peace he had being with Oz and the others, flexibility was probably wise.

"Fine, I'll tone it down. December twenty-eighth. Then he can go fuck himself in the pizza shack's ball pit, which I'll personally tell him."

"No, you need to chill until he grants you the identity."

"At the end of the six months."

"Reread the terms of your servitude. Your conservator *may* grant it to you in six months. *May.* He doesn't have to. Nothing compels him except for your good behavior. So you're not fully released until Robert says you are. Ergo, for your own good, stop being a dick." Santino glanced to Tinks. "Are you all right?"

Tinks had paused over the table. He took a deep breath. "I'm thinking."

"Why waste excess brain power when he's going to clear the table anyway?" Oz shrugged. "I never do when I'm on his team. Throw the cue ball out the window. That fucker will still win."

"What happens if he won't grant the Natalie identity to me in six months?"

"What do you think? You go back to CryoLife."

"And then what?"

"I have no idea. None of us do. Even Chuckles the Pot Dealer has never met a single person who's been transferred to CryoLife." He nodded toward Oz. "Don't you think there's a reason for that?"

So Santino also considered this lack of evidence as proof to CryoLife's ulterior motives. As a means to an end, perhaps a little give was a good idea.

If believing in Santa Claus could potentially kill me, I guess it's safer to not believe.

He should at least keep his excuses intact by calling Shelly and going to lunch with her.

"Okay, I'll be more careful. Tomorrow I'll—"

"Oh, God! Make it stop! Make it stop!"

Andrew took a quick step away from the billiard table to see Tinks on the ground. He held his head and rocked on his knees, bellowing the phrases between howls. Every muscle in his body was in spasm, and Andrew wondered if someone could explode from their own skin. But he could do no more than wonder. He felt immobilized with his hand clenched around the pool cue. Everyone else had the same reaction as the bar was silent except for the screaming.

And whatever is playing inside your head. He couldn't stop his stare.

"Move!" Oz had been cautious regarding physical contact with Andrew, but now he pushed him aside to get to Tinks. "Someone call an ambulance."

Ambulance? What was an ambulance? Nothing registered beyond Tinks's cries. The sound shattered each of Andrew's thoughts as they neared completion.

"Stop! Stop! Stop!" Tinks smashed his head against the concrete floor.

Santino slid to his knees and took Tinks's head into his lap to prevent him from beating it in. Tinks struggled violently to free himself, clawing at Santino's hands and trying to push away. Santino held firm, though he quickly discontinued the verbal comfort he'd attempted as everything was drowned out.

On the ground Oz searched through the pockets of Tinks's jacket and pants. "Where's your pen, brother? Do you have it with you?"

Tinks's response was to vomit over Santino's lap. The sour smell of the bile and acid turned Andrew's own stomach. He covered his mouth with his palm.

"Make it stop!" Tinks wailed, his face covered in vomit and blood. "God, make it stop!"

"Find the fucking pen, Oz!" The goo in Santino's lap made it more difficult to keep Tinks secure. Santino held one side of his neck and his other hand gripped Tinks's hair, vomit oozing between his fingers. "Find the fucking—"

"I've got it!"

Oz had pulled Tinks's wallet from his pocket. He unfolded it and slipped out a foil package the size of a toothpick. After he broke the foil's seal, he removed an autoinjector pen.

"Hold on, just hold on." Oz put the pen to Tinks's thigh, trying to steady him with one hand as he clicked the button at its end to activate the needle. He held the pen in place and shared a horrified look with Santino until finally Tinks's muscles released.

Andrew didn't feel like he took another breath until they heard the sirens. He knew he should do something, anything besides standing there paralyzed. But he didn't know how to handle an emergency situation. Santino and Oz looked like they knew exactly what to do.

As Tinks relaxed into what appeared to be semi-conscious whimpering, Santino moved his head onto a folded jacket. They both uncurled his body, leaving him on his side. Tinks's mouth opened as he moaned, and Andrew could see that the blood was coming from both his nose and broken teeth. Through the film of vomit his skin was beginning to bruise. But while the image served to heighten Andrew's nausea, the other two men stayed near their friend.

Oz sat in the mess, slime saturating the knees of his pants and flecked across his forearms. His hand pressed Tinks's shoulder. "It'll be okay. They're almost here."

As a constant showman, in everything Oz did there was a sense of the action being completed with the awareness of someone watching. Even when he'd revealed the emotional story behind his death, the way in which he conducted himself was cognizant of an audience. Andrew struggled and failed to remember an instance at which he'd seen the "unobserved Oz." It was like turning at the right instant to see the sun sparkle on the water. Without the distortion of his focus being on the world, the sight of simply unguarded Oz felt similar to hearing his name spoken for the first time.

Hearing my name is seeing June Celebration *in a centerfold – the visibility and appreciation of the entire piece, corner to corner. But in all actuality, that painting is seven feet high. And seeing you this way is how it'd be to look at it from that true perspective.*

Andrew felt very small. Not because he hadn't done anything to help Tinks, but for the first time since he'd emerged into this existence, the lens through which he viewed the world had inverted. Something was more important than himself and his individual set of problems. And amid the CryoLife/Robert bullshit, there really was honest, unadulterated compassion in the world.

And it comes from you. A sense of warmth spread through Andrew's chest as he watched Oz beside Tinks.

The rigid hold the incident had on him loosened when the paramedics carried Tinks out on a stretcher. Andrew dropped the pool cue he'd held and followed Oz and Santino through the front door. The three of them stood together while the ambulance whirled away.

"Who knew Chopin could be so dangerous?" Oz said it in a slow monotone, as if he were in a daze.

"Deadly. He could've killed himself. If I hadn't been holding his head, his brains would've been on the floor."

"I guess having a damaged brain is better than having one grated on a concrete floor."

"I think he'd disagree with you."

A reflective silence passed between Santino and Oz, and Andrew wondered if they'd forgotten he was still present. Or perhaps they were angry that he'd done nothing—

"That's how I feel sometimes." Oz's words were barely audible, and he stared at the ground.

He still had that vulnerable look about him, but Andrew was reminded of his comments regarding his purposeful self-destruction. Before it hadn't bothered him much, since then Oz had been no more than an entertaining alternate plan. Also, the brashness with which he'd said it made Andrew feel the statement was another attention-getter. But insinuating in this open moment that there were times he'd rather not exist, wrenched a piece of Andrew's soul. He felt a panic as if the seven-foot canvas leaned forward, threatening to crush him.

"No. Don't leave me." He turned to Oz and wrapped his arms around his neck. "Please don't leave me."

Andrew wanted to cry, but he refused to release the tears. How would he make it alone if Oz left completely? Fifteen minutes earlier, altering the schedule of seeing his friends had felt unbearable. That temporary adjustment now seemed petty. What if Oz disappeared? What if he felt so defeated that he couldn't take it anymore?

There would be nothing left. Absolutely nothing.

Being held by Oz was very different from when Robert had held him. There was something about the way Robert would almost seize him, curling his knuckles to grasp him with the tips of his fingers. It was a frantic, anguished hug, as if to prevent his Natalie from leaving him – snagging Andrew with a double barbed fish hook. Robert made him feel weak, dependent, owned.

Oz's embrace wasn't one of possession. His left hand curved around Andrew's shoulder blade, and his right rested at his mid-back. He could pull away without being snared. Andrew also felt his shoulders roll forward a little, which was something Robert had never done despite also being taller. Oz brought Andrew in, enfolding him without anxiety. Deliberate, but not desperate – a fantastic difference.

"I'm not going anywhere," Oz said.

They were just words. Logically meaningless. Oz could detour to Pooler on the way home, check out his gun from Red, and shoot himself. The assurance made Andrew feel better though.

He'd had his eyes squeezed closed, first imagining worst-case scenarios of being alone, and then his mind had wandered to how comfortable it was being in Oz's arms. How he didn't lose track of the seconds he was touched, since he hadn't felt the need to measure them. But with the relief from his promise to remain, Andrew opened his eyes.

Santino was staring at him. *Man with a Pipe* expression again – his eyebrows looked as if they were trying to frown and rise together, causing furrows across his forehead.

Andrew abruptly removed his arms from Oz's neck and took a step back.

Commence another awkward intermission.

Santino was the first to speak: "I suppose we can now agree there are worse things than a two hour pizza party."

"You smell like someone ralphed on you. Let's also agree that you need to be hosed down like a bitch in a wet t-shirt contest."

"If there were a wet t-shirt contest, you wouldn't be interested in bitches being hosed." From his peripheral vision, Andrew saw Santino put an arm around Oz's shoulder.

He knew that Oz was looking at him, but couldn't bring himself to meet his eyes.

"Just because I wouldn't be interested in the results doesn't mean I wouldn't enthusiastically blast people with a high-powered water hose," Oz said, but his tone was without its usual swagger.

"Let's go home." Santino nudged Andrew forward and the three of them walked off into the night.

Chapter 33

In the week that separated Tinks's attack and his return to the bar, Andrew had the reluctant outing with Robert, Shelly, Clark, and their hell-beast children.

Putting in my time. Another inmate on the chain gang.

But he tried to refrain from thinking of it that way. As Santino had said, obviously there were worse things than a pizza party. There was Tinks's suffering. The potential of Robert finding out about Andrew's lies and taking him away to CryoLife. Or Oz leaving forever, though he'd said he wouldn't.

While comforted at the time, the horrible thought of Oz disappearing continued to surface in Andrew's mind, along with the other ideas that he'd been trying to riddle out for weeks. That night when Andrew finally drummed up the courage to make eye contact with Oz as he'd dropped him off at the apartment, there'd been a look of confusion on his face.

Well, what do you want me to say? What do you want me to do? Andrew remained in the passenger seat as the car idled.

Do you want me to try and explain? To hug you again? To tell you how extraordinary it felt?

He definitely wanted something. Possibly needed something.

"I don't understand," Oz said.

"I'm sorry, I don't either." But Andrew reached across and touched Oz's cheek, which he hadn't done since the day of his haircut. Another anchor while he figured things out. "When I know, I'll tell you."

He'd opened the car door, stepped out, and shut it without saying more.

You can't keep doing this. Think, Andrew.

But it was hard to think. He could block out the cheesy pop music, screaming children, and inane chatter between the other adults. But it was difficult to concentrate when he could still almost feel Oz's arms around him.

My ear was against his face, and when he told me he wasn't going to leave me I could both hear and feel him speak. And his breath did smell like pine trees, but the collar of his shirt was cigarettes and something fresh … Laundry detergent? Cologne? Something that made me wish I had more space in my lungs to breathe him in. It reminded me of—

Splat.

One of Shelly's spawn had thrown a slice of pizza at his chest. The child hooted from across the table, pulling its feet up to squat in the chair like an ape.

"Carter!" Shelly yelled. "You've stained Natty's shirt! Look what you've done!"

He is looking, you idiot. Hence the laughter. Andrew peeled the slice off and considered flinging it back.

"Tell her you're sorry!"

"Sowwie." Shelly's children didn't use the letter "R." Apparently, this was viewed as cute and not stupid.

"It's fine."

"So, the new hair is starting to grow on me, Natty." Shelly leaned across the table and Andrew tried to hide his disgust at that hideous nickname and with Shelly herself.

He hadn't lied to Robert about the state she was in. This engorged person looked like a snake who'd swallowed a large egg. Her appearance hadn't bothered him when it hadn't been so obvious. It was similar to the old feeling of looking at Oz, only instead of seeing in the bloated, reptilian Shelly what *he* wanted to be, she was an image of what Robert wanted for him. And while that would never happen, it was still sickening.

"Yeah, I like it," he said.

"I've gotten used to it too, but I still prefer it longer." Robert sat beside him. He reached over and touched a piece of Andrew's hair, rubbing the strands between his thumb and first finger. "You'll grow it out, won't you?"

"I don't think so."

"I really—"

Splat.

Another slice hit almost the same place as the first before dropping into Andrew's lap. The monkey-child bounced with glee.

"Carter! Stop it, you naughty boy!"

"Sowwie."

"Rob, you men don't understand." Shelly slugged Clark playfully. "We have so much to do, why would we bother with hair? Natty, I bet it takes you half the time to fix it."

It did take less time. Hours of excruciating worry ending with a poor result had been replaced by minutes of moderate anxiety concluding in a half decent pass. He'd never go back to the long hair. Ever.

"Well, just so you don't think about doing that, Shell," Clark said. "I like your hair the way it is."

"You wouldn't want me to put the time I spend styling my hair into something else?"

"You waste enough time on the internet looking at mason jars and tissue paper crafts as it is."

This is what you want me to be. Andrew shook his head so Robert would remove his hand. *A fat milk cow that spends her days raising hellions, curling hair, and glue-gunning ribbon onto clothespins.*

What did Oz want him to be? He'd never said. He'd never insinuated. He just … was. Like he didn't mind Andrew moving in a separate orbit.

We spend a lot of time together already, but what would all day with you be like?

Whenever Robert had time off from work Andrew was subjected to Oz's constant presence. But he hadn't become exhausted with him yet. Being around him was invigorating, since he didn't have to put so much energy into placating the Natalie fantasy and also—

Don't even think about it. Andrew shot the child a glare as it raised a pizza slice. It giggled and lowered its weapon.

"Would you like that, Nat?" Robert nudged him.

"What?"

"When Shell goes, like last time, they'll drop the boys at our place."

"Why?"

"So we can watch them until she and Clark come home from the hospital."

Shelly nodded. "You used to love when the boys would stay over. Not as much as Clark and I loved it, but …"

When she trailed off and gave a sidelong look to her husband, Andrew felt like he threw up in his mouth.

"I don't think so."

"Why not?" Robert turned to him.

We don't have enough fucking Benadryl.

"There's not enough room." Thank God for small apartments.

"No problem, you can stay at our house then," Clark said. "It'd be better for the boys to not be out of their element anyway. Of course, you can bring Simon with you."

"Simon's still staying with my mom for a while."

Shelly tipped her head. "Your mom? Natty, I thought you said he was at baseball camp."

"That's where I thought he was." Andrew shrugged.

No one said anything, and he was about to drift back to his thoughts when Robert put an arm around him.

"You call us to come over and watch the boys. We'll be there whenever you need us."

Fuck. We're at climbing Annapurna levels.

"That's great! Takes such a load off my mind that the boys will be taken care of …"

As Shelly droned, Andrew's attention moved away from Fat Bandit's Pizza Shack and how he would overcome monkeysitting Shelly's flock. There was Robert's hand on his shoulder with the usual possessive firmness.

But instead of beginning another count he thought of Oz touching the same shoulder, his hand flat and relaxed, gently bringing Andrew closer. The feeling simmered under Robert's thick fingers digging into his skin. If Santino hadn't been there with that look of worry, what could've happened? Would he have pulled back only to look at Oz? In doing so, would he have been able to make a solid decision about how he felt?

Perhaps that's what he needed to make up his mind – to be in that situation uninterrupted.

The next time I see him. I'll have some excuse, I'll do it again, and we'll see what happens.

Robert's grip eased, making it easier to imagine the hand wasn't his.

My temple to his shoulder and I can feel that it's a full embrace. When Robert touches me, it's like only the muscles in his arms are firing. But Oz wanted me close to him with everything. And it was gin and cigarettes and clean laundry on the line. Maybe I would've stayed there for hours. Never left, never—

Splat.

A third stain on what was a pristine polo. But this time—

"Soww—"

Andrew pulled the pizza slice off his shirt and threw it across the table.

Splat.

Hard. Across the child's face before dropping onto its plate. And the sauce-covered baboon's mouth dropped open as it screamed.

"Sowwie" you dumb motherfucking—

Robert's hold tightened and he twisted Andrew to look at him. "Natalie! What's wrong with you?" He looked across the table where Shelly was cleaning the boy's face with a napkin between pecking its cheeks with kisses. "Is he okay? I'm sorry."

"He's fine." Clark smoothed his son's hair and turned a harsh look to Andrew. "I don't care what you do with your child, but don't touch my son."

"I didn't touch him. That jackass has been throwing shit at me—"

"Watch your language, this is a family place."

"And you let him keep on doing it. 'Sowwie.' 'Sowwie.' 'Sowwie.' Fuck that."

"Rob, control your wife."

"Control your child and teach him to talk like a human being instead of a fucking—"

When Robert stood, he drew Andrew with him so quickly that he almost fell. "We're leaving."

"Good. I didn't want—"

"I don't care." Robert looped a rigid arm around Andrew. He looked over his shoulder as he propelled him out of the room, his tone milder. "I'm sorry, Clark. And Shell. Very sorry."

"I'm not."

Robert didn't reply and pulled Andrew outside the building.

En route to the car, Andrew regretted nailing the little crotch fungus with a pizza slice and losing his temper.

I should've chucked it at Clark or Shelly. It's not the kid's fault they haven't taught him to behave. He's yet another person stuck in a shit situation. Like Simon. Like me.

But besides the slight guilt of beaming the toddler instead of its parents, Andrew could hear Santino's scolding in his head. He was playing with fire and had just shot a stream of lighter fluid into the flames.

And it wasn't only the possibility of return to CryoLife and the potential disappearance his friends had alluded to. As Robert released him once they were at the vehicle, the other more terrifying punishment jumped to mind.

Oh, my God. This is it. That's what he's going to do. Throw me in the car and do it right here, right now.

He shrank along the car door as Robert towered over him.

"Natalie, what the hell is wrong with you? A five-year-old throws a slice of pizza, and you flip out?"

"But you saw him. He started it. And they weren't doing a damn thing."

"They were disciplining their child as they saw fit. You had no right to do that!"

Andrew didn't want to apologize. The only thing he'd done wrong was refraining from throwing the pizza at Clark and Shelly instead. Or in addition to. But the way Robert was looking at him and shaking conveyed that an apology was necessary to try and avoid the dire consequences Andrew feared.

"I'm sorry."

"You should be. And you'll be calling them tomorrow to apologize yourself."

"Okay."

Robert's shoulders drooped, and Andrew released a breath he'd been holding. "I don't understand. How are you going to get better if you don't start … I mean, what's so wrong with children, Nat? You used to love them. You never would've hurt Carter before, ever."

A pizza slice to the face isn't going to scar the cretin. Maybe he'll learn what his parents obviously aren't willing to teach him.

"They make me uncomfortable, Robert. I'm sorry."

"Why do they make you uncomfortable?"

"I don't know."

"Does Simon make you uncomfortable?"

"Yes."

"Why?"

Andrew shrugged. "I'm a private person and like to take a shit in peace?"

"Natalie, the language needs to stop." Robert let out a long exhale before looking at him. "Is this because of Michael? You're hurting because of him?"

"Who?"

It occurred to him after the crushed look came into Robert's eyes. Fuck. It'd slipped his mind. But how was he supposed to remember the infant's name? It wasn't around or anything.

"Who?" Robert repeated, though not in anger. "Our baby, Nat."

"I'm sorry, I forgot."

"How could you forget? His pictures are on the walls at home, and you have a whole scrapbook full of footprints, his hospital cap, fingernail clippings and God knows what else. He's been sitting on the shelf in our living room since you came back."

Andrew tried not to find it entertaining that Robert's words made him think of a gargoyle.

"Why are you smiling? Do you think that's funny?" Robert snapped. "I fail to see the humor in you forgetting about our son."

"I know, it's not funny."

"Then why were you smiling?"

You're an idiot, Robert. An idiot.

But then a lie. A lovely lie that stank of Natalie:

"I was thinking about him. I'm sorry, I miss him."

As he'd hoped, the Natalie stench rolled over every faux pas. It was like the humid air that levitated over a landfill. Robert was blind to his deficiencies again.

"It's okay, hon," he said in his usual level voice.

Andrew hated it, but to complete his stirring performance he allowed a hug. He used the time spent clenched in Robert's meaty claws to continue his catalogue of what made an embrace from Oz far more desirable.

Chapter 34

Tinks first came back to the bar the night Andrew was with Robert and Natalie's friends. Oz hadn't been too worried about him once he'd been admitted to the hospital as he immediately began to receive reports from his network. His sources reported that besides the teeth, Tinks had broken his nose and fractured his skull seven times. But he'd be okay, and wasn't under the care of CryoLife doctors.

Oz had been more concerned about Andrew. Besides the current outing with Robert, his outburst after Tinks's fit weighed on his mind. At first, it'd been wonderful. He'd never had someone throw themselves at him and beg him not to leave. It made him feel so wanted.

And that it was you?

He hadn't been able to curb his feelings about Andrew, but he'd been careful in keeping his distance. Oz knew of Andrew's general aversion to touch – he'd described the counting, the claustrophobia, the walls closing in on him whenever Robert was near. And Oz had caught the palpable discomfort when Santino or Tinks neared the invisible boundary of his space. Sure, there was the occasional time when Andrew would touch his hand or lean close, but nothing with any frequency.

Yet suddenly there he was. His arms around Oz's neck and his chest heaving with panic.

Have I ever been so overwhelmed with something this amazing before? In front of the dry erase boards, in my other world, and at my prime. He'd pulled him close, feeling awful for being happy when Andrew was upset.

"I'm not going anywhere," he'd said.

The proofs and conjectures once fell like raindrops, and I could pull complicated ideas out of the sky. But there's never been anything as perfect as this.

However, just after Andrew had relaxed in his arms, he tensed and pulled away. Sharp and quick. And then he wouldn't even look at Oz, like he was ashamed or hadn't meant to embrace him.

Oz had felt Santino's arm around his shoulder, and hot, bitter tears clouded his eyes. He wanted to shrug his friend away, but also cry in his arms. What the fuck? Nothing was fair. What had happened to any of them, or their suffering. He'd lost everything until Andrew. Somehow Andrew eclipsed what'd been the most significant thing in his past life and made it worth losing in exchange for him.

So why can't I have you? What's the point of this? Why don't we let each other pound our heads into a concrete floor if heartache is all that's left.

At the bar, he'd pulled away from Santino's arm, pushing everything to the back of his mind in favor of another stupid joke to diffuse the situation. There hadn't been much awkwardness between them since, but on the night of Tinks's return Santino had begun lecturing him about it.

"I'm glad you sided with me that he should be cautious. That does help, but it's going to become more dangerous as the conservatorship expiration moves closer. Robert isn't going to let you have him so easily."

Moot. Andrew won't let me have him either.

"The way he talks about Robert being so devoted to the idea of recapturing this perfect family in a perfect world … When his vision is in jeopardy, he'll act."

"I'll fucking kill him," Oz said.

"You may not get that chance. Robert could spirit Andrew away, and you'd never see him again." Santino edged closer. "That's why I'm telling you, as a friend, that you cannot sink into this. For God's sake, Oz, don't lose yourself in him. Don't be so stupid as to fall in love with what you can't have. He could be gone tomorrow."

"Anything and everything could be gone tomorrow. No one knows that better than us." He chose to ignore Santino's comments about love since he didn't know what he was talking about. "You can't spend time today being paranoid about the future."

"It's not paranoia to be cautious and go about things in a patient, logical way. I'm worried about you. I see how you look at him, and how attached you're becoming to the idea—"

"Over here!"

Oz raised his hand and waved as Tinks walked into the bar.

Thank God, I can't stand this sermon anymore.

Tinks approached their table with an unusual spring to his step. Parts of his face were still purple from bruising, and his nose looked crooked, but he smiled from ear to ear. What type of drugs had they put him on to stop the music this time? From his jovial manner it was obviously a good batch –

riddled with all kinds of happy pills. He couldn't wait to fill the prescription and see what was in it.

"Hey guys, where's Andrew?"

"Choking down pizza at Fat Bandit's. Probably trying not to kill small children." Oz smiled and kicked the legs of the chair beside him. "Sit. How are you?"

"Actually, will you step outside with me a minute?" Tinks moved the chair under the table. "I have something to show you."

Without waiting for them, Tinks crammed his hands inside the pockets of the black down vest he wore and marched to the side exit. Oz traded a look with Santino before they followed.

The security light above the door illuminated the alley. Tinks rocked on his heels and his eyes gleamed.

"What's with the shit-eating grin?" Oz removed his cigarette pack and lighter. "And that gay life preserver?"

"Life preserver, did you say?" Tinks's smile spread and they could see his teeth, including the two new ones. "The irony of your words, my friend ..."

He unzipped the vest and held it open. The inside was lined with two dozen flat bundles, each about the size of a dollar bill. Black wire connected the tops of the packages.

Oz caught his breath, and the cigarette fell from his lips.

"What's that, Tinks?" Santino took a step back.

"C4. Twenty-four pounds." He zipped the vest, patted the front, and gave Oz a wink. "You're not the only one with far-reaching connections."

Hiding the explosives loosened Oz's mind.

"What the fuck are you doing with twenty-four pounds of C4 in a vest? Are you insane?"

"This is possibly the sanest thing I've ever done." His broad grin faded. "It's not going to happen to me again. I'm not going to let it."

"So you'll blow yourself up next time? Twenty-four pounds of C4 will take down a fucking building! Even if you're a miserable bastard, you can't kill a bunch of people!"

"That's where you come in." Tinks looked at them. "When it happens next time, you get everyone out. Then I'll do it."

"But your sedative pen. We can be quicker about that. It seemed to calm you down," Santino pleaded.

"Calm me down?" Tinks yelled, the bruises on his face growing darker. "Sure, it calmed me down after I'd beaten my fucking face in. It keeps me from finishing the job. It sets me up for the next time, and the next time, and the fucking next time!" He took a breath. "I'm tired, guys. I'm tired of waiting. I want it to be done."

"Tinks, it's your right to kill yourself, but you can't endanger anyone else. If it happens again, take your shot and use a gun. If you can get twenty-four pounds of C4, you can get a gun. Fuck, I'll give you one of mine." Oz didn't want Tinks to kill himself either, but this line of reasoning could buy time. Time to create a plan. "Just take that thing off."

"No, I've thought this through." He ran the tip of his tongue across his bottom lip and met Oz's eyes. "If I blow myself up, no one will put me back together. They won't be able to find the pieces of my brain to try. Not my family. Not anyone."

There hadn't been more to say in protest. The prospect of continually being saved was terrible. And by the time CryoLife took its talons out, who knew who or what you might be? Tinks's skewed logic came from wanting to be left at peace.

"So, neither of you have anything to worry about. Or Andrew – you can tell him the plan, or I will." Tinks's smile returned. "C4 is the safest explosive. The only thing that'll set it off is my ignition switch. And I give you my word that I'll wait until you, and anyone else who happens to be around, are safe before I ignite it."

He didn't receive a response.

"I get that you're shocked. But you've got to understand – for me this is a life preserver. When I wear it, I feel in control. I feel free." Tinks punched Santino's arm. "Let's play snooker. I think I could even take you tonight."

He walked back out the alley toward the bar's entrance and when he turned the corner, Santino grabbed Oz's shoulder. The large hand squeezed sharply, causing him to wince.

"Oz, I know you're not a proponent of the antipsychotics, but when you fill his prescription, give him the hard stuff, and we can talk him out of this."

"I don't think it will help. It had no effect on him last time. He's not psychotic."

"What do you call strolling around with twenty-four pounds of explosives in a vest? It's not normal!"

But Oz knew there was no convincing Tinks, and he understood why.

If I'm ever certain it's coming back, that's what I'll do. I can't go through it again. And while I have the capability, I'll completely destroy myself.

He was positive that despite the hostility between them, Brigman would intervene, if only to "fix" his mistake. In the past decade had his father discovered a combination of molecules, a brain tissue pattern that made one want to be a doctor? Want to follow orders without disagreement?

Oz shuddered. No. He'd never allow that to happen. He would take matters into his own hands and trade his entire marijuana inventory for his own explosives.

But we're not there yet. He shook out his right hand before removing a new cigarette from his pack. *I still open milk caps like a regular person and can button my own shirts. I get why you want to do it though, Tinks.*

"He's decided." Oz lit his cigarette. "I'll check out whatever they're giving him and increase the pain meds."

"We cannot allow him to wear a suicide vest. He doesn't think clearly when the music comes back. With how intense the pain is he won't be able to wait. He'll blow it immediately. Innocent people—"

"So we'll switch it out."

"Switch it out?"

"We'll get enough pot and vodka in him, and then we'll change the vest for a safe one. We'll bury the real one in your yard."

"And when the music returns and he isn't able to blow himself up on the spot?"

Oz took a long drag before responding. "We'll give him the shot, drive him out to the middle of nowhere, and return his vest if he wants it."

"But—"

"I don't want him to die either, but if he's ready it's his decision. You'd better believe that when I go out, I'll be doing so giving the finger to CryoLife myself, if I can."

He shoved both hands in his pockets as Santino studied him.

Several moments into the quiet, his friend finally spoke: "Is that why you're being so reckless with Andrew?"

"Is what why? And I'm no more reckless than I usually am. I like being reckless. Cheerfully reckless."

"Are you sick?"

"I do have a habit of interpreting innocent things with sexual innuendo. It's just so *hard* not to."

"Oz." Santino stepped closer and put a hand on his arm. "It wouldn't be the same as before. I'd make sure he couldn't—"

Oz shrugged him off with a laugh. "I'm way too many G&Ts short of having this discussion with you. And it's not necessary anyway." He removed his cigarette and flicked it to the ground. "I'm peachy, brother. Or cantaloupey. Or pineappley. Whatever suits you."

"I only want you to know that if it ever does come to that, or if you feel—"

"Has it occurred to you that a man plastered with twenty-four pounds of C4 is expecting us? That's not the type of person we should keep waiting."

Oz turned and walked up the alley alone. He appreciated the sentiments, but he had no faith in the legal system. If he'd thought making Santino his medical proxy would block Brigman, he would've done it a long time ago. There'd be no stopping him.

Except for Tinks's ingenious plan. That'd work. Shreds of this oh-so-perfect body you created for me raining from the sky. Jigsaw me together again, you fucker.

But that wasn't for a while, and possibly never. Oz was fine, and Santino was wrong. The strain in his hands had absolutely nothing to do with how he felt about Andrew.

Chapter 35

"Thanks for letting me come by, Shell," Robert said. "I appreciate it."

"Not a problem. I was going to call you anyway."

He watched her across the kitchen. She removed the glass carafe from the coffeemaker and poured a black stream into a mug before shuffling over. He smiled as he accepted the cup and cradled it in his hands.

This was how things were supposed to be. Husband at work, wife at home. Sounds of children playing in the other room. Sunlight streaming into a clean, lemon floor cleaner scented kitchen. Shelly sat opposite him, visibly attentive to everything he had to say. His life used to be like this.

"I've been so worried about Natty lately, Rob."

"I was shocked she didn't call and apologize to you and Clark. I specifically told her to."

"Perhaps she forgot, and we forgive her anyway. Carter was a bit rambunctious that night."

"Carter is five. Natalie is twenty-eight. And she never would've done that before."

It wasn't like Robert hadn't been irritated by the child's behavior. Shelly and Clark had a lax parenting style he didn't agree with. At the first pizza throw, Robert would've taken Simon out and they would've left. Natalie's reaction from the beginning struck him as odd. She'd pulled the first two slices off her shirt with an angry grimace and set them on the table.

Before you would've burst into tears because he'd stained your blouse. You'd run into the restroom and spend twenty minutes crying and trying to scrub out the stain. Of course, that's when you wore beautiful clothes instead of these men's shirts.

"Is it the medication?" Shelly asked. "I assume they have her on something."

"What she's on should be keeping her calm and helping her think. I've spoken to the doctor since it doesn't seem to be working, but I don't know how much they can do."

"She's almost a different person."

"That's what I wanted to talk to you about." Robert took a swallow of the coffee. "I understand you two have your confidences, and I don't want to infringe on your friendship, but I'm at my wit's end. I need to know if you have any insight on what's bothering her."

"Believe me, if I knew, I'd tell you."

"Does she act differently around you? I thought she might let her guard down and tell you what she obviously won't tell me. I can't seem to reach her."

"When she came over she was very strange. More quiet. Agitated. She did freak out before she left—"

"Wait. What do you mean 'when she came over?' You make it sound like she's only been here once."

"Well, that's all she has been. I've invited her but—"

"So you spend all your time outside? How much shopping can two women do?"

"Rob, what are you talking about? I haven't been out with Natty. She came to the house one time weeks ago, and I haven't seen her since …"

It felt like something high in his chest sank to his stomach. *Then where have you been, Natalie?*

"Did she tell you she's been spending time with me? I can't even get hold of her for a phone conversation. She texts me every now and then, but she won't answer when I call."

He hated to admit the truth to Shelly. It made it seem he'd lost control of his wife. But maybe he had … "She goes out every afternoon and most evenings. She always says she's with you."

"Well, you can ask Clark. I've been here the entire time."

"Do you know where she might be going?"

"No. I can't believe she'd lie to you."

"The list of what I can't believe is getting longer and longer."

Robert leaned back in his chair and closed his eyes. Where had Natalie been? What had she been doing? He tried to think. Another friend perhaps? Evie? Maryann? Imogene? Should he call them and ask if they'd been secretly gallivanting with his wife for weeks? But Natalie knew he didn't mind her other friends, so why wouldn't she tell the truth of which friend she was with?

She could be going out alone, but where besides someone's house could she be for such long stretches? Hours spent in an art museum? Feeding pigeons at the park? The zoo? Was this another "brain tissue alteration" – Natalie was now compelled to spend eight hours watching iguanas at the fucking zoo?

"It'll be okay, Rob." Shelly patted his leg. "Maybe she just needs to be alone."

"Alone where? And why?"

"It actually makes sense to me."

He looked at her and gave an exasperated laugh. "By all means explain it. I've been trying to figure her out for weeks."

"It might not be something a man would understand." She shifted in her chair. "After my miscarriage before Carter, I wanted to be alone a lot, even away from Natty. And I'd take long walks in the cemetery where it was peaceful and people wouldn't bother me."

"You're saying you think she's upset because of Michael?" Now there were two people outside of him who'd drawn that conclusion – a mental health professional and Natalie's best friend.

"She's devastated. I told you, when she came over here the one time she had a break down about it."

"She did?"

"Yes. I'll admit, it was kind of my fault. When she showed up wearing that awful sweatshirt I thought maybe she was trying to hide ... Well, you know. So I made the horrible mistake of asking her when she was due. And she completely lost it."

"And she said it was about Michael?"

"I had to tell her it wasn't her fault." Shelly nodded. "I've never seen her so upset, Rob. When she wouldn't return my calls or texts for days, I thought she was furious with me. But it was so painful that she couldn't talk to me, I guess. And that's probably why she hasn't come back to the house. Seeing my babies probably reminds her. Seeing *me* probably reminds her."

This scenario made him feel better. He'd been shocked when Natalie hadn't remembered Michael's name the night of the pizza disaster. Was the callousness a shield? Was she spending her days trying to block him out because of the overwhelming pain? Lying to be alone and suffer privately with her grief?

"I might've mentioned to you," he said. "But I have Michael's urn on the shelf in our living room. I haven't put a plaque on it yet. I wanted her to have input on the inscription."

"Yes, you told me that, but have you told her?"

"We had an argument after dinner the other night and I did."

"But before that?"

"No, I guess I assumed she knew what it was. You've seen it, it looks like an urn."

"Urns have inscriptions." Shelly put her hand on his leg. "Rob, what if she's been spending the last weeks trying to find him? Going from cemetery to cemetery looking for him?"

Robert felt enveloped with guilt. This was his fault, his doing. He should have been more persistent in getting Natalie to talk about her grief. He should've discussed a plaque for the urn with her immediately.

Instead you've been wandering. Too depressed to reach out for help. Searching for our—

"But wait," Robert said. "I told her where Michael was two days ago. She still went out yesterday and the day before. So that doesn't fit."

"After doing it for so long you don't think she'd get into a pattern? Finding out where his ashes are doesn't fix everything either. If she's been that occupied with locating him, what's going to fill her time? More sadness." Shelly pulled a tissue from a half empty box on the table. "Poor Natty. And the rest makes sense too."

"What rest?"

"I've known her for sixteen years. She'd never cut her hair. She'd never wear that ugly stuff she does now. She's trying to be someone else. Trying to get as far away from being Michael's mother as she can so it can't be her fault—"

"She's acting like a man. Men can't have children and if she's a man, she couldn't have had Michael and can't be responsible for him dying," Robert interrupted. He felt a flush of energy at having found the answer. And, yes, it did make sense. She was traumatized by the death of their son – more troubled than he even thought possible.

"And this man persona can't feel the pain. The horrible pain of losing a baby." Shelly grabbed more tissues from the box and pressed them to her face. "Oh, Natty."

He reached over and touched her shaking shoulder. "It's okay, Shell."

"But what are we going to do? She's going to ruin herself and she won't talk to us. I'm losing my best friend all over."

And I'm losing my wife. What are we going to do?

He could return to CryoLife for assistance. His meetings with Zuniga still happened; his next session was at the end of the week, but they'd said he could call in case of emergency.

Their answer for everything is meds though. And the damn pills don't work. She doesn't need pills.

What else was there? Something with more impact than additional ineffective—

"Mama." Carter stood in the kitchen doorway, a dump truck dangling from one hand. "Is you alwight?"

Shelly was crying too heavily to respond, so Robert turned to the child and smiled. "Mama's fine, Carter. She saw something sad on the TV."

"I saw a pig on the TV. I told Mama I wanted the pig, but she said no and got me this twuck." He waved the toy in his mother's direction. "Twucks and pigs awe diffwent. This isn't a pig."

Shelly hiccupped and took several breaths before she could reply. "I don't want a pig in this house, Carter."

"Pigs is useful. They gwow bacon. Twucks gwow …" The boy stopped. "Nothing. Think about the pig, Mama."

And he trotted off.

No wonder you blew up at him. Every child must remind you of our boys. Of Michael. And you're probably just as angry as you are sad sometimes.

"This pig nonsense." Shelly removed another tissue and dabbed at her eyes. She sniffled, yet smiled. "Where he gets—"

"Shell, you said you felt the same way after your miscarriage, right?"

"Not exactly the same. My depression didn't get this far."

"What stopped it? What helped you get over it?"

She tipped her head from side to side, and he could see her chew the inside of her cheek as she thought.

Don't say something stupid like "time." I waited sixteen months to get her back. I'm sick of waiting. I'm tired of my son being away from me. Of having a broken family. This needs to end, and it needs to end—

"I don't think I felt better until Carter." Shelly looked toward the door where the boy had been. "I blamed myself and felt like a failure. I didn't reach the level of creating some alter identity to deal with the pain, but who knows what may have happened?"

Again, a thought he'd had originally and that Zuniga hadn't disagreed with. To move on and heal from the loss of Michael, she needed to direct her attention away from the pain and into another baby.

"But you've got to be careful, Rob. You have to show her you understand what she's going through and be sweet to her. But not evasive. I was so upset it was the last thing I wanted. I wasn't thinking clearly, but neither is Natty."

Sweet, but not evasive. What did that mean? Empathize, but press the issue? Be forceful? Would it make her feel desirable, more like a woman if he took her passionately in his arms? He could do that, sure.

But Shelly was also right – it wasn't only sex. There was an emotional struggle going on as well. Before he took the physical steps, he had to convey his understanding of her pain, or else what would he be but a well-intentioned rapist?

"How did Clark show you he understood?"

"He found me walking alone one day. And he walked with me." Shelly smiled. "He didn't have to say anything. He just stayed beside me. That was enough."

Yes, he could do that as well. Shelly and Natalie were so similar, that would work. He'd follow her tomorrow and "stay beside her." What an excellent idea. His only regret was not having spoken with Shelly sooner.

Chapter 36

For approximately the past ten years, Oz had only spent time in his basement to tend his marijuana plants. Twelve racks of flats in various growth phases were organized under HID lamps, and two high-powered fans pushed the lamp-generated heat from the foliage. It was always hot and muggy, but the atmosphere wasn't his sole purpose for not remaining long.

Pushed behind the water heater sat a shelf full of books that he tried to forget but hadn't the heart to destroy. When he didn't leave the basement quick enough, his eyes strayed to the shelf and he'd feel those prickles down his spine.

You should've tossed the books in too.

The only brutal act Oz had ever committed was to pry the dry erase board in his basement from the wall. Equations had still been written on it when he'd marched it into the backyard. He'd thrown it repeatedly until the board was broken in pieces. Then he'd lit the fragments on fire.

Ah, if I'd had Tinks's C4 then. That would've been better than fire. And maybe I would've included the books. I could've hugged them to my chest, hit the ignition switch and – no more pain.

They were still there though – covered in dust and waiting. *What are you doing? Why are you doing this?*

He pulled a large volume from the shelf and brought it to an empty rack.

Mathematics hadn't been discussed since he'd originally told Andrew about his past life, but earlier in the day, the topic had resurfaced between them.

Andrew had spent the afternoon in Oz's pharmacy. He'd sat on the empty chair in his office and gone on and on about a single painting that Rothko had completed in 1970. It'd been the first time Oz had been alone with him since the pizza party incident, and it was nice to have Andrew to himself. He loved to listen to him talk.

Andrew could talk for hours about art the way Oz wished he was still able to elaborate on mathematics. How he spoke of Gorky, Rothko, and Picasso was how Oz thought of topology, and if Andrew got excited enough about it, Oz felt the electricity that sizzled on the surface of his skin leap over. He'd forget he ever died, and that he was missing what had once been an instrumental part of himself.

That morning the voltage had been crackling in the pharmacy. Oz was focused on his every word, although trying not to appear like he was. Until Andrew stopped mid-sentence.

"I'm sorry. I'm boring you."

"What gave you that idea?"

"Who wouldn't be bored?"

"I wouldn't. Look."

Oz pulled down the collar of his shirt. He pointed to an upside-down "U" symbol in the equation engraved on his skin.

"This is set-theoretic intersection. And I could've given you an eight-hour dissertation on it. Eight hours on one symbol. If you didn't interrupt me, or ask questions." He released his collar and smiled. "So you're quite fortunate that I'm no longer able to tell you anything but its name."

"What makes you so sure you could never do math again?"

"I do math all the time. I punch numbers into a calculator. I divide by twos and threes to mix medication. I play Keno."

"But art. With mathematics. Like what you love. Have you tried?"

Oz had swiveled his chair to look at the computer. "Yes, I have. So drop it." He laced his fingers and bent his wrists to relieve the stiffness before moving the mouse. He typed random numbers into the open spreadsheet. "Tell me more about your paintings. Talk about that."

Several seconds of silence and the input of more fake data later, Andrew spoke. "I think you should try. Maybe not with something as complicated as the Hodge conjecture. Start small. But try again."

"Tell me more about your paintings. Talk about that," Oz repeated.

Andrew's prodding had nagged him the rest of the day. Oz had tried, and he'd failed. Seeing the expressions, the phrases, the equations empty – being faced with the wide expanse of nothingness, prime for the genesis of order and meaning, and having no ideas, just a blank mind. A stupid mind. It'd been devastating.

You need to prove to yourself and to him that it's over. I can't tolerate goading to fix an unfixable problem.

Oz opened *Theorems of Finite Abelian Groups* to a random page and stared at the symbols.

At first sight, it'd been another language. But he persisted in keeping his eyes glued to the pages. He turned to another section and another. He rifled through the entire book, looking for anything he could comprehend. He used to understand. In the past, this, and not grade school math on the calculator had bored him.

But after an hour of searching, the contents of the book degenerated from another language to squiggles on a page – cave drawings. He closed the cover and folded his arms across it.

There, he'd tried and failed. Again.

The part of his brain where the sublime knowledge and natural ability lived, was gone. It was as if Brigman had taken a wood burning pen to it. His father had used a nine hundred degree soldering tip to burn away Oz's talent, and it'd never grow back. Brain cells didn't regenerate. It was wicked mockery that he retained the passion. Retribution for everything horrible he'd done in both his lives. His beautiful art …

What was the purpose of anything? Sure, he helped his friends in various ways and that gave him some kind of meaning, but it wasn't much of one. He'd been wild for mathematics. Passionate, and absolutely intoxicated as he'd never been for anything else before, or since. It'd been the reason he lived.

He pictured Andrew, briefly sensing that feeling of being wanted and holding him close. Had he ever been so fulfilled that he couldn't expand a fraction more without bursting?

It was as artificial as everything else though. Never real. Nothing was ever tangible, so that's what he ended with – nothing.

But tangible. Capable of touch. That's art. It's alive. It's something you do. You don't sit around and fucking read about it. You do it.

Oz opened his eyes.

A fat black marker rested on a shelf upstairs. He retrieved it.

He returned to the basement, uncapped the marker, and went to the empty wall space where his dry erase board had been.

"Start small."

He wrote:

V – E + F = 2

And he stared at it.

He stared at it for what felt like an hour, trying to wrap his mind around the humble concept.

Then he uncapped his marker again. He shook out his hands and put the chisel tip to the wall beside the equation. He began to draw.

Oz drew a three-dimensional cube. A soccer ball. A triangular pyramid. What appeared to be a diamond. And a shape similar to the soccer ball, but with twenty triangle faces.

He stood back to look at the graffiti.

"Explain it to me."

Oz turned his head, and Andrew was at the top of the basement stairs. Standing there, and for who knew how long. His hand rested on the railing and the HID light gave his blond hair a golden shimmer. Oz blinked a few times to ensure the figure wasn't a mirage.

And then Andrew was beside him, and they looked at the wall.

"Explain it to me," he repeated.

Oz's words caught in his throat, and when they came out they sounded hoarse. "They're spheres."

"They don't look like spheres."

It didn't matter if the words were a dig toward his sketching abilities. He was an artist of ideas, not line drawings.

He stepped to the wall and put his cheek to the cube drawing. The coldness of the ground seeped through the concrete, and the pungent marker underscored the humidity and plant smells. He brought his hand up, and dug his nails into the diamond.

"But they used to be, and could be again. They're the same sphere. The same fucking sphere!"

Oz pulled himself from the wall, tears rolling down his cheeks. He pointed at the equation.

"And if it becomes a platonic solid, it will always equal that. Always!" He drove his fist against the letters and sobbed. "$V - E + F = 2$! $V - E + F = 2$! $V - E + F = 2$! It's always the same!"

He sank to his knees, his forehead on the concrete.

"It's gorgeous. Fucking gorgeous."

A hand touched his shoulder, the backs of the fingertips smoothing his neck. The contact made his stomach flutter and his heart race. He lifted his head, expecting to meet Andrew's eyes. Possibly alarmed. Perhaps confused. Looking at him like he was crazy. And he'd understand why. He felt partially insane, which was a part of the process. But Andrew's eyes weren't on Oz. They were on the wall.

He knelt in front of it too, looking at the elegant equation. And Andrew appeared to admire the shapes and Euler's formula as if they were a genuine Rothko painting – which is what Oz felt they were.

"Yes. It is gorgeous. Fucking gorgeous."

As he did more often than not, he'd said exactly what Oz wanted to hear. Nothing more. Nothing less. Perfect.

Andrew was perfect. Oz knew he still felt bad about himself, but that would improve when he was free and could do more to change the body. Not that how he looked mattered to Oz. He was Andrew. The man who made Oz's hands shake, and who he found himself being softer with. Who he thought about in the middle of the night. Who he foolishly, juvenilely pined for.

Oz hadn't felt more turmoil within himself than right then. Kneeling together, with Andrew's fingertips on his neck and his dark eyes patiently waiting and letting Oz make the moment into whatever he needed.

But Oz had never cared about what anyone else thought. He did what he wanted. He shot his mouth off. He smoked. He drank. He both dealt and enjoyed the occasional recreational drug. Most of his actions were largely motivated by the desire to spite someone. He routinely buried feelings of friendship and quieted the voice that told him to stop. He plunged forward and did whatever he wanted to. He was after all, the coolest motherfucker there'd ever been.

Yet with Andrew, Oz felt he'd lost a part of himself. He couldn't forget how deeply he cared for him. He believed Andrew capable of unparalleled compassion. Maybe not for everyone, and not for him at first, but now, Oz wondered how far the limits extended. If Andrew knew him so well, maybe he'd be able to understand and forgive him. Once again, he couldn't control himself.

Oz realized he'd stuffed his hands in his pockets as he looked at Andrew. When he drew them out, they were eerily steady. He watched Andrew's eyes, vigilant for that frightened animal look he sometimes had when others encroached on his space.

But the look didn't come. Even when Oz curved his hands around Andrew's cheeks. Even when he leaned his head in and pressed his lips against his. Even when he scrunched closer and ran his hands through Andrew's hair as he kissed him again. And again. And again. The hand stayed where it had been on his neck, and Andrew didn't pull away.

When Oz drew back an inch or two to see his eyes, they held no fear.

He remained motionless, trying to riddle out Andrew's thoughts. He considered apologizing. Or kissing him again. Or he could tell Andrew that he loved him. That he was crazy about him. That he wanted him, needed him.

He was on the verge of doing it, until he remembered what Andrew had said when he'd initially hinted at having feelings for Oz:

"You don't suffocate me. You're independent, and don't desperately need me."

He caressed Andrew's cheek. *But I do need you. Like everything else I do, I'm out of control.*

"I'm sorry," he said and waited for a response.

"You do taste like cigarette smoke and pine trees."

"I may drink and smoke too much. A couple of my many faults. Relatively small flaws in comparison to my lack of inhibition. For which I again, apologize."

"Don't apologize." Andrew brought himself higher on his knees. He put his cheek on Oz's temple and looped his arms around his shoulders.

"Tell me I can stay with you, Oz," he whispered.

"I never said you couldn't."

That amazing feeling of having him in his arms. Made even better. Andrew was asking to stay. He breathed in the scent of his skin – it was clean and pure.

I'll stop smoking. And drinking. For you, I'll stop. So you'll continue to be perfect and unsoiled by my self-destruction.

"But you won't trap me." Andrew had pulled back and looked at him. "You promise you won't force me in any cage of any kind? To be anything or anyone I don't want to be?"

"How could I cage you? No one can cage you."

"You could try. And you can protect me, but you have to promise you won't try to trap me. You have to promise, Oz."

There was the frightened look, as if Andrew saw the cage looming already.

"You know promises are just words, don't you? There isn't a promise police that makes you abide by every one you make. People change their minds. They break promises."

"Are you saying you will?"

"No." Oz took his hand as Andrew leaned away. "I'm saying you need to trust that I won't hurt you. And you shouldn't feel compelled to drive meaningless words out of me. I'll give them to you if you want, but do you need to hear them? Don't I make you feel safe?"

He watched Andrew consider the idea. Why couldn't he leave well enough alone? Why did he to pick everything to the lowest denominator? Andrew wanted reassurance. He wanted to hear the word "yes." And his fears would've been eased.

"You do. I feel safe with you." Andrew moved in so they were almost nose to nose. "Robert doesn't make me feel safe."

"Has he hurt you? Has he threatened to? I don't care about the fucking conservatorship garbage, if he's touched you, or if you think he might, I won't let you go back."

"No, it's not that. I don't think he's dangerous, he's just so attached to Natalie. And I obviously and constantly fail at that. I've seen him get angry, but he's able to calm down. He acts lately like I'm hiding something from him."

"You are." Oz smiled and smoothed his thumb along Andrew's jaw.

"Yes, you're my secret. And I love the way I feel when I'm with you. I love every brilliant thought that comes out of your head."

Andrew studied the drawing in black marker on the concrete wall. His eyes traced the shapes and formula before falling back onto Oz's face. He leaned in, running his fingers through Oz's hair and kissed him. Again. And again. And again.

And Oz had been happy to be alive. Finally at peace with how he'd left the world the first time. He was complete.

Chapter 37

Robert sat in his car and watched Natalie leave the apartment a quarter after nine the next morning. He had "left for work" at eight thirty.

"Are you going out with Shell today?" he'd asked as he took his keys from the basket.

"Yes. I'll probably be gone all day."

"Shopping?"

"Maybe," she said.

Robert had hidden his smile. *I'm fully aware of what you're doing. You can't fool your husband, Nat.*

It was a brilliant plan. He had it mapped out in his head and spent the forty-five-minute wait running through it.

I'll follow her to wherever she's going and let her get secure that she's alone. That no one else in the world feels her pain. She'll be so upset, so overwrought with grief.

Maybe it was a cemetery she went to. He doubted she caught a taxi across to Bonaventure, but it'd be someplace similar. Enchanting in a dark, unsettling way with the wind blowing the drooping, slender branches of willow trees and markers lining the dirt roads.

She'd break down right in the middle of a road, falling to her knees to sob. To cry out to God, why had He taken her precious baby?

At the lowest point of her anguish, that's when I'll be there. Stepping from the shadows and wrapping her in my arms. It's okay, Nat. I'm here. I understand. How did I know? I felt it, hon. I knew you needed me, and I love you. I'll do whatever it takes to help you feel better. What can I do? Name anything. You want me to "walk beside you?" Absolutely and forever.

He'd walk with her, though he hated walking and thought it was pointless. He'd curl his arm around her waist as they walked. She might continue to cry, but he wouldn't mind. Her tears were like cleaning out an infected wound.

Then everything would be okay. It was exactly what Natalie needed. More than what she needed. He glanced at the empty passenger seat, on which he'd placed a bouquet of long stem roses to greet her after their walk. He was without a doubt the very gentleman's gentleman. And who knew where the evening would lead after that? Sweet but not evasive.

And we're ready to roll.

Robert allowed her to get some yards away before starting the car. He pulled a baseball cap tight over his ears and slipped on a pair of sunglasses. Slowly, he edged out of the parking space and trailed her.

Natalie walked five blocks east before turning down and proceeding two blocks south. He parallel parked across the street as she entered the pharmacy.

Errands first. Okay, got it.

Robert melted into his seat and took off his sunglasses to wait for her to emerge with her medication bag.

Thank you, God. For everything. For giving me my family back. For CryoLife. For excellent friends like Shelly. For additional chances to make things right. Life will be different than it used to be, but I'm willing to overlook the ways she's changed. I'll tolerate those oddities when things are on track.

He closed his eyes and thought of Natalie. Usually he remembered her glowing face with the golden hair curling around her shoulders. But he tried to substitute this image with how she looked now. Short haired and unsmiling. But still his Natalie. And he'd make her smile again. The plan was fool proof.

Paradise reclaimed. By me.

He opened his eyes, and turned toward the pharmacy.

That's when he saw them.

Robert knew this man. Not by name, but he'd seen him when he'd stopped for Natalie's medication. He was that freak with the tattoos and the piercings. The one who always had a smart ass comment to make. He'd hated it when this man had been at the register.

A person like him didn't belong in a respectable profession. Where did he belong? At a bar. A gas station. On a corner selling watches out of a trench coat. You could tell by the look in his eyes that he thought he was better than everyone else.

And his hand, his fucking tattooed hand was on Natalie's arm! And he smiled at her. Not how a friend smiled at a friend. A warm smile that started in his eyes and embraced his face.

She was smiling at him like she used to smile at Robert before the accident. Like there was no place else she wanted to be, and even if he wasn't talking, she was hanging on his every breath.

They walked to a car, and before he went to the driver's side, the man ran his hand through Natalie's hair. Through *his* Natalie's hair!

And she smoothed his cheek.

The blood boiled in Robert's brain. He watched the man curl her hair around his fingers and step closer to her.

If you kiss my wife, I swear to God I'll jump out of this car, and beat you to death! With my bare fists, I will beat you to fucking death!

But the man didn't kiss her. They continued to smile at each other before he let go of her hair and turned. Natalie caught his fingertips as he walked away, and he tipped his head to her, smiling again.

Robert felt his heart dissolving, and the effervescence stung his eyes. It was as if she couldn't bear to lose contact with him. She wanted him to know that his touch would be missed, even in its most brief absence. Hadn't she done this with Robert too? Played these coquettish games of love and affection?

The man squeezed Natalie's fingertips before releasing them and moving faster this time. Robert could tell he was pleased. His face beamed, and he pushed his hand through his hair as he opened the driver's door.

His happiness caused the remnants of Robert's empty chest to blaze anew. He'd never considered himself a violent man, but he pummeled the steering wheel.

Natalie got into the passenger seat, and the car left the parking lot. He saw the man's hand holding a cigarette out the window as the car drove away.

His carefully constructed plot to sweep his grieving wife off her feet crumbled. She wasn't spending her days in mourning for Michael. She was spending them with another man.

How could you do this to me? After all I've done for you? Robert grit his teeth until they ached. *Ten years of marriage. Two children. I've kept a roof over your head, I've provided for you. I sacrificed everything to bring you back from the dead. I've been nothing but loving and understanding of you before and after the accident. And this is how you repay me?*

No. This was not acceptable. He wiped his sleeve across his eyes and coughed. He'd follow them to whatever seedy motel or bar they were going to and demand that she come home. If force was necessary, he'd use it. He wouldn't allow this behavior to continue.

But the car was gone, and he was alone.

Or was he? Shelly hadn't been of much help, but he remembered his friend, Dr. Zuniga. His appointment was still days away, but she'd see him. Right now! Ultimately this was CryoLife's fault. His Natalie would never have cheated on him. Enough of "be patient" or "this is normal." This situation was their problem. And Dr. Zuniga would tell him what he needed to do to fix it and bring Natalie back.

*

Robert swiped his visitor's pass at the card reader outside the Center's indoor entrance through Savannah General. He almost hadn't bothered with the more peaceful eastside doors. He didn't feel peaceful. Let the protesters try to get in his way. Let them chuck a Bible at him. He'd jump their picket line and tackle the thrower. But there wasn't time for losing his temper with them. He had a more definite target in mind. The doors separated and he marched to the front desk.

"I want to see Dr. Zuniga, *now*," he said to the receptionist.

"Let me see if she's available. One—"

"No, not 'let me see if she's available.' Make her available."

The young woman cast a glance to the armed guards at the door. "Do you have an appointment, sir?"

"I don't need an appointment. Tell her it's Robert Keller."

"Hang on please."

Robert tapped his fingers on the counter as she walked to the other side of the desk and picked up the phone. When she returned, she looked toward the officers again.

"I'm sorry, Mr. Keller, but she's not in today."

"Call her cell then. I need to speak to her immediately."

"I apologize, but there's no way I can do that."

"I paid you people two million dollars. You get her on the damn phone now."

"Sir, I—"

"Fine. Get me Brigman then. Is he in?" It was ridiculous that Zuniga was probably basking on some beach while Robert was in crisis, but being thrown out of the Center wouldn't help anything.

"I believe so, let me check if he's—"

"Listen to me." Robert lowered his voice. "If that man is anywhere in this building, I don't care what he's doing, you will get him for me. This is an emergency and whatever else he's occupied with will have to wait. I don't care if he's elbows deep in someone's chest. Get him. Now."

If Brigman had been in surgery, he cleaned up fast and well. Only minutes later, Robert was in his office. The old man stood and leaned over his desk, his hand extended.

"Mr. Keller, what a pleasant—"

"No. You let me talk. You've done enough." Robert shut the door and approached the desk. "For weeks, *weeks* Zuniga has been talking patience and 'nudges' while we make our way through a cornucopia of medication.

Nothing is working. Nothing! And I cannot and will not accept any of that."

"Mr. Keller, please sit down. I'm quite—"

"Don't tell me what to do. I'm tired of people thinking they can advise me what to do. How to take care of *my* family and *my* wife."

Dr. Brigman kept his calming, monotone voice. "But you're here for answers, aren't you?"

"Yes. And you're going to give me something that will work today. Not tomorrow, not in a week. Today."

"Pills? You're thinking a different medication would help and that's what you want?"

Robert picked a glass paperweight from Brigman's desk and threw it hard past the man's face at his framed doctoral degree. The frame dropped to the floor and scattered jagged pieces of glass.

"Didn't you hear what I just said?" he roared. "I don't want pills! I want my fucking wife back!"

The doctor remained standing, unfazed by the violence.

"Have a seat then, Mr. Keller. And let's talk about how we can make that happen."

"It'd better happen. If it doesn't, I swear to God I will go public with what you did to her. A guy who hates Chinese food? A woman who wants to play piano? No, you took a beautiful, devoted, loving wife and mother, and you made her into a scheming adulteress. How will that look to the world? I'll target you and your company in any way I can!"

There wasn't a dramatic response, but Brigman's pupils shrank and the skin at the corners of his eyes grew pinched.

Good, you should be afraid. The reaction calmed Robert and, after taking a few breaths, he sat.

"Thank you." Brigman sank into his chair as well. "I'll admit to you first, Mr. Keller, that due to patient confidentiality I'm not aware of the details you may have discussed with—"

"Here's what you need to know: Natalie is not acting like herself. We've tried tons of medications without effect. She's hostile and belligerent. She seems to be going through some kind of gender crisis. She cut her hair and dressed like a boy. And now—" Robert could barely choke the words out. "She's cheating on me."

"Oh, dear. I'm so sorry. I agree with you completely; the situation has gone too far for talking." He leaned to the right where his laptop sat on an angle and typed. "Let me take a look at her file."

See, Robert, he agrees with you. Too far for talking.

"Goodness, cornucopia was right. And you're saying none of these medications impacted her behavior?"

"None. So I don't want more."

"I understand, but it doesn't make sense. Some of these drugs, Mr. Keller – you definitely should've seen a difference. Are you sure she's been taking her medication?"

"She has to have been. You said she needed the immunosuppressants to keep her brain from rejecting the body."

"She does, that's what's so odd about it." Brigman squinted at his computer screen.

"Well, I suppose they could've been tampered with. She is having the affair with that pharmacist."

"What?" The doctor flipped all attention immediately to Robert. "The pharmacist who dispenses her CryoLife medication? The one downtown here?"

"Yes."

"Are you sure it's the pharmacist? Not someone else who works there?"

"I don't know."

"Describe him to me."

"Nasty looking. Trailer trash. Ugly brown hair and eyes. Piercing on his eyebrow. Dirty tattoos over his arms. One of them was on his neck – a bunch of Satanic symbols probably. He's disgusting and I don't—"

"That's him." Brigman's lips drew tight together, and he kept his eyes fixated on his desk.

"So you think that's possible? That he wasn't giving her the right medication?"

It took the doctor a few seconds more to redirect his stare and focus on Robert. "Based on what you're telling me, I'd say it's highly likely, Mr. Keller. And on behalf of CryoLife, I sincerely apologize. Believe me, this issue will be addressed."

"It's the pharmacist's fault then?" Transferring blame made Robert feel better. The medication might've worked had Natalie been taking what she should. The pharmacist could've been meddling with the pills from the beginning. And who was to say he wasn't adding his own concoction? "Could he be giving her something that would make her do what he wants? That would make her want him?"

"There are no love potions. But could he be administering something so she isn't thinking clearly? Absolutely." Brigman looked just as upset as he felt.

Robert's thoughts crossed into murder. Serious murder. Not beating the man into the pavement or lofty threats. A real way to kill the pharmacist.

I'll find out where he lives. I'll use my father's gun and force my way into his house. I'll—

Dr. Brigman shook his head as if emerging from a daze. The anger in his expression had been replaced by coldness. "I don't think it's necessary to waste further time with this, Mr. Keller. The issue is obvious. And I also won't subject you to delays or try to placate you by suggesting more medication." The corners of his mouth curved in a slow smile. "We're friends, remember? And I feel a personal responsibility for what's happened here."

"You should. This is your fault." But it was difficult to be upset with someone who'd taken his side from the beginning. "Well, not you personally. You didn't make the pharmacist interfere with her medication. Still, it's kind of ..."

"No, you're correct. Some of that blame does lie with us. But I'm going to do everything in my power to correct this problem."

"What can you do?"

"Oh, I have many options at my disposal, but let's go back to a conversation we had right here in my office months ago. Remember how I said that despite my fancy degrees, I know how in tune you are with your wife?"

"Yes, I remember," Robert said.

"I think it's time for us to step aside so you can make the decisions you feel are right for Mrs. Keller." He folded his arms on his desk and leaned in. "Tell me what you think will fix this problem, and I will ensure you receive whatever support you need."

Especially with the pharmacist's role having come to light, Robert was still sure he knew what Natalie's problem was. He'd been married to her for ten years, which made him an expert. And Shelly had known her for sixteen, which made her opinions valid as well. Even if Natalie hadn't been wandering grief stricken, it made sense to him that her gender-confused behavior was due to Michael.

"Whatever that pharmacist did to her, Natalie is devastated about our son's death. What will fix this problem is for her to move past that grief and start acting like a woman." Robert swallowed. "To preserve my family, I need to give her another child to love."

"Is she open to that?"

"No, she's not."

He didn't know if assistance was something Brigman was capable of, let alone ethically allowed to do. For a second he regretted saying anything since—

"I can certainly help you with that." The doctor smiled and took a pen and pad from his desk. "It sounds rational to me. She can't deny her gender when she's carrying your child."

"Exactly."

Dr. Brigman tore the top sheet off the pad and held it out. "Take this. It'll be simple and will make things … more effective, shall we say? Put it in her water or food. When she wakes, she won't have any idea what happened."

"Thank you." Robert took the prescription and stood.

"Needless to say, don't try to fill it at that pharmacy. And I assure you, I will personally handle the matter of the pharmacist's unprofessional behavior."

"Don't worry, I'm never going to set foot in that pharmacy again."

After I chat with its owner.

Chapter 38

From the Cryobiotic Treatment Center, Robert drove first to see Simon at his parents' house, and then home. By the time he pulled into the parking spot he had another plan.

If possible, he was going to avoid the use of the prescription Brigman had given him. While Natalie had been standoffish, he reconsidered the latter half of Shelly's advice, that he shouldn't be evasive. Perhaps she wouldn't be averse if he was resolute. That could be what she wanted – for him to take control. And he could do that without drugging her. Still, he tucked the script into the pocket of his car's sun visor should he need it.

Robert was also going to put a better structure in place. He'd let Natalie do whatever she liked. No boundaries, no restrictions. But things were going to change.

You will grow your hair back and never cut it. You will put effort into looking beautiful for me by fixing your makeup and wearing clothes I approve of. You will treat me with respect, and you will take care of my son as a proper mother should. And if I want to touch you, I'm going to.

Most notably, Natalie wouldn't be going out anymore. If she left without his permission, he'd put the ankle monitor on her. Despite her protests, or how insulted she might feel, she really was a criminal this time. Adultery wasn't technically illegal, but it should be. He was through being a pushover.

But before Robert established these new rules he was going to do something about the pharmacist. He had to be removed if there'd be hope of turning the situation around. While Brigman said he was going to take care of it, Robert didn't trust it'd be handled severely. What was Brigman going to do? Write a letter? Pull the pharmacy from CryoLife's approval list? No. The pharmacist needed to be taught that there were consequences for his actions.

So that night, while he waited for Natalie to come home, he thought about what he would do and say. And this made him feel better, as much as it stoked his anger. He wasn't afraid of the pharmacist. The man was no threat, especially since right, truth, and goodness were on Robert's side. And those things always triumphed over evil.

When Natalie finally came to bed, he felt tight as a drum. She laid down at the edge – as far away from him as she could get.

Did you have a good day with Shelly? Oh, you're too tired to talk? Get some rest. Sleep it off. This is the end. The last time you are ever going to turn away from me.

The morning came too slowly. It was hard for him to stay in bed until the alarm went off.

When it finally buzzed, he showered and dressed as if he were going to work. When he heard Natalie bustling around the bathroom, he took a wrench to the kitchen.

Robert put the stopper in the left side of the sink and turned on the water. He added a spurt of detergent and piled in the dishes before sticking his head under the sink. He hooked the wrench onto the coupling that joined the trap to the drain pipe. It only took a turn or two before he was able to loosen it and separate the pipes. Cold dish water burbled over the rim of the trap as he rotated it, leaving the pipe open and disconnected.

He threw the wrench to the back of the cupboard and stood. When the sink filled to its rim, he turned off the water. A lot of time wouldn't be needed to deal with the pharmacist, and his sabotage should create enough of a mess to delay her departure.

He acted casual when she came out of the bathroom.

Natalie looked rested, as if she'd woken from a week of sleep. Her skin glowed and color tinged her cheeks.

"Are you going out with Shelly this afternoon?" Robert asked, and grabbed his keys to leave.

"Yes."

"Before you do, would you mind finishing the dishes I left in the sink? I didn't have enough time to do them this morning."

"Sure. I have to do these anyway." Natalie rose from the table and gathered their dirty breakfast plates.

"Have a good day, Nat."

She hadn't answered, though there'd been plenty of time to respond.

Five minutes later he was in the car, driving east. His hands clenched the steering wheel, his nails digging back into his palms.

After a fair amount of regret, Robert had decided not to hurt the pharmacist. He'd puff himself up to look large and intimidating. Scare the hell out of him. He had no intention to use it, but when he'd stopped to visit Simon he'd borrowed his father's gun; it was tucked under the driver's seat.

Perhaps he'd use that to threaten the pharmacist. Or put him against a wall. Nothing more. However, the verbal altercation still made him nervous.

You have to do this. You have to be the voice of good, Robert. Of purity. Of family values. All this man is going to get from CryoLife is a slap on the wrist. You go in, put him in his place, and walk away.

But he wanted to walk away quickly, so he pulled into the same spot he'd used the day before. Robert looked at the ceiling.

You are the only man who can do this. To stand for what's right.

To his shame, his legs felt weak. He was losing his nerve.

No, I'm doing this. Yesterday, I was ready to kill him, and we're not going that far. Today is yesterday. Think about that. Think about seeing them together.

He turned his head to the window and looked at the parking lot. The car was there. He remembered yesterday:

That pharmacist strolling out the doors with his hand on Natalie. The smug look on his face, while he guided her to his car. Pushing his hand through her hair. Through the hair he'd convinced her to hack off.

That was mine. The adrenalin released. *Everything about her is mine. And you caused her to mutilate herself.*

And the way she'd looked at him. Having fallen into his trap as a result of her grief. She adored him. Her hand to his face of her own accord. Touching him. She wanted to. It was nearly as bad as him touching her. Catching his fingertips when he tried to walk away …

You never touch me because you love me and want to feel close to me. I'm your husband, Natalie. Not him. You had no reason to touch his cheek or his hand. Except you wanted to feel his skin. You like to think about how it makes him feel when you touch him.

He remembered having her affection. How she fluttered around him lovingly. She used to caress his cheek, catch his hand. Now her perfect hands were soiled with the pharmacist's grease.

His throat grew dry from the rushed breathing. He hadn't seen them kiss, but he knew they had. The look in that man's eyes told him they had. Told him he'd wanted to. Robert hadn't kissed Natalie on the lips since the accident. She always turned away, but couldn't wipe the grimace off her face. Yet she kissed this man who must smell like cigarettes and alcohol and whatever else he did. She wanted to kiss him.

But no more. She'll kiss me and me alone.

Robert got out of the car and slammed the door, forgetting the gun. As he crossed the street, he didn't watch for cars, and one had to swerve around him.

I won't let anyone break apart my family.

He stomped over the curb and pushed open the door.

Chapter 39

Oz hummed as he stocked extra merchandise in the back room. It was a zen activity for him. Open a box, take out the merch, find a place for it. Open another box, take out different merch, find a different place. Since he sometimes forgot orders he'd placed, it was almost like Christmas when deliveries came. And like at Christmas, he shoved the empty boxes and wrappings aside for someone else to take care of.

Stocking required zero brain power. Less than punching numbers into spreadsheets. He could let his mind wander to better things. Such as how he was sure that sooner, rather than later, Andrew would come by to keep him company.

That was the reason he'd left the door propped an inch. It wasn't something he should do for security reasons, but he did it anyway. Barty was acquainted with their frequent visitor, and when Oz was in back, he appreciated being able to wave Andrew down the hallway.

He sliced open another carton with his box cutter and removed two packages of greeting cards.

It's always cats. Fat old ladies and cats. Why do people buy this shit?

But it didn't warrant a transcendental investigation. He put the cat cards by the other cat cards, making a mental note that he didn't need more cat cards.

He kicked the box into the corner and grabbed another. This one he opened with excruciating slowness. It was unlike Andrew to be late. Not that there'd been an established time. They'd been up late, and perhaps Andrew had slept in.

Last night, he'd fallen asleep in Oz's arms. His head near his side, and his arm wrapped around his chest. God, it'd felt incredible.

Oz had let him sleep as long as he could before he had to wake him. He'd forgone the cigarette he'd desperately wanted because leaning over to the nightstand might disturb Andrew. He remained as still as he could, smoothing his hair in the darkness. His hand felt weak as he curled Andrew's hair around his fingertips, but he didn't care.

It was then that the awareness hit him. He'd fallen in and done exactly what he'd promised himself he wouldn't, what Santino had begged him not to. He was submersed, and he knew he could never climb out. He belonged to Andrew.

The idea made him smirk.

"You have 'Property Of' written all over your forehead."

Yes, he did.

Maybe that was why he hadn't been able to call Andrew "brother" lately. They were no longer equals. But he hadn't chaffed at this realization. He'd only felt the warmth of Andrew's arm around him, and there was nowhere else he'd rather be.

Oz placed another greeting card box alongside the others. *For real, no more fucking cat cards.*

He slit open the next box and folded the lid.

Fuck. Just fuck. He eyed the shelf for an empty spot. *I guess I can turn them sideways and squeeze them in there. In how many ways can a pharmacist organize seven different types of cat cards in three places on a shelf?*

Oz capsized the cardboard box to dump out the smaller boxes.

Where "n" is the number of cat card boxes, "r" the finite number of spaces.

"Boss!"

He picked up the first box and approached his shelf.

"N" permute "r." Think. First take the "n" minus—

"Boss!"

Oz scowled, wedging the box in the small space. Couldn't Barty handle anything? For twenty fucking minutes? It was probably an old woman asking which were the best cough drops.

They're all the same. Jesus Christ.

"Shut the door, boss! Shut the fucking door!"

The steel door opened, smashing hard to the wall.

Oz turned around, but before he registered what was happening, two powerful hands pushed his shoulders into the wall. Fingers gripped under his collar as if they wanted to pull the bone out through his skin.

"Open your eyes! I want to know you're listening to everything I have to say."

"How does it feel to want?"

Hands brought him away from the wall, then thrust him back into it, whipping his head on the cement.

"Don't be a smart ass. Look at me when I'm talking to you!"

The room spun and Oz had to blink many times before he could center on the eyes drilling into him.

Robert held him pinned and his thick fingers dug into Oz's shoulders.

But Barty was there with his cell phone. Robert pulled Oz back and shoved him again into the wall. His skull cracked and his ears rang. He barely heard Barty, who pointed a box cutter like a weapon.

"Back off, you fucker!" the loyal technician shouted. "And get out! I'm calling the police!"

"You're calling the police?" Robert glanced at Barty with a sneer.

When he turned his glare away, Oz felt a sense of relief. It was like a short break from being waterboarded. But the eyes were back in an instant. And he wasn't sure who Robert was talking to. His voice was low and cocky.

"Go ahead. Call the police."

"Barty," Oz croaked. "Don't. Just go."

"Go?" The young man quivered, the box cutter still out in front.

"You heard him. Go. And shut the door," Robert hissed.

Terror streaked across Barty's face, and he hesitated.

"It's okay. Go." Oz tried to sound as calm as he could.

The technician backed toward the door, keeping his weapon at the ready. He edged out and closed the door except for a crack. Oz knew he'd be there listening. Cell phone out and primed.

Robert's nostrils flared, his breath heavy and erratic. Oz wiped every expression from his face and stared at Robert. They said nothing for a long time.

Then Robert let go of one shoulder. The release made Oz want to scream. His face contorted with pain. So much for appearing like a rock.

"At least you have some modicum of honor."

The strategy of calling off the alarm appeared successful. It was a sign of strength, of wanting to settle the dispute like men.

"What do you want? To beat the shit out of me like a Neanderthal?"

"I want to do more than beat you." Robert leaned his body weight into the shoulder still pinned. "But I won't have to. You're going to stay the fuck away from my wife."

"I haven't touched your wife."

"Yes. You. Have." Robert spoke each word separately.

"I saw your wife one time, two years ago. I haven't seen her since." Oz heard that faint voice telling him to stop.

"You're a liar."

"No, I'm not. Your wife is dead. She died in a car accident."

Stop, Oz. Stop.

"No, she's alive and you've been sleeping with her. But it's going to stop!"

"I don't fuck dead people. I like them warm."

Robert drew back his free arm, and hammered a fist into Oz's stomach. He released his remaining shoulder and Oz sank to the floor. He coughed, gasping for air, though each breath came out twisted.

"I saw you together!" Robert shouted. "You can't deny it!"

He crouched and took Oz by the hair. He pulled his head up and his voice dropped. "It's going to stop. You stay away from her and my family. Do you hear me?"

Oz couldn't breathe, let alone talk, but Robert demanded an answer.

"I said, do you hear me? Speak!"

"It's hard …" He swallowed. "It's hard to stop something you never started."

Robert released his head and stood. He reeled back his foot and kicked Oz in the abdomen. Oz braced himself with his wrist and coughed several splatters of blood onto the floor. The tails of Robert's shirt dribbled through the blood as he squatted and grasped Oz's hair again.

Why do you do this to yourself, Oz? Why? His entire torso burned.

"If you ever. Ever. Get within five feet of her. I will kill you." Robert locked eyes with Oz. "I will tear you limb from limb. I'll cut you into a thousand pieces and hide you in the walls of every house I build. I'll dissolve you in acid and mix your sludge with the mortar. I—"

"The rack, the wheel, the guillotine, the iron maiden, the—"

Robert drove Oz's forehead into the floor. His head spun, and when Robert spoke, the words sounded as if they came underwater.

"You think you're so funny. And you can go on thinking you are. You're a waste of time – a pathetic excuse for a human being, let alone a man. Natalie is my wife. *Mine*. This is your only warning."

Robert let go of his hair, and got to his feet. Oz saw him sweep the dust from his knees, roll his shoulders, and walk to the door. Despite his injuries, he couldn't help himself.

"Robert," he groaned.

The man halted. "You have something else clever to say? Go ahead. See where your cleverness gets you."

Oz turned his head. "Don't hurt him."

He closed his eyes when Robert's shoes approached.

"She's a woman." Robert loudly drew mucus into his mouth and launched it into Oz's face. "And I would never hurt my wife."

He left quickly this time.

Barty burst through the steel doors and knelt beside Oz.

"He's gone, boss, he's gone. Are you okay?" The young man took off his staff shirt and pressed it to Oz's face, wiping away the spit and blood. "You need to go to the hospital."

"Get my phone. It's in my side pocket." Oz tried to sit up, but his stomach screamed at him.

The technician dug out the phone.

"Who do you want me to call, the police? I have his license plate written down. They'll get him."

"Dial Andrew and give me the phone."

Barty pressed the phone to his ear. He tried to hold it, but his arm felt too heavy to move.

Please answer. Please, for the love of God answer the fucking phone!

"Hey, I'm sorry I'm late. I need to finish cleaning a mess and—"

Thank God. Robert hadn't been there. Oz closed his eyes. But relief was shortly undermined by an intense fear that turned his swollen stomach into tighter knots.

"Get out of the house. He knows, and he's been here." It hurt to talk, and his sentences were broken.

"What? Are you okay?"

"Don't worry. Just get out. Don't come here. Go to the gas station two blocks south. I'll have Santino come for you."

"Why can't you come? Oz, are you okay?" Andrew's voice sounded panicked.

"Just get out. Hurry. Leave everything and go."

"Okay. I'll see you soon."

The call disconnected. Barty, intuiting the next call, dialed Santino.

You said you'd always pick up for me. Answer! I can't go get him, and he can't come here. That's the first place Robert will look.

"Any time I'm right in the middle of something, the phone rings, and it's always you. Jesus Christ, Oz. What gutter are you lying in?"

"You need to go. Get Andrew at the gas station. On 52nd Street."

"I'm not your chauffeur. You go get him."

"I can't."

There was a pause. He thought the call had cut off. He looked to Barty, who pulled the phone away and confirmed that it was connected.

"Santino, are you there?"

"Why can't you get him?"

"You know why." Oz said the words as fast as possible. "And I'll let you gloat about being right later, but he's in trouble. Please. Please go get him."

He heard keys jingle in the background and a door close.

"Where do you want me to take him?"

"To your house. Hide him there until I have a plan."

"How badly hurt are you, Oz?"

Being reminded of his injuries brought them to another level, and the room spun. He fumbled for words, but couldn't wrap his mouth around any. Barty's voice sounded a room away.

"I'm calling an ambulance. I'll call you when I have more information."

Santino made random squawks into the phone. He couldn't understand them.

"No, do what he wants first," said Barty's far off voice. "Get the boy safe. That man was a maniac."

And then Oz's senses failed him.

Chapter 40

When Robert exited the pharmacy fifteen minutes later, the passion still coursed through him. He felt powerful and in control. Sure, things hadn't gone according to plan. He thought the man might have been badly injured. But it was his own fault.

I only intended to threaten him. But he provoked me. He dared to provoke me! To laugh at me like this is a joke.

He got in the car and sped down the street. He should've kicked him. Right in his face. He should've braced his hands on the wall and kicked until the man's teeth had broken off and his face was purple and swollen. Until his eyes were black. What quick-witted things could be said through broken, bloody stumps of one's teeth? And would Natalie want to touch his face then? Yes, he should've done more.

But unlike him, I have restraint. I have morals. Hopefully he learned something.

Robert had to get home anyway. The man could've dragged himself out of the fetal position to try and call Natalie. To "warn" her, maybe. Not that there was anything to warn her about. They were going to have a serious conversation, but he'd never hurt his Natalie.

I should've knocked him out. That wouldn't have pushed it too far.

Robert pulled into the parking space. He tightened his fists as he approached the apartment.

The first thing to go is her cell phone. To burn this last piece of rage and show her I mean business. I'm going to throw it against the wall. Shatter it. You won't see him. You won't speak to him. You won't see or speak to anyone I don't approve of.

He unlocked the apartment and listened. Where was she? He walked to the kitchen. There was the dish water on the floor, towels scattered around to sop it up. The pharmacist wasn't the only cunning one.

Then he heard Natalie's panicked breathing from the bedroom.

So you did call her. How nice. That's the last time you're ever going to talk to her. I should've kicked you in the throat so many times you couldn't speak at all. You deserve to have the air ripped out of you.

Robert thought about storming into the bedroom. But instead, he waited at the entrance of the kitchen, guarding the front door. He was tired of pursuing her. It was time for her to come to him.

And she did. A small bag in her hand, she hurried past him to leave.

"Natalie."

He saw the color drain from her face in the mirror by the door.

"Where do you think you're going?"

Her back tensed, and she faced him. She tried to look innocent, a watery smile on her face. But he was no fool.

He saw the terror in her eyes. Natalie had looked frightened before, but never to this extent. Every part of her body seemed to be shaking.

I hate it. Look at what's happened to you. I'm your husband. You shouldn't be afraid of me. This is how sick you are.

"Just out. Nowhere in particular."

"With Shelly?"

"Yes."

Robert stepped toward her. He moved slow, deliberate.

"I know that you know where I've been this morning."

"I have no idea what you're talking about." She tried to chuckle, but it fell short as he stopped within inches of her. "Why are you acting so strange?" she asked. "What's wrong?"

"You have that much audacity to ask me what's wrong?"

"Well, you're obviously upset."

"A person does get upset when he finds out his wife has been lying to him for weeks. That she's been cheating on him."

She twisted to face the door. And then she laughed.

"You're ridiculous, Robert. Do you hear yourself speak?"

Robert wasn't sure if what made him snap was that she was still trying to lie. That she'd turned away from him. Made fun of him. The laughter. That she'd been so corrupted to not understand what she was doing. It could've been all these things.

He grabbed her roughly by the arm, wrenching her around.

"Don't turn from me when I'm talking to you, Natalie!"

She tried to pull away, but he had her arm squeezed too tightly.

"Robert, let me go! You're hurting me!"

"I'm hurting you?" He jerked her arm. "What about you hurting me? What about you treating me like garbage?

What about you trying to poison our son? What about you running around with another man? I understand you're grieving, but what you've done is terrible! To me, to Simon, to our family! How could you do this to us? Answer me!"

But she was too terrified. Too intent on freeing herself. She struggled and struggled until he grabbed her other arm and held her still. He forced her to look at him, almost picking her off the ground.

"I saved you! It's because of me that you're alive! I sacrificed for you! You were dead, and I brought you back!"

"I didn't ask you to bring me back!" Natalie yelled. "I'm miserable! I'm miserable with myself! I'm miserable with you! I'm miserable with everyone except him!"

He'd been adamant that he could keep cool with her. She was his beautiful Natalie, even after the horrible things she'd done. She was sick, very sick. But—

"You shut your mouth!"

Robert struck her across the face. The blow knocked her to the carpet and he stood above her. Unstoppable.

And when she looked at him with quivering eyes, her hand to her red cheek, he felt no mercy. He wanted her to hurt. Like he'd been hurting. For over a year. And for nothing more than simply wanting his family back. From the last time he'd kissed her goodbye the morning of the car accident, he'd been a building mass of pain! She was miserable? She didn't know misery.

"I am your husband and provider, Natalie." Robert lowered his voice. "And I've had enough. It's time you started acting like my wife and give me the respect I deserve. If I need to show you what your place is, I will. I'm tired of waiting for you to find it."

Tears rolled down her cheeks, and he could see she was trying not to make a sound. Not a sob. Not a sniffle. She was paralyzed with fear. She was his. As it should be.

"Get up."

Natalie struggled to rise, her legs ungainly and movements clumsy. Before, he would've offered his hand, but he was through being a gentleman. She needed to earn his trust and generosity.

"Come on!" He yanked her arm, and she stumbled upright. He dragged her toward the bedroom.

When she saw where they were going, her strength returned. She fought him, her legs kicking and her nails tearing across his skin.

"No! Robert, no! Let me go!"

Her reaction infuriated him further. He got her to the door and moved her in front of himself. Then he pushed her shoulders hard and sent her flying back. She hit the floor, and her head knocked against the bench of her vanity.

"What? Do you think I want you when you look how he wants you to? You're not his. You're mine." Robert's fists shook as he towered over her. "Put on real clothes! Put on your fucking clothes, Natalie!"

He ripped open the closet door and tore out hangers. He threw the clothes at her as she cried on the floor.

"I don't care what you wear as long as it's yours. As long as it's not his!"

He spun around. She hadn't moved. She cowered on the floor surrounded by plastic hangers and garments.

"What are you waiting for? What part of what I said did you not understand? Put on your clothes, Natalie! You are not a man. You are a woman! You will dress and act like one. Put something on!"

He folded his arms and watched her frightened movements as she picked a blouse and skirt from the clothing massacre. She glanced at him, her shoulders pushed forward. She was waiting for him to hit her again. Which he was prepared to do. He didn't want to, but the force had been effective in getting her attention. Finally, she was listening.

Progress.

Robert watched her peel off the men's clothing. She tried to cover herself and hide her body from him.

"I told you not to turn away from me, Natalie," he warned. "You show yourself to that dirty pharmacist every day. You can damn well show yourself to your husband."

Natalie complied. She was still crying, but part of him was excited by the vulnerability. He considered taking her right there. She needed to realize that she only had control over what he allowed.

If I want you, I will have you. You don't get to decide if you're going to fulfill my expectations anymore.

He didn't need Brigman's prescription. He could easily overpower her. Make her accept him. And she might scream at first, but in the end it was necessary.

But no. Not here. It wasn't safe. The pharmacist might storm in and try to win her back. Robert needed to take her out of Savannah and hole up for a week or so. He'd talk some sense into her now that she was frightened enough to obey. And he'd do it there.

Natalie finished dressing and shrank on the floor. He pulled a suitcase from the closet and threw it on the bed.

"Pack something."

"What ... what do you want me to pack?"

"Clothes. And everything on your vanity. We're going away. And hurry. Move!" Robert commanded as she crawled across the carpet and piled random clothes into the suitcase.

She was taking too long. He walked to the vanity and grabbed different makeup cases and her hair brush. He took a bottle of her perfume and a couple pairs of shoes. She flinched when he came near her and dumped everything in on top of the clothes.

"That's good enough." He zipped the suitcase and picked it up in one hand.

With the other, he took her wrist. "And if you make any scene on the way, it'll be much worse for you. I promise you that."

Robert slung the bag she'd been trying to run away with over his shoulder and pulled her out of the apartment.

Chapter 41

Oz woke in a hospital room. The space around his bed was lined with a curtain, and that was all he could see – the pale yellow fabric with honeycomb shaped mesh at the top. He tried to swivel his head to look around as he felt for the controls on the railing.

"Don't move. You have a concussion and three skull fractures. And that's just your head."

What grogginess he'd felt vanished. He turned and winced, the sharp movement sending a razor through his brain.

"One would think that over thirty years of ignoring my direction would've taught you to listen. Yet here you are, in another mess you could've avoided were it not for your poor judgment."

"What are you doing here?" Oz brought his palms to his face and covered his eyes. His head was killing him. Worse than a hangover. "Get out. I'm in no mood to listen to your bullshit."

Rather than leaving, Brigman seemed to settle further into the chair by Oz's bed. He crossed one leg over the other and spoke without facing him. "I was going to visit you anyway, so I'll thank you for delivering yourself to me. I'm a busy man."

"Too many brains to scramble and far too little time. Ruining lives is more than a full-time occupation."

"I'm very disappointed in you, Osborne."

Oz lay his head back on the pillow and answered in a monotone voice. "I can't convey how mind-blowing that statement is. If my mind were my dick, I'd be calling you Cinnamon and slipping you a fifty."

"Do you understand you could've been seriously harming people by tampering with medication?"

"Here's a fun fact – I *could've been* seriously harming people while you frequently and with no intentions of stopping, *continue to* seriously harm people."

"If you wanted to prescribe medication, you should've become a real doctor. Your behavior is unethical, illegal—"

"Yes, I've been a naughty, naughty boy. Can you cut the shit, Sister Agnes? Give me my penance and get the fuck out."

Brigman glanced at him. "Are you that arrogant to think you're going to get away with this?"

"I just don't care anymore." It wasn't true. Perhaps a week or so ago it had been, but now that there was Andrew, there was a great deal to care about. He'd have to come up with a plan to get out of this situation, but first he needed to call Santino to make sure Andrew was safe. "For the third time, get out."

But the doctor still didn't move. "I've decided to forgive you. I wasn't going to, but I will."

Every muscle in his face hurt, but Oz laughed anyway. "*You* are going to forgive *me*? After you robbed me of everything, you're going to forgive me?"

"I did the right thing even though you feel I've wronged you. My only mistake was in not providing you more guidance after I brought you back to help you adjust. For that I'm sorry. But for saving you when you were on the verge of death? I won't apologize for that."

"People are so afraid of dying. So afraid of the end. You know what goes on forever? Numbers. Numbers go on forever. It's immortality, and the only discipline that deals in the infinite."

"No one wants to die. Even you didn't want to die. Don't lie to yourself."

"See, this is what you've always failed to fucking understand. Every other creative expression will fade with the ages – languages and music change, the meanings of paintings change. But mathematics and a great mathematician transcend time and lives forever." Oz glared at him. "Someday your fucking 'advances' will be forgotten. Supplanted. But the truth behind geometry, behind topology is eternal. You may think you helped, but I had my chance at immortality, and you took it away from me."

The doctor stood, a file in his hand.

Thank God. Oz lifted his head, slower this time, and looked at the side table. Where was his phone? And his cigarettes.

"So actually, if you've lost your opportunity to figuratively exist forever, you should thank me for continuing to buy you time to make yourself less of an embarrassment." Brigman removed two glossy documents and approached him. "It really was convenient for you to not only come see me, but to do so with a head injury. Go ahead, take a peek, although it won't mean anything to you."

Oz accepted the documents and turned them over. There were two MRI brain scans – one sagittal, the other axial.

And Brigman was right, any anomalies that may have existed blended into the normal structures. Not that it mattered. He could take a guess.

"Have you been having some difficulty with your hands? Those scans tell me you have."

Here we go. Oz tossed the papers off the bed and folded his arms as the old clock resumed its ticking. How much time? More than before, since it was being diagnosed earlier. But how would he tell Andrew? And how long should he wait until he bowed out like he should've done previously? One big, glorious explosion.

"So that's why you're going to *forgive* my transgressions? You'll be rid of me anyway? How about thanking me for that convenience too."

And he should thank Robert. If the man hadn't lost his fucking mind and given Oz three skull fractures and a concussion, he would've kept rationalizing and ignoring the signs. Now he could plan for the inevitable.

"No, I'm going to forgive you because you're my son. I'll always care about you, no matter how difficult you make it."

"Hand me your handkerchief, Papa. I'm getting teary-eyed."

"You've made a valiant effort in trying to be unlovable." The left side of Brigman's upper lip twitched as he combed his eyes over Oz's face. "Do you realize how much work I put into that body?"

"Yes, Pygmalion. You reminded me of that frequently." He rolled his eyes to the ceiling. "How you couldn't stop licking my face and jacking your junk because I was so perfect and—"

"Ten years, and you've destroyed it."

"It's been a riot."

"Well, unlike you, I'm capable of learning from my mistakes and we've come a long way in ten years. This time—"

Oz sat straight up. "No! There's no way I'll allow you to touch me. If I'm going to die, it'll be with dignity. Not recreated into some other type of monster by you!"

"I don't make monsters. And like I said, there've been many advances over the past decade." Brigman nodded. "I've always known there was a possibility that we'd come to this juncture again, Osborne. So I've spent a lot of time thinking about what I'll do differently."

"You won't do anything. *This time* I have more than a fucking document to stop you."

He had Santino. He had Tinks. He had Andrew. His friends wouldn't let—

"Not right now you don't." The doctor smiled.

Oz turned to the gray plastic rail and hit the nurse call button repeatedly.

"Don't bother. You're not in Savannah General. I had them bring you down the hall to the Center. I was worried about you, and wanted you nearby in case something happened." Brigman knelt to retrieve the documents Oz had swept off the bed. "You can never tell with internal injuries. One minute you're fine, and the next—"

Oz's head thumped and his abdomen burned, but he pushed aside the agony and flung the blanket off the bed, quickly throwing his legs over the side to escape.

"No, no," his father said. Oz felt his shoulders seized, but the pain radiating through his core was curtailed by the sharp, forceful stab to his neck. "You need to rest. I insist. Just relax."

Oz tried to move forward; however, he found that he couldn't. Suddenly there was nothing and he'd lost all control. Like when the HFT failed, or waking in CryoLife's clutches. He couldn't move. He couldn't speak. He couldn't blink.

I can't breathe.

He fell onto the bed and met the doctor's eyes.

"These last minutes are your penance, Osborne. When succinylcholine is used in a lethal injection, they first administer a sedative so you're not awake while you suffocate."

No coherent thoughts. Because there was no air. No relief from oxygen. He needed a breath, to gasp, to take in just a trace amount – but nothing. Every muscle was frozen.

Oz felt Brigman's hand on his hair, but he couldn't concentrate. Fear. And fear. And fear.

I can't breathe. I can't breathe. I can't breathe!

"I'm confident we'll work out all your deficiencies this time." The doctor smoothed his cheek. "I'll see you again soon."

Language deteriorated. The feelings on his skin grew numb. Thoughts became dim. And the world spun away from him for a second time.

Chapter 42

Andrew recalled seeing Santino run up to the apartment as Robert's car had pulled out of the parking lot three weeks before. His mind returned to this image like a skip in a DVD. He kept seeing it replay. He couldn't bear to think of anything else. There was nothing and even the art had left him. He felt dead inside. Dead and dirty.

He hadn't known where Robert was taking him. He'd been too fearful to ask, and the scenery blurred together. They'd driven in silence for a long time and only stopped once. With the car idling, Robert had waited for something. Andrew wasn't sure what. He'd been too scared to look at him. Robert had ceased to be someone he recognized. There was no telling what he could or was planning to do.

He remembered the car parking and being pulled out of the passenger seat. Robert's hold was hard, but nothing compared to the crushing grasp earlier. He'd been nudged up some steps and into a small brown room.

He fled to a corner and huddled near the floor, trying to make himself as small as possible. His cheek felt fat and swollen. It hurt to do so, but he pressed his face to the wall.

When he'd felt Robert's shadow, he brought his arms to cover his head. His body shook. What would he do now? Hit him again? Kick him? Or worse? God, not "worse." Anything but "worse." Murder. But please God, not "worse."

Andrew felt Robert close to him, his hand on his leg, moving it forward.

A familiar strap slid around his ankle and locked into place. He'd heard a sharp beep. Then Robert released him and stood.

"We're staying here for a while. If you try to leave, Natalie, I'll find you. And there will be consequences."

Andrew still couldn't tear his eyes from his knees. He heard Robert cross the room, call in to work and say that Natalie was sick, and he needed to be home. For a week. Maybe more, but he appreciated them being so understanding.

These words had sounded like the old Robert, but the stinging of Andrew's cheek and presence of the ankle monitor reminded him that he was being held captive by a volatile stranger.

"You are sick," Robert said after ending the call. "That's why you're here. So it's not a lie."

Andrew didn't respond.

"You can come out of that corner. I'm not going to hurt you, as long as you behave. I didn't want to hurt you before." Robert sighed. "I know it's not your fault. He's been rubbing off on you. You wouldn't have pushed me if it hadn't been for him."

Him. Oz. Andrew swallowed. But he'd seen the blood stains on the ends of Robert's shirt. "What did you do to him?"

"I taught him a valuable lesson about trying to break apart a family. He actually had the nerve to deny everything."

"Deny everything?"

"I told him straight, I said, 'Stay away from my wife.' And he denied ever having touched you. Ever having seen you in the past two years. Even when I told him I'd seen you together. He insisted you were dead."

Andrew felt a small smile on the inside. He knew what Oz had meant. Oz hadn't touched Natalie. He hadn't seen her in the past two years. And wherever Robert had seen them, in whatever context, they'd been Oz and Andrew. Natalie was dead. He hoped Oz had had enough sense to not push it, but he knew him too well for that.

"What did you do to him?" he repeated.

"I beat his head into a cement wall."

"Did you kill him?"

Even though Oz had called after the attack, could his injuries have been fatal?

Andrew's throat felt thick; his chest burned worse than the cheek. Part of him didn't want to hear. He wasn't sure he could bear it. Beating his head into a cement wall? He imagined Robert throwing Oz against it. His skull fracturing as his neck whipped back and forth. Blood in his beautiful hair and spotting his white coat. Oz on the floor, beaten and motionless. Dying. The warm hands that had caressed his skin and hair growing cold. His eyes forever closed.

"Natalie, look at me, so I know you're listening."

He turned his face. Robert sat in a chair by a small round table, his legs open and shoes flat on the floor. His elbows rested on his knees, and his face was in his hands.

Andrew thought of how he'd first seen Oz in the bar. His chair tipped back, his legs on the table and crossed at the ankles.

His arms behind his head, and a cigarette dangling from his lips as he smiled. Laughter in his eyes, because if he wasn't saying something amusing, he was thinking it. So cool, so lighthearted and relaxed. Robert had never looked this way. Even before today, when Andrew thought he knew him.

Robert appeared stern and cross. There was no longer the manic frenzy in his eyes, but when he spoke, the low tone of his voice was more terrifying.

"You're going to be here a while. And when we leave, if that pharmacist gives you anything to hurt the baby, I won't want to, but I'll ensure he's permanently taken care of."

Andrew's thoughts caught on his last sentence. "The baby?"

"You're unwell, Natalie. Everyone agrees. I wish you'd come to me instead of trying to deal with it alone. Things may not have gotten out of hand."

"What are you talking about?"

"This gender crisis you're going through … blaming yourself for Michael's death. I'm going to fix you though. I'm going to make you feel like the woman you are." Robert smiled. "You'll feel so much better when we're a family and you have a new Michael."

Andrew's mind went blank, and he felt like he'd walked into a freezer.

"You will not turn away from me again, Natalie. Ever. You have three options. You can cooperate. You can be difficult. Or …" He took a bottle of pills from his pocket and clapped it on the table. "You can go to sleep."

Now, three weeks later, Andrew couldn't remember what decision he'd made. After Robert displayed the pill bottle, the Santino replay had started. And that's all he saw. Whatever was going on around him or with him, he was locked in the car's passenger seat, watching Santino run to the apartment door.

Santino must have parked down the street. He'd run from the outer curb, his coat billowing behind him like a cape. He'd come right away. Too late, but he'd come. And the last time Andrew saw him, he'd skidded to a halt at the door, almost slipping on the mat.

The clip reversed itself, and Santino was stepping onto the curb. To the doormat. Back to the curb. To the doormat. Andrew turned this loop around his head. He didn't feel he was speaking. He didn't feel he was eating, drinking, or moving, though he must've been. He didn't feel like Robert was having sex with him, although he was. He didn't see the pregnancy tests chucked in the garbage. Only Santino trying to save him. Over and over. Failing. Over and over again.

Until one morning, Robert kissed his temple. And his breath carried the scent of stale refrigerators, instead of smoke and an evergreen forest.

"Good girl. Very good." Robert spoke to him like he was a dog. A bitch who'd done her duty. "We'll go home tomorrow."

His shoe was on the curb, but Santino stopped running.

Andrew looked at the ceiling as if seeing it for the first time. It was a cream colored ceiling that'd seen a lazy attempt at skip trowel texturing. The large knife edge gouges and patterns reminded him of something. *Something.* He felt like he'd woken and his mind was clearing. "Where am I?"

"You're in the same place you've been for the past three weeks."

"Where is here?" Events were slow in coming together. What had happened?

"Pooler. You're in Pooler, love." Robert stroked his cheek, which no longer felt bruised.

Andrew couldn't remember when his swollen face had stopped hurting. But Robert's fingertips were rough and cold. The touch rubbed Andrew like sandpaper.

"But we're going home tomorrow. You did it. We did it. And everything will be okay."

"Pooler?"

"Uh huh."

Pooler. There was a tickle in his brain. *Pooler.* "I want to look out the window. Can I look out the window?"

Robert laughed.

"You could've been looking out the window. You could've been watching television, listening to the radio, reading a book. You're the one who wanted to stay curled on the bed for hours."

Andrew sat up and felt awful inside. Awful everywhere. Awful and wrong. Loose. Filthy. Violated. He hadn't thought it was possible to hate the body more than he had, but he wanted to drink acid. Stick a fucking funnel down his throat and pour drain cleaner into his stomach.

He looked back at the ceiling. There it was. The half-assed mud technique hinted at the familiar.

Franz Kline. Oyster Liver.

Hulking smears and scrapes of black on a tan surface. The gummy underside of a pried up old tile. Layered, rough skid marks with the scent of burning rubber practically rising from the canvas. Damage. Damaging. Damaged. Worse than feeling like *Beta nu* or *Blue Nude*. He saw *Oyster Liver* in the ceiling, and he felt it inside himself.

It couldn't be true. But he knew it was. His worst nightmare. There was a nasty, sordid thing growing inside him. A tapeworm. A fucking tumor.

He felt violently ill. He turned his head off the side of the bed and vomited on the floor.

Robert petted his back as he coughed. His hand might've been a hot brand sinking into Andrew's skin.

"It's okay, hon. Here, sit."

"No, the window."

He pulled away from Robert, still coughing. His gag reflex sputtered, trying to bring out more.

Andrew stepped into the moist, sticky vomit. But he didn't care. He stumbled to the window and tore open the curtains.

And there it was. Off in the distance. Less than a mile away. Like a lighthouse.

A long concrete building on a rise. The empty parking lot. The dirty blue pickup truck on the side of the building. The gun range.

"It's a beautiful day." Robert wrapped his arm around Andrew and pulled him close. "I'm sorry I had to be more forceful with you than I usually am, but it's what you needed to come around. And there was no time to waste."

Robert caught his eye and laughed. "I found all sorts of paperwork in your bag. Attorneys, doctors, name changes? God, you were sick. Andrew? Come now."

The use of his name struck a cord. Robert said it like a punch line. A joke. So different from how he'd first heard it. From how Oz said it. He remembered so vividly, and it had been weeks that felt like eons ago. Those caramel eyes holding his ...

"Andrew."

Oz's hand curved around his face, his thumb stroking his cheek.

"Andrew."

And that night in his basement only days before Robert had taken him. He'd watched Oz's mind working as they knelt on the concrete floor.

Pre-dawn with its solid shapes rising out of chaotic brushstrokes. Soap bubbles of blue and red blocks, a yellow square, red circle, and one partially formed orange rectangle. He imagined this freely formed mosaic and thought of how Oz had first described mathematical art to him:

"The creation of beings, of worlds, of universes without limitations ... Reality being born, and folding in on itself to be born again at my command."

His thought process might've turned in the same way when he stood before the empty wall with the black marker in his hand, or in front of his first dry erase board – with his first problem. With the Hodge conjecture a hundred thousand times before. Andrew could see him sifting through options, trying to decide how to respond.

You think too much. You're handsome when you're thinking, but you do it too much, Andrew had thought. *Just tell me. I've known you have for weeks. Say aloud that you love me.*

Oz hadn't. But he'd kissed him. And while that feeling had been up there with the other high points since Oz had entered his life, it was unique in being incomparable. There wasn't a painting or a perception that he could think of. The lightbulb within his head received too high of a surge and exploded. Nothing could be seen except for Oz.

As Robert's butchering of Andrew's name couldn't drive Oz's voice from his head, his rough touches couldn't replace those first kisses. Andrew felt their imprint and they erased the ugliness that was Robert's hands on him.

And he also remembered giving in and not thinking about it anymore himself. Not plotting his moves and only considering the impact of Oz's usefulness. He'd pulled Oz close and it'd been electric, like holding a battery in his mouth.

Andrew had curled his fingers around Oz's sandy hair. *I don't care. I'll go with you wherever you want me to. I'll walk into any cage you hold open, just to be near you. I'd let you trap me.*

In a way, Andrew had been trapped already, but he hadn't been scared by it. He felt connected to this man, tied to him on the same current, on the same artery. And he'd never be able to back away of his own choice.

That was the key phrase – "of his own choice." He was literally trapped in a cage now. A cage within a cage. Locked inside the hotel room with his captor. Trapped in the body with its new occupant.

But there was an island in the distance. He'd been marooned, but he was going to get back to Oz. If he was alive, which he had to be.

"And you might've tried to go through with it. Getting this different identity. But now you know what you are." Robert reached over and put a hand on his stomach. "You're a wife and mother. That's your place."

Andrew didn't respond. It didn't matter what Robert said. He could make it to the gun range before Robert located him, despite the ankle monitor. Red would help him get it off and then they'd destroy it. His location would disappear. *He* would disappear. And Red would hide him until Oz came.

Oz would bring vials of poison to erase the *Oyster Liver* feeling and purge the revolting thing from him. And they'd run away. Anywhere. Somewhere Robert couldn't find them. Oz had said that if Robert hurt him, he wouldn't let him go back. And was there any way in which Robert could've injured him more? The only thing that kept him from wishing he was dead was the thought of being safe in Oz's arms. As if none of this had happened.

Andrew lowered his eyes to the bottom of the window.

It was sealed. The entire way around. The only way out would be to break it. How else could he get free? There were no other windows in either the main room or bathroom. Without turning his head, he glanced to the door. Maybe it was a lock he could pick? But no, it was a card reading door. Still—

Hinge pins. Twice Robert had broken into the bathroom at their apartment by removing the pins from the hinge. He'd used a hammer, but there had to be something in the room that would work to strike the pins up from the bottom. He scanned his surroundings. Maybe a pen, a fork? Were the hinges rusty? He couldn't see from across the room.

In order to try, he had to get Robert out. Blood pounded in his ears, but Andrew felt no further conflict about lying.

He bent and coughed, holding his stomach.

"Are you okay? Sit." Robert guided him to the bed.

Andrew sat and tried to look queasy. Tried to look green.

"I'm not feeling well. Can you get me something?"

"What do you need?"

"Something for the nausea." He swayed, blinking repeatedly as if he were dizzy. "It's horrible. I don't know why."

"Yes, you do. It's normal." The most horrible, chilling look – the glowing, proud face of an expectant father. If there'd been anything left in Andrew's stomach it would've come up.

"But it's bad. A ginger ale. Please … sweetheart?" He choked on the endearment.

Take the bait, you fucking bastard, and leave!

"Okay, you lie down."

Andrew lay back and covered his eyes with his arm. Robert rose from the bed and walked to the door. His nerves tensed and he tried not to move.

"Natalie, I'm locking this door. It doesn't open from the inside."

"I hardly feel I can move my fingers. Please, go."

Robert left, but Andrew waited. He remained where he was for several moments before sitting up. A new vigor filled him.

He slid to the floor and crawled to the window. He cautiously looked across the parking lot below. There he was. The captor. The rapist. The devil. Leaving the building. Climbing into the car. Driving away.

It'd been too simple. Having been practically catatonic for the past three weeks, Robert had been lulled into the sense of security that Andrew wouldn't try to escape. Robert trusted him, but Robert had always trusted too easily. And he'd get the ankle monitor off. If he had to saw through his leg, he'd get it off. But first, the hinge pins.

Andrew ran to the door and inspected the hinge. It looked new enough and the pins might come easily. He snatched a pen from the desk and slammed it under the top pin. The head budged slightly, so he hit the pen up again. And again. And—

Snap. The pen broke as the pin was halfway there.

He dragged over a chair, climbed it, and tried to pull the pin's dome.

Nothing.

Something to make it slide. Something to free it.

Andrew dashed into the bathroom and returned with the cheap liquid soap dispenser. He worked the pump over the pin and tried to pry it out. It wriggled a fraction more due to the slime, but stayed fast.

From atop the chair he surveyed the room, his panic rising. Robert wouldn't stay gone long, and this was his only chance. There had to be another tool. A couple hits would work. Something thin and sturdy, something—

Natalie's suitcase was open on the floor, and shoved inside the inner pocket were a pair of shoes. Delicate silver laced sandals with a five-inch stiletto heel.

For the first time, I love you. Thank God.

He jumped off the chair and grabbed one of the shoes. Holding it by the middle, he rammed the heel up into the hinge.

The pin popped out and sailed into the poorly-textured ceiling. With a push to the top of the door, the whole thing tilted.

No, bring it in. Bring it in! You don't have time to worry about the bottom.

Andrew curled his fingers in the gap he'd created and pulled the door toward him. The wood creaked and he hung his entire body weight on the perch until finally—

Crack. The door broke in half.

He climbed over the jagged wood, ran down the hall and stairs, and rushed out of the building. Once outside, he took a breath. He smiled for the first time in three weeks. He was free.

He ran.

Chapter 43

The crisp, fresh air filling Andrew's lungs felt amazing. He kept the concrete building with its blue truck in his sights. He ran toward Oz. Toward everything he wanted, and reclaiming what mattered to him. He started to feel better.

Until the anklet began beeping.

Oh, my God.

Robert knew of his escape. He was probably tearing back, foaming at the mouth.

Andrew ran faster. His legs ached, his sides burned, but he couldn't stop. As the beeping reminded him, he was being chased. He just didn't know how close Robert was or how much of a lead he had. His shoes slapped the pavement, and he veered to the right, only a hundred yards from the building.

He thought he heard a car engine behind him, but he barreled through the door into the moist, dark room. As usual, Red was in his booth, watching *I Love Lucy* and smoking marijuana.

"Red! Red!" He beat the call bell with his hand. "Red!"

"I'm coming, I'm coming. Lay off my damn bell, will ya?"

But Andrew hammered on it, so sure he'd heard a car on his heels. There was nowhere to hide if Robert burst through the door. He'd drag him out and throw him in the car. Never, ever would he have the chance to be free.

"What, what?" Red finally stumbled out and his jaw dropped.

Andrew realized why. He wore Natalie's clothes, and he knew how horrified he must look.

"Andrew? What's wrong? Is Oz with you?"

"No, but Robert's after me! You've got to hide me!"

"Come back quick!" Red hit the button on the counter and the door unlocked.

Andrew ran through the door and turned the corner into the booth. He collided with Red. And as bad as the obese man smelled, as greasy as his clothes and skin were, Andrew hugged him close. He was familiar. He could be trusted and wouldn't hurt him. He would've sobbed into the dirty tank top if there'd been time. Red. Radiant, grotesque Red.

"What's that beeping?" Red clapped Andrew on the back.

"The ankle monitor!" He held out his leg. "Help me get it off! If I get it off, he can't track me!"

Red squatted to examine the anklet. He pulled at it, testing its strength and trying to determine how it was fastened.

"These newfangled things."

"There's no time! Shoot it off me! Shoot it off!"

"I don't think that's necessary. We'll shoot the hell out of that black box afterward. Calm down, boy. Get in here."

He nudged Andrew into the other room where Lucy was on the television and smoke curled from a bong near an olive couch. Andrew sat on the couch and tried to stop shivering.

Red came back in the room with Oz's .22, Caroline, and a lug wrench in his hands.

"Hold still. This may hurt."

"I don't care. If this doesn't work, you're going to help me cut my leg off. Or shoot it off. It's coming off! I'm not going to let him take me!"

"Shh, shh," Red said. "You're going to be okay. No one is taking you anywhere you don't want to go."

"You don't understand. He'll call the police, they'll drag me out."

"Pfft, the police. Do you know how many guns are in this place? Trust me, you're not going anywhere. If that motherfucker sets a toe in here and starts to cause trouble, I'll shoot him myself. Hold still, goddamn it!"

Andrew steadied his leg at the knee as Red took the socket off the lug wrench. When he pulled back the strap with a large thumb, the opposite side bit into Andrew's skin. The end of the wrench slid under the black strap, and Red twisted the tool. Andrew felt like his ankle was being severed as the strap cut tighter and tighter. He ground his teeth and held his breath. Red gave a powerful jerk of the lug wrench and the rivets finally gave way.

Again, he was free.

But the monster still lived. The light flashed red, and the box beeped. Before Red could do it, Andrew snatched the gun. He didn't bother to check if it was loaded. For a short moment, there was the beeping and Lucille Ball. Then he fired. And there was only Lucy.

Now he was free.

He sighed and sank into the couch.

"What do you want me to do with it?"

"I don't care. Burn it. Bury it."

"I don't have time for that shit." Red tossed the broken ankle monitor against the wall. It bounced into a garbage can that looked like it hadn't been emptied for months. He held his lower back as he got out of the crouched position he'd been in. "I'm getting too old for this."

Since the worst was over, Andrew calmed. He inhaled before speaking, his throat scratchy from the running and panic.

"Can I use your phone to call Oz?"

"Sure." Red waddled to the television and retrieved a cell phone from the top. He tossed it to Andrew. "If he answers, tell that fucker I'm running out of weed. I've been trying to reach him for days and I'm on my reserves."

Andrew scrolled through Red's contact list until he found Oz's name. He pressed call. He waited.

The phone rang.

Pick up, Oz, pick up.

The phone rang again.

He wanted to hear Oz's voice more than he'd ever wanted to hear anything.

The phone rang a third time.

And then, mid-fourth ring—

The beep to leave a voicemail.

He tried again. Ring. Ring. Ring. Ri—voicemail.

"You said you've been trying to reach him for days?" Andrew asked as he called again.

"Yep. Left messages and everything. No response."

A cold fear iced through him. Robert hadn't said he'd killed Oz, but there'd been the blood on his shirt. And beating his head into a cement wall? Was he dead? He couldn't be. Someone would've called Red, right? He was just busy. Maybe looking for Andrew.

As connected as I am to you – I'd feel it if you were gone.

Andrew tried to speak around the knot in his throat. "Who else's number do you have? Santino? Tinks?"

"I've got—"

A loud bang came from outside the room. The sound of a door being torn off its hinges and glass shattering.

"Natalie! Where are you? I know you're in here!"

Andrew dropped the phone and looked to Red. His eyes circled the room until he felt dizzy.

"Come out right now, you fucking bitch!"

There was another crash, and he heard the call bell's dying bleat.

"Jesus!" Red opened the door and shuffled out.

"What's your problem, mister? I'm trying to run a fucking business here and you come in throwing around my shit! Look at my door, you're going to pay for that!"

"You're going to pay! Send her out! I know she's in there! Natalie!"

"I don't have anybody here but me, jackass. Me and about forty loaded guns. So you need to back the fuck out, before I shove the longest one in your asshole!"

That's right. It's okay, Andrew, it's going to be okay. You're safe.

"No."

Robert's voice dropped and he heard the distinct click of a gun safety being taken off.

"I'm not leaving without my wife. And I will stop anyone who tries to keep her from me."

Oh, God. He's going to come in. He's going to rape me, right here.

"Let's cool off, mister, okay? You don't want to be doing something you'll regret. It's against the law to point a gun at someone, even if it's not loaded."

"Believe me, it's loaded." A gunshot sounded.

Andrew grew lightheaded from the panic.

He's killed Red. Poor Red, who was only trying to help me.

"And you know what's also against the law?" Robert continued. "Holding a hostage. You turn her out here, or I'll blow your head off and find her myself."

"I told you, I don't have anyone back there. I don't know anyone by that name."

Another gunshot.

"Natalie! If you don't want me to kill your friend, show yourself! I don't want to, but I will!"

"Mister, there is no one here—"

"Shut up, you fat fuck!"

Another gunshot.

"Natalie! This is your last chance! If you come out, I won't punish you! I wouldn't endanger the life of our baby! I'm an excellent father!"

Another gunshot.

"And husband!"

Another gunshot.

"We have a perfect family! And we're going to be happy!"

There was a pause.

"I can't do it without you, honey! Come out! If you try to run away with that motherfucker, I'll find you! I will always find you! And I'll kill him next time! You know I will! Natalie!"

Andrew glanced at the phone on the ground. He looked at Oz's .22 beside Red's bong. He took the gun and cradled it to his chest.

Do it. It'll be over quickly. Put it to your head and pull the trigger. If you don't do it, Robert will take you. He'll imprison you. He'll make you have this child, and then he'll rape you again. And he'll keep raping you. You don't want that. Your life is over. There's nothing left for you.

Unless Oz was alive. And he realized that even if his life meant nothing to him, it mattered to Oz. What would he do if Andrew killed himself?

I've caused pain to so many people by existing. By being what I am. But finally there's someone I mean something to. And I can't give that up. I won't. And if he finds value in me, then I'm worth fighting for.

"Natalie! I'm tired of this game! Get your—"

"Promise you won't hurt me." Andrew lowered Caroline and walked to the door. "I got scared, Robert. I'll come out if you won't hurt me."

"When have I hurt you? Come out here." Robert's answer was still a yell, but it was less frantic and not at full lung capacity. "You have no reason to be afraid of me."

No reason?

"But I'm not just scared for me." Andrew used his next shout to cover the noise of pushing the safety off the .22. "Promise you won't hurt me or the baby! Please lower your gun!"

Another pause.

"It's lowered. Come out here. Now."

Andrew walked out of the room into Red's booth. He imagined Oz's voice in his head as he'd placed the final clip in Andrew's hand on their first day at the range:

"Take down whatever motherfucker you want."

Robert stood in front of the bullet-proof glass with his gun lowered. Andrew stepped to the closed window in the middle and slid it aside.

"Scc that wasn't hard, Natalie," Robert said with a smile.

"My name is Andrew."

Andrew brought Caroline above the counter and as he'd done weeks before, he fired ten rounds without care to aim.

Chapter 44

Red leaned down and pressed his fat fingers to Robert's neck.

"He's dead."

After emptying the .22's entire magazine, Andrew had dropped the gun and sunk to his knees sobbing. He'd held his stomach at first, until he remembered what resided within it. Then he brought his hands to his face and continued to cry. Red had stood behind him, patting his shoulder until he was able to compose himself.

When Andrew could get up, they circled the counter. Robert lay on the concrete floor, five red splotches saturating his chest. Most of the blood pooled underneath his body.

Andrew looked into Robert's wide, unblinking eyes and nudged his arm with the toe of his shoe.

He didn't see the man Natalie had loved, who, despite his faults, had just sought to reunite the family he'd lost.

You're a rapist. Not just of my body, but you tried to rape me of my identity. You deserved to die, and I'd do it again. I wish I'd had more bullets.

But he also saw something else in the body on the floor, someone else. Yes, Robert had been a man corrupted into doing inhumane things, but he'd been more than that. Somewhere there was an eight-year-old shadow of him.

An orphan.

He couldn't feel guilty about it though. Simon was better off with his grandparents. He was better off never knowing the person his father really was. What had Oz eloquently called Brigman? A "sugar-crusted shit rag." So was Robert.

But now you'll never know. You're welcome.

Andrew looked away from Robert's body toward Red.

"What are you going to do?" Red asked.

"I guess I probably shouldn't tell you that."

"Why not? He came in here with a gun and threatened us both. You had every right to take him out."

"I doubt it'll be seen that way." Andrew glanced to Red. "How much time can you give me?"

"I'm not touching him. And this is a gun range. I wouldn't be able to pay my bills if shots weren't being fired. If you want to go, then go. No one will chase you for a while."

"Good."

He knelt and reached into the pocket of Robert's slacks, removing his car keys. A moment's hesitation later, he pushed the body up slightly and also took his wallet.

"Now that will look bad. Fleeing the scene and robbing him. Just sayin'."

"Who knows how much fuel is in the car?" Andrew let Robert's body go and it flopped into the puddle of blood. He stood and walked to the door.

"When you find Oz, tell him he owes me extra Skunk Special for this bullshit."

"I promise it'll be the first thing I'll tell him." Andrew turned and smiled. "Thanks for everything, Red."

Red returned the gesture. "Take care of yourself, kid."

*

Andrew hated to drive. Being behind the wheel brought back memories of the initial accident. He remembered slamming into the dash and being pinned under the wheel.

But I've killed a man. Nothing can pin me anymore. Nothing.

He'd flown down the highway at top speed without fear and despite the pouring rain. It'd been such a hot day that steam rose from the asphalt as he parked outside Oz's house.

Andrew cut the engine and ran up the walk. The door remained unanswered after he knocked and rang the bell multiple times.

God, I hope you're not sick, or maybe you're too injured to come to the door?

After circling to the side, he found a partially open window. He pushed it higher and pulled himself over the wet ledge.

"Oz?" He cupped his hands around his mouth to shout. "Where are you?"

But he wasn't there. Andrew searched the rooms, including the basement. Math textbooks were spread across his desk, but his marijuana plants were dry and sorry looking.

Of course, if you were really hurt, Santino wouldn't let you stay here alone. You're at his house.

Andrew left through the front door, covering his head with his arms to try and keep off the rain. In the car, he shook the water from his hair before pulling out.

How badly injured must you be if you haven't been able to come home for three weeks? But don't worry. You'll get this ... this awful thing out of me before it becomes worse. You'll help me figure out what to do about killing Robert. And then I'll stay with you. You can come home and whatever he did to you, I'll take care of you, Oz.

The idea was fantastic, overwriting so much of the ugly situation. Robert had expected Andrew to take care of him and Simon. There'd been no choice. But he wanted to care for Oz. He wanted to lie in bed with Oz's head in his lap and run his hands through his hair. To wrap his arms around his chest and be held close. To feel the warmth of his breath as he said Andrew's name before kissing him.

Santino opened the door after only two knocks. He stared at Andrew as if he were a ghost.

"Andrew?"

The clothes. The God-awful clothes.

Andrew crossed the threshold and scanned the living room. "Where's Oz?"

He'd expected Oz to be on the couch, his feet kicked up on the coffee table and a highball glass in his hand. But the couch was empty. And the house didn't smell like his cigarettes.

Andrew turned to Santino.

He looked different. There were dark circles under his eyes and his face was slack. He'd seemed ten feet tall before, but now his posture sagged and his hands were shoved deep in his pockets.

"Where's Oz, Santino?"

"He's gone."

"Gone?" There was a sharp pain in the back of Andrew's throat, and he struggled to contain a sob. "He's dead?"

Santino took so long in answering. He stood there, wetting his lips while his eyes filled with tears.

For Andrew, the room spun. He wanted to drop to his knees and scream. Rip the hair from his head and beat his fists into the ground until they bled.

Never again would Oz swagger through the door, a gin in his hand and a smirk on his face. Or tap his cigarette ash while a snarky comment sailed unfiltered from his head. His hand wouldn't be there for Andrew to catch as he tried to leave the room. No chest to lean his cheek against or hair to curl his fingers around. A hundred thousand tiny things were lost. The future held pockets of time that could've been spent with him and would remain forever empty.

In the back of his mind, the overshadowing image and feeling – *Untitled (Black on Grey)*. The multiform's deep black descending into gray, a thin aura of white separating the sections. Darkness and death. The end of everything.

I should've turned the gun on myself. Why didn't I do it when I had the chance? I can't make it alone. Without him there's nothing. Nothing—

"He's not dead," Santino said. "Worse."

Andrew held his breath. What had been "worse" for him had already happened. But what was "worse" for Oz? For Santino? For Tinks?

Santino nodded. "CryoLife has him."

*

"Your optimism is inspiring, but naïve."

Half an hour later, Tinks sat with them in Santino's living room. It was evident that Oz's absence had impacted him as well, but the sadness on his face was different from the despair that weighed on Santino. Tinks appeared to have the cold acceptance of defeat, while Santino still seemed to be reeling from the shock and loss.

"It's not naïve. If he's not dead, we could still save him."

"No, you don't understand, Andrew." Tinks turned to Santino and was able to catch his lax eye contact. "And *you* don't want to hear this. But he is dead."

"You don't know that," Andrew insisted.

"He's been gone for three weeks. They admitted him to Savannah General with—"

Tinks stopped when Santino cleared his throat. He'd barely spoken and his voice was slow and stumbling, as if he wasn't fully cognizant of their presence.

"After I didn't reach you in time, I went to the hospital. I saw him there. Unconscious in the bed. They said he'd be okay. That they'd call when he woke so I could come get him. I left, to try and find you. I knew if you weren't there, he'd be upset. I tried. To find you." Santino choked on the words and brought his hands to his face. "But when they didn't call for so long I came back. And Oz was gone. The bed empty. He was already gone."

Tinks stood and crossed the room. He sat next to Santino on the couch and put an arm around his shoulder as he hunched over. Tears fell through his fingers onto the carpet. And everyone was silent until Santino raised his head. Again, he spoke as if to no one.

"I called everyone. Tapped every person I knew of in his network to find out what had happened. They'd transferred him to the CryoLife building at Brigman's request."

"But that doesn't mean he's dead. They could be holding him and—"

"Why?" Tinks looked at Andrew. "For what reason would they hold onto him? Why keep him alive? Or rather, why keep anything but his brain alive? He's gone. If and when he walks out those doors, he could be anything. But you can be damn sure he won't be the person he was. Oz is dead."

"He never wanted this." Santino covered his mouth with his hand, his eyes still watery. "He didn't want to be reanimated. And I promised him I wouldn't let that happen. I promised him."

"But we don't know. I see your point, Tinks. I do. But maybe they haven't done it yet. Maybe we could still save him."

Tinks turned and raised an eyebrow. "What are you imagining? We storm their castle and find him chained in a dungeon? Is that what you're expecting? He's dead, Andrew. He's a brain in a fucking jar. Where will you find him? In inventory. Floating in some fucking green goo. That's what you'll be strapping to your fucking steed as you ride off into the sunset. A brain in a goddamn jar."

He was right. Probably. But it was the uncertainty that kept Andrew believing. Until he saw it, it wasn't real and he hovered over that translucent sliver of white hope. No, Oz wasn't shackled in a CryoLife dungeon. But he wasn't an organ swimming in a vat of preservative either.

"We could try," Andrew said. "He'd want us to try. He'd want us to—"

"He'd want to die. He was my best friend." Santino bit his lower lip and continued. "He'd rather die than let his father bring him back. Even if he is … gone. We could still try to give him what he'd want."

There was another silence as each of them sorted the options. Finally, Tinks was the first to speak:

"If we break in, there's a chance we won't make it out. Do you understand that, Andrew?"

What they feared had become of Oz could happen to any of them. Death and reanimation. Or just death. But what waited for Andrew if he did nothing? Loneliness. A return to being an unloved freak. Without even Robert to pseudo-love the outer Natalie shell, he had no support. And, considering the circumstances behind there being no Robert, sooner or later the police would be after him. So then there was jail time. And during that, the "worse" would come to fruition. *Oyster Liver* expanding and leaving the canvas to devour what little of life remained.

He imagined how it'd be. Whether in an orange jumpsuit or street clothes. Though he knew it was there, he couldn't feel it. Yet. He could cut his hair. He could change his name. But he wouldn't be able to cloak the alien inside, warping the body for its own use. Robert was dead, but the child would continue to take control and rape his identity. That mass would grow bigger and bigger and—

"Yes, I know." Andrew shoved the thoughts from his head. "But if he's not alive, neither am I."

Chapter 45

Though Red had cautioned him in removing Robert's wallet from his corpse, Andrew was glad he'd done it. In the midst of trying to concoct a plan to break into the Center—

"It's a goddamn fortress." Tinks had his hands in his hair. "There's the protesters and the guards at front. And if we're able to force our way in, we won't get far enough to find him."

"What about the east entrance connected to the hospital?"

"It's secure. Steel doors. You need a swipe."

Andrew had folded open Robert's wallet, and there it gleamed – the visitor's pass that'd enabled him to continue avoiding the activists when he made his visits to Zuniga and Brigman.

There was no further reason to delay their plan. Every second counted to both save Oz and avoid premature capture by the authorities, who'd be seeking Robert's murderer. Armed with the visitor's pass and Tinks's vest, Santino drove them to Savannah General.

As Santino parked the car and unbuckled his seatbelt, Tinks reached from the backseat and touched the man's arm.

"Not you," he said.

"Why?" Santino asked and Andrew could see his face starting to fold.

"You're not ready to die. I am. So is he." Tinks tipped his head in Andrew's direction and then smiled. "Also, best case scenario, having the engine running would be helpful."

Santino cupped his hand under his nose to hide his mouth. Without saying anything, he put his other hand atop Tinks's and squeezed it before turning to Andrew.

They regarded each other for a few moments, and it crossed Andrew's mind that perhaps, somewhere inside, Santino was angry with him. After all, if Andrew had never lived, there wouldn't have been a Robert to take revenge on Oz, and Oz would've never fallen into CryoLife's hands. He'd still be playing snooker, drinking, and making road trips to South Carolina for cadavers with his best friend. Santino had a right to be furious and blame Andrew for taking that away.

It really is my fault.

"I'm sorry," Andrew said.

"For what?"

"For existing. If I hadn't, he'd—"

"I knew Oz for seven years. And he existed all that time. But with you, he actually lived." Santino gave a broken smile, but there was warmth in it. "And never apologize for having existed. You are not some freak of nature or CryoLife mistake. You're the man who made my best friend come alive. And that's what I always wanted for him."

Andrew didn't know what to say.

"If I don't see you, it was my pleasure to have known you." He extended his hand. "Andrew."

He was still lost for words. But he leaned over the console and hugged him. It was a different embrace compared to Robert or Oz – a firm hug between friends. Equal male friends. Santino squeezed his shoulders, patting his upper back a couple times. And he experienced that remarkable feeling of acceptance and belonging. He was "one of the guys."

"Thanks, Santino," Andrew said.

He hung on to the man until Tinks tapped his arm. When he released him, they both smiled.

Tinks opened his door and Andrew unbuckled his seatbelt, doing the same.

Once more Tinks leaned in the car. "Don't forget to keep the engine running."

*

The visitor's pass worked perfectly, and the side mouth of the steel beast opened.

"No going back." Tinks turned to Andrew. "You're sure?"

"Yes."

"And surrender isn't an option. Either we find him alive and are able to escape, or I'm blowing the place. With you and everyone else in it."

"What do you think it feels like to explode?" He'd been curious but hadn't wanted to ask in front of Santino. "Will it hurt?"

"If you're worried about that, go back to the car."

"I'm not worried about it. I just wonder."

"It won't hurt if you stay close to me. There's too much C4 for it to be anything but a flash." Tinks stepped inside the doors. "Are you coming?"

A flash in comparison to the nightmare within me. And still only a possibility. Oz could be alive.

Andrew followed him, and the doors slid closed behind them.

They made their way quickly to Dr. Brigman's office, where luck continued to be in their favor. Tinks pulled on the handle and pushed the door open. They stepped inside and Brigman looked up from his computer monitor as Andrew locked the door.

"Well, isn't this an unexpected surprise." The doctor remained seated. "Two of my old patients come to visit me and—"

Andrew had wondered how it would be coming face to face with this man again. Though he'd never witnessed Brigman's true cruelty, he remembered Oz speaking of it. This man hadn't only damaged them all, but he'd wounded Oz. Even before taking away his mathematical ability, Brigman had deeply injured him. And for the exact same reason that Robert had hurt Andrew – not living up to expectations. When he saw Brigman, he saw Robert. And it filled him with anger.

"Cut your shit!" Andrew took a step toward the desk. "We're here for Oz. Where is he?"

"Excuse me, Mrs. Keller, but—"

"Don't call me that. Don't ever call me that. My name is Andrew."

The doctor gave a slow smile. His eyes ran down Andrew's body, stopping on his midsection. "I think you'll feel differently about that in a few months. But okay, *Andrew*."

Andrew charged forward, reaching for Brigman. He was going to grasp him by the hair and slam his face into those fucking framed degrees. Then he'd throw him to the floor, take that computer and drive it into his chest. He'd use one of the metal corners to butcher him. Pounding, piece by fucking—

"Wait." Tinks grabbed his arm to restrain him. "It's not necessary."

"Ah, Mr. Tinks. How's the Polonaise treating you? Well?"

Andrew was surprised that Tinks didn't release him and only smiled.

"That's very funny. Excruciatingly funny. You know something else that's also excruciatingly funny?" He removed his hand from Andrew and unzipped his black vest. He held both sides open, proudly displaying the lining of the two dozen flat packages. "Twenty-four pounds of C4. Well, maybe excruciatingly funny was the wrong phrase. Just excruciating works fine."

The doctor pushed his rolling chair back.

"Sit, please. No need to be so hasty."

But Brigman edged toward the door.

"I said sit down!" Tinks snapped out a plastic piece that'd been hanging from the inside of the vest. The ignition switch. He held it with his thumb hovering above a button on the end.

"I'll blow it right now if you don't sit your ass in that chair!"

"Okay, I'm listening." Brigman backed up and sat, his eyes on Tinks's chest. "What is it you want?"

Tinks tilted his head toward Andrew. "You heard the man, you son-of-a-bitch. Where's our friend?"

"He's not finished yet." Brigman shrank into his chair. "He won't be for a couple more months."

Andrew understood Tinks's expression when he looked at him.

But no, he still could be alive.

"Take us to him," Andrew shouted. "We want to see him."

The doctor resumed sole eye contact with Tinks.

Tinks wrinkled his forehead and darted a glance to Andrew, before nodding. "Yes. Take us. Wherever Oz is in this madhouse, you're going to lead us there. Past every security door."

Brigman stood, visibly shaking as he came around the desk.

"Can he be moved?" Andrew asked.

"No. I told you, he's not finished."

"Not whatever you're trying to make him into. *Him*. The real him. Is he in any position to—"

The doctor shook his head. "I got rid of all that."

"I got rid of all that." Andrew felt a weight in his chest. He squeezed his eyes shut until they ached. *Oz's hair. His eyes. His smile. His arms. His hands. All of that is gone?*

No further confirmation was needed. Oz was dead. And like the fog slowly dissipating when he'd first woken into this nightmare, the last of Andrew's fiercely preserved hope faded away.

When he opened his eyes, Tinks obviously felt the same, as he'd removed the ignition switch.

"No, wait, wait," Brigman protested. "Wouldn't you want to see him? I have a new one. You might—"

"I don't want a new one!" Andrew's fists were at his sides. "I want Oz how he was! There was nothing wrong with him! Nothing! He was perfect the way he was!"

"It is him. I promise."

"Your promises are shit! You're shit!"

"No, I swear." The doctor looked between the two of them. "It looks just like him. I'm going to put everything back exactly the way it was before. Come look at him, you'll see. You'll be absolutely satisfied. We'll ..." He gave a nervous chuckle. "We'll walk out of here as good friends and you can have him in a couple—"

"Shut up." Tinks held up his hand for silence. "You forget who you're talking to. We're your previous experiments, not your customers. Do you think we're going to allow you to manipulate us and continue to damage our friend? No one is walking out as friends. No one is walking out at all." He put his hand to the door handle. "If you want to buy yourself five more minutes on this planet by taking us to whatever is left of Oz, do it. But you've destroyed your last life."

Tinks pulled open the door, and Brigman solemnly walked through it.

*

It wasn't a long journey. Tinks and Andrew flanked Brigman on either side as he led the way down the hall of Jackson Pollack tiles, past the offices and into the patient wing. He stopped before the last door on the right – coincidentally, across from what had been Andrew's room.

"In there."

"You go first." Tinks removed the ignition switch from the vest. "This better be the one."

Brigman walked into the room, and once they saw there was no ambush they entered as well.

It was plain. No cards, no balloons for well wishes. There was just a body completely covered under a white sheet and hooked to four machines.

Andrew remained near the wall, paralyzed as he watched the sheet. It rose slowly.

"Shut the door," Tinks ordered.

He moved against the door to close it, his eyes fixated on the breathing figure. He couldn't speak and every thought left his mind except:

Up and down. Up and down.

"Is it in any state to be seen, Brigman? Am I going to lift that sheet to find a bunch of gore? If that's—"

"A bunch of gore?" The doctor interrupted Tinks and walked across to the bed. "I don't make 'gore.'"

"You make shells to house damaged brains in nine months. You've only had him for three weeks."

"But I knew, like last time, that he'd need another one sooner or later. So I'd started—"

"You're a sick fuck."

"You may not understand or appreciate what I do, but I save lives. I make perfection. And only perfection."

Andrew shut his eyes as Brigman folded down the top of the sheet.

"There. Tell me that's not perfect. You never saw him before he started vandalizing himself. I can't believe what he did to that body in only ten years—"

"As you seem to have forgotten, I'll bring your attention to the vest I'm wearing. It has twenty-four pounds of explosives that I intend to detonate. So, I'd appreciate if you'd shut the fuck up about my friend. And my appreciation is something you should want right now."

Andrew felt Tinks's hand in his, and he allowed himself to be led further into the room. When Tinks stopped, so did he. But he was still afraid, more of what he'd see on the hospital bed than of the death awaiting him.

"It's okay. It's not him. But it looks like him. Say goodbye," Tinks said before raising his voice. "And you, you piece of shit. We're not terrorists. All we came for is Oz. So get your ass over to that phone and call someone. Tell them to evacuate the building and that I'm blowing it in five."

"So just call and then I'll go?"

"No. Just call and I'm blowing it in five." He laughed. "If you think we're going to let you get away to restart this shit …"

Tinks's words faded into incomprehensible white noise as Andrew dared at last to open his eyes.

It is you.

For a moment, he almost smiled. Oz. Not a "bunch of gore." Not a dead body. Complete and alive. His shaggy sandy brown hair. His tan complexion. If he opened his eyes, they'd be that light caramel color. Yes, the eyebrow piercing was gone, as well as the tattoo on his neck. But these were minor, minor things. Because there was still the perfect shape of his nose and the sharp angle of his jaw line. It was really him.

The feeling of being inches from June Celebration. *After I thought I'd never see it or you again.*

Andrew reached down and touched his hair. It felt real. He smoothed his fingers across his cheek. The skin was warm, and soft. It was as if he were asleep.

What are we doing here? It's you. I can't let Tinks blow you up. You're real. You're the same. Two months he said, and you'll wake up to float through the world once more – bold, handsome, and secure. Everything will be perfect like it was when—

Andrew withdrew his hand. No, things couldn't be like they were. Was he like Natalie? No. But who was he *thinking* like?

Robert.

This wasn't Oz. It was a body that looked like him, but would never have the character he'd filled it with. It didn't have the scent of an evergreen forest on his breath or the cigarette smoke in his hair. Whatever would fill this shell might resemble Oz, but it wouldn't be him. Even if it wanted to try. Oz had been more. The person he'd been with Andrew deserved more. And so did the original.

To be able to just be who you are without baggage. Without striving for what you're not. Charming and seemingly perfect second-version Oz had lived for ten years, struggling to reclaim a purpose in the world. So would third version Oz. And fourth. And fifth. And it needed to stop.

I am not this body. And this is not you.

Andrew recovered the familiar face with the sheet and turned to Tinks, who was blocking the door.

"Did he make the call?"

"Does it look like he made the call?"

The phone dangled off the hook from the receiver and footsteps sounded outside in the hallway. Brigman was crouched in a corner, his hands clasped and his eyes closed.

"Are you ready?" Tinks stepped closer to him. He smiled and held out the ignition switch. "I'll let you do it."

Andrew accepted the plastic piece and held his thumb lightly on the button.

This is it.

He felt Tinks's arm next to him, but he tried to sense Oz. To remember being in his arms and feeling completely accepted. And while he knew it wasn't him, he took the body's hand, tucking his fingers inside its warm palm. He took his last, deep breath.

And the building exploded.

Acknowledgments

My gratitude to several on the Momentum team who played critical roles in further elevating this book. Thank you, Joel, for taking a chance on a 140-character pitch. The editing challenges set by Ashley and Tara pushed *Assimilation* further than I'd anticipated it could go. And without the marketing guidance of Michelle and Patrick, *Assimilation* couldn't have made it out into the wild.

I am deeply grateful for the contributions Jayme continues to make in my writing process, including constant support, encouragement, and food left outside my lair. Without her repeated re-readings and corrections to comma placement, *Assimilation* would've remained a random pile of words.

Also thank you to my mom for looking past the prolific use of the "f" word to read the book, and I'm glad that most of my beta readers can still maintain eye contact with me.

Last, but not least, thanks to you for downloading/picking up this book and preventing *Assimilation* from being relegated to the darkest corner at the bottom of my sock drawer.